GW00985964

THE MUMMY

Stories of the Living Corpse

Titles in this series edited by Peter Haining

Acknowledgments

The editor and publishers are grateful to the following authors, publishers and agents for permission to reprint copyright material in this collection: The Estate of Sax Rohmer for "The Mysterious Mummy"; The Executors of Jeffery Farnol for "Black Coffee"; Arkham House Publishers for "Imprisoned With The Pharaohs" by Houdini and H P Lovecraft; The Estate of Elliott O'Donnell for "The Mummy Worshippers"; Better Publications Inc for "The Flying Head" by A Hyatt Verrill; A P Watt Literary Agency and the Estate of E F Benson for "Monkeys"; BP Singer Features Inc for "The Mummy's Ghost" by Griffin Jay and Henry Sucher; A M Heath Literary Agency for "The Secret Of Sebek" by Robert Bloch; Century Hutchinson Publishing Group for "A Life For A Life" by Dennis Wheatley; Don Congdon Literary Agency for "Colonel Stonesteel's Genuine Home-Made Truly Egyptian Mummy" by Ray Bradbury.

THE MUMMY
Stories of the Living Corpse

edited by
PETER HAINING

SEVERN HOUSE PUBLISHERS

This title first published in Great Britain 1988 by
SEVERN HOUSE PUBLISHERS LTD of
40–42 William IV Street, London WC2N 4DF.

First published in the U.S.A. 1989 by
SEVERN HOUSE PUBLISHERS INC, New York

Introduction © Peter Haining 1988

British Library Cataloguing in Publication Data
Haining, Peter, *1940–*
The mummy: stories of the living corpse.
I. Title
823'.914 [F]
ISBN 0–7278–1556–3

Distributed in the U.S.A. by
Mercedes Distribution Center, Inc
62 Imlay Street, Brooklyn, New York 11231

Printed and bound in Great Britain

For
Donn Albright,
who has resurrected
some crackers!

CONTENTS

Introduction

'Clara shuddered at the sight of the cold, marble-like face, and an icy thrill ran through her bosom at the fearful conviction that this was no earthly being. The garments, the glassy eyes and rigid features spoke of ages long past when the Egyptians walked as proud masters of the Earth! Could this be the revived King Cheops of whom she had heard tell, that now stood before her?

'Even the strongest minds dread supernatural horror, and our fair fugitive turned involuntarily away! Fearing alike to remain or to advance, her mind filled with that vague sense of danger that generally attends the want of light, when Imagination pictures terrors which do not really exist and Fancy lends her aid to magnify those which do exist, she was lost to terrifying thoughts for she knew not how long.

'When Clara did at last look again, the Mummy was gone; however, in its place innumerable fantastic shapes flittered before her eyes in every corner of the gloomy vault . . .'

This dramatic passage comes from a virtually forgotten and rarely obtainable book called *The Mummy!*, written by a vivacious young lady named Jane Webb (1807–1858) and published in three volumes in 1827. Jane, recently orphaned and left almost penniless, had turned to writing as her one hope of avoiding penury, and through a combination of imagination and determination changed the course of her life.

Though *The Mummy!* qualifies as the first novel in English on the theme and its authoress undoubtedly demonstrated a precocious talent for a writer still in her teens, the book enjoys none of the fame of those other great enduring pioneer works

of horror literature such as *Dracula* and *Frankenstein*. Whatever
the reason, it is a curious state of affairs considering the
uncanny parallels which exist between the work and Mary
Shelley's novel *Frankenstein*, which had appeared less than ten
years earlier in 1818.

Like Mary Shelley, Jane was just nineteen years old when
she created her mammoth tale of the ancient Egyptian Cheops
who is revived by electricity and then influences the affairs of a
whole range of characters – from the heroine, Clara, to the
scientific genius, Dr Entwerfen, and the evil, lustful Father
Morris. Again, like *Frankenstein, The Mummy!* was intially intended to be a short story, but was fleshed-out into a novel on
the instructions of the London publisher Henry Colburn, who
saw in it a potential best-seller. And in the same way Mary
Shelley was to sublimate her own literary ambitions to those
of her lover, the poet Shelley, Jane abandoned the field of
fantasy fiction when she married an editor named John
Claudius Loudon in 1830. Thereafter, she and her husband
collaborated on a series of successful but nevertheless far from
exciting books on gardening!

Though *The Mummy!* is only occasionally mentioned in
studies of fantasy fiction, usually in no more than a footnote –
doubtless due to the scarcity of copies, there having been only
one reprint in 1872 – it does mark the beginning of a stream of
stories which have continued to this day and which are represented in this collection. Later writers' awareness of her
book must be a matter for conjecture, but Jane Webb is, I
believe, entitled to her share of credit for initiating a vogue.

The first short story, published as such, about a mummy
was conceived by that most famous of all writers in the genre
of fantasy fiction, the great American author Edgar Allan Poe
(1809–1849), who not only pioneered the science fiction and
detective tale, but is credited with having inaugurated the
modern short story of horror as well. Indeed, his various tales
of fear and the supernatural demonstrate ideas and plot devices that have been used over and over again by Poe's suc-
cessors in the century and a quarter since he was writing
them.

The subject of galvanism – the practice of applying electric
currents to reanimate the dead – which Mary Shelley had so

successfully explored in *Frankenstein*, was still very much in the public mind when Poe wrote his story, "Some Words With A Mummy", in 1845. Though occasionally light-hearted in tone, the tale displays Poe's familiarity with the attempts then being made by the more daring scientists to revive the dead, as well as his grasp of ancient Egyptian history in general and mummies in particular. Whether or not he had recourse to consult historical sources for fine details, the unique story is clearly the work of his own amazingly fertile imagination.

"Some Words With A Mummy" described what happens when a group of savants, who are preparing to dissect an Egyptian mummy, decide instead to give it an electric shock. At this, the mummy comes dramatically alive and proceeds to deliver a quite devastating diatribe to the assembled company. The story makes, I think, a perfect starting point for our anthology.

The earliest short story about a mummy to appear in an English magazine, as far as I have been able to trace, was "My New Year's Eve Among The Mummies". It appeared in January 1880 in the *Belgravia Magazine* – one of a number of monthly journals of tales and essays which flourished during the Victorian era – credited to a writer with the strange name J. Arbuthnot Wilson. The author was, in fact, Grant Allen (1848–1899), a very cosmopolitan soul who, born in Canada of French/Irish parents and raised in America and France, taught in Jamaica for a while before finally settling in England to make a living from his pen.

Allen initially wrote scientific essays under the penname J Arbuthnot Wilson, but, when he also tried his hand at fiction and became popular with readers, he revealed his true identity to other editors and went on to produce a string of successful novels of high adventure and fantasy, such as *The Beckoning Hand* (1887) and *The Great Taboo* (1891). "My New Year's Eve Among The Mummies" was later published again, in 1884, under Grant Allen's own name in a collection of his work suitably entitled *Strange Stories*. To the best of my knowledge it has been unobtainable for the last one hundred years.

Another writer whose work was beginning to appear in magazines at this time was a young medical practitioner called Arthur Conan Doyle (1859–1930), who hoped one day to make his name as an historical novelist but instead was destined for immortality through his creation of Sherlock Holmes. Conan Doyle's first story, "The Mystery of Sasassa Valley", had been published in 1879, and by 1892 he was contributing a variety of unusual and imaginative stories to publications like *Temple Bar, Cassell's Saturday Journal* and even the *Belgravia*. Among these were two stories that both demonstrated his interest in Egyptology and featured mummies.

In 1890 Conan Doyle wrote "The Ring of Thoth" for the *Cornhill Magazine*. It was a story about an Egyptian priest who, having survived for a thousand years due to an elixir, was now desperately searching for an antidote among an exhibition of mummies in Paris. Then, in 1892, for *Harper's Magazine* he wrote "Lot No. 249", which featured a recently reanimated mummy that terrorised an English neighbourhood. It is the second of these stories which I have selected for this collection, as "The Ring of Thoth" appeared in my earlier book, *Movie Monsters*, where I explained its part in the making of the 1932 Boris Karloff movie, *The Mummy*.

If Sherlock Holmes is undeniably the foremost literary detective, then Flaxman Low, the central figure in my fourth selection, "The Story of Baelbrow", first published in 1899, was the first of a long line of psychic detectives of whom Algernon Blackwood's John Silence and Sax Rohmer's Morris Klaw are probably today the best-known.

Low, an Oxford-educated psychologist, has a very practical approach to stories of supernatural happenings, which makes him ideally suited to investigate the strange events taking place at a stone mansion called Baelbrow on the East Anglian coast. The psychic influences of an old burial mound and a reanimated mummy combine to establish this particular story as one of the best from his casebook.

The tales in this series are credited as being the work of 'E and H Heron' which, again, is actually a pseudonym: that of the popular novelist Hesketh Prichard (1876–1922) and his mother, Kate. The son was actually the major contributor to the partnership, but he insisted on sharing the credit with his parent who apparently suggested several of the plots. Hesketh on his own originated a ruthless bandit character named Don Q, whose magazine adventures were for a time as popular with many readers as those of Sherlock Holmes himself.

The last year of the nineteenth century saw the publication of what was only the second full-length novel since Jane Webb's *The Mummy!* to feature one of the reanimated ancients from the land of Egypt. It was not to be long, though, before this new work, *Pharos the Egyptian* by Guy Boothby and published by Ward Lock, was followed by several more.

Guy Boothby (1867–1905), an Australian by birth, had begun his writing career 'down under' in 1894 when he published *On The Wallaby*, but he found more lasting success when he moved to England the following year. Here he started what became a series of books about the sinister Dr Nikola and his search for immortality, which quickly earned a huge following among the general public. They were, to all intents and purposes, direct forerunners of Sax Rohmer's more famous Fu Manchu series.

Boothby was deeply interested in the history of Ancient Egypt and *Pharos the Egyptian* was just one of several novels based on this theme. *The Curse of the Snake* (1902) also pursued the same subject. Among Boothby's short stories it is therefore not surprising to find one dealing with our particular aspect of Egyptian history, and "A Professor of Egyptology", written in 1904, is a clever variation on the theme in which a modern woman is 'transported' back in time to resolve an ancient murder.

Hard on the heels of Boothby's book came *The Jewel of the Seven Stars* (1903) about the reawakening of the mummy of Queen Tera, a novel by Bram Stoker (1847–1912), the famous author of *Dracula*; *The Mummy and Miss Nitocris* (1906), in which two victims of an Egyptian princess plot her murder in contemporary Britain, written by the prolific George Griffith (1857–1906); and, perhaps the most dramatic of all, *The Yellow God* (1908), featuring Asiki, a beautiful but vicious priestess tracking her victims across two thousand years, created by the great storyteller Sir Henry Rider Haggard (1856–1925). Haggard also wrote an entertaining novella about a London bank clerk suddenly thrust back into ancient Egypt, *Smith and the Pharaohs* (1920).

However, where the mummy in fiction was concerned,

overshadowing all these names at this time was Sax Rohmer (1883–1959). He wrote a short story on the theme in 1903, when he was just twenty years old, and followed this with further tales and two excellent novels, *Brood of the Witch Queen* (1918) and *She Who Sleeps* (1928). Rohmer is famous, of course, for his creation of Dr Fu Manchu, the fiendish Oriental mastermind bent on world domination, who made his debut in the first of thirteen novels in 1913. He had begun writing at the turn of the century, and it was in 1903 that he made one of his very first sales with a story called "The Mysterious Mummy", which until recently was believed to have been lost. The 'loss' was partly attributable to the circumstances of its being published under Rohmer's real name, A Sarsfield Ward, and partly to the fact that no one, apparently, could locate the issue of the magazine in which it had appeared. I quote from Cay Van Ash's biography of Sax Rohmer, *Master of Villainy* (1972), in which he said, 'No trace has yet been found of "The Mysterious Mummy" which he (Sax) wrote for *Pearson's Magazine.*'

But as a result of diligent delving in the vast newspaper and magazine archives of the British Museum at Colindale in London, the redoubtable researcher W O G Lofts has located the story in the December 'Christmas Extra Number' edition of *Pearson's* published in 1903, and it therefore makes a welcome reappearance in these pages.

Sax Rohmer retained this interest in mummies all his life, as the two novels already mentioned bear witness: the first featured the evil, reanimated son of a witch, and the second a carefully perpetrated fraud involving an old Egyptian tomb. One of Rohmer's excellent Morris Klaw adventures in *The Dream Detective* (1920) also features the dramatic case of "The Headless Mummies".

The cinema was still very much in its infancy – and the number of fantasy films which had been produced very small – when the first mummy made an appearance on the screen. In the light of Jane Webb's pioneer achievement, it was perhaps appropriate that the filmmaker should have been English, though his chosen story was of French origin.

The concept of featuring a mummified corpse was seen as an ideal one by early filmmakers, both because it somehow embodied all the terrors of death, as well as having a human shape. No doubt, even with the limited facilities at their disposal in the early years of the twentieth century, a convincing mummy was an easier monster to depict on the screen than, say, a shape-changing vampire, a werewolf or a ghost.

The man who brought the first mummy to the screen was the scientific instrument-maker turned pioneer film producer Robert Paul, who in 1897 designed and built his own Animatographe projector, which enabled him to shoot in slow motion, introduce trick effects and even create animation sequences. Among his early pictures was a dramatic adaptation of Lord Bulwer-Lytton's famous historical novel *The Last Days of Pompeii*, produced in 1897; and then, in 1902, he chanced upon a story called "The Mummy's Foot" by Théophile Gautier and assigned it to one of his directors, Walter R Booth, to turn into a picture, utilising the camera tricks available at what was then the first indoor studio in England, situated near London.

Théophile Gautier (1811–1872) was a painter and writer who was fascinated with ancient Egyptian history. Among his earliest successes was a story called "One of Cleopatra's Nights" (1845), and other stories from his pen include a vampire short story, "Clarimonde" (1855), and two novels about the supernatural, *Avatar* (1857) and *Spirite* (1866). "The Mummy's Foot" (1863), though, is the one widely regarded as his most imaginative piece of short fiction.

Unfortunately, no record exists of the names of the actors who appeared in Robert Paul's ten-minute production of the story about the discovery of an Egyptian princess's mummified foot in a junk shop and the unexpected effect it has on the young man who purchases it. Paul, for reasons best known to himself, eschewed the author's title for his picture, releasing it instead as *The Haunted Curiosity Shop*. The indications are that it was a success with audiences, who apparently enjoyed the neat twist to the end of Gautier's story which Walter Booth faithfully retained in the film. I will not spoil your enjoyment of the story by even hinting at it here!

It was not long before Robert Paul's movie was followed by others generating a public interest in Egyptology in general, and mummies in particular, that has never flagged to this day.

The French filmmakers Lux Pictures, for example, offered in 1909 *La Momie du Roi* (the picture was later retitled *The Mummy of the King of Rameses* for British and American audiences), and after that came *The Mummy* from Thanhouser of Germany in 1911. A year later, Essanay of Chicago produced the first American contribution, *When Soul Meets Soul*, with the early silent picture star Francis X Bushman as a reanimated ancient Egyptian. In 1915, Dorothy Bellew played a revived princess in *The Avenging Hand*, which came perilously close to plagiarising *The Haunted Curiosity Shop*; while another American company, Vitagraph, starred Antonio Moreno in *The Dust of Egypt* (1915).

Two other mummy pictures from the years of World War I are also deserving of mention: *The Undying Flame* (1917), which Maurice Tourneur, later to become the architect of several outstanding horror movies, directed for Lasky Pictures featuring Olga Petrova; and *The Eyes of the Mummy* (1918) starring the screen 'vamp' Pola Negri and the sinister Emil Jannings, released by Union Pictures.

In 1909, the first stage play to feature a mummy was launched in New York. *Cleopatra* was intended to be a lavish reconstruction of the dramatic life of the Egyptian queen, but it failed dismally as an audience pleaser. Among the backstage workers on the production was a young Englishman, Jeffery Farnol (1878–1952), who had crossed the Atlantic to employ his artistic talents as a scenery painter. Shortly after this production, however, Farnol returned to England and, discarding his brush for a pen, rapidly achieved fame with a string of romantic adventure novels, beginning with *The Broad Highway* (1910) and *The Amateur Gentleman* (1913).

Whatever the impact of *Cleopatra*'s failure on Farnol, the image of the mummy remained in his consciousness and surfaced again in one of the best of his short stories, "Black Coffee", collected in *The Shadow and Other Stories* (1929). I am delighted to be returning this atmospheric and chilling little mystery to print after so many years.

C Cutcliffe Hyne, creator of the popular adventurer Captain Kettle, had meanwhile written *The Mummy of Thompson Pratt* (1908), about a man who discovers he is a direct descendant of the mummy in the museum where he works. The same year that master of the supernatural, Algernon Blackwood, wrote *The Nemesis of Fire* about a mummy and a fire elemental that threatened to destroy an old house.

Another novel, *A King in Babylon*, which was published in 1917, proved still more interesting for it had apparently been inspired by the recent spate of mummy films. The American author Burton Stevenson recounted the weird adventures of a group of filmmakers who, when working on location in Egypt, unwittingly revived some ancient residents of the tombs.

By this time the public, intrigued by all the stories of the country's fascinating legends, were starting to visit Egypt in ever-increasing numbers. Among these tourists was the famous escapologist Harry Houdini (1874–1926), who found himself involved in a bizarre experience which he later arranged to be recounted in a story by the leading horror fiction writer H P Lovecraft (1890–1937).

The strange, reclusive author from Rhode Island, the creator of a cycle of fantasy stories known as the Cthulhu Mythos (since continued by other writers), was already interested in the myths and legends of Egypt and so proved a very willing ghost-writer of Houdini's story, which he entitled "Imprisoned With The Pharaohs". It was originally published in 1924 and is now included in this collection. Lovecraft later wrote another powerful story of the same kind, "Out of the Eons" (1935), about a mummy recovered from the sea, which still retained the power to petrify all those who looked upon it.

A British tourist amongst the visitors to Egypt at this time was Elliott O'Donnell (1872–1965), the ghost-hunter and prolific writer of both factual and fictional books on the supernatural. Some critics have suggested that the dividing line between O'Donnell's 'eye-witness' accounts and his tales of fantasy is very narrow, but I am inclined to believe that his story "The Mummy Worshippers", which he wrote in 1934 and is included here, was founded on reality. Whatever the case, the tale certainly provides a new angle on our theme.

Undeniably an author with an extensive knowledge of Egyptology and archaeology, A Hyatt Verrill (1871–1954) wrote a number of books and stories popularising his interests in these subjects in the twenties and thirties. Verrill had earlier invested a considerable time exploring in South America, and some of his best work orginates from adventures which occurred in remote parts of the country. His attention was particularly engaged by the mummification processes used by the Ancient Incas and in 1929 he published a highly colourful and exciting novel on this theme entitled *The Bridge of Light*.

Verrill followed this book with a number of short stories including "The Flying Head", which he wrote in 1939 and which is reprinted in these pages. There is something of the author himself in the character of Dr Stokes who investigates the tomb of an Inca mummy – but I am happy to record that A Hyatt Verrill ended his days peacefully at home and not as the ill-fated explorer in his chilling tale.

E F Benson (1867–1940), the English horror-story writer and another to develop an early interest in archaeology, provides an unusual variation on our theme with his tale "Monkeys", which features the mummified body of an animal, rather than a human being. Benson did, in fact, spend three years as an archaeologist in Egypt and Greece, and a number of his tales are coloured by the experiences he encountered on digs in ancient ruins.

Benson's work has enjoyed a well-deserved renaissance in the past few years through the republication and adaptation for television of his 'Lucia' series of novels, but among lovers of supernatural fiction he has long held his reputation as a master of the genre. Indeed, one of his stories, "The Bus Conductor", was used in the 1945 British movie *Dead of Night*, still regarded today as arguably the finest of all supernatural anthology films.

During the thirties and forties more films featuring the mummy were produced, primarily in Hollywood, where in 1932 the director Karl Freund set a new standard of excellence with *The Mummy*, starring the great Boris Karloff as Im-ho-tep, a high-priest of the Temple of the Sun who returns to life after 3,700 years. Superbly made up by Jack Pierce, Karloff gave an outstanding performance against which all later pictures in the genre have been judged.

Delighted with the huge success of *The Mummy*, Universal Pictures embarked on a series of sequels which included *The Mummy's Hand* (1940), starring former cowboy-star Tom

Tyler, and *The Mummy's Tomb* (1942), with another of the great horror-stars of the era, Lon Chaney, playing the revived Egyptian, Prince Kharis. Such was Chaney's impact on audiences that in 1944 Universal engaged him again for the part in two more pictures: *The Mummy's Curse* and, following immediately, *The Mummy's Ghost*, in which another of the screen's top fright-merchants, John Carradine, co-starred as the high-priest Youssef.

The combination of Chaney and Carradine made *The Mummy's Ghost* an unforgettable experience as far as I was concerned, and, having two or three times seen the film again, I can vouch that it has lost none of its appeal. It is therefore a great pleasure to include a special adaption of the screenplay by Griffin Jay and Henry Sucher in this book.

The American pulp magazines which proliferated at this time also devoted much space to mummy stories – some skilfully written and dramatic, others excruciatingly crude in their melodramatic telling.

Weird Tales, the most famous of these horror magazines, naturally enough carried some of the best, including "Spiderbite" (June 1926) by screenwriter Robert S Carr; "A Visitor From Egypt" (September 1930) by Frank Belknap Long; "Empire of the Necromancers" (September 1932) by Clark Ashton Smith; two tales by E Hoffman Price, "Tarbis of the Lake" (February 1934) and "Woman in the Case" (July 1938); and "Book of the Dead" by Frank Gruber. Others worthy of mention are Theodore Orchard's "The Red Curse of the Mummy" in the February 1929 issue of *Ghost Stories*; Arthur J Burks' "Guatemozin the Visitant" in *Strange Tales* (November 1931); and one by another scriptwriter, Jack B Creamer, "The Terror Mummy", which was published in *Strange Stories* (June 1940).

Of all the mummy stories that appeared in the pulps, however, my vote for the very best goes to "The Secret of Sebek" (November 1937) and its sequel, "The Eyes of the Mummy" (April 1938). Both were published in *Weird Tales* and both were the work of Robert Bloch (1917–), who, as probably few readers need reminding, is the author of *Psycho*, the novel Alfred Hitchcock made into one of his most famous films (starring Anthony Perkins), which has so far inspired two sequels.

Since the making of *Psycho*, Robert Bloch has become much in demand as a scriptwriter and not a few of his other stories have been adapted for the screen by both American and British film companies. "The Secret of Sebek" and its follow-up have not yet been included among this number, a surprising omission considering their chilling excellence.

Among the actors who have appeared in films based on Robert Bloch's stories is Christopher Lee, who has also followed in the footsteps of Boris Karloff and Lon Chaney by playing the revived Prince Kharis on the screen. He starred in the 1959 Hammer Films version of *The Mummy*, in which Peter Cushing played the scientist responsible for reviving him. This, in turn, lead to two more sequels, *The Curse of the Mummy's Tomb* (1964) and *The Mummy's Shroud* (1967).

Hammer Films also made several pictures based on the works of Dennis Wheatley (1897–1977), whose series of Black Magic novels have sold outstandingly well. For a number of years the author was a near-neighbour of Christopher Lee and they became close friends. After Lee's success in the leading role of *The Mummy*, Wheatley suggested the actor should star in an adaptation of the short story "A Life For A Life", one of Wheatley's own which dealt with a similar theme. Lee, who was anxious to avoid becoming type-cast – it was beginning to happen with his several appearances as *Dracula* – declined the invitation, however. From the cinema-goers' point of view it is an opportunity missed to see what would have undoubtedly been a superb performance, but I am delighted to include Wheatley's story in this collection for everyone to enjoy.

And so to the final selection, "Colonel Stonesteel's Genuine Home-Made Truly Egyptian Mummy", unquestionably the most original mummy story appearing in this book, by today's most inventive fantasy writer, Ray Bradbury (1920–). Los Angeles-based Bradbury has for a number of years been interested in mummies – particularly those to be found across the nearby border with Mexico in the small town of Guanajuato. After his first visit to the sleepy community in 1947, he was inspired to write a chilling short story called "The Next In Line", which was published later that year. It has since stimulated into print a lavish if rather gruesome book of photographs entitled *The Mummies of Guanajuato* (1978).

However, while the Bradbury story here is quite different in theme and atmosphere, it is every bit as engrossing; and, as this marks its first appearance in book form, it provides the best possible finale to the anthology. Readers, I can confidently predict, will long remember Colonel Stonesteel – just as I am sure they will many of the other adventurers and dead men brought 'alive' in these pages. It has been an enjoyable task reviving them all for your pleasure and, I hope, more than the occasional *frisson* of fear . . .

Peter Haining
Boxford, Suffolk
July 1988.

SOME WORDS WITH A MUMMY

By Edgar Allan Poe

The symposium of the preceding evening had been a little too much for my nerves. I had a wretched headache, and was desperately drowsy. Instead of going out, therefore, to spend the evening, as I had proposed, it occurred to me that I could not do a wiser thing than just eat a mouthful of supper and go immediately to bed.

A *light* supper, of course. I am exceedingly fond of Welsh rabbit. More than a pound at once, however, may not at all times be advisable. Still, there can be no material objection to two. And really between two and three, there is merely a single unit of difference. I ventured, perhaps, upon four. My wife will have it five; but, clearly, she has confounded two very distinct affairs. The abstract number, five, I am willing to admit; but, concretely, it has reference to bottles of brown stout, without which, in the way of condiment, Welsh rabbit is to be eschewed.

Having thus concluded a frugal meal and donned my night-cap, with the serene hope of enjoying it till noon the next day, I placed my head upon the pillow, and through the aid of a capital conscience, fell into a profound slumber forthwith.

But when were the hopes of humanity fulfilled? I could not have completed my third snore when there came a furious ringing at the street-door bell, and then an impatient thumping at the knocker, which awakened me at once. In a minute afterward, and while I was still rubbing my eyes, my wife thrust in my face a note from my old friend, Doctor Ponnonner. It ran thus:

'Come to me, by all means, my dear good friend, as soon as you receive this. Come and help us to rejoice. At last, by long persevering diplomacy, I have gained the assent of the Directors of the City Museum, to my examination of the Mummy – you know the one I mean. I have permission to unswathe it, and open it, if desirable. A few friends only will be present – you, of course. The Mummy is now at my house, and we shall begin to unroll it at eleven to-night.

'Yours ever,

PONNONNER.'

By the time I had reached the 'Ponnonner', it struck me that I was as wide awake as a man need be. I leaped out of bed in an ecstasy, overthrowing all in my way; dressed myself with a rapidity truly marvellous; and set off, at the top of my speed, for the doctor's.

There I found a very eager company assembled. They had been awaiting me with much impatience; the Mummy was extended upon the dining-table; and the moment I entered, its examination was commenced.

It was one of a pair brought, several years previously, by Captain Arthur Sabretash, a cousin of Ponnonner's, from a tomb near Eleithias, in the Lybian Mountains, a considerable distance above the Thebes on the Nile. The grottoes at this point, although less magnificent than the Theban sepulchres, are of higher interest, on acount of affording more numerous illustrations of the private life of the Egyptians. The chamber from which our specimen was taken, was said to be very rich in such illustrations – the walls being completely covered with fresco-paintings and bas-reliefs, while statues, vases, and Mosaic work of rich patterns, indicated the vast wealth of the deceased.

The treasure had been deposited in the Museum precisely in the same condition in which Captain Sabretash had found it; – that is to say, the coffin had not been disturbed. For eight years it had thus stood, subject only externally to public inspection. We had now, therefore, the complete Mummy at our disposal; and to those who are aware how very rarely the unransacked antique reaches our shores, it will be evident, at once, that we had great reason to congratulate ourselves upon our good fortune.

Approaching the table, I saw on it a large box, or case, nearly seven feet long, and perhaps three feet wide, by two feet and a half deep. It was oblong – not coffin-shaped. The material was at first supposed to be the wood of the sycamore (*platanus*), but upon cutting into it, we found it to be pasteboard, or, more properly, *paper-mâché*, composed of papyrus. It was thickly ornamented with paintings, representing funeral scenes, and other mournful subjects – interspersed among which, in every variety of position, were certain series of hieroglyphical characters, intended, no doubt, for the name of the departed. By good luck, Mr Gliddon formed one of our party; and he had no difficulty in translating the letters, which were simply phonetic, and represented the word, *Allamistakeo*.

We had some difficulty in getting this case open without injury; but, having at length accomplished the task, we came to a second, coffin-shaped, and very considerably less in size than the exterior one, but resembling it precisely in every other respect. The interval between the two was filled with resin, which had, in some degree, defaced the colours of the interior box.

Upon opening this latter, (which we did quite easily,) we arrived at a third case, also coffin-shaped, and varying from the second one in no particular, except in that of its material, which was cedar, and still emitted the peculiar and highly aromatic odour of that wood. Between the second and the third case there was no interval – the one fitting accurately within the other.

Removing the third case, we discovered and took out the body itself. We had expected to find it, as usual, enveloped in frequent rolls or bandages of linen; but, in place of these, we found a sort of sheath, made of papyrus, and coated with a layer of plaster, thickly gilt and painted. The paintings represented subjects connected with the various supposed duties of the soul, and its presentation to different divinites, with numerous identical human figures, intended, very probably, as portraits of the persons embalmed. Extending from head to foot, was a columnar, or perpendicular inscription, in phonetic hieroglyphics, giving again his name and titles, and the names and titles of his relations.

Around the neck thus ensheathed, was a collar of

cylindrical glass beads, diverse in colour, and so arranged as to form images of deities, of the scarabæus, etc., with the winged globe. Around the small of the waist was a similar collar or belt.

Stripping off the papyrus, we found the flesh in excellent preservation, with no perceptible odour. The colour was reddish. The skin was hard, smooth and glossy. The teeth and hair were in good condition. The eyes (it seemed) had been removed, and glass ones substituted, which were very beautiful, and wonderfully life-like, with the exception of somewhat too determined a stare. The fingers and the nails were brilliantly gilded.

Mr Gliddon was of opinion, from the redness of the epidermis, that the embalmment had been effected altogether by asphaltum; but, on scraping the surface with a steel instrument, and throwing into the fire some of the powder thus obtained, the flavour of camphor and other sweet-scented gums became apparent.

We searched the corpse very carefully for the usual openings through which the entrails are extracted, but, to our surprise, we could discover none. No member of the party was at that period aware that entire or unopened mummies are not infrequently met. The brain it was customary to withdraw through the nose; the intestines through an incision in the side; the body was then shaved, washed, and salted; then laid aside for several weeks, when the operation of embalming, properly so called, began.

As no trace of an opening could be found, Doctor Ponnonner was preparing his instruments for dissection, when I observed that it was then past two o'clock. Hereupon it was agreed to postpone the internal examination until the next evening; and we were about to separate for the present, when some one suggested an experiment or two with the Voltaic pile.

The application of electricity to a mummy three or four thousand years old at the least, was an idea, if not very sage, still sufficiently original, and we all caught it at once. About one-tenth in earnest and nine-tenths in jest, we arranged a battery in the doctor's study, and conveyed thither the Egyptian.

It was only after much trouble that we succeeded in laying bare some portions of the temporal muscle which appeared of less stony rigidity than other parts of the frame, but which, as we had anticipated, of course, gave no indication of galvanic susceptibility when brought in contact with the wire. This, the first trial, indeed, seemed decisive, and, with a hearty laugh at our own absurdity, we were bidding each other good night, when my eyes, happening to fall upon those of the Mummy, were there immediately riveted in amazement. My brief glance, in fact, had sufficed to assure me that the orbs which we had all supposed to be glass, and which were originally noticeable for a certain wild stare, were now so far covered by the lids, that only a small portion of the *tunica albuginea* remained visible.

With a shout I called attention to the fact, and it became immediately obvious to all.

I cannot say that I was *alarmed* at the phenomenon, because 'alarmed' is, in my case, not exactly the word. It is possible, however, that, but for the brown stout, I might have been a little nervous. As for the rest of the company, they really made no attempt at concealing the downright fright which possessed them. Doctor Ponnonner was a man to be pitied. Mr Gliddon, by some peculair process, rendered himself invisible. Mr Silk Buckingham I fancy, will scarcely be so bold as to deny that he made his way, upon all fours, under the table.

After the first shock of astonishment, however, we resolved, as a matter of course, upon further experiment forthwith. Our operations were not directed against the great toe of the right foot. We made an incision over the outside of the exterior *os sesamoideum pollicis pedis*, and thus got at the root of the *abductor* muscle. Re-adjusting the battery, we now applied the fluid to the bisected nerves, when, with a movement of exceeding life-likeness, the Mummy first drew up its right knee so as to bring it nearly in contact with the abdomen, and then, straightening the limb with inconceivable force, bestowed a kick upon Doctor Ponnonner, which had the effect of discharging that gentleman, like an arrow from a catapult, through a window into the street below.

We rushed out *en masse* to bring in the mangled remains of the victim, but had the happiness to meet him upon the

staircase, coming up in an unaccountable hurry, brimful of
the most ardent philosophy, and more than ever impressed
with the necessity of prosecuting our experiments with rigour
and with zeal.

It was by his advice, accordingly, that we made, upon the
spot, a profound incision into the tip of the subject's nose,
while the doctor himself, laying violent hands upon it, pulled
it into vehement contact with the wire.

Morally and physically – figuratively and literally – was the
effect electric. In the first place, the corpse opened its eyes,
and winked very rapidly for several minutes, as does Mr
Barnes in the pantomime; in the second place, it sneezed; in
the third, it sat upon end; in the fourth, it shook its fist in
Doctor Ponnonnor's face; in the fifth, turning to Messieurs
Gliddon and Buckingham, it addressed them, in very capital
Egyptian, thus:-

'I must say, gentlemen, that I am as much surprised as I am
mortified, at your behaviour. Of Doctor Ponnonner nothing
better was to be expected. He is a poor little fat fool who *knows*
no better. I pity and forgive him. But you, Mr Gliddon – and
you, Silk – who have travelled and resided in Egypt until one
might imagine you to the manor born – you, I say, who have
been so much among us that you speak Egyptian fully as well,
I think, as you write your mother tongue – you, whom I have
always been led to regard as the firm friend of the mummies –
I really did anticipate more gentlemanly conduct from *you*.
What am I to think of your standing quietly by and seeing me
thus unhandsomely used? What am I to suppose by your
permitting Tom, Dick and Harry to strip me of my coffins,
and my clothes, in this wretchedly cold climate! In what light
(to come to the point) am I to regard your aiding and abetting
that miserable little villain, Doctor Ponnonner, in pulling me
by the nose?'

It will be taken for granted, no doubt, that upon hearing
this speech under the circumstances, we all either made for
the door, or fell into violent hysterics, or went off in a general
swoon. One of these three things was, I say, to be expected.
Indeed each and all of these lines of conduct might have been
very plausibly pursued. And, upon my word, I am at a loss to
know how or why it was that we pursued neither the one nor

the other. But, perhaps, the true reason is to be sought in the spirit of the age, which proceeds by the rule of contraries altogether, and is now usually admitted as the solution of everything in the way of paradox and impossibility. Or perhaps, after all, it was only the Mummy's exceedingly natural and matter-of-course air that divested his words of the terrible. However this may be, the facts are clear, and no member of our party betrayed any very particular trepidation, or seemed to consider that anything had gone very especially wrong.

For my part I was convinced it was all right, and merely stepped aside, out of the range of the Egyptian's fist. Doctor Ponnonner thrust his hands into his breeches' pockets, looked hard at the Mummy, and grew excessively red in the face. Mr Gliddon stroked his whiskers and drew up the collar of his shirt. Mr Buckingham hung down his head, and put his right thumb into the left corner of his mouth.

The Egyptian regarded him with a severe countenance for some minutes, and at length, with a sneer, said:-

'Why don't you speak, Mr Buckingham? Did you hear what I asked you, or not? *Do* take your thumb out of your mouth!'

Mr Buckingham, hereupon, gave a slight start, took his right thumb out of the left corner of his mouth, and, by way of indemnification, inserted his left thumb in the right corner of the aperture above-mentioned.

Not being able to get an answer from Mr B, the figure turned peevishly to Mr Gliddon, and, in a peremptory tone, demanded in general terms what we all meant.

Mr Gliddon replied at great length, in phonetics; and but for the deficiency of American printing-offices in hieroglyphical type, it would afford me much pleasure to record here, in the original, the whole of his very excellent speech.

I may as well take this occasion to remark, that all the subsequent conversation in which the Mummy took a part, was carried on in primitive Egyptian, through the medium (so far as concerned myself and other untravelled members of the company) – through the medium, I say, of Messieurs Gliddon and Buckingham, as interpreters. These gentlemen spoke the mother-tongue of the mummy with inimitable fluency and grace; but I could not help observing that (owing, no doubt, to the introduction of images entirely modern, and, of course, entirely novel to the stranger,) the two travellers were reduced, occasionally, to the employment of sensible forms for the purpose of conveying a particular meaning. Mr Gliddon, at one period, for example, could not make the Egyptian comprehend the term 'politics', until he sketched upon the wall, with a bit of charcoal, a little carbuncle-nosed gentleman, out at elbows, standing upon a stump, with his left leg drawn back, his right arm thrown forward, with his fist shut, the eyes rolled up toward heaven, and the mouth open at an angle of ninety degrees. Just in the same way Mr Buckingham failed to convey the absolutely modern idea, 'whig', until, (at Doctor Ponnonner's suggestion,) he grew very pale in the face, and consented to take off his own.

It will be readily understood that Mr Gliddon's discourse turned chiefly upon the vast benefits accruing to science from the unrolling and disembowelling of mummies; apologizing, upon this score, for any disturbance that might have been occasioned *him*, in particular, the individual mummy called Allamistakeo; and concluding with a mere hint (for it could scarcely be considered more), that, as these little matters were not explained, it might be as well to proceed with the investigation intended. Here Doctor Ponnonner made ready his instruments.

In regard to the latter suggestions of the orator, it appears that Allamistakeo had certain scruples of conscience, the nature of which I did not distinctly learn; but he expressed himself satisfied with the apologies tendered, and, getting down from the table, shook hands with the company all round.

When this ceremony was at an end, we immediately busied ourselves in repairing the damages which our subject had sustained from the scalpel. We sewed up the wound in his temple, bandaged his foot, and applied a square inch of black plaster to the tip of his nose.

It was now observed that the Count (this was the title, it seems, of Allamistakeo), had a slight fit of shivering – no doubt from the cold. The doctor immediately repaired to his wardrobe, and soon returned with a black dress coat, made in

Jennings' best manner, a pair of sky-blue plaid pantaloons with straps, a pink gingham *chemise*, a flapped vest of brocade, a white sack overcoat, a walking cane with a hook, a hat with no brim, patent-leather boots, straw-coloured kid gloves, an eye-glass, a pair of whiskers, and a waterfall cravat. Owing to the disparity of size between the Count and the doctor (the proportion being as two to one), there was some little difficulty in adjusting these habiliments upon the person of the Egyptian; but when all was arranged, he might have been said to be dressed. Mr Gliddon, therefore, gave him his arm, and led him to a comfortable chair by the fire, while the doctor rang the bell upon the spot and ordered a supply of cigars and wine.

The conversation soon grew animated. Much curiosity was, of course, expressed in regard to the somewhat remarkable fact of Allamistakeo's still remaining alive.

'I should have thought,' observed Mr Buckingham, 'that it is high time you were dead.'

'Why,' replied the Count, very much astonished, 'I am little more than seven hundred years old! My father lived a thousand, and was by no means in his dotage when he died.'

Here ensued a brisk series of questions and computations, by means of which it became evident that the antiquity of the Mummy had been grossly misjudged. It had been five thousand and fifty years, and some months, since he had been consigned to the catacombs at Eleithias.

'But my remark,' resumed Mr Buckinham, 'had no reference to your age at the period of interment (I am willing to grant, in fact, that you are still a young man); and my allusion was to the immensity of time during which, by your own showing, you must have been done up in asphaltum.'

'In what?' said the Count.

'In asphaltum,' persisted Mr B.

'Ah, yes; I have some faint notion of what you mean; it might be made to answer, no doubt, – but in my time we employed scarcely anything else than the Bichloride of Mercury.'

'But what we are especially at a loss to understand,' said Doctor Ponnonner, 'is, how it happens that, having been

dead and buried in Egypt five thousand years ago, you are
here to-day all alive, and looking so delightfully well.'

'Had I been, as you say, *dead*,' replied the Count, 'it is more
than probable that dead I should still be; for I perceive you
are yet in the infancy of galvanism, and cannot accomplish
with it what was a common thing among us in the old days.
But the fact is, I fell into catalepsy, and it was considered by
my best friends that I was either dead or should be; they
accordingly embalmed me at once – I presume you are aware
of the chief principle of the embalming process?'

'Why, not altogether.'

'Ah, I perceive;- a deplorable condition of ignorance! Well,
I cannot enter into details just now: but is is necessary to
explain that to embalm (properly speaking), in Egypt, was to
arrest indefinitely *all* the animal functions subjected to the
process. I use the word 'animal' in its widest sense, as including the physical not more than the moral and *vital* being. I
repeat that the leading principle of embalmment consisted,
with us, in the immediately arresting, and holding in
perpetual *abeyance, all* the animal functions subjected to the
process. To be brief, in whatever condition the individual was,
at the period of embalmment, in that condition he remained.
Now, as it is my good fortune to be of the blood of the
Scarabœus, I was embalmed *alive*, as you see me at present.'

'The blood of the Scarabœus!' exclaimed Doctor
Ponnonner.

'Yes. The Scarabœus was the *insignium*, or the 'arms', of a
very distinguished and very rare patrician family. To be 'of
the blood of the Scarabœus,' is merely to be one of that family
of which the Scarabœus is the *insignium*. I speak figuratively.'

'But what has this to do with your being alive?'

'Why it is the general custom in Egypt, to deprive a corpse –
before embalmment, of its bowels and brains; the race of
Scarabœi alone did not coincide with the custom. Had I not
been a Scarabœus, therefore, I should have been without
bowels and brains; and without either it is inconvenient to
live.'

'I perceive that,' said Mr Buckingham; 'and I presume that
all the *entire* mummies that come to hand are of the race of
Scarabœi.'

'Beyond doubt.'

'I thought,' said Mr Gliddon, very meekly, 'that the Scarbœus was one of the Egyptian gods.'

'One of the Egyptian *what*?' exclaimed the mummy starting to its feet.

'Gods!' repeated the traveller.

'Mr Gliddon, I really am astonished to hear you talk in this style,' said the Count, resuming his seat. 'No nation upon the face of the earth has ever acknowledged more than *one god*. The Scarabœus, the Ibis, etc., were with us (as similar creatures have been with others), the symbols, or *media*, through which we offered worship to the Creator too august to be more directly approached.'

There was here a pause. At length the colloquy was renewed by Doctor Ponnonner.

'It is not improbable, then, from what you have explained,' said he, 'that among the catacombs near the Nile, there may exist other mummies of the Scarabœus tribe, in a condition of vitality.'

'There can be no question of it,' replied the Count; 'all the Scarabœi embalmed accidentally while alive, are alive. Even some of those *purposely* so embalmed, may have been overlooked by their executors, and still remain in the tombs.'

'Will you be kind enough to explain,' I said, 'what you mean by "purposely so embalmed?"'

'With great pleasure,' he said. 'The usual duration of man's life, in my time, was about eight hundred years. Few men died, unless by most extraordinary accident, before the age of six hundred; few lived longer than a decade of centuries; but eight were considered the natural term. After the discovery of the embalming principle, as I have already described it to you, it occurred to our philosophers that a laudable curiosity might be gratified, and, at the same time, the interests of science much advanced, by living this natural term in instalments. In the case of history, indeed, experience demonstrated that something of this kind was indispensable. An historian, for example, having attained the age of five hundred, would write a book with great labour and then get himself carefully embalmed; leaving instructions to his executors *pro tem.*, that they should cause him to be revivified after the lapse of a certain period – say five or six hundred years. Resuming existence at the expiration of this time, he would invariably find his great work converted into a species of hazard note-book – that is to say, into a kind of literary arena for the conflicting guesses, riddles, and personal squabbles of whole herds of exasperated commentators. These guesses, etc., which passed under the name of annotations, or emendations, were found so completely to have enveloped, distorted, and overwhelmed the text, that the author had to go about with a lantern to discover his own book. When discovered, it was never worth the trouble of the search. After rewriting it throughout, it was regarded as the bounden duty of the historian to set himself to work, immediately, in correcting, from his own private knowledge and experience, the traditions of the day concerning the epoch at which he had originally lived. Now this process of re-scription and personal rectification, pursued by various individual sages, from time to time, had the effect of preventing our history from degenerating into absolute fable.'

'I beg your pardon,' said Doctor Ponnonner at this point, laying his hands gently upon the arms of the Egyptian – 'I beg your pardon, sir, but may I presume to interrupt you for one moment?'

'By all means, *sir*,' replied the Count, drawing up.

'I merely wished to ask you a question,' said the doctor. 'You mentioned the historian's personal correction of *traditions* respecting his own epoch. Pray, sir, upon an average, what proportion of these Kabbala were usually found to be right?'

'The Kabbala, as you properly term them, sir, were generally discovered to be precisely on a par with the facts recorded in the un-rewritten histories themselves; that is to say, not one individual iota of either was ever known, under any circumstances, to be not totally and radically wrong.'

'But since it is quite clear,' resumed the doctor, 'that at least five thousand years have elapsed since your entombment, I take it for granted that your histories at that period, if not your traditions, were sufficiently explicit on that one topic of universal interest, the Creation, which took place, as I presume you are aware, only about ten centuries before.'

'Sir!' said the Count Allamistakeo.

The doctor repeated his remarks, but it was only after much additional explanation that the foreigner could be made to comprehend them. The latter at length said, hesitatingly:

'The ideas you have suggestd are to me, I confess, utterly novel. During my time I never knew any one to entertain so singular a fancy as that the universe (or this world if you will have it so), ever had a beginning at all. I remember once, and once only, hearing something remotely hinted by a man of many speculations concerning the origin *of the human race;* and by this individual the very word *Adam* (or Red Earth), which you make use of, was employed. He employed it, however, in a generical sense, with reference to the spontaneous germination from rank soil (just as a thousand of the lower *genera* of creatures are germinated) – the spontaneous germination, I say, of five vast hordes of men, simultaneously upspringing in five distinct and nearly equal divisions of the globe.'

Here, in general, the company shrugged their shoulders, and one or two of us touched our foreheads with a very significant air. Mr Silk Buckingham, first glancing slightly at the occiput and then at the siniciput of Allamistakeo, spoke as follows:

'The long duration of human life in your time, together with the occasional practice of passing it, as you have explained, in instalments, must have had, indeed, a strong tendency to the general development and conglomeration of knowledge. I presume, therefore, that we are to attribute the marked inferiority of the old Egyptians in all particulars of science, when compared with the moderns, and more especially with the Yankees, altogether to the superior solidity of the Egyptian skull.'

'I confess again,' replied the Count, with much suavity, 'that I am somewhat at a loss to comprehend you; pray, to what particulars of science do you allude?'

Here our whole party, joining voices, detailed, at great length, the assumptions of phrenology and the marvels of animal magnetism.

Having heard us to an end, the Count proceeded to relate a few anecdotes, which rendered it evident that prototypes of Gall and Spurzheim had flourished and faded in Egypt so long

ago as to have been nearly forgotten, and that the manœuvres
of Mesmer were really very contemptible tricks when put in
collation with the positive miracles of the Theban *savans*, who
created lice, and a great many other similar things.

I here asked the Count if his people were able to calculate
eclipses. He smiled rather contemptuously, and said they
were.

This put me a little out; but I began to make other inquiries
in regard to his astronomical knowledge, when a member of
the company, who had never as yet opened his mouth,
whispered in my ear, that for information on this head I had
better consult Ptolemy, (whoever Ptolemy is), as well as
Plutarch *de facie lunæ*.

I then questioned the Mummy about burning-glasses and
lenses and, in general, about the manufacture of glass; but I
had not made an end of my queries before the silent member
again touched me quietly on the elbow, and begged me, for
God's sake, to take a peep at Diodorus Siculus. As for the
Count, he merely asked me, in the way of reply, if we moderns
possessed any such microscopes as would enable us to cut
cameos in the style of the Egyptians. While I was thinking
how I should answer this question, little Doctor Ponnonner
committed himself in a very extraordinary way.

'Look at our architecture!' he exclaimed, greatly to the
indignation of both the travellers, who pinched him black and
blue to no purpose.

'Look!' he cried, with enthusiasm, 'at the Bowling-green
Fountain in New York! Or, if this be too vast a contemplation,
regard for a moment the Capitol at Washington, D.C.!' – and
the good little medical man went on to detail, very minutely,
the proportions of the fabric to which he referred. He explained that the portico alone was adorned with no less than
four and twenty columns, five feet in diameter, and ten feet
apart.

The Count said that he regretted not being able to remember, just at that moment, the precise dimensions of any
one of the principal buildings of the City of Aznac, whose
foundations were laid in the night of Time, but the ruins of
which were still standing, at the epoch of his entombment, in a
vast plain of sand to the westward of Thebes. He recollected,

however (talking of porticoes), that one affixed to an inferior palace in a kind of suburb called Carnac, consisted of a hundred and forty-four columns, thirty-seven feet each in circumference, and twenty-five feet apart. The approach of this portico, from the Nile, was through an avenue two miles long, composed of sphynxes, statues and obelisks, twenty, sixty, and a hundred feet in height. The palace itself (as well as he could remember) was, in one direction, two miles long, and might have been, altogether, about seven in circuit. Its walls were richly painted all over, within and without, with hieroglyphics. He would not pretend to *assert* that even fifty or sixty of the Doctor's Capitols might have been built within these walls, but he was by no means sure that two or three hundred of them might not have been squeezed in with some trouble. That palace at Carnac was an insignificant little building after all. He (the Count) however, could not conscientiously refuse to admit the ingenuity, magnificence, and superiority of the fountain at the Bowling-green, as described by the Doctor. Nothing like it, he was forced to allow, had ever been seen in Egypt or elsewhere.

I here asked the Count what he had to say to our railroads.

'Nothing,' he replied, 'in particular.' They were rather slight, rather ill-conceived, and clumsily put together. They could not be compared, of course, with the vast, level, direct, iron-grooved causeways, upon which the Egyptians conveyed entire temples and solid obelisks of a hundred and fifty feet in altitude.

I spoke of our gigantic mechanical forces.

He agreed that we knew something in that way, but inquired how I should have gone to work in getting up the imposts on the lintels of even the little palace at Carnac.

This question I concluded not to hear, and demanded if he had any idea of Artesian wells; but he simply raised his eyebrows; while Mr Gliddon winked at me very hard and said, in a low tone, that one had been recently discovered by the engineers employed to bore for water in the Great Oasis.

I then mentioned our steel; but the foreigner elevated his nose, and asked me if our steel could have executed the sharp carved work seen on the obelisks, and which was wrought altogether by edge-tools of copper.

This disconcerted us so greatly that we thought it advisable to vary the attack to Metaphysics. We sent for a copy of a book called the 'Dial', and read out of it a chapter or two about something which is not very clear, but which the Bostonians call the Great Movement or Progress.

The Count merely said that Great Movements were awfully common things in his day, and as for Progress, it was at one time quite a nuisance, but it never progressed.

We then spoke of the great beauty and importance of Democracy, and were at much trouble in impressing the Count with a due sense of the advantages we enjoyed in living where there was suffrage *ad libitum*, and no king.

He listened with marked interest, and in fact seemed not a little amused. When we had done he said that, a great while ago there had occurred something of a very similar sort. Thirteen Egyptian provinces determined all at once to be free, and so set a magnificent example to the rest of mankind. They assembled their wise men, and concocted the most ingenious constitution it is possible to conceive. For a while they managed remarkably well; only their habit of bragging was prodigious. The thing ended, however, in the consolidation of the thirteen states, with some fifteen or twenty others, in the most odious and insupportable despotism that ever was heard of upon the face of the Earth.

I ask what was the name of the usurping tyrant.

As well as the Count could recollect it was *Mob*.

Not knowing what to say to this, I raised my voice, and deplored the Egyptian ignorance of steam.

The Count looked at me with much astonishment, but made no answer. The silent gentleman, however, gave me a violent nudge in the ribs with his elbows – told me I had sufficiently exposed myself for once – and demanded if I was really such a fool as not to know that the modern steam engine is derived from the invention of Hero, through Solomon de Caus.

We were now in imminent danger of being discomfited; but, as good luck would have it, Doctor Ponnonner, having rallied, returned to our rescue, and inquired if the people of Egypt would seriously pretend to rival the moderns in the all important particular of dress.

The Count, at this, glanced downwards to the straps of his pantaloons, and then taking hold of the end of one of his coattails, held it up close to his eyes for some minutes. Letting it fall, at last, his mouth extended itself very gradually from ear to ear; but I do not remember that he said anything in the way of reply.

Hereupon we recovered our spirits, and the Doctor, approaching the Mummy with great dignity, desired it to say candidly, upon its honour as a gentleman, if the Egyptians had comprehended at *any* period the manufacture of either Ponnonner's lozenges, or Brandreth's pills.

We looked, with profound anxiety, for an answer; but in vain. It was not forthcoming. The Egyptian blushed and hung down his head. Never was triumph more consummate; never was defeat borne with so ill a grace. Indeed, I could not endure the spectacle of the poor Mummy's mortification. I reached my hat, bowed to him stiffly, and took leave.

Upon getting home I found it past four o'clock, and went immediately to bed. It is now ten, A.M. I have been up since seven, penning these memoranda for the benefit of my family and of mankind. The former I shall behold no more. My wife is a shrew. The truth is, I am heartily sick of this life and of the nineteenth century in general. I am convinced that everything is going wrong. Besides, I am anxious to know who will be President in 2045. As soon, therefore, as I shave and swallow a cup of coffee, I shall just step over to Ponnonner's and get embalmed for a couple of hundred years.

MY NEW YEAR'S EVE AMONG
THE MUMMIES

by Grant Allen

I have been a wanderer and a vagabond on the face of the earth for a good many years now, and I have certainly had some odd adventures in my time; but I can assure you, I never spent twenty-four queerer hours than those which I passed some twelve months since in the great unopened Pyramid of Abu Yilla.

The way I got there was itself a very strange one. I had come to Egypt for a winter tour with the Fitz-Simkinses, to whose daughter Editha I was at that precise moment engaged. You will probably remember that old Fitz-Simkins belonged originally to the wealthy firm of Simkinson and Stokoe, worshipful vintners; but when the senior partner retired from the business and got his knighthood, the College of Heralds opportunely discovered that his ancestors had changed their fine old Norman name for its English equivalent some time about the reign of King Richard I; and they immediately authorized the old gentleman to resume the patronymic and the armorial bearings of his distinguished forefathers. It's really quite astonishing how often these curious coincidences crop up at the College of Heralds.

Of course it was a great catch for a landless and briefless barrister like myself – dependent on a small fortune in South American securities, and my precarious earnings as a writer of burlesque – to secure such a valuable prospective property as Editha Fitz-Simkins. To be sure, the girl was undeniably plain; but I have known plainer girls than she was, whom forty thousand pounds converted into My Ladies: and if Editha hadn't really fallen over head and ears in love with me, I suppose old Fitz-Simkins would never have consented to such a match. As it was, however, we had flirted so openly and so desperately during the Scarborough season, that it would have been difficult for Sir Peter to break it off: and so I had come to Egypt on a tour of insurance to secure my prize, following in the wake of my future mother-in-law, whose lungs were supposed to require a genial climate – though in my private opinion they were really as creditable a pair of pulmonary appendages as ever drew breath.

Nevertheless, the course of true love did not run so smoothly as might have been expected. Editha found me less ardent than a devoted squire should be; and on the very last night of the old year she got up a regulation lovers' quarrel, because I had sneaked away from the boat that afternoon under the guidance of our dragoman, to witness the seductive performances of some fair Ghawázi, the dancing girls of a neighbouring town. How she found it out heaven only knows, for I gave that rascal Dimitri five piastres to hold his tongue: but she did find it out somehow, and chose to regard it as an offence of the first magnitude: a mortal sin only to be expiated by three days of penance and humiliation.

I went to bed that night, in my hammock on deck, with feelings far from satisfactory. We were moored against the bank at Abu Yilla, the most pestiferous hole between the cataracts and the Delta. The mosquitoes were worse than the ordinary mosquitoes of Egypt, and that is saying a great deal. The heat was oppressive even at night, and the malaria from the lotus beds rose like a palpable mist before my eyes. Above all, I was getting doubtful whether Editha Fitz-Simkins might not after all slip between my fingers. I felt wretched and feverish: and yet I had delightful interlusive recollections, in between, of that lovely little Gháziyah, who danced that exquisite, marvellous, entrancing, delicious, and awfully oriental dance that I saw in the afternoon.

By Jove, she *was* a beautiful creature. Eyes like two full moons; hair like Milton's Penseroso; movements like a poem of Swinburne's set to action. If Editha was only a faint picture of that girl now! Upon my word, I was falling in love with a Gháziyah!

Then the mosquitoes came again. Buzz – buzz – buzz. I make a lunge at the loudest and biggest, a sort of prima donna in their infernal opera. I kill the prima donna, but ten more shrill performers come in its place. The frogs croak dismally in the reedy shallows. The night grows hotter and hotter still. At last, I can stand it no longer. I rise up, dress myself lightly, and jump ashore to find some way of passing the time.

Yonder, across the flat, lies the great unopened Pyramid of Abu Yilla. We are going to-morrow to climb to the top; but I will take a turn to reconnoitre in that direction now. I walk across the moonlit fields, my soul still divided between Editha and the Gháziyah, and approach the solemn mass of huge, antiquated granite blocks standing out so grimly against the pale horizon. I feel half awake, half asleep, and altogether feverish: but I poke about the base in an aimless sort of way, with a vague idea that I may perhaps discover by chance the secret of its sealed entrance, which has ere now baffled so many pertinacious explorers and learned Egyptologists.

As I walk along the base, I remember old Herodotus's story, like a page from the 'Arabian Nights', of how King Rhampsinitus built himself a treasury, wherein one stone turned on a pivot like a door; and how the builder availed himself of this his cunning device to steal gold from the king's storehouse. Suppose the entrance to the unopened Pyramid should be by such a door. It would be curious if I should chance to light upon the very spot.

I stood in the broad moonlight, near the north-east angle of the great pile, at the twelfth stone from the corner. A random fancy struck me, that I might turn this stone by pushing it inward on the left side. I leant against it with all my weight, and tried to move it on the imaginary pivot. Did it give way a fraction of an inch? No, it must have been mere fancy. Let me try again. Surely it is yielding! Gracious Osiris, it has moved an inch or more! My heart beats fast, either with fever or excitement, and I try a third time. The rust of centuries on the pivot wears slowly off, and the stone turned ponderously round, giving access to a low dark passage.

It must have been madness which led me to enter the

forgotten corridor, alone, without torch or match, at that hour of the evening; but at any rate I entered. The passage was tall enough for a man to walk erect, and I could feel, as I groped slowly along, that the wall was composed of smooth polished granite, while the floor sloped away downward with a slight but regular descent. I walked with trembling heart and faltering feet for some forty or fifty yards down the mysterious vestibule: and then I felt myself brought suddenly to a standstill by a block of stone placed right across the pathway. I had had nearly enough for one evening, and I was preparing to return to the boat, agog with my new discovery, when my attention was suddenly arrested by an incredible, a perfectly miraculous fact.

The block of stone which barred the passage was faintly visible as a square, by means of a struggling belt of light streaming through the seams. There must be a lamp or other flame burning within. What if this were a door like the outer one, leading into a chamber perhaps inhabited by some dangerous band of outcasts? The light was a sure evidence of human occupation: and yet the outer door swung rustily on its pivot as though it had never been opened for ages. I paused a moment in fear before I ventured to try the stone: and then, urged on once more by some insane impulse, I turned the massive block with all my might to the left. It gave way slowly like its neighbour, and finally opened into the central hall.

Never as long as I live shall I forget the ecstasy of terror, astonishment, and blank dismay which seized upon me when I stepped into that seemingly enchanted chamber. A blaze of light first burst upon my eyes, from jets of gas arranged in regular rows tier above tier, upon the columns and walls of the vast apartment. Huge pillars, richly painted with red, yellow, blue and green decorations, stretched in endless succession down the dazzling aisles. A floor of polished syenite reflected the splendour of the lamps, and afforded a base for red granite sphinxes and dark purple images in porphyry of the cat-faced goddess Pasht, whose form I knew so well at the Louvre and the British Museum. But I had no eyes for any of these lesser marvels, being wholly absorbed in the greatest marvel of all: for there, in royal state and with mitred head, a living Egyptian king, surrounded by his coiffured court, was

banqueting in the flesh upon a real throne, before a table
laden with Memphian delicacies!

I stood transfixed with awe and amazement, my tongue and
my feet alike forgetting their office, and my brain whirling
round and round, as I remember it used to whirl when my
health broke down utterly at Cambridge after the Classical
Tripos. I gazed fixedly at the strange picture before me, taking
in all its details in a confused way, yet quite incapable of
understanding or realizing any part of its true import. I saw
the king in the centre of the hall, raised on a throne of granite
inlaid with gold and ivory; his head crowned with the peaked
cap of Rameses, and his curled hair flowing down his
shoulders in a set and formal frizz. I saw priests and warriors
on either side, dressed in the costumes which I had often
carefully noted in our great collections; while bronze-skinned
maids, with light garments round their waists, and limbs
displayed in graceful picturesqueness, waited upon them, half
nude, as in the wall paintings which we had lately examined
at Karnak and Syene. I saw the ladies, clothed from head to
foot in dyed linen garments, sitting apart in the background,
banqueting by themselves at a separate table; while dancing
girls, like older representatives of my yesternoon friends, the
Ghawázi, tumbled before them in strange attitudes, to the
music of four-stringed harps and long straight pipes. In short,
I beheld as in a dream the whole drama of everyday Egyptian
royal life, playing itself out anew under my eyes, in its real
original properties and personages.

Gradually, as I looked, I became aware that my hosts were
no less surprised at the appearance of their anachronistic
guest than was the guest himself at the strange living
panorama which met his eyes. In a moment music and
dancing ceased; the banquet paused in its course, and the king
and his nobles stood up in undisguised astonishment to survey
the strange intruder.

Some minutes passed before any one moved forward on
either side. At last a young girl of royal appearance, yet
strangely resembling the Gháziyah of Abu Yilla, and recalling
in part the laughing maiden in the foreground of Mr Long's
great canvas at the previous Academy, stepped out before the
throng.

'May I ask you,' she said in Ancient Egyptian, 'who you are, and why you come hither to disturb us?'

I was never aware before that I spoke or understood the language of the hieroglyphics: yet I found I had not the slightest difficulty in comprehending or answering her question. To say the truth, Ancient Egyptian, though an extremely tough tongue to decipher in its written form, becomes as easy as love-making when spoken by a pair of lips like that Pharaonic princess's. It is really very much the same as English, pronounced in a rapid and somewhat indefinte whisper, and with all the vowels left out.

'I beg ten thousand pardons for my intrusion,' I answered apologetically: 'but I did not know that this Pyramid was inhabited, or I should not have entered your residence so rudely. As for the points you wish to know, I am an English tourist, and you will find my name upon this card;' saying which I handed her one from the case which I had fortunately put into my pocket, with conciliatory politeness. The princess examined it closely, but evidently did not understand its import.

'In return,' I continued, 'may I ask you in what august presence I now find myself by accident?'

A court official stood forth from the throng, and answered in a set heraldic tone: 'In the presence of the illustrious monarch, Brother of the Sun, Thothmes the Twenty-seventh, king of the Eighteenth Dynasty.'

'Salute the Lord of the World,' put in another official in the same regulation drone.

I bowed low to his Majesty, and stepped out into the hall. Apparently my obeisance did not come up to Egyptian standards of courtesy, for a suppressed titter broke audibly from the ranks of bronze-skinned waiting-women. But the king graciously smiled at my attempt, and turning to the nearest nobleman, observed in a voice of great sweetnes and self-contained majesty: 'This stranger, Ombos, is certainly a very curious person. His appearance does not at all resemble that of an Ethiopian or other savage, nor does he look like the pale-faced sailors who come to us from the Achaian land beyond the sea. His features, to be sure, are not very different from theirs; but his extraordinary and singularly inartistic dress shows him to belong to some other barbaric race.'

I glanced down at my waistcoat, and saw that I was wearing my tourist's check suit, of grey and mud colour, with which a Bond Street tailor had supplied me just before leaving town, as the latest thing out in fancy tweeds. Evidently these Egyptians must have a very curious standard of taste not to admire our pretty and graceful style of male attire.

'If the dust beneath your Majesty's feet may venture upon a suggestion,' put in the officer whom the king had addressed, 'I would hint that this young man is probably a stray visitor from the utterly uncivilized lands of the North. The headgear which he carries in his hand obviously betrays an Arctic habitat.'

I had instinctively taken off my round felt hat in the first moment of surprise, when I found myself in the midst of this strange throng, and I was standing now in a somewhat embarrassed posture, holding it awkwardly before me like a shield to protect my chest.

'Let the stranger cover himself,' said the king.

'Barbarian intruder, cover yourself,' cried the herald. I noticed throughout that the king never directly addressed anybody save the higher officials around him.

I put on my hat as desired. 'A most uncomfortable and silly form of tiara indeed,' said the great Thothmes.

'Very unlike your noble and awe-spiring mitre, Lion of Egypt,' answered Ombos.

'Ask the stranger his name,' the king continued.

It was useless to offer another card, so I mentioned it in a clear voice.

'An uncouth and almost unpronounceable designation truly,' commented his Majesty to the Grand Chamberlain beside him. 'These savages speak strange languages, widely different from the flowing tongue of Memnon and Sesostris.'

The chamberlain bowed his assent with three low genuflexions. I began to feel a little abashed at these personal remarks, and I *almost* think (though I shouldn't like it to be mentioned in the Temple) that a blush rose to my cheek.

The beautiful princess, who had been standing near me meanwhile in an attitude of statuesque repose, now appeared anxious to change the current of the conversation. 'Dear father,' she said with a respectful inclination, 'surely the stranger, barbarian though he be, cannot relish such pointed allusions to his person and costume. We must let him feel the grace and delicacy of Egyptian refinement. Then he may perhaps carry back with him some faint echo of its cultured beauty to his northern wilds.'

'Nonsense, Hatasou,' replied Thothmes XXVII testily. 'Savages have no feelings, and they are as incapable of appreciating Egyptian sensibility as the chattering crow is incapable of attaining the dignified reserve of the sacred crocodile.'

'Your Majesty is mistaken,' I said, recovering my self-possession gradually and realizing my position as a freeborn Englishman before the court of a foreign despot – though I must allow that I felt rather less confident than usual, owing to the fact that we were not represented in the Pyramid by a British Consul – 'I am an English tourist, a visitor from a modern land whose civilization far surpasses the rude culture of early Egypt; and I am accustomed to respectful treatment from all other nationalities, as becomes a citizen of the First Naval Power in the World.'

My answer created a profound impression. 'He has spoken to the Brother of the Sun,' cried Ombos in evident perturbation. 'He must be of the Blood Royal in his own tribe, or he would never have dared to do so!'

'Otherwise,' added a person whose dress I recognized as that of a priest, 'he must be offered up in expiation to Amon-Ra immediately.'

As a rule I am a decent truthful person, but under these alarming circumstances I ventured to tell a slight fib with an air of nonchalant boldness. 'I am a younger brother of our reigning king,' I said without a moment's hesitation; for there was nobody present to gainsay me, and I tried to salve my conscience by reflecting that at any rate I was only claiming consanguinity with an imaginary personage.

'In that case,' said King Thothmes, with more geniality in his tone, 'there can be no impropriety in my addressing you personally. Will you take a place at our table next to myself, and we can converse together without interrupting a banquet which must be brief enough in any circumstances? Hatasou, my dear, you may seat yourself next to the barbarian prince.'

I felt a visible swelling to the proper dimensions of a Royal Highness as I sat down by the king's right hand. The nobles resumed their places, the bronze-skinned waitresses left off standing like soldiers in a row and staring straight at my humble self, the goblets went round once more, and a comely maid soon brought me meat, bread, fruits and date wine.

All this time I was naturally burning with curiosity to inquire who my strange host might be, and how they had preserved their existence for so many centuries in this undiscovered hall; but I was obliged to wait until I had satisfied his Majesty of my own nationality, the means by which I had entered the Pyramid, the general state of affairs throughout the world at the present moment, and fifty thousand other matters of a similar sort. Thothmes utterly refused to believe my reiterated assertion that our existing civilization was far superior to the Egyptian; 'because,' he said, 'I see from your dress that your nation is utterly devoid of taste or invention;' but he listened with great interest to my account of modern society, the steam-engine, the Permissive Prohibitory Bill, the telegraph, the House of Commons, Home Rule, and other blessings of our advanced era, as well as to a brief *résumé* of European history from the rise of the Greek culture to the Russo-Turkish war. At last his questions were nearly exhausted, and I got a chance of making a few counter inquiries on my own account.

'And now,' I said, turning to the charming Hatasou, whom I thought a more pleasing informant than her august papa, 'I should like to know who *you* are.'

'What, don't you know?' she cried with unaffected surprise. 'Why, we're mummies.'

She made this astonishing statement with just the same quiet unconsciousness as if she had said, 'we're French,' or 'we're Americans.' I glanced round the walls, and observed behind the columns, what I had not noticed till then – a large number of empty mummy-cases, with their lids placed carelessly by their sides.

'But what are you doing here?' I asked in a bewildered way.

'Is it possible,' said Hatasou, 'that you don't really know

the object of embalming? Though your manners show you to be an agreeable and well-bred young man, you must excuse my saying that you are shockingly ignorant. We are made into mummies in order to preserve our immortality. Once in every thousand years we wake up for twenty-four hours, recover our flesh and blood, and banquet once more upon the mummied dishes and other good things laid by for us in the Pyramid. To-day is the first day of a millennium, and so we have waked up for the sixth time since we were first embalmed.'

'The *sixth* time?' I inquired incredulously. 'Then you must have been dead six thousand years.'

'Exactly so.'

'But the world has not yet existed so long,' I cried, in a fervour of orthodox horror.

'Excuse me, barbarian prince. This is the first day of the three hundred and twenty-seven thousandth millennium.'

My orthodoxy received a severe shock. However, I had been accustomed to geological calculations, and was somewhat inclined to accept the antiquity of man; so I swallowed the statement without more ado. Besides, if such a charming girl as Hatasou had asked me at that moment to turn Mohammedan, or to worship Osiris, I believe I should incontinently have done so.

'You wake up only for a single day and night, then?' I said.

'Only for a single day and night. After that, we go to sleep for another millennium.'

'Unless you are meanwhile burned as fuel on the Cairo Railway,' I added mentally. 'But how,' I continued aloud, 'do you get these lights?'

'The Pyramid is built above a spring of inflammable gas. We have a reservoir in one of the side chambers in which it collects during the thousand years. As soon as we awake, we turn it on at once from the tap, and light it with a lucifer match.

'Upon my word,' I interposed, 'I had no notion you Ancient Egyptians were acquainted with the use of matches.'

'Very likely not. "There are more things in heaven and earth, Cephrenes, than are dreamt of in your philosophy," as the bard of Philæ puts it.'

Further inquiries brought out all the secrets of that strange tomb-house, and kept me fully interested till the close of the banquet. Then the chief priest solemnly rose, offered a small fragment of meat to a deified crocodile, who sat in a meditative manner by the side of his deserted mummy-case, and declared the feast concluded for the night. All rose from their places, wandered away into the long corridors or side-aisles, and formed little groups of talkers under the brilliant gas-lamps.

For my part, I strolled off with Hatasou down the least illuminated of the colonnades, and took my seat beside a marble fountain, where several fish (gods of great sanctity, Hatasou assured me) were disporting themselves in a porphyry basin. How long we sat there I cannot tell, but I know that we talked a good deal about fish, and gods, and Egyptian habits, and Egyptian philosophy, and, above all, Egyptian love-making. The last-named subject we found very interesting, and when once we got fully started upon it, no diversion afterwards occurred to break the even tenour of the conversation. Hatasou was a lovely figure, tall, queenly, with smooth dark arms and neck of polished bronze: her big black eyes full of tenderness, and her long hair bound up into a bright Egyptian headdress, that harmonized to a tone with her complexion and her robe. The more we talked, the more desperately did I fall in love, and the more utterly oblivious did I become of my duty to Editha Fitz-Simkins. The mere ugly daughter of a rich and vulgar brand-new knight, for-sooth, to show off her airs before me, when here was a Princess of the Blood Royal of Egypt, obviously sensible to the attentions which I was paying her, and not unwilling to receive them with a coy and modest grace.

Well, I went on saying pretty things to Hatasou, and Hatasou went on deprecating them in a pretty little way, as who should say, 'I don't mean what I pretend to mean one bit;' until at last I may confess that we were both evidently as far gone in the disease of the heart called love as it is possible for two young people on first acquaintance to become. There-fore, when Hatasou pulled forth her watch – another piece of mechanism with which antiquaries used never to credit the Egyptian people – and declared that she had only three more hours to live, at least for the next thousand years, I fairly broke down, took out my handkerchief, and began to sob like a child of five years old.

Hatasou was deeply moved. Decorum forbade that she should console me with too much *empressement*; but she ventured to remove the handkerchief gently from my face, and suggested that there was yet one course open by which we might enjoy a little more of one another's society. 'Suppose,' she said quietly, 'you were to become a mummy. You would then wake up, as we do, every thousand years; and after you have tried it once, you will find it just as natural to sleep for a millennium as for eight hours. Of course,' she added with a slight blush, 'during the next three or four solar cycles there would be plenty of time to conclude any other arrangements you might possibly contemplate, before the occurrence of another glacial epoch.'

This mode of regarding time was certainly novel and somewhat bewildering to people who ordinarily reckon its lapse by weeks and months; and I had a vague consciousness that my relations with Editha imposed upon me a moral necessity of returning to the outer world, instead of becoming a millennial mummy. Besides, there was the awkward chance of being converted into fuel and dissipated into space before the arrival of the next waking day. But I took one look at Hatasou, whose eyes were filling in turn with sympathetic tears, and that look decided me. I flung Editha, life, and duty to the dogs, and resolved at once to become a mummy.

There was no time to be lost. Only three hours remained to us, and the process of embalming, even in the most hasty manner, would take up fully two. We rushed off to the chief priest, who had charge of the particular department in question. He at once acceded to my wishes, and briefly explained the mode in which they usually treated the corpse.

That word suddenly aroused me. 'The corpse!' I cried; 'but I am alive. You can't embalm me living,'

'We can,' replied the priest, 'under chloroform.'

'Chloroform!' I echoed, growing more and more astonished: 'I had no idea you Egyptians knew anything about it.'

'Ignorant barbarian!' he answered with a curl of the lip; 'you imagine yourself much wiser than the teachers of the world. If you were versed in all the wisdom of the Egyptians, you would know that chloroform is one of our simplest and commonest anæsthetics.'

I put myself at once under the hands of the priest. He brought out the chloroform, and placed it beneath my nostrils, as I lay on a soft couch under the central court. Hatasou held my hand in hers, and watched my breathing with an anxious eye. I saw the priest leaning over me, with a clouded phial in his hand, and I experienced a vague sensation of smelling myrrh and spikenard. Next, I lost myself for a few moments, and when I again recovered my senses in a temporary break, the priest was holding a small greenstone knife, dabbled with blood, and I felt that a gash had been made across my breast. Then they applied the chloroform once more; I felt Hatasou give my hand a gentle squeeze; the whole panorama faded finally from my view; and I went to sleep for a seemingly endless time.

When I awoke again, my first impression led me to believe that the thousand years were over, and that I had come to life once more to feast with Hatasou and Thothmes in the Pyramid of Abu Yilla. But second thoughts, combined with closer observation of the surroundings, convinced me that I was really lying in a bedroom of Shepheard's Hotel at Cairo. An hospital nurse leant over me, instead of a chief priest; and I noticed no tokens of Editha Fitz-Simkins's presence. But when I endeavoured to make inquiries upon the subject of my whereabouts, I was peremptorily informed that I mustn't speak, as I was only just recovering from a severe fever, and might endanger my life by talking.

Some weeks later I learned the sequel of my night's adventure. The Fitz-Simkinses, missing me from the boat in the morning, at first imagined that I might have gone ashore for an early stroll. But after breakfast time, lunch time, and dinner time had gone past, they began to grow alarmed, and sent to look for me in all directions. One of their scouts, happening to pass the Pyramid, noticed that one of the stones near the north-east angle had been displaced, so as to give access to a dark passage, hitherto unknown. Calling several of his friends, for he was afraid to venture in alone, he passed down the corridor, and through a second gateway into the central hall. There the Fellahin found me, lying on the ground, bleeding profusely from a wound on the breast, and in an advanced stage of malarious fever. They brought me back to the boat, and the Fitz-Simkinses conveyed me at once to Cairo, for medical attendance and proper nursing.

Editha was at first convinced that I had attempted to commit suicide because I could not endure having caused her pain, and she accordingly resolved to tend me with the utmost care through my illness. But she found that my delirious remarks, besides bearing frequent reference to a princess, with whom I appeared to have been on unexpectedly intimate terms, also related very largely to our *casus belli* itself, the dancing girls of Abu Yilla. Even this trial she might have borne, setting down the moral degeneracy which led me to patronize so degrading an exhibition as a first symptom of my approaching malady: but certain unfortunate observations, containing pointed and by no means flattering allusions to her personal appearance – which I contrasted, much to her disadvantage, with that of the unknown princess – these, I say, were things which she could not forgive; and she left Cairo abruptly with her parents for the Riviera, leaving behind a stinging note, in which she denounced my perfidy and emptyheartedness with all the flowers of feminine eloquence. From that day to this I have never seen her.

When I returned to London and proposed to lay this account before the Society of Antiquaries, all my friends dissuaded me on the grounds of its apparent incredibility. They declare that I must have gone to the Pyramid already in a state of delirium, discovered the entrance by accident, and sunk exhausted when I reached the inner chamber. In answer, I would point out three facts. In the first place, I undoubtedly found my way into the unknown passage – for which achievement I afterwards received the gold medal of the Société Khédiviale, and of which I retain a clear recollection, differing in no way from my recollection of the subsequent events. In the second place, I had in my pocket, when found, a ring of Hatasou's, which I drew from her finger just before I took the chloroform, and put into my pocket as a keepsake. And in the third place, I had on my breast the wound which I saw the priest inflict with a knife of greenstone, and the scar may be seen on the spot to the present day. The absurd hypothesis of my medical friends, that I was wounded by falling against a sharp edge of rock, I must at once reject as unworthy of a moment's consideration.

My own theory is either that the priest had not time to complete the operation, or else that the arrival of the Fitz-Simkins' scouts frightened back the mummies to their cases an hour or so too soon. At any rate, there they all were, ranged around the walls undisturbed, the moment the Fellahin entered.

Unfortunately, the truth of my account cannot be tested for another thousand years. But as a copy of this book will be preserved for the benefit of posterity in the British Museum, I hereby solemnly call upon Collective Humanity to try the veracity of this history by sending a deputation of archæologists to the Pyramid of Abu Yilla, on the last day of December, Two thousand eight hundred and seventy-seven. If they do not then find Thothmes and Hatasou feasting in the central hall exactly as I have described, I shall willingly admit that the story of my New Year's Eve among the Mummies is a vain hallucination, unworthy of credence at the hands of the scientific world.

LOT No. 249

by Sir Arthur Conan Doyle

Of the dealings of Edward Bellingham with William Monkhouse Lee, and of the cause of the great terror of Abercrombie Smith, it may be that no absolute and final judgement will ever be delivered. It is true that we have the full and clear narrative of Smith himself, and such corroboration as he could look for from Thomas Styles the servant, from the Reverend Plumptree Peterson, Fellow of Old's, and from such other people as chanced to gain some passing glance at this or that incident in a singular chain of events. Yet, in the main, the story must rest upon Smith alone, and the most will think that it is more likely that one brain, however outwardly sane, has some subtle warp in its texture, some strange flaw in its workings, than that the path of Nature has been overstepped in open day in so famed a centre of learning and light as the University of Oxford. Yet when we think how narrow and how devious this path of Nature is, how dimly we can trace it, for all our lamps of science, and how from the darkness which girds it round great and terrible possibilities loom every shadowly upwards, it is a bold and confident man who will put a limit to the strange by-paths into which the human spirit may wander.

In a certain wing of what we will call Old College in Oxford there is a corner turret of an exceeding great age. The heavy arch which spans the open door has bent downwards in the centre under the weight of its years, and the grey, lichen-blotched blocks of stone are bound and knitted together with withes and strands of ivy, as though the old mother had set

herself to brace them up against wind and weather. From the
door a stone stair curves upward spirally, passing two landings, and terminating in a third one, its steps all shapeless and
hollowed by the tread of so many generations of the seekers
after knowledge. Life has flowed like water down this winding
stair, and, waterlike, has left these smooth-worn grooves behind it. From the long-gowned, pedantic scholars of
Plantagenet days down to the young bloods of a later age, how
full and strong had been that tide of young, English life. And
what was left now of all those hopes, those strivings, those
fiery energies, save here and there in some old-world
churchyard a few scratches upon a stone, and perchance a
handful of dust in a mouldering coffin? Yet here were the
silent stair and the grey, old wall, with bend and saltire and
many another heraldic device still to be read upon its surface,
like grotesque shadows thrown back from the days that had
passed.

In the month of May, in the year 1884, three young men
occupied the sets of rooms which opened on to the separate
landings of the old stair. Each set consisted simply of a sitting-
room and of a bedroom, while the two corresponding rooms
upon the ground-floor were used, the one as a coal-cellar, and
the other as the living-room of the servant, or scout, Thomas
Styles, whose duty it was to wait upon the three men above
him. To right and to left was a line of lecture-rooms and of
offices, so that the dwellers in the old turret enjoyed a certain
seclusion, which made the chambers popular among the more
studious undergraduates. Such were the three who occupied
them now – Abercrombie Smith above, Edward Bellingham
beneath him, and William Monkhouse Lee upon the lowest
storey.

It was ten o'clock on a bright, spring night, and
Abercrombie Smith lay back in his arm-chair, his feet upon
the fender, and his briar-root pipe between his lips. In a
similar chair, and equally at his ease, there lounged on the
other side of the fireplace his old school friend Jephro Hastie.
Both men were in flannels, for they had spent their evening
upon the river, but apart from their dress no one could look at
their hard-cut, alert faces without seeing that they were
open-air men – men whose minds and tastes turned naturally

to all that was manly and robust. Hastie, indeed, was stroke of his college boat, and Smith was an even better oar, but a coming examination had already cast its shadow over him and held him to his work, save for a few hours a week which health demanded. A litter of medical books upon the table, with scattered bones, models, and anatomical plates, pointed to the extent as well as the nature of his studies, while a couple of single-sticks and a set of boxing-gloves above the mantelpiece hinted at the means by which, with Hastie's help, he might take his exercise in its most compressed and least-distant form. They knew each other very well – so well that they could sit now in that soothing silence which is the very highest development of companionship.

'Have some whisky,' said Abercrombie Smith at last between two cloudbursts. 'Scotch in the jug and Irish in the bottle.'

'No, thanks. I'm in for the sculls. I don't drink liquor when I'm training. How about you?'

'I'm reading hard. I think it best to leave it alone.'

Hastie nodded, and they relapsed into a contented silence.

'By the way, Smith,' asked Hastie, presently, 'have you made the acquaintance of either of the fellows on your stair yet?'

'Just a nod when we pass. Nothing more.'

'Hum! I should be inclined to let it stand at that. I know something of them both. Not much, but as much as I want. I don't think I should take them to my bosom if I were you. Not that there's much amiss with Monkhouse Lee.'

'Meaning the thin one?'

'Precisely. He is a gentlemanly little fellow. I don't think there is any vice in him. But then you can't know him without knowing Bellingham.'

'Meaning the fat one?'

'Yes, the fat one. And he's a man whom I, for one, would rather not know.'

Abercrombie Smith raised his eyebrows and glanced across at his companion.

'What's up then?' he asked. 'Drink? Cards? Cad? You used not to be censorious.'

'Ah! you evidently don't know the man, or you wouldn't

ask. There's something damnable about him – something reptilian. My gorge always rises at him. I should put him down as a man with secret vices – an evil liver. He's no fool, though. They say that he is one of the best men in his line that they have ever had in the college.'

'Medicine or classics?'

'Eastern languages. He's a demon at them. Chillingworth met him somewhere above the second cataract last long, and he told me that he just prattled to the Arabs as if he had been born and nursed and weaned among them. He talked Coptic to the Copts, and Hebrew to the Jews, and Arabic to the Bedouins, and they were all ready to kiss the hem of his frock-coat. There are some old hermit Johnnies up in those parts who sit on rocks and scowl and spit at the casual stranger. Well, when they saw this chap Bellingham, before he had said five words they just lay down on their bellies and wriggled. Chillingworth said that he never saw anything like it. Bellingham seemed to take it as his right, too, and strutted about among them and talked down to them like a Dutch uncle. Pretty good for an undergrad. of Old's, wasn't it?'

'Why do you say you can't know Lee without knowing Bellingham?'

'Because Bellingham is engaged to his sister Eveline. Such a bright little girl, Smith! I know the whole family well. It's disgusting to see that brute with her. A toad and a dove, that's what they always remind me of.'

Abercrombie Smith grinned and knocked his ashes out against the side of the grate.

'You show every card in your hand, old chap,' said he. 'What a prejudiced, green-eyed, evil-thinking old man it is! You have really nothing against the fellow except that.'

'Well, I've known her ever since she was as long as that cherry-wood pipe, and I don't like to see her taking risks. And it is a risk. He looks beastly. And he has a beastly temper, a venemous temper. You remember his row with Long Norton?'

'No; you always forget that I am a freshman.'

'Ah, it was last winter. Of course. Well, you know the towpath along by the river. There were several fellows going along it, Bellingham in front, when they came on an old market-woman coming the other way. It had been raining –

you know what those fields are like when it has rained – and
the path ran between the river and a great puddle that was
nearly as broad. Well, what does this swine do but keep the
path, and push the old girl into the mud, where she and her
marketings came to terrible grief. It was a blackguard thing to
do, and Long Norton, who is as gentle a fellow as ever
stepped, told him what he thought of it. One word led to
another, and it ended in Norton laying his stick across the
fellow's shoulders. There was the deuce of a fuss about it, and
it's a treat to see the way in which Bellingham looks at Norton
when they meet now. By Jove, Smith, it's nearly eleven
o'clock!'

'No hurry. Light your pipe again.'

'Not I. I'm supposed to be in training. Here I've been
sitting gossiping when I ought to have been safely tucked up.
I'll borrow your skull, if you can share it. Williams has had
mine for a month. I'll take the little bones of your ear, too, if
you are sure you won't need them. Thanks very much. Never
mind a bag, I can carry them very well under my arm. Good
night, my son, and take my tip as to your neighbour.'

When Hastie, bearing his anatomical plunder, had
clattered off down the winding stair, Abercrombie Smith
hurled his pipe into the wastepaper basket, and drawing his
chair nearer to the lamp, plunged into a formidable, green-
covered volume, adorned with great, coloured maps of that
strange, internal kingdom of which we are the hapless and
helpless monarchs. Though a freshman at Oxford, the student
was not so in medicine, for he had worked for four years at
Glasgow and at Berlin, and this coming examination would
place him finally as a member of his profession. With his firm
mouth,   broad   forehead,   and   clear-cut,   somewhat
hard-featured face, he was a man who, if he had no brilliant
talent, was yet so dogged, so patient, and so strong that he
might in the end overtop a more showy genius. A man who
can hold his own among Scotchmen and North Germans is
not a man to be easily set back. Smith had left a name at
Glasgow and at Berlin, and he was bent now upon doing as
much at Oxford, if hard work and devotion could accomplish
it.

He had sat reading for about an hour, and the hands of the

noisy carriage clock upon the side-table were rapidly closing together upon the twelve, when a sudden sound fell upon the student's ear – a sharp, rather shrill sound, like the hissing intake of a man's breath who gasps under some strong emotion. Smith laid down his book and slanted his ear to listen. There was no one either side or above him, so tht the interruption came certainly from the neighbour beneath – the same neighbour of whom Hastie had given so unsavoury an account. Smith knew him only as a flabby, pale-faced man of silent and studious habits, a man whose lamp threw a golden bar from the old turret even after he had extinguished his own. This community in lateness had formed a certain silent bond between them. It was soothing to Smith when the hours stole on towards dawning to feel that there was another so close who set as small a value upon his sleep as he did. Even now, as his thoughts turned towards him, Smith's feelings were kindly. Hastie was a good fellow, but he was rough, strong-fibred, with no imagination or sympathy. He could not tolerate departures from what he looked upon as the model type of manliness. If a man could not be measured by a public-school standard, then he was beyond the pale with Hastie. Like so many who are themselves robust, he was apt to confuse the constitution with the character, to ascribe to want of principle what was really a want of circulation. Smith, with his stronger mind, knew his friend's habit, and made allowance for it now as his thoughts turned towards the man beneath him.

There was no return of the singular sound, and Smith was about to turn to his work once more, when suddenly there broke out in the silence of the night a hoarse cry, a positive scream – the call of a man who is moved and shaken beyond all control. Smith sprang out of his chair and dropped his book. He was a man of fairly firm fibre, but there was some-thing in this sudden, uncontrollable shriek of horror which chilled his blood and pringled in his skin. Coming in such a place and at such an hour, it brought a thousand fantastic possibilities into his head. Should he rush down, or was it better to wait? He had all the national hatred of making a scene, and he knew so little of his neighbour that he would not lightly intrude upon his affairs. For a moment he stood in doubt and even as he balanced the matter there was a quick rattle of footsteps upon the stairs, and young Monkhouse Lee, half-dressed and as white as ashes, burst into his room.

'Come down!' he gasped. 'Bellingham's ill.'

Abercrombie Smith followed him closely downstairs into the sitting-room which was beneath his own, and intent as he was upon the matter in hand, he could not but take an amazed glance around him as he crossed the threshold. It was such a chamber as he had never seen before – a museum rather than a study. Walls and ceiling were thickly covered with a thousand strange relics from Egypt and the East. Tall, angular figures bearing burdens or weapons stalked in an uncouth frieze round the apartments. Above were bull-headed, stork-headed, cat-headed, owl-headed statues, with viper-crowned, almond-eyed monarchs, and strange, beetle-like deities cut out of the blue Egyptian lapis lazuli. Horus and Isis and Osiris peeped down from every niche and shelf, while across the ceiling a true son of Old Nile, a great, hanging-jawed crocodile, was slung in a double noose.

In the centre of this singular chamber was a large, square table, littered with papers, bottles, and the dried leaves of some graceful, palm-like plant. These varied objects had all been heaped together in order to make room for a mummy case, which had been conveyed from the wall, as was evident from the gap there, and laid across the front of the table. The mummy itself, a horrid, black, withered thing, like a charred head on a gnarled bush, was lying half out of the case, with its claw-like hand and bony forearm resting upon the table. Propped up against the sarcophagus was an old, yellow scroll of papyrus, and in front of it, in a wooden armchair, sat the owner of the room, his head thrown back, his widely opened eyes directed in a horrified stare to the crocodile above him, and his blue, thick lips puffing loudly with every expiration.

'My God! he's dying!' cried Monkhouse Lee, distractedly.

He was a slim, handsome young fellow, olive-skinned and dark-eyed, of a Spanish rather than of an English type, with a Celtic intensity of manner which contrasted with the Saxon phlegm of Abercrombie Smith.

'Only a faint, I think,' said the medical student. 'Just give me a hand with him. You take his feet. Now on to the sofa.

Can you kick all those little wooden devils off? What a litter it is! Now he will be all right if we undo his collar and give him some water. What has he been up to at all?'

'I don't know. I heard him cry out. I ran up. I know him pretty well, you know. It is very good of you to come down.'

'His heart is going like a pair of castanets,' said Smith, laying his hand on the breast of the unconscious man. 'He seems to me to be frightened all to pieces. Chuck the water over him! What a face he has got on him!'

It was indeed a strange and most repellent face, for colour and outline were equally unnatural. It was white, not with the ordinary pallor of fear, but with an absolutely bloodless white, like the under side of a sole. He was very fat, but gave the impression of having at some time been considerably fatter, for his skin hung loosely in creases and folds, and was shot with a meshwork of wrinkles. Short, stubbly brown hair bristled up from his scalp, with a pair of thick, wrinkled ears protruding at the sides. His light-grey eyes were still open, the pupils dilated and the balls projecting in a fixed and horrid stare. It seemed to Smith as he looked down upon him that he had never seen Nature's danger signals flying so plainly upon a man's countenance, and his thoughts turned more seriously to the warning which Hastie had given him an hour before.

'What the deuce can have frightened him so?' he asked.

'It's the mummy.'

'The mummy? How, then?'

'I don't know. It's beastly and morbid. I wish he would drop it. It's the second fright he has given me. It was the same last winter. I found him just like this, with that horrid thing in front of him.'

'What does he want with the mummy, then?'

'Oh, he's a crank, you know. It's his hobby. He knows more about these things than any man in England. But I wish he wouldn't! Ah, he's beginning to come to.'

A faint tinge of colour had begun to steal back into Bellingham's ghastly cheeks, and his eyelids shivered like a sail after a calm. He clasped and unclasped his hands, drew a long, thin breath between his teeth, and suddenly jerking up his head, threw a glance of recognition around him. As his eyes fell upon the mummy, he sprang off the sofa, seized the roll of papyrus, thrust it into a drawer, turned the key, and then staggered back on to the sofa.

'What's up?' he asked. 'What do you chaps want?'

'You've been shrieking out and making no end of a fuss,' said Monkhouse Lee. 'If our neighbour here from above hadn't come down, I'm sure I don't know what I should have done with you.'

'Ah, it's Abercrombie Smith,' said Bellingham, glancing up at him. 'How very good of you to come in! What a fool I am! Oh, my God, what a fool I am!'

He sank his head on to his hands, and burst into peal after peal of hysterical laughter.

'Look here! Drop it!' cried Smith, shaking him roughly by the shoulder.

'Your nerves are all in a jangle. You must drop these little midnight games with mummies, or you'll be going off your chump. You're all on wires now.'

'I wonder,' said Bellingham, 'whether you would be as cool as I am if you had seen – '

'What then?'

'Oh, nothing. I meant that I wonder if you could sit up at night with a mummy without trying your nerves. I have no doubt that you are quite right. I dare say that I have been taking it out of myself too much lately. But I am all right now. Please don't go, though. Just wait for a few minutes until I am quite myself.'

'The room is very close,' remarked Lee, throwing open the window and letting in the cool night air.

'It's balsamic resin,' said Bellingham. He lifted up one of the dried palmate leaves from the table and frizzled it over the chimney of the lamp. It broke away into heavy smoke wreaths, and a pungent, biting odour filled the chamber. 'It's the sacred plant – the plant of the priests,' he remarked. 'Do you know anything of Eastern languages, Smith?'

'Nothing at all. Not a word.'

The answer seemed to lift a weight from the Egyptologist's mind.

'By the way,' he continued, 'how long was it from the time that you ran down, until I came to my senses?'

'Not long. Some four or five minutes.'

'I thought it could not be very long,' said he, drawing a long breath. 'But what a strange thing unconsciousness is! There is no measurement to it. I could not tell from my own sensations if it were seconds or weeks. Now that gentleman on the table was packed up in the days of the eleventh dynasty, some forty centuries ago, and yet if he could find his tongue, he would tell us that this lapse of time has been but a closing of the eyes and a reopening of them. He is a singularly fine mummy, Smith.'

Smith stepped over to the table and looked down with a professional eye at the black and twisted form in front of him. The features, though horribly discoloured, were perfect, and two little nut-like eyes still lurked in the depths of the black, hollow sockets. The blotched skin was drawn tightly from bone to bone, and a tangled wrap of black, coarse hair fell over the ears. Two thin teeth, like those of a rat, overlay the shrivelled lower lip. In its crouching position, with bent joints and craned head, there was a suggestion of energy about the horrid thing which made Smith's gorge rise. The gaunt ribs, with their parchment-like covering, were exposed, and the sunken, leaden-hued abdomen, with the long slit where the embalmer had left his mark; but the lower limbs were wrapped round with coarse, yellow bandages. A number of little clove-like pieces of myrrh and of cassia were sprinkled over the body, and lay scattered on the inside of the case.

'I don't know his name,' said Bellingham, passing his hand over the shrivelled head. 'You see the outer sarcophagus with the inscription is missing. Lot 249 is all the title he has now. You see it printed on his case. That was his number in the auction at which I picked him up.'

'He has been a very pretty sort of fellow in his day,' remarked Abercrombie Smith.

'He has been a giant. His mummy is six feet seven in length, and that would be a giant over there, for they were never a very robust race. Feel these great knotted bones, too. He would be a nasty fellow to tackle.'

'Perhaps these very hands helped to build the stones into the pyramids,' suggested Monkhouse Lee, looking down with disgust in his eyes at the crooked, unclean talons.

'No fear. This fellow has been pickled in natron, and looked after in the most approved style. They did not serve hodsmen in that fashion. Salt or bitumen was enough for them. It has been calculated that this sort of thing cost about seven hundred and thirty pounds in our money. Our friend was a noble at the least. What do you make of that small inscription near his feet, Smith?'

'I told you that I know no Eastern tongue.'

'Ah, so you did. It is the name of the embalmer, I take it. A very conscientious worker he must have been. I wonder how many modern works will survive four thousand years?'

He kept on speaking lightly and rapidly, but it was evident to Abercrombie Smith that he was still palpitating with fear. His hands shook, his lower lip trembled, and look where he would, his eye always came sliding round to his gruesome companion. Through all his fear, however, there was a suspicion of triumph in his tone and manner. His eyes shone, and his footstep, as he paced the room, was brisk and jaunty. He gave the impression of a man who has gone through an ordeal, the marks of which he still bears upon him, but which has helped him to his end.

'You're not going yet?' he cried, as Smith rose from the sofa.

At the prospect of solitude, his fears seemed to crowd back upon him, and he stretched out a hand to detain him.

'Yes, I must go. I have my work to do. You are all right now. I think that with your nervous system you should take up some less morbid study.'

'Oh, I am not nervous as a rule; and I have unwrapped mummies before.'

'You fainted last time,' observed Monkhouse Lee.

'Ah, yes, so I did. Well, I must have a nerve tonic or a course of electricity. You are not going, Lee?'

'I'll do whatever you wish, Ned.'

'Then I'll come down with you and have a shakedown on your sofa. Good night, Smith. I am so sorry to have disturbed you with my foolishness.'

They shook hands, and as the medical student stumbled up the spiral and irregular stair he heard a key turn in a door, and the steps of his two new acquaintances as they descended to the lower floor.

In this strange way began the acquaintance between Edward

Bellingham and Abercrombie Smith, an acquaintance which the latter, at least, had no desire to push further. Bellingham, however, appeared to have taken a fancy to his rough-spoken neighbour, and made his advances in such a way that he could hardly be repulsed without absolute brutality. Twice he called to thank Smith for his assistance, and many times afterwards he looked in with books, papers and such other civilities as two bachelor neighbours can offer each other. He was, as Smith soon found, a man of wide reading, with catholic tastes and an extraordinary memory. His manner, too, was so pleasing and suave that one came, after a time, to overlook his repellent appearance. For a jaded and wearied man he was no unpleasant companion, and Smith found himself, after a time, looking forward to his visits, and even returning them.

Clever as he undoubtedly was, however, the medical student seemed to detect a dash of insanity in the man. He broke out at times into a high, inflated style of talk which was in contrast with the simplicity of his life.

'It is a wonderful thing,' he cried, 'to feel that one can command powers of good and of evil – a ministering angel or a demon of vengeance.' And again, of Monkhouse Lee, he said, 'Lee is a good fellow, an honest fellow, but he is without strength or ambition. He would not make a fit partner for a man with a great enterprise. He would not make a fit partner for me.'

At such hints and innuendoes stolid Smith, puffing solemnly at his pipe, would simply raise his eyebrows and shake his head, with little interjections of medical wisdom as to earlier hours and fresher air.

One habit Bellingham had developed of late which Smith knew to be a frequent herald of a weakening mind. He appeared to be for ever talking to himself. At late hours of the night, where there could be no visitor with him, Smith could still hear his voice beneath him in a low, muffled monologue, sunk almost to a whisper, and yet very audible in the silence. This solitary babbling annoyed and distracted the student, so that he spoke more than once to his neighbour about it. Bellingham, however, flushed up at the charge, and denied curtly that he had uttered a sound; indeed, he showed more annoyance over the matter than the occasion seemed to demand.

Had Abercrombie Smith had any doubt as to his own ears he had not to go far to find corroboration. Tom Styles, the little wrinkled man-servant who had attended to the wants of the lodgers in the turret for a longer time than any man's memory could carry him, was sorely put to it over the same matter.

'If you please, sir, said he, as he tidied down the top chamber one morning, 'do you think Mr Bellingham is all right, sir?'

'All right, Styles?'

'Yes, sir. Right in his head, sir.'

'Why should he not be, then?'

'Well, I don't know, sir. His habits has changed of late. He's not the same man he used to be, though I make free to say that he was never quite one of my gentlemen, like Mr Hastie or yourself, sir. He's took to talkin' to himself something awful. I wonder it don't disturb you. I don't know what to make of him, sir.'

'I don't know what business it is of yours, Styles.'

'Well, I takes an interest, Mr Smith. It may be forward of me, but I can't help it. I feel sometimes as if I was mother and father to my young gentlemen. It all falls on me when things go wrong and the relations come. But Mr Bellingham, sir. I want to know what it is that walks about his room sometimes when he's out and when the door's locked on the outside.'

'Eh? you're talking nonsense, Styles.'

'Maybe so, sir; but I heard it more'n once with my own ears.'

'Rubbish, Styles.'

'Very good, sir. You'll ring the bell if you want me.'

Abercrombie Smith gave little heed to the gossip of the old man-servant, but a small incident occurred a few days later which left an unpleasant effect upon his mind, and brought the words of Styles forcibly to his memory.

Bellingham had come up to see him late one night, and was entertaining him with an interesting account of the rock tombs of Beni Hassan in Upper Egypt, when Smith, whose hearing was remarkably acute, distinctly heard the sound of a door opening on the landing below.

'There's some fellow gone in or out of your room,' he remarked.

Bellingham sprang up and stood helpless for a moment, with the expression of a man who is half-incredulous and half-afraid.

'I surely locked it. I am almost positive that I locked it,' he stammered. 'No one could have opened it.'

'Why, I hear someone coming up the steps now,' said Smith.

Bellingham rushed out through the door, slammed it loudly behind him, and hurried down the stairs. About half-way down Smith heard him stop, and thought he caught the sound of whispering. A moment later the door beneath him shut, a key creaked in a lock, and Bellingham, with beads of moisture upon his pale face, ascended the stairs once more, and re-entered the room.

'It's all right,' he said, throwing himself down in a chair. 'It was that fool of a dog.' He had pushed the door open. I don't know how I came to forget to lock it.

'I didn't know you kept a dog,' said Smith, looking very thoughtfully at the disturbed face of his companion.

'Yes, I haven't had him long. I must get rid of him. He's a great nuisance.'

'He must be, if you find it so hard to shut him up. I should have thought that shutting the door would have been enough, without locking it.'

'I want to prevent old Styles from letting him out. He's of some value, you know, and it would be awkward to lose him.'

'I am a bit of a dog-fancier myself,' said Smith, still gazing hard at his companion from the corner of his eyes. 'Perhaps you'll let me have a look at it.'

'Certainly. But I am afraid it cannot be to-night; I have an appointment. Is that clock right? Then I am a quarter of an hour late already. You'll excuse me, I am sure.'

He picked up his cap and hurried from the room. In spite of his appointment, Smith heard him re-enter his own chamber and lock his door upon the inside.

This interview left a disagreeable impression upon the medical student's mind. Bellingham had lied to him, and lied so clumsily that it looked as if he had desperate reasons for concealing the truth. Smith knew that his neighbour had no dog. He knew, also, that the step which he had heard upon the stairs was not the step of an animal. But if it were not, then what could it be? There was old Styles's statement about the something which used to pace the room at times when the owner was absent. Could it be a woman? Smith rather inclined to the view. If so, it would mean disgrace and expulsion to Bellingham if it were discovered by the authorities, so that his anxiety and falsehoods might be accounted for. And yet it was inconceivable that an undergraduate could keep a woman in his rooms without being instantly detected. Be the explanation what it might, there was something ugly about it, and Smith determined, as he turned to his books, to discourage all further attempts at intimacy on the part of his soft-spoken and ill-favoured neighbour.

But his work was destined to interruption that night. He had hardly caught up the broken threads when a firm, heavy footfall came three steps at a time from below, and Hastie, in blazer and flannels, burst into the room.

'Still at it!' said he, plumping down into his wonted armchair. 'What a chap you are to stew! I believe an earthquake might come and knock Oxford into a cocked hat, and you would sit perfectly placid with your books among the ruins. However, I won't bore you long. Three whiffs of baccy, and I am off.'

'What's the news, then?' asked Smith, cramming a plug of bird's-eye into his briar with his forefinger.

'Nothing very much. Wilson made 70 for the freshmen against the eleven. They say that they will play him instead of Buddicomb, for Buddicomb is clean off colour. He used to be able to bowl a little, but it's nothing but half-volleys and long hops now.'

'Medium right,' suggested Smith, with the intense gravity which comes upon a 'varsity man when he speaks of athletics.

'Inclining to fast, with a work from leg. Comes with the arm about three inches or so. He used to be nasty on a wet wicket. Oh, by the way, have you heard about Long Norton?'

'What's that?'

'He's been attacked.'

'Attacked?'

'Yes, just as he was turning out of the High Street, and within a hundred yards of the gate of Old's.'

'But who – '

'Ah, that's the rub! If you said "what", you would be more grammatical. Norton swears that it was not human, and, indeed, from the scratches on his throat, I should be inclined to agree with him.'

'What, then? Have we come down to spooks?'

Abercrombie Smith puffed his scientific contempt.

'Well, no; I don't think that is quite the idea, either. I am inclined to think that if any showman has lost a great ape lately, and the brute is in these parts, a jury would find a true bill against it. Norton passes that way every night, you know, about the same hour. There's a tree that hangs low over the path – the big elm from Rainy's garden. Norton thinks the thing dropped on him out of the tree. Anyhow, he was nearly strangled by two arms, which, he says, were as strong and as thin as steel bands. He saw nothing; only those beastly arms that tightened and tightened on him. He yelled his head nearly off, and a couple of chaps came running, and the thing went over the wall like a cat. He never got a fair sight of it the whole time. It gave Norton a shake up, I can tell you. I tell him it has been as good as a change at the seaside for him.'

'A garrotter, most likely,' said Smith.

'Very possibly. Norton says not; but we don't mind what he says. The garrotter had long nails, and was pretty smart at swinging himself over walls. By the way, your beautiful neighbour would be pleased if he heard about it. He had a grudge against Norton, and he's not a man, from what I know of him, to forget his little debts. But hallo, old chap, what have you got in your noddle?'

'Nothing,' Smith answered curtly.

He had started in his chair, and the look had flashed over his face which comes upon a man who is struck suddenly by some unpleasant idea.

'You looked as if something I had said had taken you on the raw. By the way, you have made the acquaintance of Master B. since I looked in last, have you not? Young Monkhouse Lee told me something to that effect.'

'Yes; I know him slightly. He has been up here once or twice.'

'Well, you're big enough and ugly enough to take care of yourself. He's not what I should call exactly a healthy sort of

Johnny, though, no doubt, he's very clever, and all that. But you'll soon find out for yourself. Lee is all right; he's a very decent little fellow. Well, so long, old chap! I row Mullins for the Vice-Chancellor's pot on Wednesday week, so mind you come down, in case I don't see you before.'

Bovine Abercrombie Smith laid down his pipe and turned stolidly to his books once more. But with all the will in the world, he found it very hard to keep his mind upon his work. It would slip away to brood upon the man beneath him, and upon the little mystery which hung round his chambers. Then his thoughts turned to this singular attack of which Hastie had spoken, and to the grudge which Bellingham was said to owe the object of it. The two ideas would persist in rising together in his mind, as though there were some close and intimate connection between them. And yet the suspicion was so dim and vague that it could not be put down in words.

'Confound the chap!' cried Smith, as he shied his book on pathology across the room. 'He has spoiled my night's reading, and that's reason enough, if there were no other, why I should steer clear of him in the future.'

For ten days the medical student confined himself so closely to his studies that he neither saw nor heard anything of either of the men beneath him. At the hours when Bellingham had been accustomed to visit him, he took care to sport his oak, and though he more than once heard a knocking at his outer door, he resolutely refused to answer it. One afternoon, however, he was descending the stairs when, just as he was passing it, Bellingham's door flew open, and young Monkhouse Lee came out with his eyes sparkling and a dark flush of anger upon his olive cheeks. Close at his heels followed Bellingham, his fat, unhealthy face all quivering with malignant passion.

'You fool!' he hissed. 'You'll be sorry.'

'Very likely,' cried the other. 'Mind what I say. It's off! I won't hear of it!'

'You've promised, anyhow.'

'Oh, I'll keep that! I won't speak. But I'd rather little Eva was in her grave. Once for all, it's off. She'll do what I say. We don't want to see you again.'

So much Smith could not avoid hearing, but he hurried on,

for he had no wish to be involved in their dispute. There had been a serious breach between them, that was clear enough, and Lee was going to cause the engagement with his sister to be broken off. Smith thought of Hastie's comparison of the toad and the dove, and was glad to think that the matter was at an end. Bellingham's face when he was in a passion was not pleasant to look upon. He was not a man to whom an innocent girl could be trusted for life. As he walked, Smith wondered languidly what could have caused the quarrel, and what the promise might be which Bellingham had been so anxious that Monkhouse Lee should keep.

It was the day of the sculling match between Hastie and Mullins, and a stream of men were making their way down to the banks of the Isis. A May sun was shining brightly, and the yellow path was barred with the black shadows of the tall elm-trees. On either side the grey colleges lay back from the road, the hoary old mothers of minds looking out from their high, mullioned windows at the tide of young life which swept so merrily past them. Black-clad tutors, prim officials, pale, reading men, brown-faced, straw-hatted young athletes in white sweaters or many-coloured blazers, all were hurrying towards the blue, winding river which curves through the Oxford meadows.

Abercrombie Smith, with the intuition of an old oarsman, chose his position at the point where he knew that the struggle, if there were a struggle, would come. Far off he heard the hum which announced the start, the gathering roar of the approach, the thunder of running feet, and the shouts of the men in the boats beneath him. A spray of half-clad, deep-breathing runners shot past him, and craning over their shoulders, he saw Hastie pulling a steady thirty-six, while his opponent, with a jerky forty, was a good boat's length behind him. Smith gave a cheer for his friend, and pulling out his watch, was starting off again for his chambers, when he felt a touch upon his shoulder, and found that young Monkhouse Lee was beside him.

'I saw you there,' he said, in a timid, deprecating way. 'I wanted to speak to you, if you could spare me a half-hour. This cottage is mine. I share it with Harrington of King's. Come in and have a cup of tea.'

'I must be back presently,' said Smith. 'I am hard on the
grind at present. But I'll come in for a few minutes with
pleasure. I wouldn't have come out only Hastie is a friend of
mine.'

'So he is of mine. Hasn't he a beautiful style? Mullins
wasn't in it. But come into the cottage. It's a little den of a
place, but it is pleasant to work in during the summer
months.'

It was a small, square, white building, with green doors
and shutters, and a rustic trellis-work porch, standing back
some fifty yards from the river's bank. Inside, the main room
was roughly fitted up as a study – deal table, unpainted
shelves with books, and a few cheap oleographs upon the
wall. A kettle sang upon a spirit stove, and there were tea
things upon a tray on the table.

'Try that chair and have a cigarette,' said Lee. 'Let me
pour you out a cup of tea. It's so good of you to come in, for
I know that your time is a good deal taken up. I wanted to
say to you that, if I were you, I should change my rooms at
once.'

'Eh?'

Smith sat staring with a lighted match in one hand and his
unlit cigarette in the other.

'Yes; it must seem very extraordinary, and the worst of it
is that I cannot give my reasons, for I am under a solemn
promise – a very solemn promise. But I may go so far as to
say that I don't think Bellingham is a very safe man to live
near. I intend to camp out here as much as I can for a time.'

'Not safe! What do you mean?'

'Ah, that's what I mustn't say. But do take my advice and
move your rooms. We had a grand row to-day. You must have
heard us, for you came down the stairs.'

'I saw that you had fallen out.'

'He's a horrible chap, Smith. That is the only word for him.
I have had doubts about him ever since that night when he
fainted – you remember, when you came down. I taxed him
to-day, and he told me things that made my hair rise, and
wanted me to stand in with him. I'm not straight-laced, but I
am a clergyman's son, you know, and I think there are some
things which are quite beyond the pale. I only thank God that

I found him out before it was too late, for he was to have married into my family.'

'This is all very fine, Lee,' said Abercrombie Smith curtly. 'But either you are saying a great deal too much or a great deal too little.'

'I give you a warning.'

'If there is real reason for warning, no promise can bind you. If I see a rascal about to blow a place up with dynamite no pledge will stand in my way of preventing him.'

'Ah, but I cannot prevent him, and I can do nothing but warn you.'

'Without saying what you warn me against.'

'Against Bellingham.'

'But that is childish. Why should I fear him, or any man?'

'I can't tell you. I can only entreat you to change your rooms. You are in danger where you are. I don't even say that Bellingham would wish to injure you. But it might happen, for he is a dangerous neighbour just now.'

'Perhaps I know more than you think,' said Smith, looking keenly at the young man's boyish, earnest face. 'Suppose I tell you that someone else shares Bellingham's rooms.'

Monkhouse Lee sprang from his chair in uncontrollable excitement.

'You know, then?' he gasped.

'A woman.'

Lee dropped back again with a groan.

'My lips are sealed,' he said. 'I must not speak.'

'Well, anyhow,' said Smith, rising, 'it is not likely that I should allow myself to be frightened out of rooms which suit me very nicely. It would be a little too feeble for me to move out all my goods and chattels because you say that Bellingham might in some unexplained way do me an injury. I think that I'll just take my chance, and stay where I am, and as I see that it's nearly five o'clock, I must ask you to excuse me.'

He bade the young student adieu in a few curt words, and made his way homeward through the sweet spring evening, feeling half-ruffled, half-amused, as any other strong, unimaginative man might who has been menaced by a vague and shadowy danger.

There was one little indulgence which Abercrombie Smith always allowed himself, however closely his work might press upon him. Twice a week, on the Tuesday and the Friday, it was his invariable custom to walk over to Farlingford, the residence of Doctor Plumptree Peterson, situated about a mile and a half out of Oxford. Peterson had been a close friend of Smith's elder brother, Francis, and as he was a bachelor, fairly well-to-do, with a good cellar and a better library, his house was a pleasant goal for a man who was in need of a brisk walk. Twice a week, then, the medical student would swing out there along the dark country roads and spend a pleasant hour in Peterson's comfortable study, discussing, over a glass of old port, the gossip of the 'varsity or the latest developments of medicine or of surgery.

On the day which followed his interview with Monkhouse Lee, Smith shut up his books at a quarter past eight, the hour when he usually started for his friend's house. As he was leaving his room, however, his eyes chanced to fall upon one of the books which Bellingham had lent him, and his conscience pricked him for not having returned it. However repellent the man might be, he should not be treated with discourtesy. Taking the book, he walked downstairs and knocked at his neighbour's door. There was no answer; but on turning the handle he found that it was unlocked. Pleased at the thought of avoiding an interview, he stepped inside, and placed the book with his card upon the table.

The lamp was turned half down, but Smith could see the details of the room plainly enough. It was all much as he had seen it before – the frieze, the animal-headed gods, the hanging crocodile, and the table littered over with papers and dried leaves. The mummy case stood upright against the wall, but the mummy itself was missing. There was no sign of any second occupant of the room, and he felt as he withdrew that he had probably done Bellingham an injustice. Had he a guilty secret to preserve, he would hardly leave his door open so that all the world might enter.

The spiral stair was as black as pitch, and Smith was slowly making his way down its irregular steps, when he was suddenly conscious that something had passed him in the darkness. There was a faint sound, a whiff of air, a light brushing past his elbow, but so slight that he could scarcely be certain of it. He stopped and listened, but the wind was rustling among the ivy outside, and he could hear nothing else.

'Is that you, Styles?' he shouted.

There was no answer, and all was still behind him. It must have been a sudden gust of air, for there were crannies and cracks in the old turret. And yet he could almost have sworn that he heard a footfall by his very side. He had emerged into the quadrangle, still turning the matter over in his head, when a man came running swiftly across the smooth-cropped lawn.

'Is that you, Smith?'

'Hullo, Hastie!'

'For God's sake come at once! Young Lee is drowned! Here's Harrington of King's with the news. The doctor is out. You'll do, but come along at once. There may be life in him.'

'Have you brandy?'

'No.'

'I'll bring some. There's a flask on my table.'

Smith bounded up the stairs, taking three at a time, seized the flask, and was rushing down with it, when, as he passed Bellingham's room, his eyes fell upon something which left him gasping and staring upon the landing.

The door, which he had closed behind him, was now open, and right in front of him, with the lamp-light shining upon it, was the mummy case. Three minutes ago it had been empty. He could swear to that. Now it framed the lank body of its horrible occupant, who stood, grim and stark, with his black, shrivelled face towards the door. The form was lifeless and inert, but it seemed to Smith as he gazed that there still lingered a lurid spark of vitality, some faint sign of consciousness in the little eyes which lurked in the depths of the hollow sockets. So astounded and shaken was he that he had forgotten his errand, and was still staring at the lean, sunken figure when the voice of his friend below recalled him to himself.

'Come on, Smith!' he shouted. 'It's life and death, you know. Hurry up! Now, then,' he added, as the medical student reappeared, 'let us do a sprint. It is well under a mile, and we should do it in five minutes. A human life is better worth running for than a pot.'

Neck and neck they dashed through the darkness, and did not pull up until panting and spent, they had reached the little cottage by the river. Young Lee, limp and dripping like a broken water-plant, was stretched upon the sofa, the green scum of the river upon his black hair, and a fringe of white foam upon his leaden-hued lips. Beside him knelt his fellow-student, Harrington, endeavouring to chafe some warmth back into his rigid limbs.

'I think there's life in him,' said Smith, with his hand to the lad's side. 'Put your watch glass to his lips. Yes, there's dimming on it. You take one arm, Hastie. Now work it as I do, and we'll soon pull him round.'

For ten minutes they worked in silence, inflating and depressing the chest of the unconscious man. At the end of that time a shiver ran through his body, his lips trembled, and he opened his eyes. The three students burst out into an irrepressible cheer.

'Wake up, old chap. You've frightened us quite enough.'

'Have some brandy. Take a sip from the flask.'

'He's all right now,' said his companion Harrington. 'Heavens, what a fright I got! I was reading here, and he had gone out for a stroll as far as the river, when I heard a scream and a splash. Out I ran, and by the time I could find him and fish him out, all life seemed to have gone. Then Simpson couldn't get a doctor, for he has a game-leg, and I had to run, and I don't know what I'd have done without you fellows. That's right, old chap. Sit up.'

Monkhouse Lee had raised himself on his hands, and looked wildly about him.

'What's up?' he asked. 'I've been in the water. Ah, yes; I remember.'

A look of fear came into his eyes, and he sank his face into his hands.

'How did you fall in?'

'I didn't fall in.'

'How then?'

'I was thrown in. I was standing by the bank, and something from behind picked me up like a feather and hurled me in. I heard nothing, and I saw nothing. But I know what it was, for all that.'

'And so do I,' whispered Smith.

Lee looked up with a quick glance of surprise.

'You've learned then?' he said. 'You remember the advice I gave you?'

'Yes, and I begin to think that I shall take it.'

'I don't know what the deuce you fellows are talking about,' said Hastie, 'but I think, if I were you, Harrington, I should get Lee to bed at once. It will be time enough to discuss the why and the wherefore when he is a little stronger. I think, Smith, you and I can leave him alone now. I am walking back to college; if you are coming in that direction, we can have a chat.'

But it was little chat that they had upon their homeward path. Smith's mind was too full of the incidents of the evening, the absence of the mummy from his neighbour's rooms, the step that passed him on the stair, the reappearance – the extraordinary, inexplicable reappearance of the grisly thing – and then this attack upon Lee, corresponding so closely to the previous outrage upon another man against whom Bellingham bore a grudge. All this settled in his thoughts, together with the many little incidents which had previously turned him against his neighbour, and the singular circumstances under which he was first called in to him. What had been a dim suspicion, a vague, fantastic conjecture, had suddenly taken form, and stood out in his mind as a grim fact, a thing not to be denied. And yet, how monstrous it was! how unheard of! how entirely beyond all bounds of human experience. An impartial judge, or even the friend who walked by his side, would simply tell him that his eyes had deceived him, that the mummy had been there all the time, that young Lee had tumbled into the river as any other man tumbles into a river, and the blue pill was the best thing for a disordered liver. He felt that he would have said as much if the positions had been reversed. And yet he could swear that Bellingham was a murderer at heart, and that he wielded a weapon such as no man had ever used in all the grim history of crime.

Hastie had branched off to his rooms with a few crisp and emphatic comments upon his friend's unsociability, and Abercrombie Smith crossed the quadrangle to his corner turret with a strong feeling of repulsion for his chambers and their associations. He would take Lee's advice, and move his quarters as soon as possible, for how could a man study when his ear was straining for every murmur or footstep in the room below? He observed, as he crossed over the lawn, that the light was still shining in Bellingham's window, and as he passed up the staircase the door opened, and the man himself looked out at him. With his fat, evil face he was like some bloated spider fresh from the weaving of his poisonous web.

'Good evening,' said he. 'Won't you come in?'

'No,' cried Smith fiercely.

'No? You are as busy as ever? I wanted to ask you about Lee. I was sorry to hear that there was a rumour that something was amiss with him.'

His features were grave, but there was the gleam of a hidden laugh in his eyes as he spoke. Smith saw it, and he could have knocked him down for it.

'You'll be sorrier still to hear that Monkhouse Lee is doing very well, and is out of all danger,' he answered. 'Your hellish tricks have not come off this time. Oh, you needn't try to brazen it out. I know all about it.'

Bellingham took a step back from the angry student, and half-closed the door as if to protect himself.

'You are mad,' he said. 'What do you mean? Do you assert that I had anything to do with Lee's accident?'

'Yes,' thundered Smith. 'You and that bag of bones behind you; you worked it between you. I tell you what it is, Master B, they have given up burning folk like you, but we still keep a hangman, and, by George! if any man in this college meets his death while you are here, I'll have you up, and if you don't swing for it, it won't be my fault. You'll find that your filthy Egyptian tricks won't answer in England.'

'You're a raving lunatic,' said Bellingham.

'All right. You just remember what I say, for you'll find that I'll be better than my word.'

The door slammed, and Smith went fuming up to his chamber, where he locked the door upon the inside, and spent half the night in smoking his old briar and brooding over the strange events of the evening.

Next morning Abercrombie Smith heard nothing of his

neighbour, but Harrington called upon him in the afternoon
to say that Lee was almost himself again. All day Smith stuck
fast to his word, but in the evening he determined to pay the
visit to his friend Doctor Peterson upon which he had started
the night before. A good walk and a friendly chat would be
welcome to his jangled nerves.

Bellingham's door was shut as he passed, but glancing back
when he was some distance from the turret, he saw his
neighbour's head at the window outlined against the lamp-
light, his face pressed apparently against the glass as he gazed
out into the darkness. It was a blessing to be away from all
contact with him, if but for a few hours, and Smith stepped
out briskly, and breathed the soft spring air into his lungs.
The half-moon lay in the west between two Gothic pinnacles,
and threw upon the silvered street a dark tracery from the
stonework above. There was a brisk breeze, and light, fleecy
clouds drifted swiftly across the sky. Old's was on the very
border of the town, and in five minutes Smith found himself
beyond the houses and between the hedges of a May-scented,
Oxfordshire lane.

It was a lonely and little-frequented road which led to his
friend's house. Early as it was, Smith did not meet a single
soul upon his way. He walked briskly along until he came to
the avenue gate, which opened into the long, gravel drive
leading up to Farlingford. In front of him he could see the
cosy, red light of the windows glimmering through the foliage.
He stood with his hand upon the iron latch of the swinging
gate, and he glanced back at the road along which he had
come. Something was coming swiftly down it.

It moved in the shadow of the hedge, silently and furtively,
a dark, crouching figure, dimly visible against the black
background. Even as he gazed back at it, it had lessened its
distance by twenty paces, and was fast closing upon him. Out
of the darkness he had a glimpse of a scraggy neck, and of two
eyes that will ever haunt him in his dreams. He turned, and
with a cry of terror he ran for his life up the avenue. There
were the red lights, the signals of safety, almost within a
stone's-throw of him. He was a famous runner, but never had
he run as he ran that night.

The heavy gate had swung into place behind him but he

heard it dash open again before his pursuer. As he rushed madly and wildly through the night, he could hear a swift, dry patter behind him, and could see, as he threw back a glance, that this horror was bounding like a tiger at his heels, with blazing eyes and one stringy arm out-thrown. Thank God, the door was ajar. He could see the thin bar of light which shot from the lamp in the hall. Nearer yet sounded the clatter from behind. He heard a hoarse gurgling at his very shoulder. With a shriek he flung himself against the door, slammed and bolted it behind him, and sank half-fainting on to the hall chair.

'My goodness, Smith, what's the matter?' asked Peterson appearing at the door of his study.

'Give me some brandy.'

Peterson disappeared, and came rushing out again with a glass and a decanter.

'You need it,' he said, as his visitor drank off what he poured out for him. 'Why, man, you are as white as a cheese.'

Smith laid down his glass, rose up, and took a deep breath.

'I am my own man again now,' said he. 'I was never so unmanned before. But, with your leave, Peterson, I will sleep here to-night, for I don't think I could face that road again except by daylight. It's weak, I known, but I can't help it.'

Peterson looked at his visitor with a very questioning eye.

'Of course you shall sleep here if you wish. I'll tell Mrs Burney to make up the spare bed. Where are you off to now?'

'Come up with me to the window that overlooks the door. I want you to see what I have seen.'

They went up to the window of the upper hall whence they could look down upon the approach to the house. The drive and the fields on either side lay quiet and still, bathed in the peaceful moonlight.

'Well, really, Smith,' remarked Peterson, 'it is well that I know you to be an abstemious man. What in the world can have frightened you?'

'I'll tell you presently. But where can it have gone? Ah, now, look, look! See the curve of the road just beyond your gate.'

'Yes, I see; you needn't pinch my arm off. I saw someone pass. I should say a man, rather thin, apparently, and tall, very tall. But what of him? And what of yourself? You are still shaking like an aspen leaf.'

'I have been within hand-grip of the devil, that's all. But come down to your study, and I shall tell you the whole story.'

He did so. Under the cheery lamp-light with a glass of wine on the table beside him, and the portly form and florid face of his friend in front, he narrated, in their order, all the events, great and small, which had formed so singular a chain, from the night on which he had found Bellingham fainting in front of the mummy case until this horrid experience of an hour ago.

'There now,' he said as he concluded, 'that's the whole, black business. It is monstrous and incredible, but it is true.'

Doctor Plumptree Peterson sat for some time in silence with a very puzzled expression upon his face.

'I never heard of such a thing in my life, never!' he said at last. 'You have told me the facts. Now tell me your inferences.'

'You can draw your own.'

'But I should like to hear yours. You have thought over the matter, and I have not.'

'Well, it must be a little vague in detail, but the main points seem to me to be clear enough. This fellow Bellingham, in his Eastern studies, has got hold of some infernal secret by which a mummy—or possibly only this particular mummy—can be temporarily brought to life. He was trying this disgusting business on the night when he fainted. No doubt the sight of the creature moving had shaken his nerve, even though he had expected it. You remember that almost the first words he said were to call out upon himself as a fool. Well, he got more hardened afterwards, and carried the matter through without fainting. The vitality which he could put into it was evidently only a passing thing, for I have seen it continually in its case as dead as this table. He has some elaborate process, I fancy, by which he brings the thing to pass. Having done it, he naturally bethought him that he might use the creature as an agent. It has intelligence and it has strength. For some purpose he took Lee into his confidence; but Lee, like a decent Christian, would have nothing to do with such a business. Then they had a row, and Lee vowed that he would tell his sister of Bellingham's true character. Bellingham's game was to prevent him, and he nearly managed it, by setting this creature of his on his track. He had already tried its powers upon another man—Norton—towards whom he had a grudge. It is the merest chance that he has not two murders upon his soul. Then, when I taxed him with the matter, he had the strongest reasons for wishing to get me out of the way before I could convey my knowledge to anyone else. He got his chance when I went out, for he knew my habits and where I was bound for. I have had a narrow shave, Peterson, and it is mere luck you didn't find me on your doorstep in the morning. I'm not a nervous man as a rule, and I never thought to have the fear of death put upon me as it was to-night.'

'My dear boy, you take the matter too seriously,' said his companion. 'Your nerves are out of order with your work, and you make too much of it. How could such a thing as this stride about the streets of Oxford, even at night, without being seen?'

'It has been seen. There is quite a scare in the town about an escaped ape, as they imagine the creature to be. It is the talk of the place.'

'Well, it's a striking chain of events. And yet, my dear fellow, you must allow that each incident in itself is capable of a more natural explanation.'

'What! even my adventure of to-night?'

'Certainly. You come out with your nerves all unstrung, and your head full of this theory of yours. Some gaunt, half-famished tramp steals after you, and seeing you run, is emboldened to pursue you. Your fears and imagination do the rest.'

'It won't do, Peterson; it won't do.'

'And again, in the instance of your finding the mummy case empty, and then a few moments later with an occupant, you know that it was lamp-light, that the lamp was half turned down, and that you had no special reason to look hard at the case. It is quite possible that you may have overlooked the creature in the first instance.'

'No, no; it is out of the question.'

'And then Lee may have fallen into the river, and Norton been garrotted. It is certainly a formidable indictment that you have against Bellingham; but if you were to place it before a police magistrate, he would simply laugh in your face.'

'I know he would. That is why I mean to take the matter into my own hands.'

'Eh?'

'Yes; I feel that a public duty rests upon me, and, besides, I must do it for my own safety, unless I choose to allow myself to be hunted by this beast out of the college, and that would be a little too feeble. I have quite made up my mind what I shall do. And first of all, may I use your paper and pens for an hour?'

'Most certainly. You will find all that you want upon that side-table.'

Abercrombie Smith sat down before a sheet of foolscap, and for an hour, and then for a second hour his pen travelled swiftly over it. Page after page was finished and tossed aside while his friend leaned back in his armchair, looking across at him with patient curiosity. At last, with an exclamation of satisfaction, Smith sprang to his feet, gathered his papers up into order, and laid the last one upon Peterson's desk.

'Kindly sign this as a witness,' he said.

'A witness? Of what?'

'Of my signature, and of the date. The date is the most important. Why, Peterson, my life might hang upon it.'

'My dear Smith, you are talking wildly. Let me beg you to go to bed.'

'On the contrary, I never spoke so deliberately in my life. And I will promise to go to bed the moment you have signed it.'

'But what is it?'

'It is a statement of all that I have been telling you to-night. I wish you to witness it.'

'Certainly,' said Peterson, signing his name under that of his companion. 'There you are! But what is the idea?'

'You will kindly retain it, and produce it in case I am arrested.'

'Arrested? For what?'

'For murder. It is quite on the cards. I wish to be ready for every event. There is only one course open to me, and I am determined to take it.'

'For Heaven's sake, don't do anything rash!'

'Believe me, it would be far more rash to adopt any other course. I hope that we won't need to bother you, but it will ease my mind to know that you have this statement of my motives. And now I am ready to take your advice and to go to roost, for I want to be at my best in the morning.'

Abercrombie Smith was not an entirely pleasant man to have as an enemy. Slow and easy-tempered, he was formidable when driven to action. He brought to every purpose in life the same deliberate resoluteness which had distinguished him as a scientific student. He had laid his studies aside for a day, but he intended that the day should not be wasted. Not a word did he say to his host as to his plans, but by nine o'clock he was well on his way to Oxford.

In the High Street he stopped at Clifford's, the gunmakers, and bought a heavy revolver, with a box of central-fire cartridges. Six of them he slipped into the chambers, and half-cocking the weapon, placed it in the pocket of his coat. He then made his way to Hastie's rooms, where the big oarsman was lounging over his breakfast, with the *Sporting Times* propped up against the coffee-pot.

'Hullo! What's up?' he asked. 'Have some coffee?'

'No, thank you. I want you to come with me, Hastie, and do what I ask you.'

'Certainly, my boy.'

'And bring a heavy stick with you.'

'Hullo!' Hastie stared. 'Here's a hunting crop that would fell an ox.'

'One other thing. You have a box of amputating knives. Give me the longest of them.'

'There you are. You seem to be fairly on the war trail. Anything else?'

'No; that will do.' Smith placed the knife inside his coat, and led the way to the quadrangle. 'We are neither of us chickens, Hastie,' said he. 'I think I can do this job alone, but I take you as a precaution. I am going to have a little talk with Bellingham. If I have only him to deal with, I won't, of course, need you. If I shout, however, up you come and lam out with your whip as hard as you can lick. Do you understand?'

'All right. I'll come if I hear you bellow.'

'Stay here, then. I may be a little time, but don't budge
until I come down.'

'I'm a fixture.'

Smith ascended the stairs, opened Bellingham's door and
stepped in. Bellingham was seated behind his table, writing.
Beside him, among his litter of strange possessions, towered
the mummy case, with its sale number 249 still stuck upon its
front, and its hideous occupant stiff and stark within it. Smith
looked very deliberately round him, closed the door, and then,
stepping across to the fireplace, struck a match and set the fire
alight. Bellingham sat staring, with amazement and rage
upon his bloated face.

'Well, really now, you make yourself at home,' he gasped.

Smith sat himself deliberately down, placing his watch
upon the table, drew out his pistol, cocked it, and laid it in his
lap. Then he took the long amputating knife from his bosom,
and threw it down in front of Bellingham.

'Now, then,' said he, 'just get to work and cut up that
mummy.'

'Oh, is that it?' said Bellingham with a sneer.

'Yes, that is it. They tell me that the law can't touch you.
But I have a law that will set matters straight. If in five
minutes you have not set to work, I swear by the God who
made me that I will put a bullet through your brain!'

'You would murder me?'

Bellingham had half-risen, and his face was the colour of
putty.

'Yes.'

'And for what?'

'To stop your mischief. One minute has gone.'

'But what have I done?'

'I know and you know.'

'This is mere bullying.'

'Two minutes are gone.'

'But you must give reasons. You are a madman – a
dangerous madman. Why should I destroy my own property?
It is a valuable mummy.'

'You must cut it up, and you must burn it.'

'I will do no such thing.'

'Four minutes are gone.'

Smith took up the pistol and he looked towards Bellingham with an inexorable face. As the secondhand stole round, he raised his hand, and the finger twitched upon the trigger.

'There! there! I'll do it!' screamed Bellingham.

In frantic haste he caught up the knife and hacked at the figure of the mummy, ever glancing round to see the eye and the weapon of his terrible visitor bent upon him. The creature crackled and snapped under every stab of the keen blade. A thick, yellow dust rose up from it. Spices and dried essences rained down upon the floor. Suddenly, with a rending crack, its backbone snapped asunder, and it fell, a brown heap of sprawling limbs, upon the floor.

'Now into the fire!' said Smith.

The flames leaped and roared as the dried and tinder-like debris was piled upon it. The little room was like the stokehole of a steamer and the sweat ran down the faces of the two men; but still the one stooped and worked, while the other sat watching him with a set face. A thick, fat smoke oozed out from the fire, and a heavy smell of burned resin and singed hair filled the air. In a quarter of an hour a few charred and brittle sticks were all that was left of Lot No. 249.

'Perhaps that will satisfy you,' snarled Bellingham, with hate and fear in his little grey eyes as he glanced back at his tormentor.

'No; I must make a clean sweep of all your materials. We must have no more devil's tricks. In with all these leaves! They may have something to do with it.'

'And what now?' asked Bellingham, when the leaves also had been added to the blaze.

'Now the roll of papyrus which you had on the table that night. It is in that drawer, I think.'

'No, no,' shouted Bellingham. 'Don't burn that! Why, man, you don't know what you do. It is unique; it contains wisdom which is nowhere else to be found.'

'Out with it!'

'But look here, Smith, you can't really mean it. I'll share the knowledge with you. I'll teach you all that is in it. Or, stay, let me only copy it before you burn it!'

Smith stepped forward and turned the key in the drawer.

Taking out the yellow, curled roll of paper, he threw it into the fire, and pressed it down with his heel. Bellingham screamed, and grabbed at it; but Smith pushed him back and stood over it until it was reduced to a formless, grey ash.

'Now, Master B.,' said he, 'I think I have pretty well drawn your teeth. You'll hear from me again, if you return to your old tricks. And now good morning, for I must go back to my studies.'

And such is the narrative of Abercrombie Smith as to the singular events which occurred in Old College, Oxford, in the spring of '84. As Bellingham left the university immediately afterwards, and was last heard of in the Sudan, there is no one who can contradict his statement. But the wisdom of men is small, and the ways of Nature are strange, and who shall put a bound to the dark things which may be found by those who seek for them?

THE STORY OF BAELBROW

by E & H Heron

It is a matter for regret that so many of Mr Flaxman Low's reminiscences should deal with the darker episodes of his experiences. Yet this is almost unavoidable, as the more purely scientific and less strongly marked cases would not, perhaps, contain the same elements of interest for the general public, however valuable and instructive they might be to the expert student. It has also been considered better to choose the completer cases, those that ended in something like satisfactory proof, rather than the many instances where the thread broke off abruptly amongst surmisings, which it was never possible to subject to convincing tests.

North of a low-lying strip of country on the East Anglian coast, the promontory of Bael Ness thrusts out a blunt nose into the sea. On the Ness, backed by pinewoods, stands a square, comfortable stone mansion, known to the countryside as Baelbrow. It has faced the east winds for close upon three hundred years, and during the whole period has been the home of the Swaffam family, who were never in anywise put out of conceit of their ancestral dwelling by the fact that it had always been haunted. Indeed, the Swaffams were proud of the Baelbrow Ghost, which enjoyed a wide notoriety, and no one dreamt of complaining of its behaviour until Professor Van der Voort of Louvain laid information against it, and sent an urgent appeal for help to Mr Flaxman Low.

The Professor, who was well acquainted with Mr Low, detailed the circumstances of his tenancy of Baelbrow, and the unpleasant events that had followed thereupon.

It appeared that Mr Swaffam, senior, who spent a large portion of his time abroad, had offered to lend his house to the Professor for the summer season. When the Van der Voorts arrived at Baelbrow, they were charmed with the place. The prospect, though not very varied, was at least extensive, and the air exhilarating. Also the Professor's daughter enjoyed frequent visits from her betrothed – Harold Swaffam – and the Professor was delightfully employed in overhauling the Swaffam library.

The Van der Voorts had been duly told of the ghost, which lent distinction to the old house, but never in any way interfered with the comfort of the inmates. For some time they found this description to be strictly true, but with the beginning of October came a change. Up to this time and as far back as the Swaffam annals reached, the ghost had been a shadow, a rustle, a passing sigh – nothing definite or troublesome. But early in October strange things began to occur, and the terror culminated when a housemaid was found dead in a corridor three weeks later. Upon this the Professor felt that it was time to send for Flaxman Low.

Mr Low arrived upon a chilly evening when the house was already beginning to blur in the purple twilight, and the resinous scent of the pines came sweetly on the land breeze. Van der Voort welcomed him in the spacious, fire-lit hall. He was a stout man with a quantity of white hair, round eyes emphasised by spectacles, and a kindly, dreamy face. His life-study was philology, and his two relaxations chess and the smoking of a big bowled meerschaum.

'Now, Professor,' said Mr Low when they had settled themselves in the smoking-room, 'how did it all begin?'

'I will tell you,' replied Van der Voort, thrusting out his chin, and tapping his broad chest, and speaking as if an unwarrantable liberty had been taken with him. 'First of all, it has shown itself to me!'

Mr Flaxman Low smiled and assured him that nothing could be more satisfactory.

'But not at all satisfactory!' exclaimed the Professor. 'I was sitting here alone, it might have been midnight – when I hear something come creeping like a little dog with its nails, tick-tick, upon the oak flooring of the hall. I whistle, for I think it is the little "Rags" of my daughter, and afterwards opened the door, and I saw' – he hesitated and looked hard at Low through his spectacles, 'something that was just disappearing into the passage which connects the two wings of the house. It was a figure, not unlike the human figure, but narrow and straight. I fancied I saw a bunch of black hair, and a flutter of something detached, which may have been a handkerchief. I was overcome by a feeling of repulsion. I heard a few clicking steps, then it stopped, as I thought, at the museum door. Come, I will show you the spot.'

The Professor conducted Mr Low into the hall. The main staircase, dark and massive, yawned above them, and directly behind it ran the passage referred to by the Professor. It was over twenty feet long, and about midway led past a deep arch containing a door reached by two steps. Van der Voort explained that this door formed the entrance to a large room called the Museum, in which Mr Swaffam, senior, who was something of a dilettante, stored the various curios he picked up during his excursions abroad. The Professor went on to say that he immediately followed the figure, which he believed had gone into the museum, but he found nothing there except the cases containing Swaffam's treasures.

'I mentioned my experience to no one. I concluded that I had seen the ghost. But two days after, one of the female servants coming through the passage, in the dark, declared that a man leapt out at her from the embrasure of the Museum door, but she released herself and ran screaming into the servants' hall. We at once made a search but found nothing to substantiate her story.

'I took no notice of this, though it coincided pretty well with my own experience. The week after, my daughter Lena came down late one night for a book. As she was about to cross the hall, something leapt upon her from behind. Women are of little use in serious investigations – she fainted! Since then she has been ill and the doctor says "run down".' Here the Professor spread out his hands. 'So she leaves for a change to-morrow. Since then other members of the household have been attacked in much the same manner, with always the same result, they faint and are weak and useless when they recover.

'But, last Wednesday, the affair became a tragedy. By that time the servants had refused to come through the passage except in a crowd of three or four, – most of them preferring to go round by the terrace to reach this part of the house. But one maid, named Eliza Freeman, said she was not afraid of the Baelbrow Ghost, and undertook to put out the lights in the hall one night. When she had done so, and was returning through the passage past the Museum door, she appears to have been attacked, or at any rate frightened. In the grey of the morning they found her lying beside the steps dead. There was a little blood upon her sleeve but no mark upon her body except a small raised pustule under the ear. The doctor said the girl was extraordinarily anæmic, and that she probably died from fright, her heart being weak. I was surprised at this, for she had always seemed to be a particularly strong and active young woman.'

'Can I see Miss Van der Voort to-morrow before she goes?' asked Low, as the Professor signified he had nothing more to tell.

The Professor was rather unwilling that his daughter should be questioned, but he at last gave his permission, and next morning Low had a short talk with the girl before she left the house. He found her a very pretty girl, though listless and startlingly pale, and with a frightened stare in her light brown eyes. Mr Low asked if she could describe her assailant.

'No,' she answered. 'I could not see him for he was behind me. I only saw a dark, bony hand, with shining nails, and a bandaged arm pass just under my eyes before I fainted.'

'Bandaged arm? I have heard nothing of this.'

'Tut – tut, mere fancy!' put in the Professor impatiently.

'I saw the bandages on the arm,' repeated the girl, turning her head wearily away, 'and I smelt the antiseptics it was dressed with.'

'You have hurt your neck,' remarked Mr Low, who noticed a small circular patch of pink under her ear.

She flushed and paled, raising her hand to her neck with a nervous jerk, as she said in a low voice: 'It has almost killed me. Before he touched me, I knew he was there! I felt it!'

When they left her the Professor apologised for the unreliability of her evidence, and pointed out the discrepancy between her statement and his own.

'She says she sees nothing but an arm, yet I tell you it had no arms! Preposterous! Conceive a wounded man entering this house to frighten the young women! I do not know what to make of it! Is it a man, or is it the Baelbrow Ghost?'

During the afternoon when Mr Low and the Professor returned from a stroll on the shore, they found a dark-browed young man with a bull neck, and strongly marked features, standing sullenly before the hall fire. The Professor presented him to Mr Low as Harold Swaffam.

Swaffam seemed to be about thirty, but was already known as a far-seeing and successful member of the Stock Exchange.

'I am pleased to meet you, Mr Low,' he began, with a keen glance, 'though you don't look sufficiently high-strung for one of your profession.'

Mr Low merely bowed.

'Come, you don't defend your craft against my insinuations?' went on Swaffam. 'And so you have come to rout out our poor old ghost from Baelbrow? You forget that he is an heirloom, a family possession! What's this about his having turned rabid, eh, Professor?' he ended, wheeling round upon Van der Voort in his brusque way.

The Professor told the story over again. It was plain that he stood rather in awe of his prospective son-in-law.

'I heard much the same from Lena, whom I met at the station,' said Swaffam. 'It is my opinion that the women in this house are suffering from an epidemic of hysteria. You agree with me, Mr Low?'

'Possibly. Though hysteria could hardly account for Freeman's death.'

'I can't say as to that until I have looked further into the particulars. I have not been idle since I arrived. I have examined the Museum. No one has entered it from the outside, and there is no other way of entrance except through the passage. The flooring is laid, I happen to know, on a thick layer of concrete. And there the case for the ghost stands at present.' After a few moments of dogged reflection, he swung round on Mr Low, in a manner that seemed peculiar to him when about to address any person. 'What do you say to this plan, Mr Low? I propose to drive the Professor over to Ferryvale, to stop there for a day or two at the hotel, and I will also dispose of the servants who still remain in the house for, say, forty-eight hours. Meanwhile you and I can try to go further into the secret of the ghost's new pranks?'

Flaxman Low replied that this scheme exactly met his views, but the Professor protested against being sent away. Harold Swaffam, however, was a man who liked to arrange things in his own fashion, and within forty-five minutes he and Van der Voort departed in the dogcart.

The evening was lowering, and Baelbrow, like all houses built in exposed situations, was extremely susceptible to the changes of the weather. Therefore, before many hours were over, the place was full of creaking noises as the screaming gale battered at the shuttered windows, and the tree-branches tapped and groaned against the walls.

Harold Swaffam on his way back was caught in the storm and drenched to the skin. It was, therefore, settled that after he had changed his clothes he should have a couple of hours' rest on the smoking-room sofa, while Mr Low kept watch in the hall.

The early part of the night passed over uneventfully. A light burned faintly in the great wainscotted hall, but the passage was dark. There was nothing to be heard but the wild moan and whistle of the wind coming in from the sea, and the squalls of rain dashing against the windows. As the hours advanced, Mr Low lit a lantern that lay at hand, and, carrying it along the passage tried the Museum door. It yeilded, and the wind came muttering through to meet him. He looked round at the shutters and behind the big cases which held Mr Swaffam's treasures, to make sure that the room contained no living occupant but himself.

Suddenly he fancied he heard a scraping noise behind him, and turned round, but discovered nothing to account for it. Finally, he laid the lantern on a bench so that its light should fall through the door into the passage, and returned again to the hall, where he put out the lamp, and then once more took up his station by the closed door of the smoking-room.

A long hour passed, during which the wind continued to roar down the wide hall chimney, and the old boards creaked as if furtive footsteps were gathering from every corner of the house. But Flaxman Low heeded none of these; he was awaiting for a certain sound.

After a while, he heard it – the cautious scraping of wood on wood. He leant forward to watch the Museum door. Click, click, came the curious dog-like tread upon the tiled floor of the Museum, till the thing, whatever it was, paused and listened behind the open door. The wind lulled at the moment, and Low listened also, but no further sound was to be heard, only slowly across the broad ray of light falling through the door grew a stealthy shadow.

Again the wind rose, and blew in heavy gusts about the house, till even the flame in the lantern flickered; but when it steadied once more, Flaxman Low saw that the silent form had passed through the door, and was now on the steps outside. He could just make out a dim shadow in the dark angle of the embrasure.

Presently, from the shapeless shadow came a sound Mr Low was not prepared to hear. The thing sniffed the air with the strong, audible inspiration of a bear, or some large animal. At the same moment, carried on the draughts of the hall, a faint, unfamiliar odour reached his nostrils. Lena Van der Voort's words flashed back upon him – this, then, was the creature with the bandaged arm!

Again, as the storm shrieked and shook the windows, a darkness passed across the light. The thing had sprung out from the angle of the door, and Flaxman Low knew that it was making its way towards him through the illusive blackness of the hall. He hesitated for a second; then he opened the smoking-room door.

Harold Swaffam sat up on the sofa, dazed with sleep.

'What has happened? Has it come?'

Low told him what he had just seen. Swaffam listened half-smilingly.

'What do you make of it now?' he said.

'I must ask you to defer that question for a little,' replied Low.

'Then you mean me to suppose that you have a theory to fit all these incongruous items?'

'I have a theory, which may be modified by further

knowledge,' said Low. 'Meantime, am I right in concluding from the name of this house that it was built on a barrow or burying-place?'

'You are right, though that has nothing to do with the latest freaks of our ghost,' returned Swaffam decidedly.

'I also gather that Mr Swaffam has lately sent home one of the many cases now lying in the Museum?' went on Mr Low.

'He sent one, certainly, last September.'

'And you have opened it,' asserted Low.

'Yes; though I flattered myself I had left no trace of my handiwork.'

'I have not examined the cases,' said Low. 'I inferred that you had done so from other facts.'

'Now, one thing more,' went on Swaffam, still smiling. 'Do you imagine there is any danger − I mean to men like ourselves? Hysterical women cannot be taken into serious account.'

'Certainly; the gravest danger to any person who moves about this part of the house alone after dark,' replied Low.

Harold Swaffam leant back and crossed his legs.

'To go back to the beginning of our conversation, Mr Low, may I remind you of the various conflicting particulars you will have to reconcile before you can present any decent theory to the world?'

'I am quite aware of that.'

'First of all, our original ghost was a mere misty presence, rather guessed at from vague sounds and shadows − now we have a something that is tangible, and that can, as we have proof, kill with fright. Next Van der Voort declares the thing was a narrow, long and distinctly armless object, while Miss Van der Voort has not only seen the arm and hand of a human being, but saw them clearly enough to tell us that the nails were gleaming and the arm bandaged. She also felt its strength. Van der Voort, on the other hand, maintained that it clicked along like a dog − you bear out this description with the additional information that it sniffs like a wild beast. Now what can this thing be? It is capable of being seen, smelt, and felt, yet it hides itself, successfully in a room where there is no cavity or space sufficient to afford covert to a cat! You still tell me that you believe that you can explain?'

'Most certainly,' replied Flaxman Low with conviction.

'I have not the slightest intention or desire to be rude, but as a mere matter of common sense, I must express my opinion plainly. I believe the whole thing to be the result of excited imaginations, and I am about to prove it. Do you think there is any further danger to-night?'

'Very great danger to-night,' replied Low.

'Very well; as I said, I am going to prove it. I will ask you to allow me to lock you up in one of the distant rooms, where I can get no help from you, and I will pass the remainder of the night walking about the passage and hall in the dark. That should give proof one way or the other.'

'You can do so if you wish, but I must at least beg to be allowed to look on. I will leave the house and watch what goes on from the window in the passage, which I saw opposite the Museum door. You cannot, in any fairness, refuse to let me be a witness.'

'I cannot, of course,' returned Swaffam. 'Still, the night is too bad to turn a dog out into, and I warn you that I shall lock you out.'

'That will not matter. Lend me a macintosh, and leave the lantern lit in the Museum, where I placed it.'

Swaffam agreed to this. Mr Low gives a graphic account of what followed. He left the house and was duly locked out, and, after groping his way round the house, found himself at length outside the window of the passage, which was almost opposite to the door of the Museum. The door was still ajar and a thin band of light cut out into the gloom. Further down the hall gaped black and void. Low, sheltering himself as well as he could from the rain, waited for Swaffam's appearance. Was the terrible yellow watcher balancing itself upon its lean legs in the dim corner opposite, ready to spring out with its deadly strength upon the passer-by?

Presently Low heard a door bang inside the house, and the next moment Swaffam appeared with a candle in his hand, an isolated spread of weak rays against the vast darkness behind. He advanced steadily down the passage, his dark face grim and set, and as he came Mr Low experienced that tingling sensation, which is so often the forerunner of some strange experience. Swaffam passed on towards the other end of the passage. There was a quick vibration of the Museum door as a lean shape with a shrunken head leapt out into the passage after him. Then all together came a hoarse shout, the noise of a fall and utter darkness.

In an instant, Mr Low had broken the glass, opened the window, and swung himself into the passage. There he lit a match and as it flared he saw by its dim light a picture painted for a second upon the obscurity beyond.

Swaffam's big figure lay with outstretched arms, face downwards, and as Low looked a crouching shape extricated itself from the fallen man, raising a narrow vicious head from his shoulder.

The match spluttered feebly and went out, and Low heard a flying step click on the boards, before he could find the candle Swaffam had dropped. Lighting it, he stooped over Swaffam and turned him on his back. The man's strong colour had gone, and the wax-white face looked whiter still against the blackness of hair and brows, and upon his neck under the ear was a little raised pustule, from which a thin line of blood was streaked up to the angle of his cheekbone.

Some instinctive feeling prompted Low to glance up at this moment. Half extended from the Museum doorway were a face and bony neck – a high-nosed, dull-eyed, malignant face, the eye-sockets hollow, and the darkened teeth showing. Low plunged his hand into his pocket, and a shot rang out in the echoing passage-way and hall. The wind sighed through the broken panes, a ribbon of stuff fluttered along the polished flooring, and that was all, as Flaxman Low half dragged, half carried Swaffam into the smoking-room.

It was some time before Swaffam recovered consciousness. He listened to Low's story of how he had found him with a red angry gleam in his sombre eyes.

'The ghost has scored off me,' he said, with an odd, sullen laugh, 'but now I fancy it's my turn! But before we adjourn to the Museum to examine the place, I will ask you to let me hear your notion of things. You have been right in saying there was real danger. For myself I can only tell you that I felt something spring upon me, and I knew no more. Had this not happened I am afraid I should never have asked you a second time what your idea of the matter might be,' he added with a sort of sulky frankness.

'There are two main indications,' replied Low. 'This strip of yellow bandage, which I have just now picked up from the passage floor, and the mark on your neck.'

'What's that you say?' Swaffam rose quickly and examined his neck in a small glass beside the mantelshelf.

'Connect those two, and I think I can leave you to work it out for yourself,' said Low.

'Pray let us have your theory in full,' requested Swaffam shortly.

'Very well,' answered Low good-humouredly – he thought Swaffam's annoyance natural in the circumstances – 'The long, narrow figure which seemed to the Professor to be armless is developed on the next occasion. For Miss Van der Voort sees a bandaged arm and a dark hand with gleaming – which means, of course, gilded – nails. The clicking sound of the footsteps coincides with these particulars, for we know that sandals made of strips of leather are not uncommon in company with gilt nails and bandages. Old and dry leather would naturally click upon your polished floor.'

'Bravo, Mr Low! So you mean to say that this house is haunted by a mummy!'

'That is my idea, and all I have seen confirms me in my opinion.'

'To do you justice, you held this theory before to-night – before, in fact, you had seen anything for yourself. You gathered that my father had sent home a mummy, and you went on to conclude that I had opened the case?'

'Yes. I imagine you took off most of, or rather all, the outer bandages, thus leaving the limbs free, wrapped only in the inner bandages which were swathed round each separate limb. I fancy this mummy was preserved on the Theban method with aromatic spices, which left the skin olive-coloured, dry and flexible, like tanned leather, the features remaining distinct, and the hair, teeth, and eyebrows perfect.'

'So far, good,' said Swaffam. 'But now, how about the intermittent vitality? The postule on the neck of those whom it attacks? And where is our old Baelbrow ghost to come in?'

Swaffam tried to speak in a rallying tone, but his excitement and lowering temper were visible enough, in spite of the attempts he made to suppress them.

'To begin at the beginning,' said Flaxman Low, 'everybody who, in a rational and honest manner, investigates the phenomena of spiritism will, sooner or later, meet in them some perplexing element, which is not to be explained by any of the ordinary theories. For reasons into which I need not now enter, this present case appears to me to be one of these. I am led to believe that the ghost which has for so many years given dim and vague manifestations of its existence in this house is a vampire.'

Swaffam threw back his head with an incredulous gesture.

'We no longer live in the middle ages, Mr Low! And besides, how could a vampire come here?' he said scoffingly.

'It is held by some authorities on these subjects that under certain conditions a vampire may be self-created. You tell me that this house is built upon an ancient barrow, in fact, on a spot where we might naturally expect to find such an elemental psychic germ. In those dead human systems were contained all the seeds for good and evil. The power which causes these psychic seeds or germs to grow is thought, and from being long dwelt on and indulged, a thought might finally gain a mysterious vitality, which could go on increasing more and more by attracting to itself suitable and appropriate elements from its environment. For a long period this germ remained a helpless intelligence, awaiting the opportunity to assume some material form, by means of which to carry out its desires. The invisible is the real; the material only subserves its manifestation. The impalpable reality already existed, when you provided for it a physical medium for action by unwrapping the mummy's form. Now, we can only judge of the nature of the germ by its manifestation through matter. Here we have every indication of a vampire intelligence touching into life and energy the dead human frame. Hence the mark on the neck of its victims, and their bloodless and anæmic condition. For a vampire, as you know, sucks blood.'

Swaffam rose, and took up the lamp.

'Now, for proof,' he said bluntly. 'Wait a second, Mr Low. You say you fired at this appearance?' And he took up the pistol which Low had laid down on the table.

'Yes, I aimed at a small portion of its foot which I saw on the step.'

Without more words, and with the pistol still in his hand, Swaffam led the way to the Museum.

The wind howled round the house, and the darkness, which precedes the dawn, lay upon the world, when the two men looked upon one of the strangest sights it has ever been given to men to shudder at.

Half in and half out of an oblong wooden box in a corner of the great room, lay a lean shape in its rotten yellow bandages, the scraggy neck surmounted by a mop of frizzled hair. The toe strap of a sandal and a portion of the right foot had been shot away.

Swaffam, with a working face, gazed down at it, then seizing it by its tearing bandages, he flung it into the box, where it fell into a life-like posture, its wide, moist-lipped mouth gaping up at them.

For a moment Swaffam stood over the thing; then with a curse he raised the revolver and shot into the grinning face again and again with a deliberate vindictiveness. Finally he rammed the thing down into the box, and, clubbing the weapon, smashed the head into fragments with a vicious energy that coloured the whole horrible scene with a suggestion of murder done.

Then, turning to Low, he said: 'Help me to fasten the cover on it.'

'Are you going to bury it?'

'No, we must rid the earth of it,' he answered savagely. 'I'll put it into the old canoe and burn it.'

The rain had ceased when in the daybreak they carried the old canoe down to the shore. In it they placed the mummy case with its ghastly occupant, and piled faggots about it. The sail was raised and the pile lighted, and Low and Swaffam watched it creep out on the ebb-tide, at first a twinkling spark, then a flare and waving fire, until far out to sea the history of that dead thing ended 3000 years after the priests of Armen had laid it to rest in its appointed pyramid.

A PROFESSOR OF EGYPTOLOGY

by Guy Boothby

From seven o'clock in the evening until half past, that is to say
for the half-hour preceding dinner, the Grand Hall of the
Hôtel Occidental, throughout the season, is practically a
lounge, and is crowded with the most fashionable folk
wintering in Cairo. The evening I am anxiuos to describe was
certainly no exception to the rule. At the foot of the fine
marble staircase – the pride of its owner– a well-known
member of the French Ministry was chatting with an English
Duchess whose pretty, but somewhat delicate, daughter was
flirting mildly with one of the Sirdar's Bimbashis, on leave
from the Soudan. On the right-hand lounge of the Hall an
Italian Countess, whose antecedents were as doubtful as her
diamonds, was apparently listening to a story a handsome
Greek *attaché* was telling her; in reality, however, she was
endeavouring to catch scraps of a conversation being carried
on, a few feet away, between a witty Russian and an equally
clever daughter of the United States. Almost every nationality
was represented there, but unfortunately for our prestige, the
majority were English. The scene was a brilliant one, and the
sprinkling of military and diplomatic uniforms (there was a
Reception at the Khedivial Palace later) lent an additional
touch of colour to the picture. Taken altogether, and regarded
from a political point of view, the gathering had a significance
of its own.

At the end of the Hall, near the large glass doors, a handsome, elderly lady, with grey hair, was conversing with one of
the leading English doctors of the place – a grey-haired,

clever-looking man, who possessed the happy faculty of being able to impress everyone with whom he talked with the idea that he infinitely preferred his or her society to that of any other member of the world's population. They were discussing the question of the most suitable clothing for a Nile voyage, and as the lady's daughter, who was seated next her, had been conversant with her mother's ideas on the subject ever since their first visit to Egypt (as indeed had been the Doctor), she preferred to lie back on the divan and watch the people about her. She had large, dark, contemplative eyes. Like her mother she took life seriously, but in a somewhat different fashion. One who has been bracketed third in the Mathematical Tripos can scarcely be expected to bestow very much thought on the comparative merits of Jæger, as opposed to dresses of the Common or Garden flannel. From this, however, it must not be inferred that she was in any way a blue stocking, that is, of course, in the vulgar acceptation of the word. She was thorough in all she undertook, and for the reason that mathematics interested her very much the same way that Wagner, chess, and, shall we say, croquet, interest other people, she made it her hobby, and it must be confessed she certainly succeeded in it. At other times she rode, drove, played tennis and hockey, and looked upon her world with calm, observant eyes that were more disposed to find good than evil in it. Contradictions that we are, even to ourselves, it was only those who knew her intimately, and they were few and far between, who realised that, under that apparently sober, matter-of-fact personality, there existed a strong leaning towards the mysterious, or, more properly speaking, the occult. Possibly she herself would have been the first to deny this – but that I am right in my surmise this story will surely be sufficient proof.

Mrs Westmoreland and her daughter had left their comfortable Yorkshire home in September, and, after a little dawdling on the Continent, had reached Cairo in November – the best month to arrive, in my opinion, for then the rush has not set in, the hotel servants have not had sufficient time to become weary of their duties, and what is better still, all the best rooms have not been bespoken. It was now the middle of December, and the fashionable caravanserai, upon which they had for many years bestowed their patronage, was crowded from roof to cellar. Every day people were being turned away, and the manager's continual lament was that he had not another hundred rooms wherein to place more guests. He was a Swiss, and for that reason regarded hotel-keeping in the light of a profession.

On this particular evening Mrs Westmoreland and her daught Cecilia had arranged to dine with Dr Forsyth – that is to say, they were to eat their meal at his table in order that they might meet a man of whom they had heard much, but whose acquaintance they had not as yet made. The individual in question was a certain Professor Constanides – reputed one of the most advanced Egyptologists, and the author of several well-known works. Mrs Westmoreland was not of an exacting nature, and so long as she dined in agreeable company did not trouble herself very much whether it was with an English earl or a distinguished foreign *savant*.

'It really does not matter, my dear,' she was wont to observe to her daughter. 'So long as the cooking is good and the wine above reproach, there is absolutely nothing to choose between them. A Prime Minister and a country vicar are, after all, only men. Feed them well and they'll lie down and purr like tame cats. They don't want conversation.' From this it will be seen that Mrs Westmoreland was well acquainted with her world. Whether Miss Cecilia shared her opinions is another matter. At any rate, she had been looking forward for nearly a fortnight to meeting Constanides, who was popularly supposed to possess an extraordinary intuitive knowledge – instinct, perhaps, it should be called – concerning the localities of tombs of the Pharaohs of the Eleventh, Twelfth and Thirteenth Dynasties.

'I am afraid Constanides is going to be late,' said the Doctor, who had consulted his watch more than once. 'I hope, in that case, as his friend and your host, you will permit me to offer you my apologies.'

The Doctor at no time objected to the sound of his own voice, and on this occasion he was even less inclined to do so. Mrs Westmoreland was a widow with an ample income, and Cecila, he felt sure, would marry ere long.

'He has still three minutes in which to put in an

appearance,' observed that young lady, quietly. And then she added in the same tone, 'Perhaps we ought to be thankful if he comes at all.'

Both Mrs Westmoreland and her friend the Doctor regarded her with mildly reproachful eyes. The former could not understand anyone refusing a dinner such as she felt sure the Doctor had arranged for them; while the latter found it impossible to imagine a man who would dare to disappoint the famous Dr Forsyth, who, having failed in Harley Street, was nevertheless coining a fortune in the land of the Pharaohs.

'My good friend Constanides will not disappoint us, I feel sure,' he said, consulting his watch for the fourth time. 'Possibly I am a little fast, at any rate I have never known him to be unpunctual. A remarkable – a very remarkable man is Constanides. I cannot remember ever to have met another like him. And such a scholar!'

Having thus bestowed his approval upon him the worthy Doctor pulled down his cuffs, straightened his tie, adjusted his *pince-nez* in his best professional manner, and looked round the hall as if searching for someone bold enough to contradict the assertion he had just made.

'You have, of course, read his *Mythological Egypt,*' observed Miss Cecilia, demurely, speaking as if the matter were beyond doubt.

The Doctor looked a little confused.

'Ahem! Well, let me see,' he stammered, trying to find a way out of the difficulty. 'Well, to tell the truth, my dear young lady, I'm not quite sure that I have studied that particular work. As a matter of fact, you see, I have so little leisure at my disposal for any reading that is not intimately connected with my profession. That, of course, must necessarily come before everything else.'

Miss Cecilia's mouth twitched as if she were endeavouring to keep back a smile. At the same moment the glass doors of the vestibule opened and a man entered. So remarkable was he that everyone turned to look at him – a fact which did not appear to disconcert him in the least.

He was tall, well shaped, and carried himself with the air of one accustomed to command. His face was oval, his eyes large and set somewhat wide apart. It was only when they were directed fairly at one that one became aware of the power they possessed. The cheek bones were a trifle high, and the forehead possibly retreated towards the jet-black hair more than is customary in Greeks. He wore neither beard nor moustache, thus enabling one to see the wide, firm mouth, the compression of the lips which spoke for the determination of their possessor. Those who had an eye for such things noted the fact that he was faultlessly dressed, while Miss Cecila, who had the precious gift of observation largely developed, noted that, with the exception of a single ring and a magnificent pearl stud, the latter strangely set, he wore no jewellery of any sort.

He looked about him for Dr Forsyth, and, when he had located him, hastened forward.

'My dear friend,' he said in English, which he spoke with scarcely a trace of foreign accent, 'I must crave your pardon a thousand times if I have kept you waiting.'

'On the contrary,' replied the Doctor, effusively, 'you are punctuality itself. Permit me to have the pleasure – the very great pleasure – of introducing you to my friends, Mrs Westmoreland and her daughter, Miss Cecilia, of whom you have often heard me speak.'

Professor Constanides bowed and expressed the pleasure he experienced in making their acquaintance. Though she could not have told you why, Miss Cecilia found herself undergoing very much the same sensation as she had done when she had passed up the Throne Room at her presentation. A moment later the gong sounded, and, with much rustling of skirts and fluttering of fans, a general movement was made towards the dining-room.

As host, Dr Forsyth gave his arm to Mrs Westmoreland, Constanides following with Miss Cecilia. The latter was conscious of a vague feeling of irritation; she admired the man and his work, but she wished his name had been anything rather than what it was.

(It should be here remarked that the last Constanides she had encountered had swindled her abominably in the matter of a turquoise brooch, and in consequnce the name had been an offence to her ever since.)

Dr Forsyth's table was situated at the further end, in the

window, and from it a good view of the room could be obtained. The scene was an animated one, and one of the party, at least, I fancy, will never forget it – try how she may.

During the first two or three courses the conversation was practically limited to Cecilia and Constanides; the Doctor and Mrs Westmoreland being too busy to waste time on idle chatter. Later, they became more amenable to the discipline of the table – or, in other words, they found time to pay attention to their neighbours.

Since then I have often wondered with what feelings Cecilia looks back upon that evening. In order, perhaps, to punish me for my curiosity, she has admitted to me since that she had never known, up to that time, what it was to converse with a really clever man. I submitted to the humiliation for the reason that we are, if not lovers, at least old friends, and, after all, Mrs Westmoreland's cook is one in a thousand.

From that evening forward, scarcely a day passed in which Constanides did not enjoy some portion of Miss Westmoreland's society. They met at the polo ground, drove in the Gezîreh, shopped in the Muski, or listened to the band, over afternoon tea, on the balcony of Shepheard's Hotel. Constanides was always unobtrusive, always picturesque and invariably interesting. What was more to the point, he never failed to command attention whenever or wherever he might appear. In the Native Quarter he was apparently better known than in the European. Cecilia noticed that there he was treated with a deference such as one would only expect to be shown to a king. She marvelled, but said nothing. Personally, I can only wonder that her mother did not caution her before it was too late. Surely she must have seen how dangerous the intimacy was likely to become. It was old Colonel Bettenham who sounded the first note of warning. In some fashion or another he was connected with the Westmorelands, and therefore had more or less right to speak his mind.

'Who the man is, I am not in a position to say,' he remarked to the mother; 'but if I were in your place I should be very careful. Cairo at this time of year is full of adventurers.'

'But, my dear Colonel,' answered Mrs Westmoreland, 'you surely do not mean to insinuate that the Professor is an adventurer. He was introduced to us by Dr Forsyth, and he has written so many clever books.'

'Books, my dear madam, are not everything,' the other replied judicially, and with that fine impartiality which marks a man who does not read. 'As a matter of fact I am bound to confess that Phipps – one of my captains – wrote a novel some years ago, but only one. The mess pointed out to him that it wasn't good form, don't you know, so he never tried the experiment again. But as for this man, Constanides, as they call him, I should certainly be more than careful.'

I have been told since that this conversation worried poor Mrs Westmoreland more than she cared to admit, even to herself. To a very large extent she, like her daughter, had fallen under the spell of the Professor's fascination. Had she been asked, point blank, she would doubtless have declared that she preferred the Greek to the Englishman – though, of course, it would have seemed flat heresy to say so. And yet – well, doubtless you can understand what I mean without my explaining further.

I am inclined to believe that I was the first to notice that there was serious trouble brewing. I could see a strained look in the girl's eyes for which I found if difficult to account. Then the truth dawned upon me, and I am ashamed to say that I began to watch her systematically. We have few secrets from each other now, and she has told me a good deal of what happened during that extraordinary time – for extraordinary it certainly was. Perhaps none of us realised what a unique drama we were watching – one of the strangest, I am tempted to believe, that this world of ours has ever seen.

Christmas was just past and the New Year was fairly under way when the beginning of the end came. I think by that time even Mrs Westmoreland had arrived at some sort of knowledge of the case. But it was then too late to interfere. I am as sure that Cecilia was not in love with Constanides as I am of anything. She was merely fascinated by him, and to a degree that, happily for the peace of the world, is as rare as the reason for it is perplexing.

To be precise, it was on Tuesday, January the 3rd, that the

crisis came. On the evening of that day, accompanied by her daughter and escorted by Dr Forsyth, Mrs Westmoreland attended a reception at the palace of a certain Pasha, whose name I am obviously compelled to keep to myself. For the purposes of my story it is sufficient, however, that he is a man who prides himself on being up-to-date in most things, and for that and other reasons invitations to his receptions are eagerly sought after. In his drawing-room one may meet some of the most distinguished men in Europe, and on occasion it is even possible to obtain an insight into certain political intrigues that, to put it mildly, afford one an opportunity of reflecting on the instability of mundane affairs and of politics in particular.

The evening was well advanced before Constanides made his appearance. When he did, it was observed that he was more than usually quiet. Later, Cecilia permitted him to conduct her into the balcony, whence, since it was a perfect moonlight night, a fine view of the Nile could be obtained. Exactly what he said to her I have never been able to discover; I have, however, her mother's assurance that she was visibly agitated when she rejoined her. As a matter of fact, they returned to the hotel almost immediately, when Cecilia, pleading weariness, retired to her room.

And now this is the part of the story you will find as difficult to believe as I did. Yet I have indisputable evidence that it is true. It was nearly midnight and the large hotel was enjoying the only quiet it knows in the twenty-four hours. I have just said that Cecilia had retired, but in making that assertion I am not telling the exact truth, for though she had bade mother 'Goodnight' and had gone to her room, it was not to rest. Regardless of the cold night air she had thrown open the window, and was standing looking out into the moonlit street. Of what she was thinking I do not know, nor can she re-member. For my own part, however, I incline to the belief that she was in a semi-hypnotic condition and that for the time being her mind was a blank.

From this point I will let Cecilia tell the story herself.

How long I stood at the window I cannot say; it may have been only five minutes, it might have been an hour. Then, suddenly, an extraordinary thing happened. I knew that it was imprudent, I was aware that it was even wrong, but an overwhelming craving to go out seized me. I felt as if the house were stifling me and that if I did not get out into the cool night air, and within a few minutes, I should die. Stranger still, I felt no desire to battle with the temptation. It was as if a will infinitely stronger than my own was dominating me and that I was powerless to resist. Scarcely conscious of what I was doing I changed my dress, and then, throwing on a cloak, switched off the electric light and stepped out into the corridor. The white-robed Arab servants were lying about on the floor as is their custom; they were all asleep. On the thick carpet of the great staircase my steps made no sound. The hall was in semi-darkness and the watchman must have been absent on his rounds, for there was no one there to spy upon me. Passing through the vestibule I turned the key of the front door. Still success attended me, for the lock shot back with scarcely a sound and I found myself in the street. Even then I had no thought of the folly of this escapade. I was merely conscious of the mysterious power that was dragging me on. Without hesitation I turned to the right and hastened along the pavement, faster I think than I had ever walked in my life. Under the trees it was comparatively dark, but out in the roadway it was well-nigh as bright as day. Once a carriage passed me and I could hear its occupants, who were French, conversing merrily – otherwise I seemed to have the city to myself. Later I heard a *muezzin* chanting his call to prayer from the minaret of some mosque in the neighbourhood, the cry being taken up and repeated from other mosques. Then at the corner of a street I stopped as if in obedience to a command. I can recall the fact that I was trembling, but for what reason I could not tell. I say this to show that while I was incapable of returning to the hotel, or of exercising my normal will power, I still possessed the faculty of observation.

I had scarcely reached the corner referred to, which, as a matter of fact, I believe I should recognise if I saw it again, when the door of a house opened and a man emerged. It was Professor Constanides, but his appearance at such a place and at such an hour, like everything else that happened that night, did not strike me as being in any way extraordinary.

'You have obeyed me,' he said by way of greeting. 'That is well. Now let us be going – the hour is late.'

As he said it there came the rattle of wheels and a carriage drove swiftly round the corner and pulled up before us. My companion helped me into it and took his place beside me. Even then, unheard-of as my action was, I had no thought of resisting.

'What does it mean?' I asked. 'Oh, tell me what it means? Why am I here?'

'You will soon know,' was his reply, and his voice took a tone I had never noticed in it before.

We had driven some considerable distance, in fact, I believe we had crossed the river, before either of us spoke again.

'Think,' said my companion, 'and tell me whether you can remember ever having driven with me before?'

'We have driven together many times lately,' I replied. 'Yesterday to the polo, and the day before to the Pyramids.'

'Think again,' he said, and as he did so he placed his hand on mine. It was as cold as ice. However, I only shook my head.

'I cannot remember,' I answered, and yet I seemed to be dimly conscious of something that was too intangible to be a recollection. He uttered a little sigh and once more we were silent. The horses must have been good ones for they whirled us along at a fast pace. I did not take much interest in the route we followed, but at last something attracted my attention and I knew that we were on the road to Gizeh. A few moments later the famous Museum, once the palace of the ex-Khedive Ismail, came into view. Almost immediately the carriage pulled up in the shadow of the *Lebbek* trees and my companion begged me to alight. I did so, whereupon he said something, in what I can only suppose was Arabic, to his coachman, who whipped up his horses and drove swiftly away.

'Come,' he said, in the same tone of command as before, and then led the way towards the gates of the old palace. Dominated as my will was by his I could still notice how beautiful the building looked in the moonlight. In the daytime it presents a faded and unsubstantial appearance, but now, with its Oriental tracery, it was almost fairylike. The Professor halted at the gates and unlocked them. How he had admitted us, I cannot say. It suffices that, almost before I was aware of it, we had passed through the garden and were ascending the steps to the main entrance. The doors behind us, we entered the first room. It is only another point in this extraordinary adventure when I declare that even now I was not afraid; and yet to find oneself in such a place and at such an hour at any other time would probably have driven me beside myself with terror. The moonlight streamed in upon us, revealing the ancient monuments and the other indescribable memorials of those long-dead ages. Once more my conductor uttered his command and we went on through the second room, passed the Skekh-El-Beled and the Seated Scribe. Room after room we traversed, and to do so it seemed to me that we ascended stairs innumerable. At last we came to one in which Constanides paused. It contained numerous mummy cases and was lighted by a skylight through which the rays of the moon streamed in. We were standing before one which I remembered to have remarked on the occasion of our last visit. I could distinguish the paintings upon it distinctly. Professor Constanides, with the deftness which showed his familiarity with the work, removed the lid and revealed to me the swathed-up figure within. The face was uncovered and was strangely well-preserved. I gazed down on it, and as I did so a sensation that I had never known before passed over me. My body seemed to be shrinking, my blood to be turning to ice. For the first time I endeavoured to exert myself, to tear myself from the bonds that were holding me. But it was in vain. I was sinking – sinking – sinking – into I knew not what. Then the voice of the man who had brought me to the place sounded in my ears as if he were speaking from a long way off. After that a great light burst upon me, and it was as if I were walking in a dream; yet I knew it was too real, too true to life to be a mere creation of my fancy.

It was night and the heavens were studded with stars. In the distance a great army was encamped and at intervals the calls of the sentries reached me. Somehow I seemed to feel no wonderment at my position. Even my dress caused me no surprise. To my left, as I looked towards the river, was a large tent, before which armed men paced continually. I looked about me as if I expected to see someone, but there was no one to greet me.

'It is for the last time,' I told myself. 'Come what may, it shall be the last time!'

Still I waited, and as I did so I could hear the night wind sighing through the rushes on the river's bank. From the tent near me – for Usirtasen, son of Amenemhait – was then fighting against the Libyans and was commanding his army in person – came the sound of revelry. The air blew cold from the desert and I shivered, for I was but thinly clad. Then I hid myself in the shadow of a great rock that was near at hand. Presently I caught the sound of a footstep, and there came into view a tall man, walking carefully, as though he had no desire that the sentries on guard before the Royal tent should become aware of his presence in the neighbourhood. As I saw him I moved from where I was standing to meet him. He was none other than Sinûhît – younger son of Amenemhait and brother of Usirtasen – who was at that moment conferring with his generals in the tent.

I can see him now as he came towards me, tall, handsome, and defiant in his bearing as a man should be. He walked with the assured step of one who has been a soldier and trained to warlike exercises from his youth up. For a moment I regretted the news I had to tell him – but only for a moment. I could hear the voice of Usirtasen in the tent, and after that I had no thought for anyone else.

'Is it thou, Nofrît?' he asked as soon as he saw me.

'It is I!' I replied. 'You are late, Sinûhît. You tarry too long over the wine cups.'

'You wrong me, Nofrît,' he answered, with all the fierceness for which he was celebrated. 'I have drunk no wine this night. Had I not been kept by the Captain of the Guard I should have been here sooner. Thou art not angry with me, Nofrît?'

'Nay, that were presumption on my part, my lord,' I answered. 'Art thou not the King's son, Sinûhît?'

'And by the Holy Ones I swear that it were better for me if I were not,' he replied. 'Usirtasen, my brother, takes all and I am but the jackal that gathers up the scraps wheresoever he may find them.' He paused for a moment. 'However, all goes well with our plot. Let me but have time and I will yet be ruler of this land and of all the Land of Khem beside.' He drew himself up to his full height and looked towards the sleeping camp. It was well known that between the brothers there was but little love, and still less trust.

'Peace, peace,' I whispered, fearing lest his words might be overheard. 'You must not talk so, my lord. Should you by chance be heard you know what the punishment would be!'

He laughed a short and bitter laugh. He was well aware that Usirtasen would show him no mercy. It was not the first time he had been suspected, and he was playing a desperate game. He came a step closer to me and took my hand in his. I would have withdrawn it – but he gave me no opportunity. Never was a man more in earnest than he was then.

'Nofrît,' he said, and I could feel his breath upon my cheek, 'what is my answer to be? The time for talking is past; now we must act. As thou knowest, I prefer deeds to words, and to-morrow my brother Usirtasen shall learn that I am as powerful as he.'

Knowing what I knew I could have laughed him to scorn for his boastful speech. The time, however, was not yet ripe, so I held my peace. He was plotting against his brother, whom I loved, and it was his desire that I should help him. That, however, I would not do.

'Listen,' he said, drawing even closer to me, and speaking in a voice that showed me plainly how much in earnest he was, 'thou knowest how much I love thee. Thou knowest that there is nought I would not do for thee or for thy sake. Be but faithful to me now and there is nothing thou shalt ask in vain of me hereafter. All is prepared, and ere the moon is gone I shall be Pharaoh and reign beside Amenemhait, my father.'

'Are you so sure that your plans will not miscarry?' I asked, with what was almost a sneer at his recklessness – for recklessness it surely was to think that he could induce an army that had been admittedly successful to swerve in its allegiance to the general who had won its battles for it, and to desert in the face of the enemy. Moreover, I knew that he was wrong in believing that his father cared more for him than for Usirtasen, who had done so much for the kingdom, and who was beloved by high and low alike. But it was not in Sinûhît's nature to look upon the dark side of things. He had complete confidence in himself and in his power to bring his conspiracy against his father and brother to a successful issue. He revealed to me his plans, and, bold though they were, I could see that it was impossible that they could succeed. And in the event of his failing,what mercy could he hope to receive? I knew Usirtasen too well to think that he would show any. With all the eloquence I could command I implored him to abandon the attempt, or at least to delay it for a time. He seized my wrist and pulled me to him, peering fiercely into my face.

'Art playing me false?' he asked. 'If it is so it were better that you should drown yourself in yonder river. Betray me and nothing shall save you – not even Pharaoh himself.'

That he meant what he said I felt convinced. The man was desperate; he was staking all he had in the world upon the issue of his venture. I can say with truth that it was not my fault that we had been drawn together, and yet on this night of all others it seemed as if there were nothing left for me but to side with him or to bring about his downfall.

'Nofrît,' he said, after a short pause, 'is it nothing, thinkest thou, to be the wife of a Pharaoh? Is it not worth striving for, particularly when it can be so easily accomplished?'

I knew, however, that he was deluding himself with false hopes. What he had in his mind could never come to pass. I was like dry grass between two fires. All that was required was one small spark to bring about a conflagration in which I should be consumed.

'Harken to me, Nofrît,' he continued. 'You have means of learning Usirtasen's plans. Send me word to-morrow as to what is in his mind and the rest will be easy. Your reward shall be greater than you dream of.'

Though I had no intention of doing what he asked, I knew that in his present humour it would be little short of madness to thwart him. I therefore temporised with him, and allowed him to suppose that I would do as he wished, and then, bidding him good-night, I sped away towards the hut where I was lodged. I had not been there many minutes when a messenger came to me from Usirtasen, summoning me to his presence. Though I could not understand what it meant I hastened to obey.

On arrival there I found him surrounded by the chief officers of his army. One glance at his face was sufficient to tell me that he was violently angry with someone, and I had the

best of reasons for believing that that someone was myself.
Alas! it was as I had expected. Sinûhît's plot had been discovered; he had been followed and watched, and my meeting
with him that evening was known. I protested my innocence
in vain. The evidence was too strong against me.

'Speak, girl, and tell what thou knowest,' said Usirtasen, in
a voice I had never heard him use before. 'It is the only way
by which thou canst save thyself. Look to it that thy story
tallies with the tales of others!'

I trembled in every limb as I answered the questions he put
to me. It was plain that he no longer trusted me, and that the
favour I had once found in his eyes was gone, never to return.

'It is well,' he said when I had finished my story. 'And now
we will see thy partner – the man who would have put me –
the Pharaoh who is to be – to the sword had I not been warned
in time.'

He made a sign to one of the officers who stood by, whereupon the latter left the tent, to return a few moments later
with Sinûhît.

'Hail, brother!' said Usirtasen, mockingly, as he leaned
back in his chair and looked at him through half-shut eyes.
'You tarried but a short time over the wine cup this night. I
fear it pleased thee but little. Forgive me; on another occasion
better shall be found for thee lest thou shouldst deem us
lacking in our hospitality.'

'There were matters that needed my attention and I could
not stay,' Sinûhît replied, looking his brother in the face.
'Thou wouldst not have me neglect my duties.'

'Nay! nay! Maybe they were matters that concerned our
personal safety?' Usirtasen continued, still with the same
gentleness. 'Maybe you heard that there were those in our
army who were not well disposed towards us? Give me their
names, my brother, that due punishment may be meted out to
them.'

Before Sinûhît could reply, Usirtasen had sprung to his feet.

'Dog!' he cried, 'darest thou prate to me of matters of
importance when thou knowest thou hast been plotting
against me and my father's throne. I have doubted thee these
many months and now all is made clear. By the Gods, the
Holy Ones, I swear that thou shalt die for this ere cock-crow.'

It was at this moment that Sinûhît became aware of my presence. A little cry escaped him, and his face told me as plainly as any words could speak that he believed that I had betrayed him. He was about to speak, probably to denounce me, when the sound of voices reached us from outside. Usirtasen bade the guards to ascertain what it meant, and presently a messenger entered the tent. He was travel-stained and weary. Advancing towards where Usirtasen was seated, he knelt before him.

'Hail, Pharaoh,' he said. 'I come to three from the Palace of Titoui.'

An anxious expression came over Usirtasen's face as he heard this. I also detected beads of perspiration on the brow of Sinûhît. A moment latter it was known to us that Amenemhait was dead, and, therefore, Usirtasen reigned in his stead. The news was so sudden, and the consequences so vast, that it was impossible to realise quite what it meant. I looked across at Sinûhît and his eyes met mine. He seemed to be making up his mind about something. Then with lightning speed he sprang upon me; a dagger gleamed in the air; I felt as if a hot iron had been thrust into my breast, and after that I remember no more.

As I felt myself falling I seemed to wake from my dream – if dream it were – to find myself standing in the Museum by the mummy case, and with Professor Constanides by my side.

'You have seen,' he said. 'You have looked back across the centuries to that day when, as Nofrît, I believed you had betrayed me, and killed you. After that I escaped from the camp and fled into Kaduma. There I died; but it was decreed that my soul should never know peace till we had met again and you had forgiven me. I have waited all these years, and see – we meet at last.'

Strange to say, even then the situation did not strike me as being in any way improbable. Yet now, when I see it set down in black and white, I find myself wondering that I dare to ask anyone in their sober senses to believe it to be true. Was I in truth that same Nofrît who, four thousand years before, had been killed by Sinûhît, son of Amenemhait, because he believed that I had betrayed him? It seemed incredible, and yet, if it were a creation of my imagination, what did the dream mean? I fear it is a riddle of which I shall probably never know the answer.

My failure to reply to his question seemed to cause him pain.

'Nofrît,' he said, and his voice shook with emotion, 'think what your forgiveness means to me. Without it I am lost both here and hereafter.'

His voice was low and pleading and his face in the moonlight was like that of a man who knew the uttermost depths of despair.

'Forgive – forgive,' he cried again, holding out his hands to me. 'If you do not, I must go back to the sufferings which have been my portion since I did the deed which wrought my ruin.'

I felt myself trembling like a leaf.

'If it is as you say, though I cannot believe it, I forgive you freely,' I answered, in a voice that I scarcely recognised as my own.

For some moments he was silent, then he knelt before me and took my hand, which he raised to his lips. After that, rising, he laid his head upon the breast of the mummy before which we were standing. Looking down at it he addressed it thus:

'*Rest, Sinûhît, son of Amenemhait* – for that which was foretold for thee is now accomplished, and the punishment which was decreed is at an end. Henceforth thou mayest sleep in peace.'

After that he replaced the lid of the coffin, and when this was done he turned to me.

'Let us be going,' he said, and we went together through the rooms by the way we had come.

Together we left the building and passsed through the gardens out into the road beyond. There we found the carriage waiting for us, and we took our places in it. Once more the horses sped along the silent road, carrying us swiftly back to Cairo. During the drive not a word was spoken by either of us. The only desire I had left was to get back to the hotel and lay my aching head upon my pillow. We crossed the bridge and entered the city. What the time was I had no idea, but I was conscious that the wind blew chill as if in anti- cipation of the dawn. At the same corner whence we had started, the coachman stopped his horses and I alighted, after which he drove away as if he had received his orders before-hand.

'Will you permit me to walk with you as far as your hotel?' said Constanides, with his customary politeness.

I tried to say something in reply, but my voice failed me. I would much rather have been alone, but as he would not allow this we set off together. At the corner of the street in which the hotel is situated we stopped.

'Here we must part,' he said. Then, after a pause, he added, 'And for ever. From this moment I shall never see your face again.'

'You are leaving Cairo?' was the only thing I could say.

'Yes, I am leaving Cairo,' he replied with peculiar emphasis. 'My errand here is accomplished. You need have no fear that I shall ever trouble you again.'

'I have no fear,' I answered, though I am afraid it was only a half truth.

He looked earnestly into my face.

'Nofrît,' he said, 'for, say what you will, you are the Nofrît I would have made my Queen and have loved beyond all other women, never again will it be permitted you to look into the past as you did to-night. Had things been ordained otherwise we might have done great things together, but the gods willed that it should not be. Let it rest therefore. And now – farewell! To-night I go to the rest for which I have so long been seeking.'

Without another word he turned and left me. Then I went on to the hotel. How it came about I cannot say, but the door was open and I passed quickly in. Once more, to my joy, I found the watchman was absent from the hall.

Trembling lest anyone might see me, I sped up the stairs and along the corridor, where the servants lay sleeping just as I had left them, and so to my room. Everything was exactly as I had left it, and there was nothing to show that my absence had been suspected. Again I went to the window, and, in a feeling of extraordinary agitation, looked out. Already there were signs of dawn in the sky. I sat down and tried to think over all that had happened to me that evening, endeavouring to convince myself, in the face of indisputable evidence, that it was not real and that I had only dreamt it. Yet it would not do! At last, worn out, I retired to rest. As a rule I sleep soundly; it is scarcely, however, a matter for wonderment that I did not do so on this occasion. Hour after hour I tumbled and tossed – thinking – thinking – thinking. When I rose and looked into the glass I scarcely recognised myself. Indeed, my mother commented on my fagged appearance when we met at the breakfast table.

'My dear child, you look as if you had been up all night,' she said, and little did she guess, as she nibbled her toast, that there was a considerable amount of truth in her remark.

Later she went shopping with a lady staying in the hotel, while I went to my room to lie down. When we met again at lunch it was easy to see that she had some news of importance to communicate.

'My dear Cecilia,' she said, 'I have just seen Dr Forsyth, and he has given me a terrible shock. I don't want to frighten you, my girl, but have you heard that *Professor Constanides was found dead in bed this morning?* It is a most terrible affair! He must have died during the night!'

I am not going to pretend that I had any reply ready to offer her at that moment.

THE MYSTERIOUS MUMMY

by Sax Rohmer

It was about five o'clock on a hot August afternoon, that a tall, thin man, wearing a weedy beard, and made conspicious by an ill-fitting frock-coat and an almost napless silk hat, walked into the entrance hall of the Great Portland Square Museum. He carried no stick, and, looking about him, as though unfamiliar with the building, he ultimately mounted the principal staircase, walking with a pronounced stoop, and at intervals coughing with a hollow sound.

His gaunt figure attracted the attention of several people, among them the attendant in the Egyptan room. Hardened though he was to the eccentric in humanity, the man who hung so eagerly over the mummies of departed kings and coughed so frequently, nevertheless secured his instant attention. Visitors of the regulation type were rapidly thinning out, so that the gaunt man, during the whole of the time he remained in the room, was kept under close surveillance by the vigilant official. Seeing him go in the direction of the stairs, the attendant supposed the strange visitor to be about to leave the Museum. But that he did not immediately do so was shown by subsequent testimony.

The day's business being concluded, the staff of police who patrol nightly the Great Square Museum duly filed into the building. A man is placed in each room, it being his duty to examine thoroughly every nook and cranny; having done which, all doors of communication are closed, the officer on guard in one room being unable to leave his post or to enter another. Every hour the inspector, a sergeant, and a fireman

make a round of the entire building: from which it will be seen
that a person having designs on any of the numerous treasures of
the place would require more than average ingenuity to bring his
plans to a successful issue.

In recording this very singular case, the only incident of the
night to demand attention is that of the mummy in the Etruscan
room.

Persons familiar with the Great Portland Square Museum will
know that certain of the tombs in the Etruscan room are used as
receptacles for Egyptian mummies that have, for various
reasons, never been put upon exhibition. Anyone who has
peered under the partially raised lid of a huge sarcophagus and
found within the rigid form of a mummy, will appreciate the
feelings of the man on night duty amid surroundings so
lugubrious. The electric light, it should be mentioned, is not
extinguished until the various apartments have been examined,
and its extinction immediately precedes the locking of the door.

The constable in the Etruscan room glanced into the various
sarcophagi and cast the rays of his bull's-eye lantern into the
shadows of the great stone tombs. Satisfied that no one lurked
there, he mounted the steps leading up to the Roman gallery,
turning out the lights in the room below from the switch at the
top. The light was still burning on the ground floor, and the
sergeant had not yet arrived with the keys. It was whilst the man
stood awaiting his coming that a singular thing occurred.

From somewhere within the darkened chamber beneath,
there came the sound of a hollow cough!

By no means deficient in courage, the constable went down
the steps in three bounds, his lantern throwing discs of light on
stately statues and gloomy tombs. The sound was not repeated:
and having nothing to guide him to its source, he commenced a
second methodical search of the sarcophagi, as offering the most
likely hiding places. When all save one had been examined, the
constable began to believe that the coughing had existed only in
his imagination. It was upon casting the rays of his bull's-eye
into the last sarcophagus that he experienced a sudden sensation
of fear. It was empty; yet he distinctly remembered, from his
previous examination, that a mummy had lain there!

At the moment of making this weird discovery, he realised
that he would have done better, before commencing his search

for the man with the cough, first to turn on the light; for it must be remembered that he had extinguished the electric lamps. Determined to do so before pursuing his investigations further, he ran up the steps—to find the Roman gallery in darkness. The bright disc of a latern was approaching from the upper end, and the man ran forward.

'Who turned off the lights here?' came the voice of the sergeant.

'That's what I want to know! Somebody did it while I was downstairs!' said the constable, and gave a hurried account of the mysterious coughing and the missing mummy.

'How long has there been a mummy in this tomb?' asked the sergeant.

'There was one there a month back, but they took it upstairs. They may have brought it down again last week though, or it may have been a fresh one. You see, the other lot were on duty up to last night.'

This was quite true, as the sergeant was aware. Three bodies of picked men share the night duties at the Great Portland Square Museum, and those on duty upon this particular occasion had not been in the place during the previous two weeks.

'Very strange!' muttered the sergeant; and a moment later his whistle was sounding.

From all over the building men came running, for none of the doors had yet been locked.

'There seems to be someone concealed in the Museum: search all the rooms again!' was the brief order.

The constables disappeared, and the sergeant, accompanied by the inspector, went down to examine the Etruscan room. Nothing was found there; nor were any of the other searchers more successful. There was no trace anywhere of a man in hiding. Beyond leaving open the door between the Roman gallery and the steps of the Etruscan room, no more could be done in the matter. The gallery communicates with the entrance hall, where the inspector, together with the sergeant and fireman, spends the night, and the idea of the former was to keep in touch with the scene of these singular happenings. His action was perfectly natural; but these precautions were subsequently proved to be absolutely useless.

The night passed without any disturbing event, and the mystery of the vanishing mummy and the ghostly cough seemed likely to remain a mystery. The night-police filed out in the early morning, and the inspector, with the sergeant, returned, as soon as possible, to the Museum, to make further inquiries concerning the missing occupant of the sarcophagus.

'A mummy in the end tomb!' exclaimed the curator of Etruscan antiquities; 'my dear sir, there has been no mummy there for nearly a month!'

'But my man states that he saw one there last night!' declared the inspector.

The curator looked puzzled. Turning to an attendant, he said: 'Who was in charge of the Etruscan room immediately before six last night?'

'I was, sir!'

'Were there any visitors?'

'No one came in between five-forty and six.'

'And before that?'

'I was away at tea, sir!'

'Who was in charge then?'

'Mr Robins.'

'Call Robins.'

The commissionaire in question arrived.

'How long were you in the Etruscan room last night?'

'About half-an-hour, sir.'

'Are you sure that no one concealed himself?'

The man looked startled. 'Well, sir,' he said hesitatingly, 'I'm sorry I didn't report it before; but when Mr Barton called me, at about twenty-five minutes to six, there *was* someone there, a gent in a seedy frock-coat and a high hat, and I don't remember seeing him come out.'

'Did you search the room?'

'Yes, sir; but there was no one to be seen!'

'You should have reported the matter at once. I must see Barton.'

Barton, the head attendant, remembered speaking to Robins at the top of the steps leading to the Etruscan room. He saw no one come out, but it was just possible for a person to have done so and yet be seen by neither himself nor Robins.

'Let three of you thoroughly overhaul the room for any sign of a man having hidden there,' directed the curator briskly.

He turned to the sergeant and inspector with a smile, 'I rather fancy it will prove to be a mare's nest!' he said. 'We have had these mysteries before.'

The words had but just left his lips when a Museum official, a well-known antiquarian expert, ran up in a perfect frenzy of excitement. 'Good heavens, Peters!' he gasped. 'The Rienzi Vase has gone!'

'*What!*' came an incredulous chorus.

'The circular top of the case has been completely cut out and ingeniously replaced, and a plausible imitation of the vase substituted!'

They waited for no more, but hurried upstairs to the Vase room, which, in the Great Portland Square Museum, is really only a part of the Egyptian room. The Rienzi Vase, though no larger than an ordinary breakfast-cup, all the world knows to be of fabulous value. It seemed inconceivable that anyone could have stolen it. Yet there, in the midst of a knot of excited officials, stood the empty case, whilst the imitation antique was being passed from hand to hand.

Never before nor since has such a scene been witnessed in the Museum. The staff, to a man, had lost their wits. What is to be done? was the general inquiry. In less than half an hour the doors would have to be opened to the public, and the absence of the famous vase would inevitably be noticed. It was at this juncture, and whilst everyone was speaking at once, that one of the party, standing close to a wall-cabinet, suddenly held up a warning finger. 'Hush!' he said; 'listen!'

A sudden silence fell upon the room so that people running about in other apartments could be plainly heard. And presently, from somewhere behind the glass doors surrounding the place, came a low moan, electrifying the already excited listeners. The keys were promptly forthcoming and then was made the second astounding discovery of the eventful morning.

A man, gagged and bound, was imprisoned behind a great mummy case!

Eager hands set to work to release him, and restoratives were applied, as he seemed to be in a very weak condition. He was but partially dressed, and breathed heavily through his nose, like a man in a drunken slumber. All waited breathlessly for his return to consciousness; for certainly he, if anyone, should be in a position to furnish some clue to the deep mystery.

On regaining his senses, he had disappointingly little to tell. He was Constable Smith, who had been on night-duty in the Egyptian room. Sometime during the first hour, and not long after the alarm in the basement, he had been mysteriously pinioned as he paraded the apartment. He caught no glimpse of his opponent, who held him from behind in such a manner that he was totally unable to defend himself. Some sweet-smelling drug had been applied to his nostrils, and he remembered no more until regaining consciousness in the mummy case! That was the whole of his testimony.

In setting out the particulars of this remarkable affair, a third and final discovery must be noted. The three men who had been directed to examine the Etruscan room brought to light a bundle of old garments, containing an ancient opera-hat, a faded frock-coat, a pair of shiny trousers, and a pair of elastic-sided boots. They were wedged high up at the back of a tall statue, where they had evidently escaped the eyes of all previous searchers.

That constituted the entire data on which investigations had to be based. The Egyptain room was closed indefinitely, 'for repairs.' No further useful evidence could be obtained from anyone. Several witnesses furnished consistent descriptions of the shabby stranger with the hollow cough; but it may here be mentioned that no one of them ever set eyes upon him again. The inspector, the sergeant, and the fireman solemnly swore to having visited the Egyptian room at the end of each hour throughout the night, and to having found the constable on duty as usual! Smith swore, with equal solemnity, that he had been drugged during the first hour and subsequently confined in the mummy case.

The matter was carefully kept out of the papers, although the Museum, throughout many following days, positively bristled with detectives. As the second week drew to a close and the Egyptian room still remained locked, well-informed persons began to whisper that a scandal could no longer be avoided. There can be no doubt that, in many quarters, Constable Smith's share in the proceedings was regarded with grave suspicion. It was at this critical juncture, when it seemed inevitable that the loss of the world-famous Rienzi Vase must be made known to an unsympathetic public, that certain high authorities gave out that the vase had been removed, and that none of the night staff were in any way implicated in its disappearance!

On this announcement being made, several strange theories were mooted. Some stated that the vase had never left the Museum! Others averred that it had been pawned to a foreign government!

Whatever the real explanation, and the secret was jealously guarded by the highly-placed officials who alone knew the truth, suffice it that the Egyptian room was again thrown open and the Rienzi Vase shown to be reposing in its usual position.

Now that it again stands in its place for all to see, there can be no objection to my relating how I once held the famous Reinzi Vase in my possession for twelve days. If there be any objection . . . I am sorry. You must understand that I am no common thief – no footpad: I am a person of keenly observant character, and my business is to detect vital weaknesses in great institutions and to charge a moderately high fee for my services. Thus I discovered that a certain famous tiara in a French museum was inadequately protected, and accordingly removed it, replacing it by a substitute. The authorities refused me my fee, and all the world knows that my clever forgery was detected by the experts. That brought them to their senses; it is the genuine tiara that reposes in their cabinet now!

In the same way I removed a world-renowned, historical mummy from its resting place in Cairo, and two days later they grew suspicious of my imitation – it was the handiwork of a clever Birmingham artist – and the department was closed. The bulky character of the mummy nearly brought about my downfall, and it was only by abandoning it that I succeeded in leaving Cairo. I am not proud of that case; I was clumsy. But of the case of the Rienzi Vase I have every reason to be highly proud. That you may judge of the neatness and dispatch with which I acted, I will relate how the whole business was conducted.

You must know, then, that the first flaw I discovered in the arrangements at the Great Portland Square Museum was this: the wall-cases were badly guarded. I learnt this interesting fact one afternoon as I strolled about the Egyptian room. A certain gentleman – I will not name him – was showing a party of ladies round the apartment. He had unlocked a wall-case, and was standing with a handsome bead-necklet in his hand, explaining where and when it was found. He was only a few yards away, but with his back toward the case. Enough! The key, with others attached, was in the glass door. You will admit that this was exceedingly careless; but the presence of four charming American ladies . . . one can excuse him!

I regret to have to confess that I was somewhat awkward – the keys rattled. The whole party looked in my direction. But the immaculate man-about-town, with his cultivated manner and his very considerable knowledge of Egyptology – how should they suspect? I apologised; I had brushed against them in passing; I made myself agreeable, and the uncomfortable incident was forgotten, by them – not by me. I had a beautiful wax impression to keep my memory fresh!

The scheme formed then. I knew that a body of picked police promenaded the Museum at night, and that each of the rooms was usually in charge of the same man. I learnt, later, that there were three bodies of men, so that the same police were in the Museum but one week in every three. I made the acquaintance of seven constables and frequented eight different public-houses before I met the man of whom I was in search.

The first policeman I found, who paraded the Egyptian room at night, was short and thick-set, and I gave him up as a bad job. I learnt from him, however, who was to occupy the post during the coming week, and presently I unearthed the private bar which this latter officer, his name was Smith, used. Eureka! He was tall and thin. Incidentally, he was also surly. But the winning ways of the jovial master-plumber, who was so free with his money, ultimately thawed him.

Every night throughout the rest of the week I spent in this constable's company, studying his somewhat colourless personality. Then, one afternoon, I entered the Museum. My weedy beard, my gaunt expression, and my hollow cough – they were all in the part! I went up to the Egyptian room to assure myself that a certain mummy case had not been removed, and having found it to occupy its usual place, I descended to the Etruscan basement.

For half-an-hour I occupied myself there, but the commissionaire never budged from his seat. I knew that this particular man was only in temporary charge whilst another was at tea, for I was well posted, and wondered if his companion were ever coming back. Luckily, an incident occurred to serve my purpose. The chief attendant appeared at the head of the steps. 'Robins!' he called.

Robins ran briskly upstairs at his command, and then – in fifteen seconds my transformation was complete. Gone were the weedy grey beard and moustache – gone the seedy, black garments and the elastic-sided boots – gone the old opera-hat – and, behold, I was Constable Smith, attired in mummy wrappings!

An acrobatic spring, and the bundle of aged garments was wedged behind a tall statue, where nothing but a most minute search could reveal it. Down again, not a second to spare! Into the empty sarcophagus at the further end of the room; and, lastly, a hideous rubber mask slipped over the ruddy features of Constable Smith and attached behind the ears, my arms stiffened and my hands concealed in the wrappings, and I was a long-dead mummy – with a neat leather case hidden beneath my arched back!

Brisk work, I assure you; but one grows accustomed to it in time. The commissionaire entered the room very shortly afterwards. He had not seen me go out, but, as I expected, neither was he absolutely sure that I had not done so. He peered about suspiciously, but I did not mind. The real ordeal came a couple of hours later, when a police officer flashed his lantern into all the tombs.

For a moment my heart seemed to cease beating as the light shone on my rubber countenance. But he was satisfied, this stupid policeman, and I heard his footsteps retreating to

the door. I allowed him time to get to the top, and extinguished the light in the Etruscan room, and then . . . I
was out of my tomb and hidden in the little niche immediately
beside the foot of the stairs. I coughed loudly. Heavens! He
came back down the steps with such velocity that he was
carried halfway along the room. He began to flash his
lantern into the tombs again; but, before he had examined
the first of them, I was upstairs in the Roman gallery!

Without the electric light it was quite dark in the Etruscan
room, which is in the basement; but, being a bright night, I
knew I could find what I required in the Roman gallery
without the aid of artificial light; besides, I had not to act in
the open – someone might arrive too soon. So, thoroughly
well posted as to the situation of the switches, I extinguished
the lamps, and dodged in among the Roman stonework to
the foot of a great pillar, towering almost to the lofty roof and
surmounted by an ornate capital.

I had planned all this beforehand, you see; but I must
confess it was an awful scramble to the top. I had only just
curled up on the summit, the handle of my invaluable
leather-case held fast in my teeth, when a sergeant came
running down the gallery, almost into the arms of the
constable who was running up the steps from the Etruscan
room.

A moment's hurried conversation, and then the lights
turned on and the sound of a whistle. It was foolish, of
course; but I had expected it. From all over the building the
police arrived, and, fatigued as I was with my climb, yet
another acrobatic feat was before me.

The top of my pillar was no great distance from the stone
balustrade of the first-floor landing, on which the Egyptian
room opens, and a narrow ledge, perhaps of eleven inches,
runs all round the wall of the Roman gallery some four feet
below the ceiling. I cautiously stepped from the pillar to the
ledge – I was invisible from the other end of the place – and,
pressing my body close against the wall, reached the
balustrade. Before Constable Smith – who had left his post
and descended to the lower gallery on hearing the sergeant's
whistle – re-entered the Egyptian room, my bright, new key
had found the lock of a certain cabinet, and I was secure

behind a mummy case – whilst a little steel pin prevented the spring of the lock from shutting me in.

Poor Constable Smith! I was sorry to have to act so: but, ten minutes after the closing of the doors of communication, I came on him from behind, having silently crept from the case as he passed me, and followed him down the darkened room, the thin linen wrappings that covered my feet making no sound upon the wooden floor. I had a pad ready in my hand, saturated with the contents of a small phial that had reposed in my mummy garments.

I thrust my knee in his spine and seized his hands by a trick which you may learn for a peseta any day in the purlieus of Tangier. A muscular man, he tried hard to cope with his unseen opponent; but the pad never left his mouth and nostrils, and the few muffled cries that escaped him were luckily unheard. He soon became unconscious, and I had to work hard lest the inspector should make his round before I was ready for him. The mummy case had to be lowered on to the floor, and the heavy body tightly bound and lifted into it, then stood up again and securely locked behind the glass doors. It was hot work, and I had but just accomplished the task and climbed into the constable's uniform, when the inspector's key sounded in the door. Ah! it is an exciting progression!

The rest was easy. Wrapped up in my yellow mummy linen were the various appliances I required, and in the leather box was the imitation Rienzi Vase. The circular glass top of the case gave some trouble. So hard and thick was it that I had to desist five times and conceal my tools, owing to the hourly visits of the inspector. Poor Constable Smith began to groan toward six o'clock, and a second dose of medicine was necessary to keep him quiet for another hour or so.

I filed out with the other police in the morning, the Rienzi Vase inside my helmet. As to the sequel, it is brief. Of course the detectives tried their hands at the affair; but, pooh! I am too old a bird to leave 'clues'! It is only amateurs that do that!

My fee, and the conditions to be observed in paying it, I conveyed to the authorities privately. They thought they had a 'clue' then, and delayed another week. They actually detained my unhappy agent, a most guileless and upright person, who knew positively nothing. Oh! it was too funny! But, realising that only by the vase being returned to its place could a scandal be avoided – they met me in the matter.

THE MUMMY'S FOOT

by Théophile Gautier

I had entered, in an idle mood, the shop of one of those
curiosity vendors who are called *marchands de bric-à-brac* in that
Parisian argot which is so perfectly unintelligible elsewhere in
France.

The warehouse of my *bric-à-brac* dealer was a veritable
Capharnaum; all ages and all nations seemed to have made
their rendezvous there; an Etruscan lamp of red clay stood
upon a Boule cabinet, with ebony panels, brightly striped by
lines of inlaid brass; a duchess of the court of Louis XV
nonchalantly extended her fawn-like feet under a massive
table of the time of Louis XIII with heavy spiral supports of
oak, and carven designs of chimeras and foliage intermingled.

From disembowelled cabinets escaped cascades of silver-
lustrous Chinese silks and waves of tinsel, which an oblique
sunbean shot through with luminous beads; while portraits of
every era, in frames more or less tarnished, smiled through
their yellow varnish.

The dealer followed me closely through the tortuous way
contrived between the piles of furniture.

It was a singular face, that of the merchant. An immense
skull, polished like a knee, and surrounded by a thin aureole of
white hair, which brought out the clear salmon tint of his
complexion all the more strikingly, lent him a false aspect of
patriarchal *bonhomie*, counteracted, however, by the scintillation
of two little yellow eyes which trembled in their orbits like two
louis d'or upon quicksilver.

The curve of his nose presented an aquiline silhouette

which suggested the Oriental or Jewish type. His hands –
thin, slender, full of nerves which projected like strings upon
the finger-board of a violin, and armed with claws like those
on the terminations of bats' wings – shook with senile
trembling; but those convulsively agitated hands became
firmer than steel pincers or lobsters' claws when they lifted
any precious article – an onyx cup, a Venetian glass, or a
dish of Bohemian crystal. This strange old man had an
aspect so thoroughly rabbinical and cabalistic that he would
have been burnt on the mere testimony of his face three
centuries ago.

'Will you not buy something from me to-day, sir? Here is a
Malay kreese with blade undulating like flame; look at those
grooves contrived for the blood to run along – it is a fine
character of ferocious arm, and will look well in your collection: this two-handed sword is very beautiful – it is the
work of Josepe de la Hera; and this *colichemarde*, with its
fenestrated guard – what a superb specimen of handicraft!'

'No; I have quite enough weapons and instruments of
carnage – I want a small figure, something which will suit
me as a paper-weight; for I cannot endure those trumpery
bronzes which the stationers sell, and which may be found
on everybody's desk.'

The old gnome foraged among his ancient wares, and
finally arranged before me some antique bronzes – so-called,
at least; fragments of malachite; little Hindoo or Chinese
idols – a kind of poussah toys in jade-stone, representing the
incarnations of Brahma or Vishnoo, and wonderfully
appropriate to the very undivine office of holding papers and
letters in place.

I was hesitating between a porcelain dragon, all con-
stellated with warts – its mouth formidable with bristling
tusks and ranges of teeth – and an abominable little Mexican
fetish, representing the god Zitziliputzi *au naturel*, when I
caught sight of a charming foot, which I at first took for a
fragment of some antique Venus.

It had those beautiful ruddy and tawny tints that lend to
Florentine bronze that warm living look so much preferable
to the grey-green aspect of common bronzes, which might
easily be mistaken for statues in a state of putrefaction:

satiny gleams played over its rounded forms, doubtless
polished by the amorous kisses of twenty centuries.

'That foot will be my choice,' I said to the merchant, who
regarded me with an ironical and saturnine air, and held out
the object desired that I might examine it more fully.

I was surprised at its lightness; it was not a foot of metal,
but in sooth a foot of flesh – an embalmed foot – a mummy's
foot: on examining it still more closely the very grain of the
skin, and the almost imperceptible lines impressed upon it by
the texture of the bandages, became perceptible.

The toes were slender and delicate, and terminated by
perfectly formed nails, pure and transparent as agates; the
great toe, slightly separated from the rest, afforded a happy
contrast, in the antique style to the position of the other toes,
and lent it an aerial lightness – the grace of a bird's foot – the
sole, scarcely streaked by a few almost imperceptible cross
lines, afforded evidence that it had never touched the bare
ground, and had only come in contact with the finest matting
of Nile rushes, and the softest carpets of panther skin.

'Ha, ha! – You want the foot of the Princess Hermonthis,'
exclaimed the merchant, with a strange giggle, fixing his
owlish eyes upon me. 'Ha, ha, ha! For a paper-weight! An
original idea! Artistic idea! Old Pharaoh would certainly have
been surprised had someone told him that the foot of his
adored daughter would be used for a paper-weight after he
had had a mountain of granite hollowed out as a receptacle for
the triple coffin, painted and gilded – covered with
hieroglyphics and beautiful paintings of the Judgment of
Souls,' continued the queer little merchant, half audibly, as
though talking to himself.

'How much will you charge me for this mummy fragment?'

'Ah, the highest price I can get; for it is a superb piece.'

'Assuredly that is not a common article; but, still, how
much do you want? In the first place let me warn you that all
my wealth consists of just five louis: I can buy anything that
costs five louis, but nothing dearer.'

'Five louis for the foot of the Princess Hermonthis! That is
very little, very little indeed; 'tis an authentic foot,' muttered
the merchant, shaking his head, and imparting a peculiar
rotary motion in his eyes. 'Well, take it, and I will give you the

bandages into the bargain,' he added, wrapping the foot in an ancient damask rag.

He poured the gold coins into a sort of mediæval alms-purse hanging at his belt, repeating: 'The foot of the Princess Hermonthis, to be used for a paper-weight!'

Then, turning his phosphorescent eyes upon me, he exclaimed in a voice strident as the crying of a cat which has swallowed a fishbone: 'Old Pharaoh will not be well pleased; he loved his daughter – the dear man!'

'You speak as if you were a contemporary of his: you are old enough, goodness knows! but you do not date back to the Pyramids of Egypt,' I answered, laughingly, from the threshold.

I went home, delighted with my acquisition.

With the idea of putting it to profitable use as soon as possible, I placed the foot of the divine Princess Hermonthis upon a heap of papers scribbled over with verses, in themselves an undecipherable mosaic work of erasures; articles freshly begun; letters forgotten. The effect was charming, bizarre, and romantic.

Well satisfied with this embellishment, I went out with the gravity and pride becoming one who feels that he has the ineffable advantage over all the passers-by whom he elbows, of possessing a piece of the Princess Hermonthis, daughter of Pharaoh.

I looked upon all who did not possess, like myself, a paper-weight so authentically Egyptian, as very ridiculous people; and it seemed to me that the proper occupation of every sensible man should consist in the mere fact of having a mummy's foot upon his desk.

Happily I met some friends whose presence distracted me in my infatuation with this new acquisition: I went to dinner with them.

When I came back that evening, with my brain slightly confused by a few glasses of wine, a vague whiff of Oriental perfume delicately titillated my olfactory nerves; the heat of the room had warmed the natron, bitumen, and myrrh in which the *paraschistes*, who cut open the bodies of the dead, had bathed the corpse of the princess; it was a perfume at once sweet and penetrating – a perfume that four thousand years had not been able to dissipate.

I soon drank deeply from the black cup of sleep: for a few hours all remained opaque to me.

Yet light gradually dawned upon the darkness of my mind; dreams commenced to touch me softly in their silent flight.

The eyes of my soul were opened; and I beheld my chamber as it actually was; I might have believed myself awake but for a vague consciousness which assured me that I slept and that something fantastic was about to take place.

The odour of the myrrh had augmented in intensity: and I felt a slight headache, which I very naturally attributed to several glasses of champagne that we had drunk to the unknown gods and our future fortunes.

I peered through my room with a feeling of expectation which I saw nothing to justify: every article of furniture was in its proper place.

After a few moments, however, all this calm interior appeared to become disturbed; the woodwork cracked stealthily; the ash-covered log suddenly emitted a jet of blue flame.

My eyes accidentally fell upon the desk where I had placed the foot of the Princess Hermonthis.

Instead of remaining quiet – as behoved a foot which had been embalmed for four thousand years – it commenced to act in a nervous manner; contracted itself, and leaped over the papers like a startled frog. One would have imagined that it had suddenly been brought into contact with a galvanic battery: I could distinctly hear the dry sound made by its little heel, hard as the hoof of a gazelle.

Suddenly I saw the folds of my bed-curtain stir, and heard a bumping sound, like that caused by some person hopping on one foot across the floor. I must confess I became alternately hot and cold; that I felt a strange wind chill my back.

The bed-curtains opened and I beheld the strangest figure imaginable before me.

It was a young girl of a very deep coffee-brown complexion, like the bayadere Amani, and possessing the purest Egyptian type of perfect beauty: her eyes were almond shaped and oblique, with eyebrows so black that they seemed blue; her nose was exquisitely chiselled, almost Greek in its delicacy of outline; and she might indeed have been taken for a

Corinthian statue of bronze but for the prominence of her cheekbones and the slightly African fullness of her lips.

Her arms, slender and spindle-shaped, like those of very young girls, were encircled by a peculiar kind of metal bands and bracelets of glass beads; her hair was all twisted into little cords, and she wore upon her bosom a little idol-figure of green paste, bearing a whip with seven lashes, which proved it to be an image of Isis. Her brow was adorned with a shining plate of gold, and a few traces of paint relieved the coppery tint of her cheeks.

As for her costume, it was very odd indeed.

Fancy a *pagne* or skirt all formed of little strips of material bedizened with red and black hieroglyphics, stiffened with bitumen, and apparently belonging to a freshly unbandaged mummy.

In one of those sudden flights of thought so common in dreams I heard the hoarse falsetto of the *bric-à-brac* dealer repeating like a monotonous refrain the phrase he had uttered in his shop with so enigmatical an intonation:

'Old Pharaoh will not be well pleased: he loved his daughter, the dear man!'

One strange circumstance, which was not at all calculated to restore my equanimity, was that the apparition had but one foot; the other was broken off at the ankle!

She approached the table where the foot was starting and fidgeting about more than ever, and there supported herself upon the edge of the desk. I saw her eyes fill with pearly-gleaming tears.

Although she had not as yet spoken, I fully comprehended the thoughts which agitated her: she looked at her foot – for it was indeed her own – with an exquisitely graceful expression of coquettish sadness; but the foot leaped and ran hither and thither, as though impelled on steel springs.

Then commenced between the Princess Hermonthis and her foot – which appeared to be endowed with a special life of its own – a very fantastic dialogue in a most ancient Coptic tongue, such as might have been spoken thirty centuries ago in the syrinxes of the land of Ser: luckily, I understood Coptic perfectly well that night.

The Princess Hermonthis cried, in a voice sweet and vibrant as the tones of a crystal bell:

'Well, my dear little foot, you always flee from me; yet I always took good care of you, I bathed you with perfumed water in a bowl of alabaster; I smoothed your heel with pumice-stone mixed with palm oil; your nails were cut with golden scissors and polished with a hippopotamus tooth; I was careful to select *tatbebs* for you, painted and embroidered and turned up at the toes, which were the envy of all the young girls in Egypt: you wore on your toe rings bearing the device of the sacred scarabæus; and you supported one of the lightest bodies that a lazy foot could sustain.'

The foot replied, in a pouting and chagrined tone:

'You know well that I do not belong to myself any longer – I have been bought and paid for; the old merchant knew what he was about; he bore you a grudge for having refused to espouse him; – this is an ill turn which he has done you. The Arab who violated your royal coffin in the subterranean pits of the necropolis of Thebes was sent thither by him: he desired to prevent you from being present at the reunion of the shadowy nations in the cities below. Have you five pieces of gold for my ransom?'

'Alas, no! – my jewels, my rings, my purses of gold and silver, they were all stolen from me,' answered the Princess Hermonthis, with a sob.

'Princess,' I then exclaimed, 'I never retained anybody's foot unjustly; even though you have not got the five louis which it cost me, I present it to you gladly: I should feel unutterably wretched to think that I were the cause of so amiable a person as the Princess Hermonthis being lame.'

She turned a look of deepest gratitude upon me; and her eyes shone with bluish gleams of light.

She took her foot – which surrendered itself willingly this time – like a woman about to put on her little shoe, and adjusted it to her leg with much skill.

This operation over, she took a few steps about the room, as though to assure herself that she was really no longer lame.

'Ah, how pleased my father will be! – he who was so unhappy because of my mutilation, and who from the moment of my birth set a whole nation at work to hollow me out a tomb so deep that he might preserve me intact until that last day when souls must be weighed in the balance of Amenthi! Come with me to my father; he will receive you kindly, for you have given me back my foot.'

I thought this proposition natural enough. I arrayed myself in a dressing-gown of large-flowered pattern, which lent me a very Pharanoic aspect; hurriedly put on a pair of Turkish slippers, and informed the Princess Hermonthis that I was ready to follow her.

Before starting, Hermonthis took from her neck the little idol of green paste, and laid it on the scattered sheets of paper which covered the table.

'It is only fair,' she observed smilingly, 'that I should replace your paper-weight.'

She gave me her hand, which felt soft and cold, like the skin of a serpent; and we departed.

We passed for some time with the velocity of an arrow through a fluid and greyish expanse, in which half-formed silhouettes flitted swiftly by us, to right and left.

For an instant we saw only sky and sea.

A few moments later obelisks commenced to tower in the distance: pylons and vast flights of steps guarded by sphinxes became clearly outlined against the horizon.

We had reached our destination.

The princess conducted me to the mountain of rose-coloured granite, in the face of which appeared an opening so narrow and low that it would have been difficult to distinguish it from the fissures in the rock had not its location been marked by two stelæ wrought with sculptures.

Hermonthis kindled a torch, and led the way before me.

We traversed corridors hewn through the living rock: their walls, covered with hieroglyphics and paintings of allegorical processions, might well have occupied thousands of arms for thousands of years in their formation; these corridors, of interminable length, opened into square chambers, in the midst of which pits had been contrived, through which we descended by cramp-irons or spiral stair-ways; these pits again conducted us into other chambers, opening into other corridors, likewise decorated with painted sparrow-hawks, serpents coiled in circles.

At last we found ourselves in a hall so vast, so enormous, so immeasurable, that the eye could not reach its limits; files of monstrous columns stretched far out of sight on every side, between which winked livid stars of yellowish flame.

The Princess Hermonthis still held my hand, and graciously saluted the mummies of her acquaintance.

My eyes became accustomed to the dim twilight, and objects became discernible.

I beheld the kings of the subterranean races seated upon thrones – grand old men, though dry, withered, wrinkled like parchment, and blackened with naphtha and bitumen – all wearing *pshents* of gold, and breastplates and gorgets glittering with precious stones; their eyes immovably fixed like the eyes of sphinxes, and their long beards whitened by the snow of centuries. Behind them stood their peoples, in the stiff and constrained posture enjoined by Egyptian art, all eternally preserving the attitude prescribed by the hieratic code. Behind these nations, the cats, ibises, and crocodiles contemporary with them – rendered monstrous of aspect by their swathing bands – mewed, flapped their wings, or extended their jaws in a saurian giggle.

All the Pharaohs were there – Cheops, Chephrenes, Psammetichus, Sesostris, Amenotaph – all the dark rulers of the pyramids and syrinxes; on yet higher thrones sat Chronos and Xixouthros – who was contemporary with the deluge; and Tubal Cain, who reigned before it.

The beard of King Xixouthros had grown seven times around the granite table upon which he leaned, lost in deep reverie – and buried in dreams.

Further back, through a dusty cloud, I beheld dimly the seventy-two pre-Adamite Kings, with their seventy-two peoples – forever passed away.

After permitting me to gaze upon this bewildering spectacle a few moments, the Princess Hermonthis presented me to her father Pharaoh, who favoured me with a most gracious nod.

'I have found my foot again! I have found my foot!' cried the Princess, clapping her little hands together with every sign of frantic joy. 'It was this gentleman who restored it to me.'

The races of Kemi, the races of Nahasi – all the black, bronzed, and copper-coloured nations – repeated in chorus:

'The Princess Hermonthis has found her foot again!'

Even Xixouthros himself was visibly affected.

He raised his heavy eyelids, stroked his moustache with his fingers, and turned upon me a glance weighty with centuries.

'By Oms, the dog of Hell, and Tmei, daughter of the Sun and of Truth, this is a brave and worthy lad!' explained Pharaoh, pointing to me with his sceptre, which was terminated with a lotus-flower.

'What recompense do you desire?'

Filled with that daring inspired by dreams in which nothing seems impossible, I asked him for the hand of the Princess Hermonthis; the hand seemed to me a very proper antithetic recompense for the foot.

Pharaoh opened wide his great eyes of glass in astonishment at my witty request.

'What country do you come from? And what is your age?'

'I am a Frenchman; and I am twenty-seven years old, venerable Pharaoh.'

'Twenty-seven years old! And he wishes to espouse the Princess Hermonthis who is thirty centuries old!' cried out at once all the Thrones and all the Circles of Nations.

Only Hermonthis herself did not seem to think my request unreasonable.

'If you were even only two thousand years old,' replied the ancient King, 'I would willingly give you the Princess; but the disproportion is too great; and, besides, we must give our daughters husbands who will last well; you do not know how to preserve yourself any longer; even those who died only fifteen centuries ago are already no more than a handful of dust; behold, my flesh is solid as basalt; my bones are bars of steel!

'I shall be present on the last day of the world, with the same body and the same features which I had during my lifetime; my daughter Hermonthis will last longer than a statue of bronze.

'Then the last particles of your dust will have been scattered abroad by the winds; and even Isis herself, who was able to find the atoms of Osiris, would scarce be able to recompose your being.

'See how vigorous I yet remain, and how mighty is my

grasp,' he added, shaking my hand in the English fashion with a strength that buried my rings in the flesh of my fingers.

He squeezed me so hard that I awoke, and found my friend Alfred shaking me by the arm to make me get up.

'O you everlasting sleeper! Must I have you carried out into the middle of the street, and fireworks exploded in your ears? It is after noon; don't you recollect your promise to take me with you to see M Aguado's Spanish pictures?'

'God! I forgot all, all about it,' I answered, dressing myself hurriedly; 'we will go there at once; I have the permit lying on my desk.'

I started to find it – but fancy my astonishment when I beheld, instead of the mummy's foot I had purchased the evening before, the little green paste idol left in its place by the Princess Hermonthis!

BLACK COFFEE

by Jeffery Farnol

Professor Jarvis sat among piles of reference-books, and stacks of notes and jottings, the silence about him unbroken save for the ceaseless scratching of his pen.

Professor Jarvis hated bustle and noise of all sorts, for they destroyed that continuity of thought, that following out of proved facts to their primary hypotheses, which was to him the chief end and aim of existence; therefore he inhabited the thirtieth storey.

He had seen none but John, his valet, for nearly a month, sitting night after night, perched high above the great city, busied upon the work of which he had dreamed for years, his treatise upon 'The Higher Ethics of Philosophy', and already it neared completion. A spirit of work had come upon him these last few weeks, a spirit that was a devil, cruel, relentless, allowing of no respite from the strain of intricate thought and nerve-racking effort; hence the Profesor sat writing night after night, and had of late done with little sleep and much black coffee.

To-night, however, he felt strangely tired; he laid down his pen, and, resting his throbbing temples between his hands, stared down vacantly at the sheets of manuscript before him.

As he leaned thus, striving against a feeling of nausea that had recurred frequently the last few days, the long, close-written lines became to him 'things' endowed with sinuous life, that moved, squirming a thousand legs across the white paper.

Professor Jarvis closed his eyes and sighed wearily. 'I really must get some sleep,' he said to himself, 'I wonder when it was I slept last?' As he spoke he tried unsuccessfully to yawn and stretch himself. His glance, wandering aimlessly, paused at the lamp upon the desk before him, and as he stared at it, he noticed that the 'things' had got from the paper and were writhing and creeping up the green shade. He sighed again, and his fingers fumbled among the papers beside him for the electric bell. Almost immediately, it seemed to him, he heard John's voice rather faint and far-away, responding from the shadow that lay beyond the light of the lamp.

'John, if you are really there, be so good as to switch on the light,' said the Professor. 'John,' he continued, blinking at his valet in the sudden glare, 'when did I sleep last?'

'Why, sir, you haven't rightly slept for a week now, just a doze now and then on the couch, sir, but that's nothing; if you'll allow me to advise you, sir, the best thing you could do would be to go to bed at once.'

'Humph!' said the Professor. 'Thank you, John, but your advice, though excellent, is impracticable. I am engaged upon my last chapter, and sleep is impossible until it is finished.'

'Begging your pardon, sir,' began John, 'but if you were to try undressing and going to bed properly – '

'Don't be a fool, John!' cried the Professor, with a sudden access of anger that was strangely at variance with his usual placid manner, 'do you think I wouldn't sleep if I could? Can't you see I'm sick for sleep? I tell you I'd sleep if I could, but I can't – there can be no rest for me I know now, until I've finished my book, and that will be somewhere about dawn,' and the Professor glared up at John, his thick brows twitching, and his eyes glowing within the pale oval of his face with an unpleasant light.

'If you would only give up drinking so much black coffee, sir; they do say it's very bad for the nerves – '

'And I think they are right,' put in the Professor, and his voice was as gentle as ever. 'Yes, I think they are right. For instance, John, at this precise moment I have a feeling that there is a hand groping behind the curtains yonder. Yet this mental attitude harmonises in a manner with the subject of this last chapter, which deals with the psychic forces of nature. I allude, John, more especially to the following passage:

'"That mysterious power which some call the soul, if sufficiently educated, may cast off for a time this bodily flesh, and precipitate itself into illimitable spaces, riding upon the winds, walking upon the beds of seas and rivers, and indeed may even re-inhabit the bodies of those that have been long dead, provided they could be kept from corruption."' The Professor leaned back in his chair, and continued in the voice of one thinking aloud:

'All this was known centuries ago, notably to the priests of Isis and the early Chaldeans, and is practised to-day in some small part by the fakirs of India and the lamas of Tibet, and yet is looked upon by the ignorant world as little more than cheap trickery. By the way,' he broke off, becoming suddenly aware of John's presence, 'didn't you ask for leave of absence until to-morrow?'

'Well, yes, sir, I did,' admitted John, 'but I thought I'd put it off, seeing you are so – so busy, sir.'

'Nonsense, John, don't waste the evening, it must be getting late; just brew some more coffee in the samovar, and then you can go.' John hesitated, but, meeting the Professor's eye, obeyed; and having set the steaming samovar on a small table at his master's elbow and put the room in order, he turned to the door.

'I shall be back in the morning at eight o'clock, sir.'

'Very good, John,' said the Professor, sipping his coffee. 'Good-night, John.'

'Good-night, sir,' returned John, and, closing the door behind him, stood for a moment to shake his head. 'He isn't fit to be left alone,' he muttered, 'but I'll get back before eight to-morrow morning, yes, I'll take good care to be back before eight.' So saying, he turned, and went softly along the passage.

For a long time the Professor had sat crouched above his desk, yet in the last half-hour he had not added a single word to the page before him, for somewhere beneath his brain a small hammer seemed tap-tapping, soft and slow and regular, rendering the stillness about him but the more profound. Slowly and gradually a feeling of expectation grew upon him, a foolishly persistent expectation of something that was drawing near and nearer to him with every stroke of the hammer – something that he could neither guess at, nor hope to arrest, only, he knew that it was coming, coming, and he waited with straining ears, listening for the unknown.

Suddenly, from somewhere in the world far below, a clock chimed midnight, and as the last strokes died there was a hurry of footsteps along the corridor without, a knock, and a fumbling at the handle. As the Professor rose, the door opened, and a shortish, stoutish individual, chiefly re-markable for a round, red face, and a bristle of grey hair, trotted in, and was shaking him by the hand – talking meanwhile in that quick jerky style that was characteristic of Magnus McManus, whose researches in Lower Egypt and along the Nile during the last ten years had made his name famous.

'My dear Dick,' he began, 'good God, how ill you look! – frightful – overwork as usual, eh?'

'Why, Magnus!' exclaimed the Professor, 'I thought you were in Egypt?'

'Exactly – so I was – came back last week with a specimen – been in New York three days – must get back to the Nile at once – booked passage yesterday – sail to-morrow – noon. You see, Dick,' continued Magnus, trotting up and down the room, 'I received a cable from Tarrant – overseer of the excavations, you know – to say they've come upon a monolith – Coptic inscriptions – curious – may be important – very.'

'Yes,' nodded the Professor.

'So just looked you up, Dick – to ask you to take charge of this specimen I brought over – thought you wouldn't mind keeping it until I got back.'

'Certainly, of course,' said the Professor rather absently.

'Undoubtedly the greatest find of the age,' pursued Magnus, 'stupendous – will throw a new light on Egyptian history – there is not in the whole world, so far as is known, such another mummy.'

'A what?' exclaimed the Professor, 'did you say "mummy"?'

'To be sure,' nodded Magnus, 'though the term is inapt – this is something more than your ordinary dried-up mummy.'

'And have you – have you brought it with you, Magnus?'

'Certainly – it's waiting outside in the corridor.'

For no apparent reason the Professor shivered violently, and the nausea came upon him again.

'The deuce of a time getting it here – awkward to handle, you know,' and as he spoke Magnus turned and trotted from the room. There came a murmur of voices outside, a shuffle and stagger of approaching footsteps as of men who bore a heavy burden, and above all the excited tones of Magnus.

'Easy there – mind that corner – steady, steady, don't jar it; now, gently – so.' And Magnus reappeared, followed by four men who bent beneath something in shape between a packing-case and a coffin, which by the direction of Magnus they sat carefully down in a convenient corner.

'Now,' cried he, as soon as they were alone, drawing a small screwdriver from his pocket, 'I'm going to show you something that will make you doubt the evidence of your eyes – as I did myself at first – a wonder, Dick – that will set all the societies gaping – open-mouthed – like fools.'

One by one Magnus extracted the screws that held down the lid, while the Professor watched, wide-eyed, waiting – waiting.

'This specimen will be a revelation on the art of embalming,' continued Magnus, busy upon the last screw. 'Here is no stuffed and withered, dried-up wisp of humanity. Whoever did this was a genius – positively – there has been no disembowelling here – deuce take this screw – body is as perfect as when life first left it – and mark me, Dick – it can't be less than six thousand years old at the very least – probably older. I tell you it's beyond all wonder, but there – judge for yourself!' and with these words, Magnus laid down the screwdriver, lifted off the heavy lid and stood aside.

The Professor drew a deep breath, his fingers clutching convulsively at his chair-arms, as he stared at that which lay, or rather stood, within the glass-fronted shell or coffin.

And what he saw was an oval face framed in black hair, a face full and unshrunken, yet of a hideous ashen-grey, a high, thin, aquiline nose with delicate proud-curving nostrils, and below, a mouth, blue-lipped, yet in whose full, cruel lines lurked a ghastly mockery that carried with it a nameless horror.

'Must have been handsome at one time,' said Magnus.

'Very much so indeed – regular features and all that – pure Egyptian type, but – '

'It's – the – the face of a devil,' muttered the Professor thickly. 'I wonder what – what lies behind those eyelids; they seem as if they might lift at any moment, and if they did – Oh, I tell you it is horrible.'

Magnus laughed. 'Thought she'd astonish you – will knock science deaf and dumb – not a doubt. The setting of these stones,' he continued with a complacent air, ''round her neck – uncut emeralds they are – dates quite back to the Fifth Dynasty – yet that scarab on her breast seems even earlier still – the gold embroidery on her gown beats me – quite – and the thumb-ring by its shape would almost seem to belong to the Fifteenth Dynasty. Altogether she's a puzzle. Another peculiar thing was that – mouth and nostrils had been – plugged by a kind of cement – deuce of a time getting it out.

'The inscription upon her sarcophagus,' he ran on, 'describes her as: "Ahasuera, Princess of the House of Ra, in the reign of Raman Kau Ra," possibly another title for Seti The Second. I also came upon a papyrus – very important – and three tablets; have only had time to dip into them hastily – but from what I gather, Ahasuera appears to have been of a very evil reputation – combination of Semiramis, Cleopatra, and Messalina, multiplied by three! One of her lovers was a certain Ptomes, High Priest of the Temple of Osiris, who is spoken of as "one greatly versed in the arts and mysteries of Isis and the high Gods." When I first opened her sarcophagus, from the strange disorder of the wrappings – almost seemed as if she must have moved – also the golden death-mask that had covered her face had fallen off – which was curious – very. Upon examining this mask – found an inscription across the forehead – puzzled me for days – meaning came to me all at once – in bed – might be translated by a line of doggerel verse something like this:

> *"Isis awhile hath stayed my breath,*
> *Whoso wakes me shall find death."*

which is also curious, eh? Why, Great heavens, man! What ails you?' Magnus broke off, for he had turned and looked at his friend for the first time.

'Nothing,' returned the Professor in the same thick voice. 'Nothing – only cover it up – cover it up in God's name.'

'Certainly – to be sure,' said Magnus, staring. 'Had no idea it would affect you like that, nerves must be at sixes and sevens, should take more care of yourself, Dick, and stop that confounded black coffee.'

As the last screw was driven home, the Professor laughed, a little wildly. 'There are eighteen screws, about two and a half inches long, eh, Magnus?'

'Yes,' said Magnus and turned to stare again.

'Good,' the Professor rejoined with the same strange laugh. Magnus forced a smile.

'Why, Dick,' he began, 'you almost talk as though you imagined – '

'Those eyes,' the Professor broke in, 'they haunt me; they are the eyes of one who waits to take you unawares; they are eyes that watch and follow you behind your back – '

'Pooh! nonsense, Dick,' cried Magnus, rather hastily. 'This is nothing but imagination – sheer imagination. You ought to take a holiday or you will be suffering from hallucinations next.'

'Sit still and listen,' said the Professor, and he began to read from the manuscript before him:

'"That mysterious power which some call the soul, if sufficiently educated, may cast off for a time this bodily flesh and precipitate itself into illimitable spaces, riding upon the winds, walking upon the beds of seas and rivers, and indeed may even re-inhabit the bodies of those that have been long dead, provided that body could be kept free from corruption."'

'Humph!' said Magnus, crossing his legs. 'Well?'

'"Provided that body could be kept free from corruption."' repeated the Professor; then, raising his arm with a sudden gesture, he pointed at the thing in the corner: 'That is not death,' he said.

Magnus leaped to his feet. 'Man, are you mad,' he cried, 'what do you mean?'

'Suspended animation!' said the Professor.

For a long moment there was silence, during which the two men stared into each other's eyes; the face of Magnus had lost some of its colour, and the Professor's fingers moved nervously upon his chair-arms. Suddenly Magnus laughed, though perhaps a trifle too boisterously.

'Bosh!' he exclaimed, 'what folly are you talking, Dick? What you require is a good stiff glass of brandy and bed afterwards,' and with the knowledge and freedom of an old friend, he crossed to a corner cabinet, and took thence a decanter and glasses, pouring out a stiff peg into each.

'So you don't agree with me, Magnus?'

'Agree, no,' said Magnus, swallowing his brandy at a gulp, 'it's all nerves – damn 'em.'

The Professor shook his head. 'There are more things in heaven and earth – '

'Yes – yes, I know – I have cursed Shakespeare frequently for that same quotation.'

'But you yourself wrote a paper, Magnus, only a few years ago, on the hypnotic trances practised by the Egyptians.'

'Now, Dick,' expostulated Magnus, 'be reasonable, for heaven's sake! Is it possible that any trance could extend into six or seven thousand years? Preposterous, utterly. Come, get to bed, man, like a sensible chap – where's John?'

'I gave him leave of absence until to-morrow.'

'The deuce you did?' exclaimed Magnus, glancing round the room with an uneasy feeling. 'Well, I'll take his place – see you into bed and all that.'

'Thanks, Magnus, but it's no good,' returned the Professor, shaking his head. 'I couldn't sleep until I've finished this last chapter, and it won't take long.'

'One o'clock, by Gad!' exclaimed Magnus, glancing at his watch. 'Must hurry off, Dick – hotel – sail to-morrow, you know.'

The Professor shivered, and rose to his feet. 'Good-bye, Magnus,' he said as they shook hands. 'I hope your monolith will turn out a good find. Good-bye!'

'Thanks, old fellow,' said Magnus, returning the pressure. 'Now, no more poisonous coffee, mind.' So saying he trotted to the door, nodded, and was gone.

The Professor sat for a moment with puckered brows, then, rising hastily, crossed to the door, turned the handle, and peered out into the dim light of the corridor.

'Magnus,' he called in a hoarse whisper. 'Magnus.'

'Well?' came the answer.

'Then you don't think It will open Its eyes, do you, Magnus?'

'Good God – no!'

'Ah!' said the Professor, and closed the door.

'I wish,' said the Professor, as he took up his pen, 'I wish that I had not let John go; I feel strangely lonely to-night, and John is so very matter of fact.' So saying he bent to his writing again. His brain had grown singularly bright and clear, all his faculties seemed strung to their highest pitch, a feeling of exaltation had taken possession of him. His ideas grew luminous, intricate thoughts became coherent, the words shaping themselves beneath his pen with a subtle power and eloquence.

Yet all at once, and for no apparent reason, in the very middle of a sentence, a desire seized upon him to turn his head and look back over his shoulder at that which stood in the corner. He checked it with an effort, and his pen resumed its scratching; though all the time he was conscious that the desire was growing, and that sooner or later it would master him. Not that he expected to see anything unusual, that was absurd, of course. He began trying to remember how many screws there were holding down the lid upon that Thing, whose lips had mocked at God and man through centuries and whose eyes – ah, whose eyes – The Professor turned suddenly, and with his pen extended before him, began counting the glinting screw-heads to himself in an undertone.

'One, two, three, four, five, six – six along each side, and three along the top and bottom – eighteen in all. And they were steel screws, too, a quarter of an inch thick, and two and a half inches in length; they ought to be strong enough, and yet eighteen after all was not many; why hasn't Magnus used more of them, it would have been so much – ' The Professor checked himself, and turned back to his work; but he tried vainly to write, for now the impulse held him without respite, growing more insistent each moment, an impulse that had fear beneath it, fear born of things that move behind one. 'Ah, yes, behind one – why had he let It be placed in the corner that was directly behind his chair?' He rose and began pulling and dragging at his desk, but it was heavy, and defied his efforts; yet the physical exertion, futile though it was, seemed to calm him, but though he bent resolutely above his task – the finishing of his great book – his mind was absent, and the pen between his fingers traced idle patterns and meaningless scribbles upon the sheet before him, so he tossed it aside, and buried his face in his hands.

Could it be possible that in the darkness behind the lid with the eighteen screws the eyes were still shut, or were they – ? The Professor shivered. Ah, if he could but know, if he could only be certain – he wished John was here – John was so very matter of fact – he might have sat and watched It – yes, he had been foolish to let John go. The Professor sighed, and, opening his eyes, remained motionless – staring down at the sheet of foolscap before him – staring at the two uneven lines scrawled across it in ragged capitals that were none of his:

'Isis awhile hath stayed my breath,
Whoso wakes me shall find death.'

A sudden piping, high-pitched laugh startled him. 'Could it really be issuing from his own lips?' he asked himself, and indeed, he knew it must be so. He sat with every nerve tingling, hoping, praying for something to break the heavy silence – the creak of a footstep – a shout – a scream – anything rather than that horrible laugh; and as he waited it came again, louder, wilder than before. And now he felt it quivering between his teeth, rattling in his throat, shaking him to and fro in its grip; then, swift as it had come it was gone, and the Professor was looking down at a litter of torn paper at his feet. He reached out a trembling hand to the rack upon his desk and taking down a pipe already filled, lighted it. The tobacco seemed to soothe him, and he inhaled it deeply, watching it roll in thin clouds across the room, until he noticed that it always drifted in the same direction, to hang like a curtain above one point, an ever-moving curtain behind which were shadowy 'somethings' that moved and writhed.

The Professor got unsteadily to his legs.

'Magnus was right,' he muttered, 'I am ill, I must try to sleep – I must – I must.' But as he stood there, leaning his shaking hands upon the table-edge, the blind fear, the unreasoning dread against which he had battled so vainly all night swept over him in an irresistible wave; his breath choked, a loathing horror shook him from head to foot, yet all the time his gaze never left the great white box, with its narrow screw-heads that stared at him like little searching eyes. Something glittered upon the floor beside it, and almost before he knew he had snatched up the screwdriver. He worked feverishly until but one screw remained, and as he stopped to wipe the sweat from his cheek he was surprised to find himself singing a song he had heard at a music-hall years before, in his college days; then he held his breath as the last screw gave . . .

The oval face framed in a mist of black hair, the long voluptuous eyes with their heavy lids, the aquiline nose, the cruel curve of the nostrils, and the full-lipped sensual mouth, with its everlasting mockery: he had seen it all before, and yet as he gazed he was conscious of a change, subtle and horrible, a change that he could not define, yet which held him as one entranced. With an effort he turned away his eyes, and tried to replace the lid, but could not; he looked about him wildly, then snatching up a heavily fringed rug, covered the horror from sight.

'Magnus was right,' he repeated, 'I must sleep,' and crossing to the couch, he sank upon it and hid his face among the cushions.

A long time he lay there, but sleep was impossible, for the sound of the hammers was in his ears again, but louder now and seeming to beat upon his very brain. What was that other sound – that came to him beneath the hammer-strokes – could it be a footstep? He sat up listening, and then he noticed that the fringe upon the rug was moving. He rubbed his eyes, disbelieving, until all at once it was shaken by another movement that ran up it with a strange rippling motion. He rose, trembling, and creeping forward, tore away the rug. Then he saw and understood the change that had baffled him before; and with the knowledge, the might of his learning, the strength of his manhood, deserted him, and covering his face, Professor Jarvis rocked his body to and fro making a strange whimpering noise, like a little child; for the ashen grey was gone from the face, and the lips which had been black were blood-red. For a while the Professor continued to rock to and fro, whimpering behind his hands, till with a sudden gesture, wild and passionate, he tossed his arms above his head.

'My God!' he cried, 'I'm going mad – I am mad, oh, anything but that – not mad, no, not mad – I am not mad – no.' Chancing to catch sight of himself in a mirror, he shook his head and chuckled. 'Not mad,' he whispered to his reflection, 'oh, no.' Then he turned to the case once more, and began patting and stroking the glass.

'Oh, Eyes of Death, lift thy lashes, for I am fain to know the mystery beyond. What though I be the Priest Ptomes, even he that put this magic upon thee, yet I am come back to thee, Beloved, and my soul calleth unto thine even as in Thebes of old. Oh, Eyes of Death, lift thy lashes, for I am fain to know the mystery beyond. While thy soul slept, mine hath hungered for thee through countless ages, and now is the time of waiting accomplished. Oh, Eyes of Death, lift thy lashes, for I am fain to know the mystery beyond. Ah, God,' he broke out suddenly, 'she will not wake – I cannot wake her.' And he writhed his fingers together. All at once his aspect changed, his mouth curved with a smile of cunning, he crept to where a small mirror hung upon the wall, and, with a swift movement, hid it beneath his coat, and, crossing to his desk, propped it up before him.

'They will not open while I look and wait for it,' he said, nodding and smiling to himself. 'They are the eyes of one who waits to take you unawares, that watch and follow you behind your back, yet I shall see them, yes, I shall see them.'

From the world below came the long-drawn tooting of a steamer on the river, and with the sound, faint and far-away though it was, reason reasserted itself.

'Good heavens!' he exclaimed, trying to laugh. 'What a fool I am to let a pitiful bit of dead humanity drive me half-wild with fear, and in New York too; it seems inconceivable.' So saying the Professor crossed to the brandy, and, with his back turned resolutely, slowly drained his glass, yet even then he was vaguely conscious of eyes that watched him, followed his every movement, and with difficulty he forbore from swinging round on his heel. With the same iron will crushing down his rebellious nerves, he arranged his papers and took up his pen.

The human body after all has certain attributes of the cur,

for let that master, the mind, chastise it, and it will cringe, let him command and it will obey. So the Professor sat, his eye clear, his hand firm, scarcely noticing the mirror beside him, even when he paused to take a fresh sheet.

The sickly grey of dawn was at the windows as he paused to glance at his watch. 'Another half-hour,' he muttered, 'and my work is done, ended, fin – ' The word died upon his lips, for his glance by accident had fallen upon the mirror, and the eyes were wide open. For a long moment they looked into his ere their lids fluttered and fell.

'I am suffering from hallucinations,' he groaned. 'It is one of the results of loss of sleep, but I wish John was back; John is such a matter-of-fact – '

There was a sound behind him, a sound soft and gentle like the whisper of wind in trees, or the brushing of drapery against a wall – and it was moving across the floor behind him. A chill as of death shuddered through him, and he knew the terror that is dumb.

Scarcely daring to look, full of a dread of expectation, he lifted his eyes to the mirror. The case behind him was empty; he turned swiftly, and there, so close that he might almost touch it, was the 'Thing' he had called a pitiful bit of dead humanity. Slowly, inch by inch, it moved towards him, with a scrape and rustle of stiff draperies:

> *'Isis awhile hath stayed my breath,*
> *Whoso wakes me, shall find – death!'*

With a cry that was something between a scream and a laugh he leaped to his feet and hurled himself upon It; there was the sound of a dull blow, a gasp, and Professor Jarvis was lying upon the floor, his arms wide-tossed, and his face hidden in the folds of a rug.

Next day there was a paragraph in the papers, which read as follows:

'STRANGE DEATH

'Yesterday at his chambers in — Street, Professor Jarvis, the famous Scientist, was found dead, presumably of heart-failure. A curious feature of the case was that a mummy which had stood in a rough travelling-case in a corner on the opposite side of the room was found lying across the Professor's dead body.'

IMPRISONED WITH THE PHARAOHS

by Houdini & H P Lovecraft

Mystery attracts mystery. Ever since the wide appearance of my name as a performer of unexplained feats, I have encountered strange narratives and events which my calling has led people to link with my interests and activities. Some of these have been trivial and irrelevant, some deeply dramatic and absorbing, some productive of weird and perilous experiences and some involving me in extensive scientific and historical research. Many of these matters I have told and shall continue to tell very freely; but there is one of which I speak with great reluctance, and which I am now relating only after a session of grilling persuasion from the publishers of this magazine, who had heard vague rumours of it from other members of my family.

The hitherto guarded subject pertains to my non-professional visit to Egypt fourteen years ago, and has been avoided by me for several reasons. For one thing, I am averse to exploiting certain unmistakably actual facts and conditions obviously unknown to the myriad tourists who throng about the pyramids and apparently secreted with much diligence by the authorities at Cairo, who cannot be wholly ignorant of them. For another thing, I dislike to recount an incident in which my own fantastic imagination must have played so great a part. What I saw – or thought I saw – certainly did not take place; but is rather to be viewed as a result of my then recent readings in Egyptology, and of the speculations anent this theme which my environment naturally prompted. These imaginative stimuli, magnified by the excitement of an actual event terrible enough in itself, undoubtedly gave rise to the culminating horror of that grotesque night so long past.

In January, 1910, I had finished a professional engagement in England and signed a contract for a tour of Australian theatres. A liberal time being allowed for the trip, I determined to make the most of it in the sort of travel which chiefly interests me; so accompanied by my wife I drifted pleasantly down the Continent and embarked at Marseilles on the P & O Steamer *Malwa*, bound for Port Said. From that point I proposed to visit the principal historical localities of lower Egypt before leaving finally for Australia.

The voyage was an agreeable one, and enlivened by many of the amusing incidents which befall a magical performer apart from his work. I had intended, for the sake of quiet travel, to keep my name a secret; but was goaded into betraying myself by a fellow-magician whose anxiety to astound the passengers with ordinary tricks tempted me to duplicate and exceed his feats in a manner quite destructive of my incognito. I mention this because of its ultimate effect – an effect I should have foreseen before unmasking to a shipload of tourists about to scatter throughout the Nile valley. What it did was to herald my identity wherever I subsequently went, and deprive my wife and me of all the placid inconspicuousness we had sought. Travelling to seek curiosities, I was often forced to stand inspection as a sort of curiosity myself!

We had come to Egypt in search of the picturesque and the mystically impressive, but found little enough when the ship edged up to Port Said and discharged its passengers in small boats. Low dunes of sand, bobbing buoys in shallow water, and a drearily European small town with nothing of interest save the great De Lesseps statue, made us anxious to get on to something more worth our while. After some discussion we decided to proceed at once to Cairo and the Pyramids, later going to Alexandria for the Australian boat and for whatever Greco-Roman sights that ancient metropolis might present.

The railway journey was tolerable enough, and consumed only four hours and a half. We saw much of the Suez Canal, whose route we followed as far as Ismailiya and later had a taste of Old Egypt in our glimpse of the restored fresh-water canal of the Middle Empire. Then at last we saw Cairo glimmering through the growing dusk; a winking constellation which became a blaze as we halted at the great Gare Centrale.

But once more disappointment awaited us, for all that we beheld was European save the costumes and the crowds. A prosaic subway led to a square teeming with carriages, taxicabs, and trolley-cars and gorgeous with electric lights shining on tall buildings; whilst the very theatre where I was vainly requested to play and which I later attended as a spectator, had recently been renamed the 'American Cosmograph'. We stopped at Shepheard's Hotel, reached in a taxi that sped along broad, smartly built-up streets; and amidst the perfect service of its restaurant, elevators, and generally Anglo-American luxuries the mysterious East and immemorial past seemed very far away.

The next day, however, precipitated us delightfully into the heart of the *Arabian Nights* atmosphere; and in the winding ways and exotic skyline of Cairo, the Bagdad of Harun-al-Rashid seemed to live again. Guided by our Baedeker, we had struck east past the Ezbekiyeh Gardens along the Mouski in quest of the native quarter, and were soon in the hands of a clamorous cicerone who – notwithstanding later developments – was assuredly a master at his trade.

Not until afterward did I see that I should have applied at the hotel for a licenced guide. This man, a shaven, peculiarly hollow-voiced and relatively cleanly fellow who looked like a Pharaoh and called himself 'Abdul Reis el Drogman', appeared to have much power over others of his kind; though subsequently the police professed not to know him, and to suggest that *reis* is merely a name for any person in authority, whilst 'Drogman' is obviously no more than a clumsy modification of the word for a leader of tourists parties – *dragoman*.

Abdul led us among such wonders as we had before only read and dreamed of. Old Cairo is itself a story-book and a dream – labyrinths of narrow alleys redolent of aromatic secrets; Arabesque balconies and oriels nearly meeting above the cobbled streets; maelstroms of Oriental traffic with strange cries, cracking whips, rattling carts, jingling money, and braying donkeys; kaleidoscopes of polychrome robes, veils, turbans, and tarbushes; water-carriers and dervishes, dogs and cats, soothsayers and barbers; and over all the whining of blind beggars crouched in alcoves, and the sonorous chanting of muezzins from minarets limned delicately against a sky of deep, unchanging blue.

The roofed, quieter bazaars were hardly less alluring. Spice, perfume, incense beads, rugs, silks, and brass – old Mahmoud Suleiman squats cross-legged amidst his gummy bottles while chattering youths pulverize mustard in the hollowed-out capital of an ancient classic column – a Roman Corinthian, perhaps from neighboring Heliopolis, where Augustus stationed one of his three Egyptian legions. Antiquity begins to mingle with exoticism. And then the mosques and the museum – we saw them all, and tried not to let our Arabian revel succumb to the darker charm of Pharaonic Egypt which the museum's priceless treasures offered. That was to be our climax, and for the present we concentrated on the mediaeval Saracenic glories of the Califs whose magnificent tomb-mosques form a glittering faery necropolis on the edge of the Arabian Desert.

At length Abdul took us along the Sharia Mohammed Ali to the ancient mosque of Sultan Hassan, and the tower-flanked Babel-Azab, beyond which climbs the steep-walled pass to the mighty citadel that Saladin himself built with the stones of forgotten pyramids. It was sunset when we scaled that cliff, circled the modern mosque of Mohammed Ali, and looked down from the dizzy parapet over mystic Cairo – mystic Cairo all golden with its carven domes, its ethereal minarets and its flaming gardens.

Far over the city towered the great Roman dome of the new museum; and beyond it – across the cryptic yellow Nile that is the mother of eons and dynasties – lurked the menacing sands of the Libyan Desert, undulant and iridescent and evil with older arcana.

The red sun sank low, bringing the relentless chill of Egyptian dusk; and as it stood poised on the world's rim like that ancient god of Heliopolis – Re-Harakhte, the Horizon-Sun – we saw silhouetted against its vermeil holocaust the black outlines of the Pyramids of Gizeh – the palaeogean tombs there were hoary with a thousand years when Tut-

Ankh-Amen mounted his golden throne in distant Thebes. Then we knew that we were done with Saracen Cairo, and that we must taste the deeper mysteries of primal Egypt – the black Kem of Re and Amen, Isis and Osiris.

The next morning we visited the Pyramids, riding out in a Victoria across the island of Chizereh with its massive lebbakh trees, and the smaller English bridge to the western shore. Down the shore road we drove, between great rows of lebbakhs and past the vast Zoological Gardens to the suburb of Gizeh, where a new bridge to Cairo proper has since been built. Then, turning inland along the Sharia-el-Haram, we crossed a region of glassy canals and shabby native villages till before us loomed the objects of our quest, cleaving the mists of dawn and forming inverted replicas on the roadside pools. Forty centuries, as Napoleon had told his campaigners there, indeed looked down upon us.

The road now rose abruptly, till we finally reached our place of transfer between the trolley station and the Mena House Hotel. Abdul Reis, who capably purchased our Pyramid tickets, seemed to have an understanding with the crowding, yelling and offensive Bedouins who inhabited a squalid mud village some distance away and pestiferously assailed every traveller; for he kept them very decently at bay and secured an excellent pair of camels for us, himself mounting a donkey and assigning the leadership of our animals to a group of men and boys more expensive than useful. The area to be traversed was so small that camels were hardly needed, but we did not regret adding to our experience this troublesome form of desert navigation.

The pyramids stand on a high rock plateau, this group forming next to the northernmost of the series of regal and aristocratic cemeteries built in the neighbourhood of the extinct capital Memphis, which lay on the same side of the Nile, somewhat south of Gizeh, and which flourished between 3400 and 2000 B.C. The greatest pyramid, which lies nearest the modern road, was built by King Cheops or Khufu about 2800 B.C., and stand more than 450 feet in perpendicular height. In a line southwest from this are successively the Second Pyramid, built a generation later by King Khephren, and though slightly smaller, looking even larger because set on higher ground, and the radically smaller Third Pyramid of King Mycerinus, built about 2700 B.C. Near the edge of the plateau and due east of the Second Pyramid, with a face probably altered to form a colossal portrait of Khephren, its royal restorer, stands the monstrous Sphinx – mute, sardonic, and wise beyond mankind and memory.

Minor pyramids and the traces of ruined minor pyramids are found in several places, and the whole plateau is pitted with the tombs of dignitaries of less than royal rank. These latter were originally marked by *mastabas*, or stone bench-like structures about the deep burial shafts, as found in other Memphian cemeteries and exemplified by Perneb's Tomb in the Metropolitan Museum of New York. At Gizeh, however, all such visible things have been swept away by time and pillage; and only the rock-hewn shafts, either sand-filled or cleared out by archaeologists, remain to attest their former existence. Connected with each tomb was a chapel in which priests and relatives offered food and prayer to the hovering *ka* or vital principle of the deceased. The small tombs have their chapels contained in their stone *mastabas* or superstructures, but the mortuary chapels of the pyramids, where regal Pharaohs lay, were separate temples, each to the east of its corresponding pyramid, and connected by a causeway to a massive gate-chapel or propylon at the edge of the rock plateau.

The gate-chapel leading to the Second Pyramid, nearly buried in the drifting sands, yawns subterraneously south-east of the Sphinx. Persistent tradition dubs it the 'Temple of the Sphinx'; and it may perhaps be rightly called such if the Sphinx indeed represents the Second Pyramid's builder Khephren. There are unpleasant tales of the Sphinx before Khephren – but whatever its elder features were, the monarch replaced them with his own that men might look at the colossus without fear.

It was in the great gateway-temple that the life-size diorite statue of Khephren now in the Cairo museum was found; a statue before which I stood in awe when I beheld it. Whether the whole edifice is now excavated I am not certain, but in 1910 most of it was below ground, with the entrance heavily barred at night. Germans were in charge of the work, and the war or other things may have stopped them. I would give much, in view of my experience and of certain Bedouin whisperings discredited or unknown in Cairo, to know what has developed in connection with a certain well in a transverse gallery where statues of the Pharaoh were found in curious juxtaposition to the statues of baboons.

The road, as we traversed it on our camels that morning, curved sharply past the wooden police quarters, post office, drug store and shops on the left, and plunged south and east in a complete bend that scaled the rock plateau and brought us face to face with the desert under the lee of the Great Pyramid. Past Cyclopean masonry we rode, rounding the eastern face and looking down ahead into a valley of minor pyramids beyond which the eternal Nile glistened to the east, and the eternal desert shimmered to the west. Very close loomed the three major pyramids, the greatest devoid of outer casing and showing its bulk of great stones, but the others retaining here and there the neatly fitted covering which had made them smooth and finished in their day.

Presently we descended towards the Sphinx, and sat silent beneath the spell of those terrible unseeing eyes. On the vast stone breast we faintly discerned the emblem of Re-Harakhte, for whose image the Sphinx was mistaken in a late dynasty; and though sand covered the tablet between the great paws, we recalled what Thutmosis IV inscribed thereon, and the dream he had when a prince. It was then that the smile of the Sphinx vaguely displeased us, and made us wonder about the legends of subterranean passages beneath the monstrous creature, leading down, down, to depths none might dare hint at – depths connected with mysteries older than the dynastic Egypt we excavate, and having a sinister relation to the persistence of abnormal, animal-headed gods in the ancient Nilotic pantheon. Then, too, it was I asked myself an idle question whose hideous significance was not to appear for many an hour.

Other tourists now began to overtake us, and we moved on to the sand-choked Temple of the Sphinx, fifty yards to the southeast, which I have previously mentioned as the great gate of the causeway to the Second Pyramid's mortuary chapel on the plateau. Most of it was still underground, and although we dismounted and descended through a modern passage to its alabaster corridor and pillared hall, I felt that Adul and the local German attendant had not shown us all there was to see.

After this we made the conventional circuit of the pyramid plateau, examining the Second Pyramid and the peculiar ruins of its mortuary chapel to the east, the Third Pyramid and its miniature southern satellites and ruined eastern chapel, the rock tombs and the honeycombings of the Fourth and Fifth dynasties, and the famous Campbell's Tomb whose shadowy shaft sinks precipitously for fifty-three feet to a sinister sarcophagus which one of our camel drivers divested of the cumbering sand after a vertiginous descent by rope.

Cries now assailed us from the Great Pyramid, where Bedouins were besieging a party of tourists with offers of speed in the performance of solitary trips up and down. Seven minutes is said to be the record for such an ascent and descent, but many lusty shieks and sons of shieks assured us they could cut it to five if given the requisite impetus of liberal *baksheesh*. They did not get this impetus, though we did let Abdul take us up, thus obtaining a view of unprecedented magnificence which included not only remote and glittering Cairo with its crowned citadel background of gold-violet hills, but all the pyramids of the Memphian district as well, from Abu Roash on the north to the Dashur on the south. The Sakkara step-pyramid, which marks the evolution of the low *mastaba* into the true pyramid, showed clearly and alluringly in the sandy distance. It is close to this transition-monument that the famed tomb of Perneb was found – more than four hundred miles north of the Theban rock valley where Tut-Ankh-Amen sleeps. Again I was forced to silence through sheer awe. The prospect of such antiquity, and the secrets each hoary monument seemed to hold and brood over, filled me with a reverence and sense of immensity nothing else ever gave me.

Fatigued by our climb, and disgusted with the importunate Bedouins whose actions seemed to defy every rule of taste, we omitted the arduous detail of entering the cramped interior pasages of any of the pyramids, though we saw several of the hardiest tourists preparing for the suffocating crawl through Cheops' mightiest memorial. As we dismissed and overpaid our local bodyguard and drove back to Cairo with Abdul Reis under the afternoon sun, we half regretted the omission we had made. Such fascinating things were whispered about lower pyramid passages not in the guide books; passages whose entrances had been hastily blocked up and concealed by certain uncommunicative archaeologists who had found and begun to explore them.

Of course, this whispering was largely baseless on the face of it; but it was curious to reflect how persistently visitors were forbidden to enter the Pyramids at night, or to visit the lowest burrows and crypt of the Great Pyramid. Perhaps in the latter case it was the psychological effect which was feared – the effect on the visitor of feeling himself huddled down beneath a gigantic world of solid masonry; joined to the life he has known by the merest tube, in which he may only crawl, and which any accident or evil design might block. The whole subject seemed so weird and alluring that we resolved to pay the pryamid plateau another visit at the earliest possible opportunity. For me this opportunity came much earlier than I expected.

That evening, the members of our party feeling somewhat tired after the strenuous programme of the day, I went alone with Abdul Reis for a walk through the picturesque Arab quarter. Though I had seen it by day, I wished to study the alleys and bazaars in the dusk, when rich shadows and mellow gleams of light would add to their glamour and fantastic illusion. The native crowds were thinning, but were still very noisy and numerous when we came upon a knot of revelling Bedouins in the Suken-Nahhasin, or bazaar of the coppersmiths. Their apparent leader, an insolent youth with heavy features and saucily cocked tarbush, took some notice of us, and evidently recognized with no great friendliness my competent but admittedly supercilious and sneeringly disposed guide.

Perhaps, I thought, he resented that odd reproduction of the Sphinx's half-smile which I had often remarked with amused irritation; or perhaps he did not like the hollow and sepulchral resonance of Abdul's voice. At any rate, the exchange of ancestrally opprobrious language became very brisk; and before long Ali Ziz, as I heard the stranger called when called by no worse name, began to pull violently at

Abdul's robe, an action quickly reciprocated and leading to a spirited scuffle in which both combatants lost their sacredly cherished headgear and would have reached an even direr condition had I not intervened and separated them by main force.

My interference, at first seemingly unwelcome on both sides, succeeded at last in effecting a truce. Sullenly each belligerent composed his wrath and his attire, and with an assumption of dignity as profound as it was sudden, the two formed a curious pact of honour which I soon learned is a custom of great antiquity in Cairo – a pact for the settlement of their difference by means of a nocturnal fist fight atop the Great Pyramid, long after the departure of the last moonlight sightseer. Each duellist was to assemble a party of seconds, and the affair was to begin at midnight, proceeding by rounds in the most civilized possible fashion.

In all this planning there was much which excited my interest. The fight itself promised to be unique and spectacular, while the thought of the scene on the hoary pile overlooking the antediluvian plateau of Gizeh under the wan moon of the pallid small hours appealed to every fibre of imagination in me. A request found Abdul exceedingly willing to admit me to his party of seconds; so that all the rest of the early evening I accompanied him to various dens in the most lawless regions of the town – mostly northeast of the Ezbekiyeh – where he gathered one by one a select and formidable band of congenial cutthroats as his pugilistic background.

Shortly after nine our party, mounted on donkeys bearing such royal or tourist-reminiscent names as 'Rameses,' 'Mark Twain,' 'J P Morgan,' and 'Minnehaha,' edged through street labyrinths both Oriental and Occidental, crossed the muddy and mast-forested Nile by the bridge of the bronze lions, and cantered philosophically between the lebbakhs on the road to Gizeh. Slightly over two hours was consumed by the trip, toward the end of which we passed the last of the returning tourists, saluted the last inbound trolley-car, and were alone with the night and the past and the spectral moon.

Then we saw the vast pyramids at the end of the avenue, ghoulish with a dim atavistical menace which I had not seemed to notice in the daytime. Even the smallest of them held a hint of the ghastly – for was it not in this that they had buried Queen Nitocris alive in the Sixth Dynasty; subtle Queen Nitocris, who once invited all her enemies to a feast in a temple below the Nile, and drowned them by opening the water-gates? I recalled that the Arabs whisper things about Nitocris, and shun the Third Pyramid at certain phases of the moon. It must have been over her that Thomas Moore was brooding when he wrote a thing muttered about by Memphian boatmen:

> 'The subterranean nymph that dwells
> 'Mid sunless gems and glories hid –
> The lady of the Pyramid!'

Early as we were, Ali Ziz and his party were ahead of us; for we saw their donkeys outlined against the desert plateau at Kafrel-Haram; toward which squalid Arab settlement, close to the Sphinx, we had diverged instead of following the regular road to the Mena House, where some of the sleepy, inefficient police might have observed and halted us. Here, where filthy Bedouins stabled camels and donkeys in the rock tombs of Khephren's courtiers, we were led up the rocks and over the sand to the Great Pyramid, up whose time-worn sides the Arabs swarmed eagerly, Abdul Reis offering me the assistance I did not need.

As most travellers know, the actual apex of this structure has long been worn away, leaving a reasonably flat platform twelve yards square. On this eery pinnacle a squared circle was formed, and in a few moments the sardonic desert moon leered down upon a battle which, but for the quality of the ringside cries, might well have occurred at some minor athletic club in America. As I watched it, I felt that some of our less desirable institutions were not lacking; for every blow, feint, and defence bespoke 'stalling' to my inexperienced eye. It was quickly over, and despite my misgivings as to methods I felt a sort of proprietary pride when Abdul Reis was adjudged the winner.

Reconciliation was phenomenally rapid, and amidst the singing, fraternizing and drinking which followed, I found it difficult to realize that a quarrel had ever occurred. Oddly enough, I myself seemed to be more a centre of notice than the antagonists; and from my smattering of Arabic I judged that they were discussing my professional performances and escapes from every sort of manacle and confinement, in a manner which indicated not only a surprising knowledge of me, but a distinct hostility and scepticism concerning my feats of escape. It gradually dawned on me that the elder magic of Egypt did not depart without leaving traces, and that fragments of a strange secret lore and priestly cult-practices have survived surreptitiously amongst the fellaheen to such an extent that the prowess of a strange *hahwi* of magician is resented and disputed. I thought of how much my hollow-voiced guide Abdul Reis looked like an old Egyptian priest of Pharaoh or smiling Sphinx . . . and wondered.

Suddenly something happened which in a flash proved the correctness of my reflections and made me curse the denseness whereby I had accepted this night's events as other than the empty and malicious 'frame-up' they now showed themselves to be. Without warning, and doubtless in answer to some subtle sign from Abdul, the entire band of Bedouins precipitated itself upon me; and having produced heavy ropes, soon had me bound as securely as I was ever bound in the course of my life, either on the stage or off.

I struggled at first, but soon saw that one man could make no headway against a band of over twenty sinewy barbarians. My hands were tied behind my back, my knees bent to their fullest extent, and my wrists and ankles stoutly linked together with unyielding cords. A stifling gag was forced into my mouth, and a blindfold fastened tightly over my eyes. Then, as Arabs bore me aloft on their shoulders and began a jouncing descent of the pyramid, I heard the taunts of my late guide Adbul, who mocked and jeered delightedly in his hollow voice, and assured me that I was soon to have my 'magic powers' put to a supreme test which would quickly remove any egotism I might have gained through triumphing over all the tests offered by America and Europe. Egypt, he reminded me, is very old, and full of inner mysteries and antique powers not even conceivable to the experts of today, whose devices had so uniformly failed to entrap me.

How far or in what direction I was carried, I cannot tell; for the circumstances were all against the formation of any accurate judgment. I know, however, that it could not have been a great distance; since my bearers at no point hastened beyond a walk, yet kept me aloft a surprisingly short time. It is this perplexing brevity which makes me feel almost like shuddering whenever I think of Gizeh and its plateau – for one is oppressed by hints of the closeness to everyday tourist routes of what existed then and must exist still.

The evil abnormality I speak of did not become manifest at first. Setting me down on a surface which I reconized as sand rather than rock, my captors passed a rope around my chest and dragged me a few feet to a ragged opening in the ground, into which they presently lowered me with much rough hand-ling. For apparent eons I bumped against the stony irregular sides of a narrow hewn well which I took to be one of the numerous burial-shafts of the plateau until the prodigious, almost incredible depth of it robbed me of all bases of con-jecture.

The horror of the experience deepened with every dragging second. That any descent through the sheer solid rock could be so vast without reaching the core of the planet itself, or that any rope made by man could be so long as to dangle me in these unholy and seemingly fathomless profundities of nether earth, were beliefs of such grotesqueness that it was easier to doubt my agitated senses than to accept them. Even now I am uncertain, for I know how deceitful the sense of time becomes when one is removed or distorted. But I am quite sure that I preserved a logical consciousness that far; that at least I did not add any fullgrown phantoms of imagination to a picture hideous enough in its reality, and explicable by a type of cerebral illusion vastly short of actual hallucination.

All this was not the cause of my first bit of fainting. The shocking ordeal was cumulative, and the beginning of the later terrors was a very perceptible increase in my rate of descent. They were paying out that infinitely long rope very swiftly now, and I scraped cruelly against the rough and constricted sides of the shaft as I shot madly downward. My clothing was in tatters, and I felt the trickle of blood all over, even above the mounting and excruciating pain. My nostrils, too, were assailed by a scarcely definable menace: a creeping odour of damp and staleness curiously unlike anything I had ever smelled before, and having faint overtones of spice and incense that lent an element of mockery.

Then the mental cataclysm came. It was horrible – hideous beyond all articulate description because it was all of the soul, with nothing of detail to describe. It was the ecstasy of nightmare and the summation of the fiendish. The suddenness of it was apocalyptic and demoniac – one moment I was plunging agonizingly down that narrow well of million-toothed torture, yet the next moment I was soaring on bat-wings in the gulfs of hell; swinging free and swoopingly through illimitable miles of boundless, musty space; rising dizzily to measureless pinnacles of chilling ether, then diving gaspingly to sucking nadirs of ravenous, nauseous lower vacua. . . . Thank God for the mercy that shut out in oblivion those clawing Furies of consciousness which half unhinged my faculties, and tore harpy-like at my spirit! That one respite, short as it was, gave me the strength and sanity to endure those still greater sublimations of cosmic panic that lurked and gibbered on the road ahead.

It was very gradually that I regained my senses after that eldritch flight through stygian space. The process was infinitely painful, and coloured by fantastic dreams in which my bound and gagged condition found singular embodiment. The precise nature of these dreams was very clear while I was experiencing them, but became blurred in my recollection almost immediately afterwards, and was soon reduced to the merest outline by the terrible events – real or imaginary – which followed. I dreamed that I was in the grasp of a great and horrible paw; a yellow, hairy, five-clawed paw which had reached out of the earth to crush and engulf me. And when I stopped to reflect what the paw was, it seemed to me that it was Egypt. In the dream I looked back at the events of the preceding weeks, and saw myself lured and enmeshed little by little, subtly and insidiously, by some hellish ghoul-spirit of the elder Nile sorcery; some spirit that was in Egypt before ever man was, and that will be when man is no more.

I saw the horror and unwholesome antiquity of Egypt, and the grisly alliance it has always had with the tombs and temples of the dead. I saw phantom processions of priests with the heads of bulls, falcons, cats, and ibises; phantom processions marching interminably through subterraneous labyrinths and avenues of titanic propylaea beside which a man is as a fly, and offering unnamable sacrifice to indescribable gods. Stone colossi marched in endless night and drove herds of grinning androsphinxes down to the shores of illimitable stagnant rivers of pitch. And behind it all I saw the ineffable malignity of primordial necromancy, black and amorphous, and fumbling greedily after me in the darkness to choke out the spirit that had dared to mock it by emulation.

In my sleeping brain there took shape a melodrama of sinister hatred and pursuit, and I saw the black soul of Egypt singling me out and calling me in audible whispers; calling and luring me, leading me on with the glitter and glamour of a Saracenic surface, but ever pulling me down to the age-mad catacombs and horrors of its *dead* and abysmal pharaonic heart.

Then the dream faces took on human resemblances, and I saw my guide Abdul Reis in the robes of a king, with the sneer of the Sphinx on his features. And I knew that those features were the features of Khephren the Great, who raised the Second Pyramid, carved over the Sphinx's face in the likeness of his own and built that titanic gateway temple whose myriad corridors the archaeologists think they have dug out of the cryptical sand and the uninformative rock. And I looked at the long, lean, rigid hand of Khephren; the long, lean, rigid hand as I had seen it on the diorite statue in the Cairo Museum – the statue they had found in the terrible gateway temple – and wondered that I had not shrieked when I saw it on Abdul Reis . . . That hand! It was hideously cold, and it was crushing me; it was the cold and cramping of the sarcophagus . . . the chill and constriction of unrememberable Egypt . . . It was nighted, necropolitan Egypt itself . . . that yellow paw . . . and they whisper such things of Khephren. . . .

But at this juncture I began to awake – or at least, to assume a condition less completely that of sleep than the one just preceding. I recalled the fight atop the pyramid, the treacherous Bedouins and their attack, my frightful descent by rope through endless rock depths, and my mad swinging and plunging in a chill void redolent of aromtic putrescence. I perceived that I now lay on a damp rock floor, and that my bonds were still biting into me with unloosened force. It was very cold, and I seemed to detect a faint current of noisome air sweeping across me. The cuts and bruises I had received from the jagged sides of the rock shaft were paining me woefully, their soreness enhanced to a stinging or burning acuteness by some pungent quality in the faint draft, and the mere act of rolling over was enough to set my whole frame throbbing with untold agony.

As I turned I felt a tug from above, and concluded that the rope whereby I was lowered still reached the surface. Whether or not the Arabs still held it, I had no idea; nor had I any idea how far within the earth I was. I knew that the darkness around me was wholly or nearly total, since no ray of moonlight penetrated my blindfold; but I did not trust my senses enough to accept as evidenc of extreme depth the sensation of vast duration which had characterized my descent.

Knowing at least that I was in a space of considerable extent reached from the surface directly above by an opening in the rock, I doubtfully conjectured that my prison was perhaps the buried gateway chapel of old Khephren – the Temple of the Sphinx – perhaps some inner corridor which the guides had not shown me during my morning visit, and from which I might easily escape if I could find my way to the barred entrance. It would be a labyrinthine wandering, but no worse than others out of which I had in the past found my way.

The first step was to get free of my bonds, gag, and blindfold; and this I knew would be no great task, since subtler experts than these Arabs had tried every known species of fetter upon me during my long and varied career as an exponent of escape, yet had never succeeded in defeating my methods.

Then it occurred to me that the Arabs might be ready to meet and attack me at the entrance upon any evidence of my probable escape from the binding cords, as would be furnished by any decided agitation of the rope which they probably held. This, of course, was taking for granted that my place of confinement was indeed Khephren's Temple of the Sphinx. The direct opening in the roof, wherever it might lurk, could not be beyond easy reach of the ordinary modern entrance near the Sphinx; if in truth it were any great distance at all on the surface, since the total area known to visitors is not at all enormous. I had not noticed any such opening during my daytime pilgrimage, but knew that these things are easily overlooked amidst the drifting sands.

Thinking these matters over as I lay bent and bound on the rock floor, I nearly forgot the horrors of abysmal descent and cavernous swinging which had so lately reduced me to a coma. My present thought was only to outwit the Arabs, and I accordingly determined to work myself free as quickly as possible, avoiding any tug on the descending line which might betray an effective or even problematical attempt at freedom.

This, however, was more easily determined than effected. A few preliminary trials made it clear that little could be accomplished without considerable motion; and it did not surprise me when, after one especially energetic struggle, I began to feel the coils of falling rope as they piled up about me and upon me. Obviously, I thought, the Bedouins had felt my movements and released their end of the rope; hastening no doubt to the temple's true entrance to lie murderously in wait for me.

The prospect was not pleasing – but I had faced worse in my time without flinching, and would not flinch now. At present I must first of all free myself of bonds, then trust to ingenuity to escape from the temple unharmed. It is curious how implicitly I had come to believe myself in the old temple of Khephren beside the Sphinx, only a short distance below the ground.

That belief was shattered, and every pristine apprehension of preternatural depth and demoniac mystery revived, by a circumstance which grew in horror and significance even as I formulated my philosophical plan. I have said that the falling rope was piling up about and upon me. Now I saw that it was continuing to pile, as no rope of normal length could possibly do. It gained in momentum and became an avalanche of hemp, accumulating mountainously on the floor and half burying me beneath its swiftly multiplying coils. Soon I was completely engulfed and gasping for breath as the increasing convulsions submerged and stifled me.

My senses tottered again, and I vainly tried to fight off a menace desperate and ineluctable. It was not merely that I was tortured beyond human endurance – not merely that life and breath seemed to be crushed slowly out of me – it was the knowledge of what those unnatural lengths of rope implied, and the consciousness of what unknown and incalculable gulfs of inner earth must at this moment be surrounding me. My endless descent and swinging flight through goblin space, then, must have been real, and even now I must be lying helpless in some nameless cavern world toward the core of the planet. Such a sudden confirmation of ultimate horror was insupportable, and a second time I lapsed into merciful oblivion.

When I say oblivion, I do not imply that I was free from dreams. On the contrary, my absence from the conscious world was marked by visions of the most unutterable hideousness. God! . . . If only I had not read so much Egyptology before coming to this land which is the fountain of all darkness and terror! This second spell of fainting filled my sleeping mind anew with shivering realization of the country and its archaic secrets, and through some damnable chance my dreams turned to the ancient notions of the dead and their sojournings in soul and body beyond those mysterious tombs which were more houses than graves. I recalled, in dream-shapes which it is well that I do not remember, the peculiar and elaborate construction of Egyptian sepulchers; and the exceedingly singular and terrific doctrines which determined this construction.

All these people thought of was death and the dead. They conceived of a literal resurrection of the body which made them mummify it with desperate care, and preserve all the vital organs in canopic jars near the corpse; whilst besides the body they believed in two other elements, the soul, which after its weighing and approval by Osiris dwelt in the land of the blest, and the obscure and portentous *ka* or life-principle which wandered about the upper and lower worlds in a horrible way, demanding occasional access to the preserved body, consuming the food offerings brought by priests and pious relatives to the mortuary chapel, and sometimes – as men whispered – taking its body or the wooden double always buried beside it and stalking noxiously abroad on errands peculiarly repellent.

For thousands of years those bodies rested gorgeously encased and staring glassily upward when not visited by the *ka*, awaiting the day when Osiris should restore both *ka* and soul, and lead forth the stiff legions of the dead from the sunken houses of sleep. It was to have been a glorious rebirth – but not all souls were approved, nor were all tombs inviolate, so that certain grotesque *mistakes* and fiendish *abnormalities* were to be looked for. Even today the Arabs murmur of unsanctified convocations and unwholesome worship in forgotten nether abysses, which only winged invisible *kas* and soulless mummies may visit and return unscathed.

Perhaps the most leeringly blood-congealing legends are those which relate to certain perverse products of decadent priestcraft – *composite mummies* made by the artificial union of human trunks and limbs with the heads of animals in imitation of the elder gods. At all stages of history the sacred animals were mummified, so that consecrated bulls, cats, ibises, crocodiles and the like might return some day to greater glory. But only in the decadence did they mix the human and animal in the same mummy – only in the decadence, when they did not understand the rights and prerogatives of the *ka* and the soul.

What happened to those composite mummies is not told of – at least publicly – and it is certain that no Egyptologist ever found one. The whispers of Arabs are very wild, and cannot be relied upon. They even hint that old Khephren – he of the Sphinx, the Second Pyramid and the yawning gateway temple – lives far underground wedded to the ghoul-queen Nitocris and ruling over the mummies that are neither of man nor of beast.

It was of these – of Khephren and his consort and his strange armies of the hybrid dead – that I dreamed, and that is why I am glad the exact dream-shapes have faded from my memory. My most horrible vision was connected with an idle question I had asked myself the day before when looking at the great carven riddle of the desert and wondering with what unknown depth the temple close to it might be secretly connected. That question, so innocent and whimsical then, assumed in my dream a meaning of frenetic and hysterical madness . . . *what huge and loathsome abnormality was the Sphinx originally carven to represent?*

My second awakening – if awakening it was – is a memory of stark hideousness which nothing else in my life – save one thing which came after – can parallel; and that life has been full and adventurous beyond most men's. Remember that I had lost consciousness whilst buried beneath a cascade of falling rope whose immensity revealed the cataclysmic depth of my present position. Now, as perception returned, I felt the entire weight gone; and realized upon rolling over that although I was still tied, gagged and blindfolded, *some agency had removed completely the suffocating hempen landslide which had overwhelmed me.* The significance of this condition, of course, came to me only gradually; but even so I think it would have brought unconsciousness again had I not by this time reached such a state of emotional exhaustion that no new horror could make much difference. I was alone . . . *with what?*

Before I could torture myself with any new reflection, or make any fresh effort to escape from my bonds, an additional circumstance became manifest. Pains not formerly felt were racking my arms and legs, and I seemed coated with a profusion of dried blood beyond anything my former cuts and abrasions could furnish. My chest, too, seemed pierced by a hundred wounds, as though some malign, titanic ibis had been pecking at it. Assuredly the agency which had removed the rope was a hostile one, and had begun to wreak terrible injuries upon me when somehow impelled to desist. Yet at the time my sensations were distinctly the reverse of what one might expect. Instead of sinking into a bottomless pit of despair, I was stirred to a new courage and action; for now I felt that the evil forces were physical things which a fearless man might encounter on an even basis.

On the strength of this thought I tugged again at my bonds, and used all the art of a lifetime to free myself as I had so often done amidst the glare of lights and the applause of vast crowds. The familiar details of my escaping process commenced to engross me, and now that the long rope was gone I half regained my belief that the supreme horrors were hallucinations after all, and that there had never been any terrible shaft, measureless abyss or interminable rope. Was I after all in the gateway temple of Khephren beside the Sphinx, and had the sneaking Arabs stolen in to torture me as I lay helpless there? At any rate, I must be free. Let me stand up unbound, ungagged, and with eyes open to catch any glimmer of light which might come trickling from any source, and I could actually delight in the combat against evil and treacherous foes!

How long I took in shaking off my encumbrances I cannot tell. It must have been longer than in my exhibition performances, because I was wounded, exhausted, and enervated by the experiences I had passed through. When I was finally free, and taking deep breaths of a chill, damp, evilly spiced air all the more horrible when encountered without the screen of gag and blindfolded edges, I found that I was too cramped and fatigued to move at once. There I lay, trying to stretch a frame bent and mangled, for an indefinite period, and straining my eyes to catch a glimpse of some ray of light which would give a hint as to my position.

By degrees my strength and flexibility returned, but my eyes beheld nothing. As I staggered to my feet I peered diligently in every direction, yet met only an ebony blackness as great as that I had known when blindfolded. I tried my legs, blood-encrusted beneath my shredded trousers, and found that I could walk; yet could not decide in what direction to go. Obviously I ought not to walk at random, and perhaps retreat directly from the entrance I sought; so I paused to note the direction of the cold, fetid, natron-scented air-current which I had never ceased to feel. Accepting the point of its source as the possible entrance to the abyss, I strove to keep track of this landmark and to walk consistently toward it.

I had a match-box with me, and even a small electric flashlight; but of course the pockets of my tossed and tattered clothing were long since emptied of all heavy articles. As I walked cautiously in the blackness, the draft grew stronger and more offensive, till at length I could regard it as nothing less than a tangible stream of detestable vapour pouring out of some aperture like the smoke of the genie from the fisherman's jar in the Eastern tale. The East . . . Egypt . . .

truly, this dark cradle of civilization was ever the wellspring of horrors and marvels unspeakable!

The more I reflected on the nature of this cavern wind, the greater my sense of disquiet became; for although despite its odour I had sought its source as at least an indirect clue to the outer world, I now saw plainly that this foul emanation could have no admixture or connection whatsoever with the clean air of the Libyan Desert, but must be essentially a thing vomited from sinister gulfs still lower down. I had, then, been walking in the wrong direction!

After a moment's reflection I decided not to retrace my steps. Away from the draft I would have no landmarks, for the roughly level rock floor was devoid of distinctive configurations. If, however, I followed up the strange current, I would undoubtedly arrive at an aperture of some sort, from whose gate I could perhaps work round the walls to the opposite side of this Cyclopean and otherwise unnavigable hall. That I might fail, I well realized. I saw that this was no part of Khephren's gateway temple which tourists know, and it struck me that this particular hall might be unknown even to archaeologists, and merely stumbled upon by the inquisitive and malignant Arabs who had imprisoned me. If so, was there any present gate of escape to the known parts or to the outer air?

What evidence, indeed, did I now possess that this was the gateway temple at all? For a moment all my wildest speculations rushed back upon me, and I thought of that vivid melange of impressions – descent, suspension in space, the rope, my wounds, and the dreams that were frankly dreams. Was this the end of life for me? Or indeed, would it be merciful if this moment *were* the end? I could answer none of my own questions, but merely kept on, till Fate for a third time reduced me to oblivion.

This time there were no dreams, for the suddenness of the incident shocked me out of all thought either conscious or subconscious. Tripping on an unexpected descending step at a point where the offensive draft became strong enough to offer an actual physical resistance, I was precipitated headlong down a black flight of huge stone stairs into a gulf of hideousness unrelieved.

That I ever breathed again is a tribute to the inherent vitality of the healthy human organism. Often I look back to that night and feel a touch of actual humour in those repeated lapses of consciousness; lapses whose succession reminded me at the time of nothing more than the crude cinema melodramas of that period. Of course, it is possible that the repeated lapses never occurred; and that all the features of that underground nightmare were merely the dreams of one long coma which began with the shock of my descent into that abyss and ended with the healing balm of the outer air and of the rising sun which found me stretched on the sands of Gizeh before the sardonic and dawn-flushed face of the Great Sphinx.

I prefer to believe this latter explanation as much as I can, hence was glad when the police told me that the barrier to Khephren's gateway temple had been found unfastened, and that a sizable rift to the surface did actually exist in one corner of the still buried part. I was glad, too, when the doctors pronounced my wounds only those to be expected from my seizure, blindfolding, lowering, struggling with bonds, falling some distance – perhaps into a depression in the temple's inner gallery – dragging myself to the outer barrier and escaping from it, and experiences like that . . . a very soothing diagnosis. And yet I know that there must be more than appears on the surface. That extreme descent is too vivid a memory to be dismissed – and it is odd that no one has ever been able to find a man answering the description of my guide, Abdul Reis el Drogman – the tomb-throated guide who looked and smiled like King Khephren.

I have digressed from my connected narrative – perhaps in the vain hope of evading the telling of that final incident; that incident which of all is most certainly an hallucination. But I promised to relate it, and I do not break promises. When I recovered – or seemed to recover – my senses after that fall down the black stone stairs, I was quite as alone and in darkness as before. The windy stench, bad enough before, was now fiendish; yet I had acquired enough familiarity by this time to bear it stoically. Dazedly I began to crawl away from the place whence the putrid wind came, and with my bleeding hands felt the colossal blocks of a mighty pavement. Once my head struck against a hard object, and when I felt of it I learned that it was the base of a column – a column of unbelievably immensity – whose surface was covered with gigantic chiseled hieroglyphics very perceptible to my touch.

Crawling on, I encountered other titan columns at incomprehensible distances apart; when suddenly my attention was captured by the realization of something which must have been impinging on my subconscious hearing long before the conscious sense was aware of it.

From some still lower chasm in earth's bowels were proceeding certain *sounds*, measured and definite, and like nothing I had ever heard before. That they were very ancient and distinctly ceremonial I felt almost intuitively; and much reading in Egyptology led me to associate them with the flute, the sambuke, the sistrum, and the tympanum. In their rhythmic piping, droning, rattling and beating I felt an element of terror beyond all the known terrors of earth – a terror peculiarly dissociated from personal fear, and taking the form of a sort of objective pity for our planet, that it should hold within its depths such horrors as must lie beyond these aegipanic cacophonies. The sounds increased in volume, and I felt that they were approaching. Then – and may all the gods of all pantheons unite to keep the like from my ears again – I began to hear, faintly and afar off, the morbid and millennial tramping of the marching things.

It was hideous that footfalls so dissimilar should move in such perfect rhythm. The training of unhallowed thousands of years must lie behind that march of earth's inmost monstrosities . . . padding, clicking, walking, stalking, rumbling, lumbering, crawling . . . and all to the abhorrent discords of those mocking instruments. And then – God keep the memory of those Arab legends out of my head! – the mummies without souls . . . the meeting-place of the wandering *kas* . . . the hordes of the devil-cursed pharaonic dead of forty centuries . . . the *composite mummies* led through the uttermost onyx voids by King Khephren and his ghoul-queen Nitocris . . .

The tramping drew nearer – Heaven save me from the sound of those feet and paws and hooves and pads and talons as it commenced to acquire detail! Down limitless reaches of sunless pavement a spark of light flickered in the malodorous wind and I drew behind the enormous circumference of a Cyclopic column that I might escape for a while the horror that was stalking million-footed toward me through gigantic hypostyles of inhuman dread and phobic antiquity. The flickers increased, and the tramping and dissonant rhythm grew sickeningly loud. In the quivering orange light there stood faintly forth a scene of such stony awe that I gasped from sheer wonder that conquered even fear and repulsion. Bases of columns whose middles were higher than human sight . . . mere bases of things that must each dwarf the Eiffel Tower to insignificance . . . hieroglyphics carved by un-thinkable hands in caverns where daylight can be only a remote legend . . .

I *would not* look at the marching things. That I desperately resolved as I heard their creaking joints and nitrous wheezing above the dead music and the dead tramping. It was merciful that they did not speak . . . but God! *their crazy torches began to cast shadows on the surface of those stupendous columns. Hippopotami should not have human hands and carry torches . . . men should not have the heads of crocodiles . . .*

I tried to turn away, but the shadows and the sounds and the stench were everywhere. Then I remembered something I used to do in half-conscious nightmares as a boy, and began to repeat to myself, 'This is a dream! This is a dream!' But it was of no use, and I could only shut my eyes and pray . . . at least, that is what I think I did, for one is never sure in visions – and I know this can have been nothing more. I wondered whether I should ever reach the world again, and at times would furtively open my eyes to see if I could discern any feature of the place other than the wind of spiced putrefaction, the topless columns, and the thaumatropically grotesque shadows of abnormal horror. The sputtering glare of multiplying torches now shone, and unless this hellish place were wholly without walls, I could not fail to see some boundary or fixed landmark soon. But I had to shut my eyes again when I realized how many of the things were assembling – and when I glimpsed a certain object walking solemnly and steadily *without any body above the waist.*

A fiendish and ululant corpse-gurgle or death-rattle now

split the very atmosphere – the charnel atmosphere poisonous with naftha and bitumen blasts – in one concerted chorus from the ghoulish legion of hybrid blasphemies. My eyes, perversely shaken open, gazed for an instant upon a sight which no human creature could even imagine without panic, fear and physical exhaustion. The things had filed ceremonially in one direction, the direction of the noisome wind, where the light of their torches showed their bended heads – or the bended heads of such as had heads. They were worshipping before a great black fetor-belching aperture which reached up almost out of sight, and which I could see was flanked at right angles by two giant staircases whose ends were far away in shadow. One of these was indubitably the staircase I had fallen down.

The dimensions of the hole were fully in proportion with those of the columns – an ordinary house would have been lost in it, and any average public building could easily have been moved in and out. It was so vast a surface that only by moving the eye could one trace its boundaries . . . so vast, so hideously black, and so aromatically stinking . . . Directly in front of this yawning Polyphemus-door the things were throwing objects – evidently sacrifices or religious offerings, to judge by their gestures. Khephren was their leader; sneering King Khephren *or the guide Abdul Reis*, crowned with a golden pshent and intoning endless formulae with the hollow voice of the dead. By his side knelt beautiful Queen Nitocris, whom I saw in profile for a moment, noting that the right half of her face was eaten away by rats or other ghouls. And I shut my eyes again when I saw what objects were being thrown as offerings to the fetid aperture or its possible local deity.

It occurred to me that, judging from the elaborateness of this worship, the concealed deity must be one of considerable importance. Was it Osiris or Isis, Horus or Anubis, or some vast unknown God of the Dead still more central and supreme? There is a legend that terrible altars and colossi were reared to an Unknown One before even the known gods were worshipped. . . .

And now, as I steeled myself to watch the rapt and sepulchral adorations of those nameless things, a thought of escape flashed upon me. The hall was dim, and the columns heavy with shadow. With every creature of that nightmare throng absorbed in shocking raptures, it might be barely possible for me to creep past to the far-away end of one of the staircases and ascend unseen; trusting to Fate and skill to deliver me from the upper reaches. Where I was, I neither knew nor seriously reflected upon – and for a moment it struck me as amusing to plan a serious escape from that which I knew to be a dream. Was I in some hidden and unsuspected lower realm of Khephren's gateway temple – that temple which generations have persistently called the Temple of the Sphinx? I could not conjecture, but I resolved to ascend to life and consciousness if wit and muscle could carry me.

Wriggling flat on my stomach, I began the anxious journey toward the foot of the left-hand staircase, which seemed the more accessible of the two. I cannot describe the incidents and sensations of that crawl, but they may be guessed when one reflects on what I had to watch steadily in that malign, wind-blown torchlight in order to avoid detection. The bottom of the staircase was, as I have said, far away in shadow, as it had to be to rise without a bend to the dizzy parapeted landing above the titanic aperture. This placed the last stages of my crawl at some distance from the noisome herd, though the spectacle chilled me even when quite remote at my right.

At length I succeeded in reaching the steps and began to climb; keeping close to the wall, on which I observed decorations of the most hideous sort, and relying for safety on the absorbed, ecstatic interest with which the monstrosities watched the foul-breezed aperture and the impious objects of nourishment they had flung on the pavement before it. Though the staircase was huge and steep, fashioned of vast porphyry blocks as if for the feet of a giant, the ascent seemed virtually interminable. Dread of discovery and the pain which renewed exercise had brought to my wounds combined to make that upward crawl a thing of agonizing memory. I had intended, on reaching the landing, to climb immediately onward along whatever upper staircase might mount from there; stopping for no last look at the carrion abominations that pawed and genuflected some seventy or eighty feet below – yet a sudden repetition of that thunderous corpse-gurgle and death-rattle chorus, coming as I had nearly gained the top of the flight and showing by its ceremonial rhythm that it was not an alarm of my discovery, caused me to pause and peer cautiously over the parapet.

The monstrosities were hailing something which had poked itself out of the nauseous aperture to seize the hellish fare proffered it. It was something quite ponderous, even as seen from my height; something yellowish and hairy, and endowed with a sort of nervous motion. It was as large, perhaps, as a good-sized hippopotamus, but very curiously shaped. It seemed to have no neck, but five separate shaggy heads springing in a row from a roughly cylindrical trunk; the first very small, the second good-sized, the third and fourth equal and largest of all, and the fifth rather small, though not so small as the first.

Out of these heads darted curious rigid tentacles which seized ravenously on the excessively great quantities of unmentionable food placed before the aperture. Once in a while the thing would leap up, and occasionally it would retreat into its den in a very odd manner. Its locomotion was so inexplicable that I stared in fascination, wishing it would emerge farther from the cavernous lair beneath me.

Then it *did emerge* . . . it *did* emerge, and at the sight I turned and fled into the darkness up the higher staircase that rose behind me; fled unknowingly up incredible steps and ladders and inclined planes to which no human sight or logic guided me, and which I must ever relegate to the world of dreams for want of any confirmation. It must have been a dream, or the dawn would never have found me breathing on the sands of Gizeh before the sardonic dawn-flushed face of the Great Sphinx.

The Great Sphinx! God! That idle question I asked myself on that sun-blest morning before . . . *what huge and loathsome abnormality was the Sphinx originally carven to represent?* Accursed is the sight, be it in dream or not, that revealed to me the supreme horror – the unknown God of the Dead, which licks its colossal chops in the unsuspected abyss, fed hideous morsels by soulless absurdities that should not exist. The five-headed monster that emerged . . . that five-headed monster as large as a hippopotamus . . . the five-headed monster – *and that of which it is the merest forepaw* . . .

But I survived, and I know it was only a dream.

THE MUMMY WORSHIPPERS

by Elliott O'Donnell

One day, a few years back, I was looking at my old friend
Katebit in the Oriental Department of the British Museum.
Many, if not all my readers, have some acquaintance with
Katebit, the mummy with the golden face and head slightly
on one side. I believe in her lifetime she had some association
with the College of Amen-ra. There is something about her,
for me, that exercises a strange fascination. Maybe it is her
hands. Of course they are mere bones now, but there is
something dainty about those bones, something that suggests,
at least, that the hands of Katebit were very lovely during her
lifetime. I am peculiarly susceptible to lovely hands; and,
unhappily, one sees few of them in London. In New York and
many of the American cities it is otherwise. That, I think, is
because America is so cosmopolitan and the mixture of
nationalities often makes for feminine loveliness.

To proceed, I was standing, looking at Katebit, one
morning, when I fancied I saw her move her head. At first, it
was only a slight movement, then it became a decided to and
fro wag. This made me start. 'It is a little alarming, isn't it?' a
voice behind me whispered. I turned, and saw a man; a
shrivelled-up, sallow-faced, white-haired man, who spoke
with a foreign accent and looked very like a mummy himself.
He said tht he had often seen Katebit move her head about
like that, and that as many other people had, too, he thought
there was no doubt whatsoever but that she was obsessed by a
spirit – a Lamuki was the term he used – that often did obsess
mummies and make them do all manner of queer things.

Leaving the Museum together, we got friendly over a cup of tea at Lyons' Corner House in Tottenham Court Road. During intervals in the music, he told me his name was Bobdillo, Colonel Bobdillo, and that he had once enjoyed the privilege of visiting a mummy-worshipping society in Norwood.

'People are so in the habit of associating mummies with Egypt,' he said, 'that it is, perhaps, difficult to realise that all mummies are not Egyptian, and that mummification was at one time common in many parts of America. The society I visited was American, and the mummies they specialised in were Peruvian. Their headquarters (they had branches in various parts of London) were in Upper Norwood, and consisted of two large, adjacent, though detached, houses, the grounds of which had been thrown into one and rendered private by high stone walls and many trees. When I got there the sun was low in the sky; it was about eight o'clock in late summer, and the shadows from the trees and walls lay black all around me.

'In the centre of an open space in the grounds was a strange-looking building.' The Colonel paused, as if he were intently reviewing it in his mind's eye. Then he went on. 'The man who introduced me there, for convenience' sake I will call him Pesquillo, that is near enough to his real name, told me it was a chulpa. A chulpa is a Peruvian tomb. In this case the chulpa was a circular mass of stone and clay, faced with blocks of trachyte or basalt. The whole of the exterior was painted flaming red and yellow, an effect that was strangely startling in the waning daylight. In height it could not have been far off twenty feet. Its only visible entrance, a narrow wooden door, in accordance with custom, so I was told, faced the east. When all the members, there were about a dozen, had gathered together round the chulpa, the president, a tall, grey-haired Peruvian, with a long, much-waxed moustache, announced the programme for the evening. After the usual minutes had been read and various business discussed, the mummy of Princess Tetraqua[1] of the Inca Royal House was to be laid with much pomp and ceremony in the specially pre-

[1] That is the nearest I can get to the name he mentioned.

pared receptacle for it in the chulpa. After that they were all to join in the usual ceremony of worshipping the mummy and invoking the spirit of the dead to come to them and manifest its presence in some unmistakable manner. 'I am not at all superstitious,' the Colonel added, 'but the President spoke so seriously, and the chulpa lent such an air of ghostliness to the scene, that I admit I did feel a bit uncanny. Later – but wait.'

The Colonel paused again and graciously accepted the cigar I offered him. Then he resumed. 'I felt still more uncanny,' he said, 'when four members of the Society, all very tall men in black clothes, came out of the house, carrying a kind of stretcher, and on it, seated upon a low stool, a weird-looking figure. It was the mummy, wrapped in a llama skin. The only uncovered part of her were the hands and feet. These, despite their mummification, were beautiful. I was able to obtain a close view of them, as the stretcher, on two benches provided for the purpose, was set in our midst. French writers are very fond of describing beautiful hands and feet. Apparently beautiful hands and feet appeal especially to the French, but I doubt if Zola, du Boisgoby, Eugêne Sue or Théophile Gautier ever saw more beautiful hands and feet than those of the Princess Tetraqua. The hands were slender, with tapering fingers and long, almond-shaped nails, gleaming red with recently applied varnish. The feet were slender, too; each toe exquisitely formed, with nails as beautifully shaped as those on the fingers, and likewise gleaming red. How different to the toes of most modern women, malshaped and corn-covered through the constant wearing of boots and shoes. On her ankles, as well as her wrists, Tetraqua, like most of the Inca women, wore gold bangles. By the side of the stool, made of some highly polished American wood, upon which Tetraqua sat, were several pieces of highly coloured Peruvian pottery; and painted in brilliant red, on what looked like a piece of calico, attached to the llama skin covering her breast, was a flaming device depicting the sun. After the recital of several long prayers by the president, whilst all the members knelt, the mummy was taken, with every sign of respect, into the chulpa and there deposited.

'Then incense was burned, more prayers recited, and everyone sat on the ground, cross-legged, like so many Turks, their

eyes fixed intently on the door of the chulpa. I asked my friend
Pesquillo why they were all looking in that direction, and he
told me they were waiting for some demonstration from the
Princess. Minute after minute passed; the sun slowly sank to
rest in its bed of crimson and gold; the sky paled, the stars and
moon appeared; the shadows of the trees and walls grew
blacker, the air cooled and a gentle night breeze set all the
leaves on trees and bushes gently rustling. And still the
watchers, with eyes fixed on the door of the chulpa, sat and
waited. I grew very tired,' the Colonel added, adjusting his
long-distance pince-nez to look at the leader of the newly
arrived orchestra, who was a lady, 'of sitting in that ridiculous
attitude, and staring at that infernal door, and I was calling
down, silently, of course, maledictions by the score on those
around me, particularly on Pesquillo, for inviting me to such a
fiasco, when suddenly, in the bright moonlight, I saw the
handle of the chulpa door turn. Then, very slowly, the door
opened and the mummy appeared on the threshold. Being
within a few feet of it, I could see every detail, the llama skins,
the flaring pictorial device on the piece of cotton or calico that
covered the breast; the outlines of the eyes, nose and mouth,
painted in some dark colour on the skin concealing the face;
the bare hands and feet, the gleaming vermilion toe- and
finger-nails. That I was thrilled goes without saying. Who
wouldn't have been thrilled? I think even you, my friend,
would have been moved to some extent, despite your many
tête-à-tête with ghosts. Anything more startling than what I
now saw can hardly be imagined. Amid a strange silence,
intensified rather than broken by the ghostly rustling of
leaves, and rendered still more emphatic, perhaps, by the
brilliance of the moonlight and the blackness that lay all
around us, the mummy moved. On it came, with a curious
gliding rather than walking motion, straight towards me. I
wanted to jump up and run. I could not. Something seemed to
hold me down and keep me chained to the ground. Whilst all
around me, so it seemed, were watching breathlessly, nearer
and nearer it came, till it got right up to me, and bending
down, peered into my face. I thought then that I should have
fainted with horror, for I found myself gazing, not at mere
painted outlines of eyes, but into living eyes, the dark liquid

eyes of a woman, full of fire and passion.' The Colonel stopped rather abruptly. He seemed to be overcome with emotion. The mummy had obviously made a great impression on him, so great that when the orchestra recommenced playing its pretty leader no longer attracted his attention. The music temporarily ceasing again, he went on. 'When the mummy bent over me,' he said, 'I smelt no mustiness, nothing unpleasant, such as one usually associates with the dead, especially the long dead, but just the reverse, a delightful odour, sweet and subtle, unmistakably oriental. The Damascus and Kashmir ladies use a perfume something like it, but not nearly so fragrant and intoxicating. Raising her arms, now loosed from the llama skins, she suddenly threw them round my neck and kissed me. My friend, many women have kissed me. You may smile, but it is true.'

'I believe you,' I murmured. 'You are just the sort of man women would kiss.'

The cloud vanished from the Colonel's face. Once again, he beamed, not at me, but at the blonde leader of the orchestra. Their eyes meeting, as eyes often do, she beamed back, not at me, but at him. Presently he continued.

'I have never experienced anything like that kiss,' he sighed. 'The lips, they were soft, like satin, so warm, so fragrant, and so full of passion. I would like to have been kissed by them, always, for Eternity. Alas, it was not to be. She, the mummy, withdrew them, patted me on the cheek with a soft, cool hand, and moved away. Facing us all, she stretched out her arms, uttered three cries, so weird and unearthly that several dogs in the neighbouring premises barked and howled, and then, turning round, glided back to the chulpa. Becoming more and more shadowy and indistinct as she approached it, upon reaching its threshold she faded away altogether. Explain it as you may, my friend, I was looking at her one moment, and the next peering into space, the empty space of that gloomy portal. For some minutes I heard sobbing, the sobbing of a woman in terrible distress. It certainly seemed to come from the chulpa, and several dogs belonging to the neighbouring houses howled and whined, as if frightened. When the sobbing ceased, and the dogs, in consequence, left off their demonstrations, the President said a few prayers in some Peruvian dialect, shut and bolted the door of the chulpa, and announced the meeting at an end.

'That night, I dreamed the door of my room gently opened and a figure silently and cautiously entered. It was clad in some white, mystical garment, so transparent that I could see through it the outlines of a woman's slim body, beautifully fashioned. Approaching the bed, she leaned over me, and once again I experienced that kiss, those lips were unmistakable, they were so soft, fragrant and so full of passion. They were pressed against mine for quite a long time, but not too long, I can assure you. To be kissed to death by those lips would, indeed, be a blissful ending.'

The Colonel, pausing again, looked so sentimental that I nearly laughed outright, preventing myself only by a mighty effort. Presently, with a sigh, he continued.

'All our experiences in this world, nice as well as nasty, come to an end some time, and so it was on this occasion. The lips were withdrawn, those lovely hands ceased smoothing my cheeks and forehead, Tetraqua, for I knew it was she, left the room as noiselessly as she had entered it, and I awoke. I might have thought it was only a dream and nothing more that I had awakened from, but for two things, and those two things convinced me to the contrary, and assured me that Tetraqua actually had, in spirit form, paid me a visit. For one thing, the room was full of that sweet scent I had smelt the previous evening in the garden at Norwood. For the other, on the little round table by my bedside, was something whose like I had never seen before, except in a museum in Paris. It was one of those small golden plaques, symbolic of the sun, which were invariably inserted by the priesthood in the mouths of Inca women of the highest rank, during the process of mummification.'

THE FLYING HEAD

by A Hyatt Verrill

It was indeed strange, Dr Stokes thought, that his Indian labourers should appear so loath to dig into the mound. They worked half-heartedly, hung back, and appeared nervous and ill at ease. Dr Stokes had excavated hundreds of burial mounds in Peru and had disinterred countless Inca and pre-Inca mummies; yet never before had the Cholos showed the least hesitation in digging into graves of their forefathers and dragging out their dessicated bodies.

When the archaeologist questioned them they merely muttered and mumbled in their native Quichua, saying something unintelligible about *supay*, or devil; and when at last the posts and adobe bricks marking a grave were exposed, the men demanded their pay and deserted in a body.

'Looks as if we'd have to do the rest of the work ourselves, Tom,' Dr Stokes said to his assistant.

Presently the last of the bricks were removed, and the scientist uttered an exclamation of delight as he saw the contents of the tomb. The mummy-bundle itself was magnificent with silver and gold ornaments, and grouped about it were splendid specimens of pottery.

'By Jove!' he cried as he examined one of the jars. 'An entirely new motif! See here, Tom!'

Painted in black and scarlet upon the cream-coloured surface of the jar was a grotesque, winged figure resembling an owl, with a horribly fiendish expression on its almost-human face. Never before had Dr Stokes seen anything like it, and his enthusiasm increased when he discovered that every piece of pottery in the tomb bore the same strange design.

All impatience to learn the contents of the mummy-bundle, the two men took it from the grave and packed up the pottery. Loading their discoveries into their ramshackle car, they started on the long drive to San Isidro where, in the scientist's temporary laboratory, the mummy could be unwrapped. It was late when they arrived, but so anxious was the archaeologist to learn what might be hidden under the wrappings of the mummy, that he could not wait until morning and Tom's assistance before getting at it.

With notebook at hand he began removing the layers of coarse cotton cloth, and his enthusiasm increased at the splendid robes and ornate decorations revealed beneath. Never had he seen anything to equal it! Carefully removing and labelling each of the many gold and silver ornaments, folding the delicate robes and making copious notes, Dr Stokes chuckled with delight at the chased silver mask covering the face of the false head, and mentally preened himself on the turquoise and lapis lazuli beads.

Then, as he lifted the last of the gorgeous robes, an ejaculation of wonder came from the scientist's lips. Resting between the drawn-up knees of the mummy, and clasped in the shrunken hands, was a human head.

'By Jove!' Dr Stokes exclaimed. 'A trophy head, and a marvellously fine one at that!'

Triumphant at having made such a remarkable discovery, he stood gazing admiringly at it. The head was perfectly preserved and the eyes, apparently of some dull green, jade-like material, which had been inserted in the sockets, gave a most lifelike effect. On either side of the skull, long black hair hung from beneath a tightly fitting leather cap with long ears or tabs, and this together with the snaky locks and cold, green staring eyes, lent the mummified head a most horrible and fiendish expression. An expression of unspeakable malevolence and cruelty!

'Whoever you were, you were no beauty,' Dr Stokes muttered to himself a little grimly. 'But you're a wonderful specimen, all the same.'

Then, as he carefully moved the mummy's shrivelled hands

and lifted the head, preparatory to placing it in a case, the scientist almost dropped the gruesome thing in his sudden astonishment. He stood there staring incredulously, dumbfounded with wonder. Attached to the fearsome head was a tiny, shrivelled body! A body no larger than that of a newly born infant, but unspeakably repulsive with its covering of dark, curly hair.

For a brief instant, his first astonishment over, Dr Stokes thought that the dried body was that of a monkey attached to the trophy head as a decoration; but only a glance was needed to prove this surmise wrong. The body belonged to the head itself. It was the mummy of a strange, horrible freak; a being with the body of a hairy midget, barely a foot in length and with the head of a full-grown man!

Here, indeed, was a momentous discovery. Very carefully placing the unique specimen in a covered tray upon his laboratory table, Dr Stokes switched out the lights and went to his bedroom, highly elated at the results of his latest excavations.

He was not a nervous or excitable man, and through years of disinterring and handling the earthly remains of human beings he had come to regard bones and mummies merely as specimens. He was not addicted to day-dreaming, and there was not a trace of superstition in his makeup. Otherwise his rest might have been disturbed by most unpleasant dreams; but as it was, he slept soundly until suddenly he found himself awake, fully conscious, listening for some sound which he felt sure had awakened him. Then he heard it. A rustling, scratching noise from his laboratory, followed an instant later by a crash.

'Confound those cats!' the scientist exclaimed, leaping from his bed. 'Now one of the beasts has upset something.'

Switching on the lights he glanced about him. Upon the table was the overturned tray, the mummy of the freak beside it, and on the floor was the cover where it had fallen.

'Damn!' Dr Stokes exclaimed aloud. Then, to himself, 'Lucky it wasn't the mummy the beast knocked off. Strange I should have forgotten to close the shutters.'

Replacing the mummy in the tray, he set it upon a shelf; then armed himself with a stout stick and commenced a hunt

for the offending feline. But he could find no trace of a trespassing cat. Satisfied that the creature had been frightened
by the crash of the falling tray and had dashed out through the
barred window, he closed the wooden shutters, switched off
the light and again went to bed.

He did not know how long he had slept when he was
awakened. For an instant there was no sound, nothing to have
disturbed his slumbers. Then from the darkness came a soft,
swishing, fluttering noise, and he felt a breath of air against
his face as if some moving object had passed swiftly by.

'Bat,' was his mental comment, as he fumbled for his
flashlight. As the beam stabbed the darkness he caught a
glimpse of a shadowy, indistinct form, two feet or more across
the wings, as it flitted through the door leading to the
laboratory.

'One of those big fruit-bats,' he decided as he rose. 'Probably that's the nuisance that knocked over the tray. I'll finish
him in short order.'

But there was no sign of the bat in the laboratory. Deciding
that the creature had found a way out through some aperture
under the eaves, Dr Stokes resumed his interrupted slumbers
and slept soundly until aroused by Tom's knocking on the
outer door.

'I'll bet you sat up all night working on that mummy,' Tom
said, as Dr Stokes, in dressing gown and slippers, admitted
him. 'Still in bed at this hour and you look all ragged out.
Really, you shouldn't – '

'You're wrong, Tom,' the other interrupted. 'I went to bed
early enough, but I had a bad night. First a dratted cat came
in – I'd forgotten to close the shutters in the laboratory; then
one of those big fruit-bats, or maybe it was the bat both times.
Anyway, cat or bat, the pest made a racket. Knocked over a
tray on my table and –

'Great Scott, I'd forgotten you didn't know. Tom, my boy,
that mummy we dug up is a most marvellous discovery!
Absolutely unique. Magnificent robes and ornaments – but
nothing compared to what was buried with him. Another
mummy? Why, the most amazing mummy ever found in Peru!
Just wait till you see it.'

Anxious to witness Tom's astonishment and enthusiasm

when he saw the dessicated freak, Dr Stokes led the way to the laboratory and reached for the tray in which he had placed the mummified midget during the night. As he was on the point of lifting it down, there was an exclamation of surprise from Tom.

'Oh, I say, that *is* a find! What a magnificent trophy head!'

Dr Stokes wheeled. 'Trophy head?' he cried. 'What – '

His words died on his lips and he stood staring, dumbfounded, incredulous. Resting in the lap of the mummy, just as he had first seen it, was the mummified freak! How had the thing come there? He was positive he had placed it in the tray on the shelf after the trespassing creature of the night had upset it on the table. And he was equally positive he had *not* replaced it in its original position. Was it possible he had walked in his sleep and, while unconscious, had replaced the shrivelled midget in the mummy's lap? Or had the incidents of the night been merely a dream?

But even so, that would not explain the matter; for he had lifted the supposed trophy head from the mummy's lap and had placed it in the tray on his table before he had retired for the night. Yes, he *must* have placed it there in his sleep. That was the logical explanation.

All these thoughts flashed through his brain in a fraction of a second. Then, recovering himself with a bit of an effort, he stepped forward with a simulated chuckle.

'Trophy head!' he exclaimed. 'Just lift it carefully, Tom, and for heaven's sake don't drop it in your amazement.'

Somewhat puzzled, his assistant gingerly lifted the gruesome green-eyed thing, and a long whistle of astonishment came from his lips.

'Good Lord!' he cried. 'It's a freak! Ugh!' He shuddered. 'It's a perfect horror! I'd hate like blazes to see or meet such a nightmarish thing alive. But it's a marvellous specimen – nothing like it in the world, I suppose. But what do you make of it, Doctor? Why was the other chap buried with this hobgoblin in his lap?'

'I think the explanation is simple enough,' replied the scientist. 'The other chap, as you term him, was unquestionably a noble of high rank – his robes and wealth of gold prove that; and undoubtedly the malformed midget was his court jester, as you might term him. According to the accounts of Francisco Pizarro, the conqueror of Peru, and his fellows, dwarfs or hunchbacks or human freaks were quite commonly kept by members of the Inca court. But I believe this is the first ever to be disinterred.'

Tom had replaced the repulsive thing and was examining the other objects take from the grave and mummy-bundle.

'Gosh!' he exclaimed. 'Did you notice the resemblance between these figures on the pottery and that – that beastly midget? See, Doctor, the heads are almost identical; green eyes, hair, painting and all. And the hairy body! All that horrible thing needs is a pair of wings to make the design a perfect likeness.'

'*Hmm.* Yes, there *is* a stiking similarity,' agreed the other. 'Very likely the designs were intended to portray the creature. Somewhat conventionalized, of course. Wings added for symbolism, perhaps; or possibly, in fact I should say probably, the midget was unable to walk – don't see how he could with the immense head and undeveloped legs – and the artist felt he should be given wings to make up for his handicaps. But just look at this robe, Tom, and start cataloguing the items while I get dressed and run over to Joe's for a cup of coffee.'

Throughout the day the two men worked at the specimens, Tom numbering and cataloguing them while Dr Stokes wrote minute descriptions of each. But busily occupied as he was, a corner of his brain was ceaselessly struggling to straighten out the events of the preceding night. He fought to solve the mystery as to why the mummified freak had been in the mummy's lap, in spite of the fact that he distinctly recalled having placed it on the shelf on the other side of the room.

To Dr Stokes the only logical explanation appeared to be that he had walked in his sleep, a thing he had never done in his life before, and with the remarkable midget's mummy on his mind he had placed it where it had been found. Yet this seemingly reasonable solution of the matter did not entirely satisfy him.

As there was no other possible way to account for it he finally dismissed the matter for the time being, while he took time off for a good dinner and a pleasant evening at the home of the *alcalde*, the local mayor. But when he went to bed his thoughts reverted once more to the events of the previous night. But not for long. He was very sleepy. This time he flattered himself that no cats or bats would disturb him, for he had carefully closed and barred the shutters. Presently he was sleeping soundly.

Dr Stokes awoke from a dreamless slumber to find himself tense, expectant, listening. Something, he couldn't say what, made him feel nervous, apprehensive. Could it be, he wondered, that there had been a slight earthquake shock? Then once again he heard it – the same soft rustling sound of the night before! Something was moving about near him, flitting back and forth in the darkness; and an involuntary shudder passed over the scientist.

But the next instant he was himself again. It was only that confounded fruit-bat, or another one of its tribe. But how the deuce did the thing get in? Probably never went out, Dr Stokes decided. No doubt the beast had its hideout somewhere in the roof and was trying to get out, but found it impossible with the windows shuttered. Well, he would soon put an end to *that* nuisance.

Rising, Dr Stokes fumbled for a stout stick. Grasping the club he snapped on his flashlight and aimed a vicious blow at a flapping shadow. But the weapon swished harmlessly through the air, and the flitting creature vanished in the darkness of the doorway. Intent on knocking the thing down, the scientist shut the door and, flashing his light about the hallway, entered the laboratory and closed the door behind him.

As he did so there was a swish of air past his head. He involuntarily ducked, and the flying creature swept by within an inch of his face. Wheeling, the scientist struck blindly. There was a soft thud, an agonized cry so filled with mingled pain and anger that Dr Stokes shuddered as he heard the thing stiking the floor.

'Got him!' exulted the scientist, and swung the beam of his flashlight in the direction whence had come the sound of the creature's fall. The torch almost dropped from his hand when he staggered back wide-eyed, chills running up and down his spine. On the floor, staring up at him with green eyes ablaze with fiendish fury and hatred, was the horrible mummified freak! The thing was *alive!*

It was impossible, incredible; and for a brief instant Dr Stokes felt that he must be in the grip of a horrible nightmare. He must break this unholy spell! Controlling his shaken nerves with a tremendous effort, the scientist raised his stick for the fatal blow. Keeping his light focused upon the fearsome thing on the floor, he took a step forward.

A scream of abject terror came from the man's lips. He sprang back, the stick clattering from his hand. Chilled with horror he stood there, powerless to move. The awful head with its diminutive hairy body was advancing! With terror clutching at his heart, icy cold, while beads of cold perspiration oozed from his forehead, he stood transfixed, powerless to move as if hypnotized by the harsh, malignant green eyes in that demoniacal skull. Dr Stokes saw the long tabs of the thing's leather cap tremble and – No, *not* the flaps of the cap but wings – soft, leathery wings that were attached to the nightmarish head of the apparition!

Yet even in his mad, helpless terror the scientist noticed with vast relief that one of the thing's batlike wings was injured, torn, and useless, where the stick had struck. And so this spawn of hell, this awful being, this mummified freak that by some supernatural means had come to life, could no longer fly. But it was creeping toward its attacker!

Uttering strange, uncanny, gibbering sounds, its lips drawn back above sharp, pointed teeth, its baleful green eyes fixed upon the scientist, the loathsome, hideous monstrosity was dragging its attenuated body across the floor; pushing itself forward by its shrunken legs, balancing its great head by its batlike wings and tiny hands; moving slowly, inch by inch, but steadily toward the spot where Dr Stokes stood back against the wall, gasping, choking, dumb with utter horror.

He strove with all his will power to move, to escape, but not a muscle responded. If only he could recover his stick, could crush this devilish spawn of the nether world to a shapeless pulp! But the scientist's limbs, his arms were nerveless, limp, incapable of control. Within two feet of where he stood, the stick rested where it had fallen from his shaking hand.

At his feet, the torch lay on the floor, its beam still directed at the malignant, awful monstrosity that was moving nearer and nearer. Dr Stokes, however, was paralyzed, frozen into immobility with hypnotic terror. Yet his brain was active, his mind receptive, functioning sanely enough. Or *was* he sane? he asked himself.

Did the thing actually exist – or was it but the figment of a disordered mind? His common-sense scientific brain told him it could not be real, that a mummy thousands of years old could not be endowed with life, that a semi-human freak could not possess wings and fly. It was too preposterous, too supernatural to be real. Yet Dr Stokes' staring, horror-filled eyes contradicted the arguments in his brain. The awful thing *was* there, and it was alive, and every moment it was dragging its repulsive, fiendish being nearer; a ghastly, demoniacal thing conjured by some black magic back to life.

Nearer and nearer it crept; in the silence of the room, the scraping, shuffling sounds of the thing's movements seemed loud and distinct. It reached the fallen stick and, in a sudden mad fury seized it in its teeth and shook it as a terrier worries a rat, mouthing and growling, biting splinters from the hard, tough wood. Then, dropping the inanimate club, the ghastly thing gathered itself together, bared its needle-pointed teeth and, with a sudden harsh flap of its wings, leaped at the man!

With a shriek of abject terror the scientist came to life and sprang aside. He stepped upon the torch, reeled backward and fell heavily to the floor as the shattered light plunged the room into inky blackness. As he fell he felt the loathsome, horrible thing strike his leg, and there was a sharp stab of pain as the strong keen teeth of the devilish creature bit into his flesh.

Then he was struggling, fighting madly, clawing and striking with his fists at the misshapen, incredible, indescribably vile semi-human monster that clung to him like a leech. Heedless of the frantic blows rained upon it, the thing was crawling, dragging its way across the scientist's chest, closer and closer to his sweating throat and face.

Dr Stokes' clutching hands grasped a leathery wing, only to release their grip as fanglike teeth bit deeply into his wrists. Screaming with deadly fear, he saw the thing's eyes glowing like green fire in the blackness. In the scientist's nostrils was the musty, fetid odour of ancient, ravaged tombs. His tortured nerves gave way at last. Something seemed to snap within his mind and he sank back limp, inert, unconscious. . .

There was no response to Tom's repeated knocking on the doctor's door. Wondering, thinking it most strange that his employer should be out so early or should be sleeping so soundly, and vaguely troubled, the young assistant walked around the house. The bedroom windows were tightly shuttered, but to Tom's surprise the shutters on the laboratory windows were ajar. Raising himself on tiptoe he peered between the iron bars into the room, only to reel back, feeling faint and nauseated at what he had seen.

Lying upon the laboratory floor in a great pool of blood was the body of the scientist, an expression of unspeakable terror in his dead, glassy eyes, his head twisted horribly to one side, exposing a fearful, ragged gash in his throat.

Trembling in every limb, Tom rushed to the office of the *alcalde* and in scarcely coherent Spanish babbled that Dr Stokes had been brutally murdered. Battering down the heavy doors, the native police, with the *alcalde* and Tom, dashed through the short hallway to the laboratory.

'*Madre de Dios!*' exclaimed the first man to reach the room, and crossed himself. 'What devil's work is this?'

Steeling himself for the effort, Tom bent over the forlorn body of Dr Stokes.

'Some savage wild beast did this,' he declared, his voice shaky. 'It must have entered by the open window. Perhaps it is still here.'

Whipping out their revolvers the police began searching the room, but no trace of another living thing could be found.

The *alcalde* shook his head. 'Strange things happen,' he said in lowered tones. 'The Senor Stokes desecrated the tombs of the ancient ones. Perchance' – he glanced furtively about him – 'perchance it was no beast, no creature of flesh and blood that destroyed him. The *Indios* tell of unholy things, Senor. They tell of captive devils buried with the ancient dead to protect their bodies and their treasures from being disturbed. Perchance – *quien sabe?*'

'Nonsense!' exclaimed Tom. 'You may believe in such occult things, but I don't!'

Involuntarily Tom glanced at the mummy as he spoke. A half-suppressed ejaculation came from his lips and a cold chill ran along his spine. Resting between the knees of the mummy was the horrible mummified freak, its jade-green eyes cold and expressionless – yet with its dead, shrunken face and lips smeared with a moist, dull red!

Whether the *alcalde* or the police had noticed it, Tom could not tell. He hardly thought so. Stepping forward, breathing hard and holding his nerves under iron control, he gently drew a corner of a robe and covered the horrible, gruesome thing.

Doctor Stokes' mutilated body had been removed and was resting in its casket, awaiting the aeroplane which had been summoned to carry it to Lima, when Tom re-entered the laboratory. Clenching his teeth, summoning all his self-control, mentally cursing himself for a credulous fool, he hastily gathered the robes and ornaments taken from the mummy, flung them over the shrivelled, dessicated monstrosity, covered it with a blanket and, trembling despite himself, loaded the unwieldy bundle in the ramshackle car. Several hours later he returned, the car empty, with an indefinable feeling of vast relief.

Far out in the desert, amid the crumbling ruins of the forgotten pre-Inca city, the mummy again rested in its ancient tomb.

MONKEYS

by E F Benson

Dr Hugh Morris, while still in the early thirties of his age, had
justly earned for himself the reputation of being one of the
most dexterous and daring surgeons in his profession, and
both in his private practice and in his voluntary work at one of
the great London hospitals his record of success as an operator
was unparalleled among his colleagues. He believed that
vivisection was the most fruitful means of progress in the
science of surgery, holding, rightly or wrongly, that he was
justified in causing suffering to animals, though sparing them
all possible pain, if thereby he could reasonably hope to gain
fresh knowledge about similar operations on human beings
which would save life or mitigate suffering; the motive was
good, and the gain already immense. But he had nothing but
scorn for those who, for their own amusement, took out packs
of hounds to run foxes to death, or matched two greyhounds to
see which would give the death-grip to a single terrified hare:
that, to him, was wanton torture, utterly unjustifiable. Year in
and year out, he took no holiday at all, and for the most part
he occupied his leisure, when the day's work was over, in
study.

He and his friend Jack Madden were dining together one
warm October night at his house looking on to Regent's Park.
The windows of his drawing-room on the ground-floor were
open, and they sat smoking, when dinner was done, on the
broad window-seat. Madden was starting next day for Egypt,
where he was engaged in archæological work, and he would be
engaged throughout the winter in the excavation of a newly-

discovered cemetery across the river from Luxor, near Medinet Habu. But it was no good.

'When my eye begins to fail and my fingers to falter,' said Morris, 'it will be time for me to think of taking my ease. What do I want with a holiday? I should be pining to get back to my work all the time. I like work better than loafing. Purely selfish.'

'Well, be unselfish for once,' said Madden. 'Besides, your work would benefit. It can't be good for a man never to relax. Surely freshness is worth something.'

'Precious little if you're as strong as I am. I believe in continual concentration if one wants to make progress. One may be tired, but why not? I'm not tired when I'm actually engaged on a dangerous operation, which is what matters. And time's so short. Twenty years from now I shall be past my best, and I'll have my holiday then, and when my holiday is over, I shall fold my hands and go to sleep for ever and ever. Thank God, I've got no fear that there's an after-life. The spark of vitality that has animated us burns low and then goes out like a windblown candle, and as for my body, what do I care what happens to that when I have done with it? Nothing will survive of me except some small contribution I may have made to surgery, and in a few years' time that will be super-seded. But for that I perish utterly.'

Madden squirted some soda into his glass.

'Well, if you've quite settled that – ' he began.

'I haven't settled it, science has,' said Morris. 'The body is transmuted into other forms, worms batten on it, it helps to feed the grass, and some animal consumes the grass. But as for the survival of the individual spirit of a man, show me one title of scientific evidence to support it. Besides, if it did survive, all the evil and malice in it must surely survive too. Why should the death of the body purge that away? It's a nightmare to contemplate such a thing, and oddly enough, unhinged people like spiritualists want to persuade us for our consolation that the nightmare is true. But odder still are those old Egyptians of yours, who thought that there was something sacred about their bodies, after they were quit of them. And didn't you tell me that they covered their coffins with curses on anyone who disturbed their bones?'

'Constantly,' said Madden. 'It's the general rule in fact. Marrowy curses written in hieroglyphics on the mummy-case or carved on the sarcophagus.'

'But that's not going to deter you this winter from opening as many tombs as you can find, and rifling from them any objects of interest or value.'

Madden laughed.

'Certainly it isn't,' he said. 'I take out of the tombs all objects of art, and I unwind the mummies to find and annex their scarabs and jewellery. But I make an absolute rule always to bury the bodies again. I don't say that I believe in the power of those curses, but anyhow a mummy in a museum is an indecent object.'

'But if you found some mummied body with an interesting malformation, wouldn't you send it to some anatomical institute?' asked Morris.

'It has never happened to me yet,' said Madden, 'but I'm pretty sure I shouldn't.'

'Then you're a superstitious Goth and an anti-educational Vandal,' remarked Morris . . . 'Hullo, what's that?' He leant out of the window as he spoke. The light from the room vividly illuminated the square of lawn outside, and across it was crawling the small twitching shape of some animal. Hugh Morris vaulted out of the window, and presently returned, carrying carefully in his spread hands a little grey monkey, evidently desperately injured. Its hind legs were stiff and outstretched as if it was partially paralysed.

Morris ran his soft deft fingers over it.

'What's the matter with the little beggar, I wonder,' he said. 'Paralysis of the lower limbs: it looks like some lesion of the spine.'

The monkey lay quite still, looking at him with anguished appealing eyes as he continued his manipulation.

'Yes, I thought so,' he said. 'Fracture of one of the lumbar vertebræ. What luck for me! It's a rare injury, but I've often wondered. . . . And perhaps luck for the monkey too, though that's not very probable. If he was a man and a patient of mine, I shouldn't dare to take the risk. But, as it is . . .'

Jack Madden started on his southward journey next day, and

by the middle of November was at work on this newly-discovered cemetery. He and another Englishman were in charge of the excavation, under the control of the Antiquity Department of the Egyptian Government. In order to be close to their work and to avoid the daily ferrying across the Nile from Luxor, they hired a bare roomy native house in the adjoining village of Gurnah. A reef of low sandstone cliff ran northwards from here towards the temple and terraces of Deir-el-Bahari, and it was in the face of this and on the level below it that the ancient graveyard lay. There was much accumulation of sand to be cleared away before the actual exploration of the tombs could begin, but trenches cut below the foot of the sandstone ridge showed that there was an extensive area to investigate.

The more important sepulchres, they found, were hewn in the face of this small cliff: many of these had been rifled in ancient days, for the slabs forming the entrances into them had been split, and the mummies unwound, but now and then Madden unearthed some tomb that had escaped these marauders, and in one he found the sarcophagus of a priest of the nineteenth dynasty, and that alone repaid weeks of fruitless work. There were nearly a hundred *ushaptiu* figures of the finest blue glaze; there were four alabaster vessels in which had been placed the viscera of the dead man removed before embalming: there was a table of which the top was inlaid with squares of variously coloured glass, and the legs were of carved ivory and ebony: there were the priest's sandals adorned with exquisite silver filagree: there was his staff of office inlaid with a diaper-pattern of cornelian and gold, and on the head of it, forming the handle, was the figure of a squatting cat, carved in amethyst, and the mummy, when unwound, was found to be decked with a necklace of gold plaques and onyx beads. All these were sent down to the Gizeh Museum at Cairo, and Madden reinterred the mummy at the foot of the cliff below the tomb. He wrote to Hugh Morris describing this find, and laying stress on the unbroken splendour of these crystalline winter days, when from morning to night the sun cruised across the blue, and on the cool nights when the stars rose and set on the vapourless rim of the desert. If by chance Hugh should change his mind, there was ample room for him in this house at Gurnah, and he would be very welcome.

A fortnight later Madden received a telegram from his friend. It stated that he had been unwell and was starting at once by long sea to Port Said, and would come straight up to Luxor. In due course he announced his arrival at Cairo and Madden went across the river next day to meet him: it was reassuring to find him as vital and active as ever, the picture of bronzed health. The two were alone that night, for Madden's colleague had gone for a week's trip up the Nile, and they sat out, when dinner was done, in the enclosed courtyard adjoining the house. Till then Madden had shied off the subject of himself and his health.

'Now I may as well tell you what's been amiss with me,' he said, 'for I know I look a fearful fraud as an invalid, and physically I've never been better in my life. Every organ has been functioning perfectly except one, but something suddenly went wrong there just once. It was like this.'

He paused a moment.

'After you left,' he said, 'I went on as usual for another month or so, very busy, very serene and, I may say, very successful. Then one morning I arrived at the hospital when there was one perfectly ordinary but major operation waiting for me. The patient, a man, was wheeled into the theatre anæsthetized, and I was just about to make the first incision into the abdomen, when I saw that there was sitting on his chest a little grey monkey. It was not looking at me, but at the fold of skin which I held between my thumb and finger. I knew, of course, that there was no monkey there, and that what I saw was a hallucination, and I think you'll agree that there was nothing much wrong with my nerves when I tell you that I went through the operation with clear eyes and an unshaking hand. I had to go on: there was no choice about the matter. I couldn't say: "Please take that monkey away," for I knew there was no monkey there. Nor could I say: "Somebody else must do this, as I have a distressing hallucination that there is a monkey sitting on the patient's chest." There would have been an end of me as a surgeon and no mistake. All the time I was at work it sat there absorbed in the most part in what I was doing and peering into the wound, but now and then it looked up at me, and chattered with rage. Once it fingered a spring-forceps which clipped a severed vein, and that was the worst moment of all. . . At the end it was carried out still balancing itself on the man's chest. . . I think I'll have a drink. Strongish, please. . . Thanks.'

'A beastly experience,' he said when he had drunk. 'Then I went straight away from the hospital to consult my old friend Robert Angus, the alienist and nerve-specialist, and told him exactly what had happened to me. He made several tests, he examined my eyes, tried my reflexes, took my bood-pressure: there was nothing wrong with any of them. Then he asked me questions about my general health and manner of life, and among these questions was one which I am sure has already occurred to you, namely, had anything occurred to me lately, or even remotely, which was likely to make me visualize a monkey. I told him that a few weeks ago a monkey with a broken lumbar vertebra had crawled on to my lawn, and that I had attempted an operation – binding the broken vertebra with wire – which had occurred to me before as a possibility. You remember the night, no doubt?'

'Perfectly,' said Madden, 'I started for Egypt next day. What happened to the monkey, by the way?'

'It lived for two days: I was pleased, because I had expected it would die under the anæsthetic, or immediately afterwards from shock. To get back to what I was telling you. When Angus had asked all his questions, he gave me a good wigging. He said that I had persistently overtaxed my brain for years, without giving it any rest or change of occupation, and that if I wanted to be of any further use in the world, I must drop my work at once for a couple of months. He told me that my brain was tired out and that I had persisted in stimulating it. A man like me, he said, was no better than a confirmed drunkard, and that, as a warning, I had had a touch of an appropriate delirium tremens. The cure was to drop work, just as a drunkard must drop drink. He laid it on hot and strong: he said I was on the verge of a breakdown, entirely owing to my own foolishness, but that I had wonderful physical health, and that if I did break down I should be a disgrace. Above all – and this seemed to me awfully sound advice – he told me not to attempt to avoid thinking about what had happened to me.

If I kept my mind mind off it, I should be perhaps driving it into the subconscious, and then there might be bad trouble. "Rub it in: think what a fool you've been," he said. "Face it, dwell on it, make yourself thoroughly ashamed of yourself." Monkeys, too: I wasn't to avoid the thought of monkeys. In fact, he recommended me to go straight away to the Zoological Gardens, and spend an hour in the monkey-house.'

'Odd treatment,' interrupted Madden.

'Brilliant treatment. My brain, he explained, had rebelled against its slavery, and had hoisted a red flag with the device of a monkey on it. I must show it that I wasn't frightened at its bogus monkeys. I must retort on it by making myself look at dozens of real ones which could bite and maul you savagely, instead of one little sham monkey that had no existence at all. At the same time I must take the red flag seriously, recognize there was danger, and rest. And he promised me that sham monkeys wouldn't trouble me again. Are there any real ones in Egypt, by the way?'

'Not so far as I know,' said Madden. 'But there must have been once, for there are many images of them in tombs and temples.'

'That's good. We'll keep their memory green and my brain cool. Well, there's my story. What do you think of it?'

'Terrifying,' said Madden. 'But you must have got nerves of iron to get through that operation with the monkey watching.'

'A hellish hour. Out of some disordered slime in my brain there had crawled this unbidden thing, which showed itself, apparently substantial, to my eyes. It didn't come from outside: my eyes hadn't told my brain that there was a monkey sitting on the man's chest, but my brain had told my eyes so, making fools of them. I felt as if someone whom I absolutely trusted had played me false. Then again I have wondered whether some instinct in my subconscious mind revolted against vivisection. My reason says that it is justified, for it teaches us how pain can be relieved and death postponed for human beings. But what if my subconscious persuaded my brain to give me a good fright, and reproduce before my eyes the semblance of a monkey, just when I was putting into practice what I had learned from dealing out pain and death to animals?'

He got up suddenly.

'What about bed?' he said. 'Five hours' sleep was enough for me when I was at work, but now I believe I could sleep the clock round every night.'

Young Wilson, Madden's colleague in the excavations, returned next day and the work went steadily on. One of them was on the spot to start it soon after sunrise, and either one or both of them were superintending it, with an interval of a couple of hours at noon, until sunset. When the mere work of clearing the face of the sandstone cliff was in progress and of carting away the silted soil, the presence of one of them sufficed, for there was nothing to do but to see that the workmen shovelled industriously, and passed regularly with their baskets of earth and sand on their shoulders to the dumping-grounds, which stretched away from the area to be excavated, in lengthening peninsulas of trodden soil. But, as they advanced along the sandstone ridge, there would now and then appear a chiselled smoothness in the cliff and then both must be alert. There was great excitement to see if, when they exposed the hewn slab that formed the door into the tomb, it had escaped ancient marauders, and still stood in place and intact for the modern to explore. But now for many days they came upon no sepulchre that had not already been opened. The mummy, in these cases, had been unwound in the search for necklaces and scarabs, and its scattered bones lay about. Madden was always at pains to reinter these.

At first Hugh Morris was assiduous in watching the excavations, but as day after day went by without anything of interest turning up, his attendance grew less frequent: it was too much of a holiday to watch the day-long removal of sand from one place to another. He visited the Tomb of the Kings, he went across the river and saw the temples at Karnak, but his appetite for antiquities was small. On other days he rode in the desert, or spent the day with friends at one of the Luxor hotels. He came home from there one evening in rare good spirits, for he had played lawn-tennis with a woman on whom he had operated for malignant tumour six months before and she had skipped about the court like a two-year-old. 'God, how I want to be at work again,' he exclaimed. 'I wonder

whether I ought not to have stuck it out, and defied my brain
to frighten me with bogies.'

The weeks passed on, and now there were but two days
left before his return to England, where he hoped to resume
work at once: his tickets were taken and his berth booked. As
he sat over breakfast that morning with Wilson, there came a
workman from the excavation, with a note scribbled in hot
haste by Madden, to say that they had just come upon a
tomb which seemed to be unrifled, for the slab that closed it
was in place and unbroken. To Wilson, the news was like the
sight of a sail to a marooned mariner, and when, a quarter of
an hour later, Morris followed him, he was just in time to see
the slab prised away. There was no sarcophagus within, for
the rock walls did duty for that, but there lay there,
varnished and bright in hue as if painted yesterday, the
mummycase roughly following the outline of the human
form. By it stood the alabaster vases containing the entrails
of the dead, and at each corner of the sepulchre there were
carved out of the sandstone rock, forming, as it were, pillars
to support the roof, thick-set images of squatting apes. The
mummy-case was hoisted out and carried away by workmen
on a bier of boards into the courtyard of the excavators'
house at Gurnah, for the opening of it and the unwrapping of
the dead.

They got to work that evening directly they had fed: the
face painted on the lid was that of a girl or young woman,
and presently deciphering the hieroglyphic inscription,
Madden read out that within lay the body of A-pen-ara,
daughter of the overseer of the cattle of Senmut.

'Then follow the usual formulas,' he said. 'Yes, yes . . . ah,
you'll be interested in this, Hugh, for you asked me once
about it. A-pen-ara curses any who desecrates or meddles
with her bones, and should anyone do so, the guardians of
her sepulchre will see to him, and he shall die childless and
in panic and agony; also the guardian of her sepulchre will
tear the hair from his head and scoop his eyes from their
sockets, and pluck the thumbs from his right hand, as a man
plucks the young blade of corn from its sheath.'

Morris laughed.

'Very pretty little attentions,' he said. 'And who are the

guardians of this sweet young lady's sepulchre? Those four great apes carved at the corners?'

'No doubt. But we won't trouble them, for to-morrow I shall bury Miss A-pen-ara's bones again with all decency in the trench at the foot of her tomb. They'll be safer there, for if we put them back where we found them, there would be pieces of her hawked about by half the donkey-boys in Luxor in a few days. "Buy a mummy hand, lady? . . . Foot of a Gyppy Queen, only ten piastres, gentlemen" . . . Now for the unwinding.'

It was dark by now, and Wilson fetched out a paraffin lamp, which burned unwaveringly in the still air. The lid of the mummy-case was easily detached, and within was the slim, swaddled body. The embalming had not been very thoroughly done, for all the skin and flesh had perished from the head, leaving only bones of the skull stained brown with bitumen. Round it was a mop of hair, which with the ingress of the air subsided like a belated *soufflé*, and crumbled into dust. The cloth that swathes the body was as brittle, but round the neck, still just holding together, was a collar of curious and rare workmanship: little ivory figures of squatting apes alternated with silver beads. But again a touch broke the thread that strung them together, and each had to be picked out singly. A bracelet of scarabs and cornelians still clasped one of the fleshless wrists, and then they turned the body over in order to get at the members of the necklace which lay beneath the nape. The rotted mummy-cloth fell away altogether from the back, disclosing the shoulder-blades and the spine down as far as the pelvis. Here the embalming had been better done, for the bones still held together with remnants of muscle and cartilage.

Hugh Morris suddenly sprang to his feet.

'My God, look there!' he cried, 'one of the lumbar vertebræ, there at the base of the spine, has been broken and clamped together with a metal band. To hell with your antiquities: let me come and examine something much more modern than any of us!'

He pushed Jack Madden aside, and peered at this marvel of surgery.

'Put the lamp closer,' he said, as if directing some nurse at an operation. 'Yes: that vertebra has been broken right across and has been clamped together. No one has ever, as far as I know, attempted such an operation except myself, and I have only performed it on that little paralysed monkey that crept into my garden one night. But some Egyptian surgeon, more than three thousand years ago, performed it on a woman. And look, look! She lived afterwards, for the broken vertebra put out that bony efflorescence of healing which has encroached over the metal band. That's a slow process, and it must have taken place during her lifetime, for there is no such energy in a corpse. The woman lived long: probably she recovered completely. And my wretched little monkey only lived two days and was dying all the time.'

Those questing hawk-visioned fingers of the surgeon perceived more finely than actual sight, and now he closed his eyes as the tip of them felt their way about the fracture in the broken vertebra and the clamping metal band.

'The band doesn't encircle the bone,' he said, 'and there are no studs attaching it. There must have been a spring in it, which, when it was clasped there, kept it tight. It has been clamped round the bone itself: the surgeon must have scraped the verebra clean of flesh before he attached it. I would give two years of my life to have looked on, like a student, at that masterpiece of skill, and it was worth while giving up two months of my work only to have seen the result. And the injury itself is so rare, this breaking of a spinal vertebra. To be sure, the hangman does something of the sort, but there's no mending that! Good Lord, my holiday has not been a waste of time!'

Madden settled that it was not worth while to send the mummy-case to the museum at Gizeh, for it was of a very ordinary type, and when the examination was over they lifted the body back into it, for reinterment next day. It was now long after midnight and presently the house was dark.

Hugh Morris slept on the ground-floor in a room adjoining the yard where the mummy-case lay. He remained long awake marvelling at that astonishing piece of surgical skill performed, according to Madden, some thirty-five centuries ago. So occupied had his mind been with homage that not till now did he realize that the tangible proof and witness of the

operation would to-morrow be buried again and lost to science. He must persuade Madden to let him detach at least
three of the vertebræ, the mended one and those immediately
above and below it, and take them back to England as demonstration of what could be done: he would lecture on his exhibit
and present it to the Royal College of Surgeons for example
and incitement. Other trained eyes beside his own must see
what had been successfully achieved by some unknown
operator in the nineteenth dynasty . . . But supposing
Madden refused? He always made a point of scrupulously
reburying these remains: it was a principle with him, and no
doubt some superstition-complex – the hardest of all to combat with because of its sheer unreasonableness – was involved.
Briefly, it was impossible to risk the chance of his refusal.

He got out of bed, listened for a moment by his door, and
then softly went out into the yard. The moon had risen, for the
brightness of the stars was paled, and though no direct rays
shone into the walled enclosure, the dusk was dispersed by the
toneless luminosity of the sky, and he had no need of a lamp.
He drew the lid off the coffin, and folded back the tattered
cerements which Madden had replaced over the body. He had
thought that those lower vertebræ of which he was determined
to possess himself would be easily detached, so far perished
were the muscle and cartilage which held them together, but
they cohered as if they had been clamped, and it required the
utmost force of his powerful fingers to snap the spine, and as
he did so the severed bones cracked as with the noise of a
pistol-shot. But there was no sign that anyone in the house
had heard it, there came no sound of steps, nor lights in the
windows. One more fracture was needed, and then the relic
was his. Before he replaced the ragged cloths he looked again
at the stained fleshless bones. Shadow dwelt in the empty
eye-sockets, as if black sunken eyes still lay there, fixedly
regarding him, the lipless mouth snarled and grimaced. Even
as he looked some change came over its aspect, and for one
brief moment he fancied that there lay staring up at him the
face of a great brown ape. But instantly that illusion vanished,
and replacing the lid he went back to his room.

The mummy-case was reinterred next day, and two evenings after Morris left Luxor by the night train for Cairo, to

join a homeward-bound P & O at Port Said. There were some hours to spare before his ship sailed, and having deposited his luggage, including a locked leather despatch-case, on board, he lunched at the Café Tewfik near the quay. There was a garden in front of it with palm trees and trellises gaily clad in bougainvillias: a low wooden rail separated it from the street, and Morris had a table close to this. As he ate he watched the polychromatic pageant of Eastern life passing by: there were Egyptian officials in broad-cloth frock coats and red fezzes; barefooted splay-toed fellahin in blue gabardines; veiled women in white making stealthy eyes at passers-by; half-naked gutter-snipes, one with a sprig of scarlet hibiscus behind his ear; travellers from India with solar topees and an air of aloof British superiority; dishevelled sons of the Prophet in green turbans; a stately sheik in a white *burnous*; French painted ladies of a professional class with lace-rimmed para-sols and provocative glances; a wild-eyed dervish in an accordion-pleated skirt, chewing betel-nut and slightly foaming at the mouth. A Greek boot-black with box adorned with brass plaques tapped his brushes on it to encourage customers, an Egyptian girl squatted in the gutter beside a gramophone, steamers passing into the Canal hooted on their syrens.

Then at the edge of the pavement there sauntered by a young Italian harnessed to a barrel-organ: with one hand he ground out a popular air by Verdi, in the other he held out a tin can for the tributes of music-lovers: a small monkey in a yellow jacket, tethered to his wrist, sat on the top of his instrument. The musician had come opposite the table where Morris sat: Morris liked the gay tinkling tune, and feeling in his pocket for a piastre, he beckoned to him. The boy grinned and stepped up to the rail.

Then suddenly the melancholy-eyed monkey leaped from its place on the organ and sprang on to the table by which Morris sat. It alighted there, chattering with rage in a crash of broken glass. A flower-vase was upset, a plate clattered on to the floor. Morris's coffee-cup discharged its black contents on the tablecloth. Next moment the Italian had twitched the frenzied little beast back to him, and it fell head downwards on the pavement. A shrill hubbub arose, the waiter at

Morris's table hurried up with voluble execrations, a
policeman kicked out at the monkey as it lay on the ground,
the barrel-organ tottered and crashed on the roadway. Then
all subsided again, and the Italian boy picked up the little
body from the pavement. He held it out in his hands to
Morris.

'*E morto,*' he said.

'Serves it right, too,' retorted Morris. 'Why did it fly at me
like that?'

He travelled back to London by long sea, and day after day
that tragic little incident, in which he had had no responsible
part, began to make a sort of colouring matter in his mind
during those hours of lazy leisure on ship-board, when a man
gives about an equal inattention to the book he reads and to
what passes round him. Sometimes if the shadow of a seagull
overhead slid across the deck towards him, there leaped into
his brain, before his eyes could reassure him, the ludicrous
fancy that this shadow was a monkey springing at him. One
day they ran into a gale from the west: there was a crash of
glass at his elbow as a sudden lurch of the ship upset a laden
steward, and Morris jumped from his seat thinking that a
monkey had leaped on to his table again. There was a
cinematograph show in the saloon one evening, in which some
naturalist exhibited the films he had taken of wild life in
Indian jungles: when he put on the screen the picture of a
company of monkeys swinging their way through the trees
Morris involuntarily clutched the sides of his chair in hideous
panic that lasted but a fraction of a second, until he recalled to
himself that he was only looking at a film in the saloon of a
steamer passing up the coast of Portugal. He came sleepy into
his cabin one night and saw some animal crouching by the
locked leather despatch-case. His breath caught in his throat
before he perceived that this was a friendly cat which rose
with gleaming eyes and arched its back . . .

These fantastic unreasonable alarms were disquieting. He
had as yet no repetition of the hallucination that he saw a
monkey, but some deep-buried 'idea,' to cure which he had
taken two months' holiday, was still unpurged from his mind.
He must consult Robert Angus again when he got home, and
seek further advice. Probably that incident at Port Said had

rekindled the obscure trouble, and there was this added to it, that he knew he was now frightened of real monkeys: there was terror sprouting in the dark of his soul. But as for it having any connection with his pilfered treasure, so rank and childish a superstition deserved only the ridicule he gave it. Often he unlocked his leather case and sat poring over that miracle of surgery which made practical again long-forgotten dexterities.

But it was good to be back in England. For the last three days of the voyage no menace had flashed out on him from the unknown dusks, and surely he had been disquieting himself in vain. There was a light mist lying over Regent's Park on this warm March evening, and a drizzle of rain was falling. He made an appointment for the next morning with the specialist, he telephoned to the hospital that he had returned and hoped to resume work at once. He dined in very good spirits, talking to his manservant, and, as subsequently came out, he showed him his treasured bones, telling him that he had taken the relic from a mummy which he had seen unwrapped and that he meant to lecture on it. When he went up to bed he carried the leather case with him. Bed was comfortable after the ship's berth, and through his open window came the soft hissing of the rain on to the shrubs outside.

His servant slept in the room immediately over his. A little before dawn he woke with a start, roused by horrible cries from somewhere close at hand. Then came words yelled out in a voice that he knew:

'Help! Help!' it cried. 'O my God, my God! Ah – h – ' and it rose to a scream again.

The man hurried down and clicked on the light in his master's room as he entered. The cries had ceased: only a low moaning came from the bed. A huge ape with busy hands was bending over it; then taking up the body that lay there by the neck and the hips he bent it backwards and it cracked like a dry stick. Then it tore open the leather case that was on a table by the bedside, and with something that gleamed white in its dripping fingers it shambled to the window and disappeared.

A doctor arrived within half an hour, but too late. Handfuls of hair with flaps of skin attached had been torn from the head of the murdered man, both eyes were scooped out of their sockets, the right thumb had been plucked off the hand, and the back was broken across the lower vertebræ.

Nothing has since come to light which could rationally explain the tragedy. No large ape had escaped from the neighbouring Zoological Gardens, or, as far as could be ascertained, from elsewhere, nor was the monstrous visitor of that night ever seen again. Morris's servant had only had the briefest sight of it, and his description of it at the inquest did not tally with that of any known simian type. And the sequel was even more mysterious, for Madden, returing to England at the close of the season in Egypt, had asked Morris's servant exactly what it was that his master had shown him the evening before as having been taken by him from a mummy which he had seen unwrapped, and had got from him a sufficiently conclusive account of it. Next autumn he continued his excavations in the cemetery at Gurnah, and he disinterred once more the mummy-case of A-pen-ara and opened it. But the spinal vertebræ were all in place and complete: one had round it the silver clip which Morris had hailed as a unique achievement in surgery.

THE MUMMY'S GHOST

by Griffin Jay & Henry Sucher

Near the titanic Sphinx of Egypt, past the rows of gigantic statues of Pharaoh Rameses, lies a temple – the Temple of Arkhon. Its columns, eroded by the desert sand, having long since fallen, and the stones of its structure are scattered about. The temple has nearly crumbled but its priests have survived.

A tall, dignified Egyptian ascends the steps, entering the altar room. There he is met by the reigning Priest of Arkhon, and he bows to the withering man. As the Priest seats himself upon his throne, he announces to the visitor, Youssef Bey, that he is ready to die. He tells Youssef to take his place as High Priest and that his purpose is to journey to America to retrieve Kharis and Ananka, both of whom were shipped there previously.

Elsewhere, in the small town of Mapleton in New England, a professor of Egyptology is lecturing to a classroom of students at school. The subject of the lecture is Kharis, the Living Mummy, and as Prof. Norman progresses, the students listen in rapt attention. They are told of the secret society of Arkhon, which harbours the most sacred mummies throughout the centuries. Norman tells of Kharis' destruction:

'The Monster itself was consumed in the flames of the burial room.'

He continues, telling of Kharis' fantastic longevity due to tana leaves, and the pupils are amazed, shocked to disbelief.

'But how they could preserve life indefinitely is still a mystery,' he adds, not knowing exactly how the leaves were used.

The dismissal bell rings and the class leaves. On the outside, one of the students, Tom Herbie, is teased about his fiancée, Amina Mansori, a beautiful young lady of Egyptian descent, but Tom just passes it off. Tom goes to one of the nearby houses, stepping inside, and he finds Amina in her library. They greet each other and he playfully lifts up her pet monkey. Walking around the room, Tom happens to see a volume on the tombs of Egypt, and he becomes interested in it, remarking that Prof. Norman might like to read it. But his comments are interrupted when he sees a pained expression on Amina's face.

'Something happens to me when I think of Egypt,' she explains.

She rises from her seat and almost faints; Tom helps her to her room. He asks her to go with him to a theatre and she accepts the invitation, but adds that she must first take a rest in order to overcome her weakness.

In Egypt, at the same time, Youssef Bey and the High Priest are gazing into an urn from which vapours of mystic time are billowing, and the High Priest narrates the story of Kharis and his princess Ananka. He proceeds:

Over 3000 years ago, Ananka, daughter of Pharaoh Amenophis, died, and she was buried with great ceremony. Before her entombment, her father bade her farewell forever, and nearby, unseen among the crowd, Ananka's forbidden lover, Kharis, a prince of the royal house, looked on in tears. He refused to believe that she would no longer be with him, so he broke into the sacred altar room of one of the temples. There, he removed the coffer of tana leaves from its hiding place at the feet of the idol Isis, knowing that he could revive her with them. This act, however, angered the gods, and even the idol moved in anger. The ankh held in Isis' hand moved forward to point accusingly at Kharis. Fleeing in fear, he escaped with the leaves and withdrew to her tomb to recite the incantation for resurrection, but the scribes learned of the theft and arrested him. Brought before Amenophis, he was adjudged guilty of sacrilege and condemned to be mummified alive. It was decreed in the sacred writings of Thoth that all who defile the temple of Isis must die a terrible, agonized death. Kharis was taken to the embalming room, where he was wrapped in gauze soaked with liquid, and his tongue was cut out to prevent his unholy oaths from being heard. After the last piece of gauze was wrapped about him, he was placed in a case and taken to

an unmarked tomb near the Valley of the Seven Jackals – where Ananka
was buried. The case was lowered into it, and the slaves who
participated in the burial were slain. No one but the Priests of Arkhon
would ever know of Kharis' burial place. Immediately after, the priests
moved Kharis to a tomb at the entrance of Ananka's tomb, along with
the tana leaves he had stolen. It was ordained by Amon-Ra that Kharis
would remain immortal in order to guard Ananka from desecration. An
American archaeologist, thousands of years later, stumbled upon the two,
and they were transported to America. One priest had been recently sent
there to retrieve the two, but he had failed and he was met by a violent
death. Kharis supposedly was destroyed by fire.

'But through the secret message brought to us by the Holy
Spirit of Amon-Ra,' the High Priest says, 'we know that he is
still alive.'

The High Priest begins to tell Youssef of his duties as the
new High Priest of Arkhon, and he hands him the priestly
medallion.

'Now swear by the ancient gods of Egypt that you shall
never rest until Kharis and Princess Ananka are returned to
their rightful resting places in these tombs,' he says, pointing
to the tombs inscribed upon the medallion.

Youssef speaks the oath and the High Priest tells Youssef
the secrets of the tana leaves. As the High Priest finishes, he
sits down, collapsing in the arms of Death.

Elsewhere, that night, Professor Norman is sitting in his
study in deep contemplation, busily translating an ancient
Egyptian hieroglyphic. Suddenly his face brightens in success.
'I have it!' he jubilantly bursts forth.

Instantly, Ellen, his wife, enters the room, complaining
that it is far beyond his bedtime, but he refuses to retire,
telling her that he has discovered the secret of the tana leaves
– nine tana leaves each night during the cycle of the full moon
to keep movement in Kharis' withering limbs. Not understanding her husband's scientific find, Ellen departs for bed,
and Norman decides to try to put the knowledge to use – he
places nine of the crumbling leaves into an urn of boiling
water, and the vapours rise mystically into the air.

Nearby, in the forest Kharis is limping in his rotting rags
when he senses the precious tana leaves. He turns, heading
towards Professor Norman's house, and he comes to a fence.

He mightily crashes through, continuing onward. In Norman's home, his houseguest Amina is sleeping, but she begins to stir restlessly. As if in a trance, she arises from bed, going out of the room, and at the same time, Kharis is approaching the house. Amina goes out on the porch, walking out in the yard, and she continues into the woods nearby. Only moments later Kharis arrives, stopping before the library of Norman, and he ominously steps to the door. In the room before him, Norman sits and he seems to sense Kharis' presence. As Norman turns in horror, Kharis advances, his hand lifted at Norman's neck, and Norman moves back with fear spread across his face. Kharis seizes his neck, choking him to death, and the ancient Egyptian lifts the urn aside, leaving, and nearby, Amina sees him. She immediately faints from the sight of the walking mummy and as her arm lies on the grass, a scarab-birthmark reveals itself.

The following morning, as Tom is dressing, one of his friends rushes in excitedly.

'Norman's dead!' he chatters. 'Murdered!'

Tom then is told that Amina, found outside the house when the body was discovered, is the prime suspect. Instantly Tom speeds out to investigate.

At Norman's study, the Sheriff is examining Norman's corpse.

'Strangulation,' he mutters. 'Traces of foreign substance on his throat . . . It's mould!'

'The mummy!' someone gasps.

Ellen is brought in and tells Sheriff Elwood that Norman was working on some Egyptian hieroglyphics that night. Elwood has Amina questioned and she tells him she cannot remember what happened the night before to make her go out in the garden. Just then, Tom rushes in angrily, contending that Amina could not possibly be the murderess, for she was at the theatre with him that night when Norman was murdered. When asked what time they returned, Tom tells the Sheriff, who instantly suspects that the murder took place an hour after they returned, thereby once more pointing a condemning finger at Amina. Amina is released into Tom's custody with the reminder that she must stay in Mapleton, and the two leave. Outside, however, Amina turns, startled, and Tom inquires what is wrong. She promptly excuses herself by saying nothing but her nerves.

Soon, news of the Mummy Murder leaks out, and newspapers all around the country spread the fearful rumours. In most of the papers this gaping headline is screamed:

MUMMY BELIEVED TO BE BACK
IN NEW ENGLAND!

People are warned to stay at home in Mapleton, and plenty of guards are set up. The police caution a group of women to be careful, while in an old shack near the swamp, Youssef Bey is mumbling cryptic chants over a steaming urn. He prays to Amon-Ra for protection:

'*O Mighty Gods of Egypt, protect me with your shielding arms. Bring Kharis to me. Guide him here where I await him.*'

Prowling through the forest not far away, Kharis suddenly stops in his path, sensing Youssef's message, but he continues. At the same moment, near Kharis, Tom and Amina drive up and stop their car. Tom tells Amina that she has been acting strangely lately and his dog, Peanuts, begins to bark nervously. Amina sees Kharis coming from the distance but Tom does not and she tries to conceal seeing him. Tom kisses her but Amina sees a shadow in the bushes nearby and Peanuts barks again. Suddenly, a man bursts forth from the brush, carrying a shotgun, and he trips, apologizing for scaring them. It is Ben, one of the local farmers who are hunting for Kharis. Frightened, Amina asks to go home, and Tom drives her.

Later, Kharis limps into the field near Ben's home and Ben's dog King begins to bark too. Kharis heads towards the barn and King pursues him, biting the wrappings around his leg. The monstrous mummy enters the barn, unmindful of the dog, but Ben's wife hears the commotion and gazes out of the window above the barn. Just as she does, Ben himself returns, and he hears King barking in the barn. Readying his shotgun, Ben cautiously steps inside to meet Kharis, who attacks him. Ben emits a chilling scream, and his wife runs downstairs to the barn to find Ben murdered – and the wall torn out. King barks towards the forest.

The Sheriff is summoned and he examines Ben. Looking at the torn-out wall, he returns with a diagnosis.

'No thief killed Ben,' he says. 'And nothing human tore through that wall.'

At the shack, Kharis comes to Youssef, who thanks Amon-Ra for answering his prayers.

'Mighty Amon-Ra, I thank thee for guiding Kharis to me,' he says. Then turning to Kharis, he says, 'Come, Kharis.'

The two step out into the moonlit night.

Miles away, sometime later, inside the building inscribed **SCRIPPS MUSEUM** the guide is lecturing to a few people on Princess Ananka, while they stare with unbroken attention at the mummy of Ananka herself. As they move on to the next exhibit, Youssef remains at the mummy case. There he prays for forgiveness for allowing the unbelieving heretics to look upon Ananka. After midnight, the night watchman peeks into the room, and, seeing no one there, moves on. Unnoticed, Youssef steps out of the darkness. The drowsy night watchman retires for the night to a small room in the nearby rear of the museum, and he hangs his cap on the hand of a Greek statue. Taking his shoes off, he reclines in his favourite chair to read a mystery novel, and for background music, turns the radio on.

Kharis, outside, gropes to the delivery entrance of the museum, banging on the metallic door, but in vain.

The night watchman is confronted by a mystery announcer instead of music, and the unknowingly prophetic man declares in sombre tones:

'This is the hour of death! The forces of evil stand at the threshold . . . A man will die tonight!'

Kharis manages to force his entrance into the museum and he limps to the chamber where Ananka lies. There, Youssef is burning two urns of incense at the head and foot of her mummy case.

'The hour of fulfilment is here. Behold Ananka, the princess of your forbidden love!'

Youssef gestures towards the hideous mummy lying lifelessly in the case and Kharis gently touches the wrappings about her deathly face.

At that same instant, Amina awakens from a sound sleep and screams hysterically. Her housekeeper, Mrs Drake, rushes in to try to calm her.

Kharis sees the magnificent ugliness of his bride, and the structure beneath the wrappings of Ananka crumble into thin air. Angered, he hurls the case upon its side, and Youssef offers no hindrance to Kharis' actions, for he too knows that Ananka's spirit has moved to another body.

'Our old mission will be fulfilled,' he promises Kharis.

The sound of Kharis' destructive spell has meanwhile brought the night watchman forward, armed with a loaded pistol. Finding only Youssef, he orders him to back away, but Youssef stands immobile, a wicked smile confidently spread across his lips. As the watchman approaches Youssef, the reason for his confidence makes itself known. Kharis moves from the shadows, attacking the old man, who is almost instantly slain. The watchman falls limply to the floor and Youssef leads Kharis away.

At her home, Amina is weeping and babbling about 'a strange feeling she had been struck by, and Mrs Drake comforts her.

'I could feel his hands touching me,' she cries, telling of her sensing someone touching her face.

Mrs Drake tells her that it was only a nightmare.

The following morning Tom goes to Sheriff Elwood, begging him to let Amina go free, but he flatly refuses, saying she is still a suspect – although the Mummy has been declared the murderer.

'Just to make things a little more involved,' he tells Tom, 'a man was murdered in the Scripps Museum last night.'

A police investigator is called in to diagnose the murder, and this man, the Inspector, begins to question Dr Hyatt, the curator of the Egyptian section. He inquires if there were anything else that occurred out of the ordinary, and Hyatt tells him in reply that the mummy of Ananka has vanished in a remarkable manner – *the body was stolen from inside the wrappings, which were untouched!* The Inspector sees an inscription on the side of the overturned case and asks Hyatt to decipher it. He obliges:

'Herein rests, and must forever rest, the Princess Ananka, third daughter of Amenophis.'

Continuing, he reads a passage indirectly mentioning reincarnation, and the Inspector decides to go to Mapleton to recheck the Norman murder. He requests that Hyatt accompany him to facilitate translation if necessary.

Soon the Inspector, Hyatt and the Sheriff and his men are gathered in Norman's home to examine the Mad Mummy Murder Mystery, and they question everyone. The Sheriff forms a plan to trap Kharis should he return – a pit would be dug in the floor, in Kharis' probable path, and they would summon him with tana leaves. Coming for the lifegiving fluid, he would fall into the pit and be trapped. But how to summon Kharis remains a mystery.

At his finacée's home, Tom talks to Amina, asking her to go with him to his house, away from the Mummy, but she is reluctant to break the Sheriff's orders.

'My family is busy getting out the heirloom jewels for the bride,' he tells her, cryptically proposing.

She recognizes this and chatters, 'Bride? Oh, no!'

She refuses to endanger Tom by marrying him but is finally persuaded. Suddenly Mrs Drake appears and tells Amina it is time to go to bed. Tom departs, leaving Peanuts with Amina to act as a watchdog.

Later that night, Youssef and Kharis are in the abandoned shack near the swamp edge, and Youssef is attempting to find the whereabouts of Ananka's spirit, while Kharis stands by anxiously. Everything done unsuccessfuly, Youssef resorts to prayer:

'Show me her dwelling place, O Amon-Ra. Shed your light upon the darkness of my groping. Hear my prayer.'

Instantly, the shutter of the window is opened by an unseen force, for there is no wind, and a mystic moonbeam is focused on the medallion of Youssef. He realizes its implications and dispatches Kharis again.

'By the light of the sign you will know her,' he says. 'Go.'

Meanwhile, the Sheriff and the Inspector are questioning Ellen about her husband, and they ask her where he was sitting the fateful night. She points out the seat and Hyatt is told to sit there. As the interrogation continues, she is asked about the tana leaves.

'He was excited about something,' she recalls. 'I think it was something about "nine".'

'Nine!' Hyatt jubilantly exclaims. 'Nine tana leaves, that's what he meant!'

The Sheriff sends Ellen away and Hyatt places nine crumbling tana leaves in the boiling urn, planning to summon Kharis into their trap.

In the forest far away, Kharis seems to sense the aroma, and he turns, limping toward the house. In Amina's room nearby, Peanuts whimpers, and Amina herself awakens, rising hypnotically. She goes out of the door to the patio and sees Kharis nearing her. She immediately faints and he bends awkwardly down beside her. Peanuts is barking helplessly as Kharis carries Amina away. Passing near his home, Kharis and Ananka-Amina are sighted by a man, who promptly calls Tom on the telephone. Tom is awakened by the call and when he hears of Amina's abduction he swiftly leaps up, instructing the caller to summon the police also.

The Sheriff is giving instructions to his men about the ten-foot pit, and he dismisses them to their outside posts. The Inspector, however, stops him, contending that all of the men are needed at the pit to catch the maddened mummy. The Sheriff accedes to his wishes.

Kharis is carrying Amina across a wooden bridge and he turns off the side, going down a swampside path. Peanuts chases him, barking angrily, and far behind, Tom is following Peanuts, through the high brush and weeds.

Mrs Drake, having learned of Amina's kidnapping, becomes hysterical and rushes wildly to Norman's home, where she almost dashes into the pit made for Kharis, but the Sheriff stops her in time. They take her inside to calm her and to hear her story.

Tom races across the bridge. He catches up with Peanuts, who obediently guides him in Kharis' tracks. He follows the dog in earnest pursuit.

Kharis reaches the shack, carrying Amina inside, and he sets her upon a table in the middle of the room. Near the door,

Youssef stands, looking on enviously as the beautiful raven-haired lovely – Kharis' bride – lies unconscious.

'And the sign, Ananka,' Youssef says, pointing to the scarab-birthmark of Ananka. 'She's beautiful, Kharis – as she was centuries ago. The will of Amon-Ra has been done.'

Mrs Drake tells the Sheriff her tale and they race after Kharis, who has long since gone.

Presently, Amina awakens and, looking around, she sees the face of Kharis. Gasping at the sight, she asks where she is and why she is there. Youssef tells her that she is the Princess Ananka, but she confesses she knows nothing of any such person.

'Centuries ago, you died an accursed death,' he says.

'No!' she says.

Tom nears the shack while the Sheriff's men are yet far behind him in pursuit.

Youssef fills a hypodermic needle with tana fluid for embalming and straps Amina to the table. As he is about to inject the serum into her veins, he hesitates. A tiny, whispering voice inside his head warns him not to do it, but to keep Amina for himself. It almost convinces him, but he remembers that it was his sacred pledge.

'O Mighty Isis,' he mumbles, 'protect me in this hour of temptation.'

Youssef hears the voice again, and it tells him to use tana leaves on Amina to make her immortal, instead of embalming her in horrible wrapping. He surrenders to temptation and unties her, lifting a cup of tana liquid to her lips.

'Here in this cup is my gift of life to you,' he tells her. 'I will make you immortal. We will not return to Egypt.'

Kharis overhears Youssef's treachery, and his ashen face becomes aglow with anger. He slowly moves toward Youssef.

'Has any other man offered the gift of eternal life to his bride?' he asks her proudly.

Kharis suddenly strikes the cup from Youssef's hands and he flees in terror from Kharis. Vainly, Youssef tries to convince Kharis that they will return to Egypt, but Kharis knows the truth. Kharis pursues him, seizing him, and Youssef is hurled to the ground below – and his death.

As Youssef's body strikes the ground, it falls before Tom,

who rushes to the shack. There he is confronted by Kharis, and a battle between the two begins. Tom seizes an axe, swinging it at his would-be murderer, but in vain. Kharis strikes him, knocking him backwards into unconsciousness. Peanuts runs to Tom.

Kharis ascends the ramp to the shack and lifts Amina up in his arms. Her hair has turned grey in the brief interval! He carries her out to the back, down a series of ladders, and the Sheriff and his men arrive at last. They rush into the shack, which they find abandoned, except for Egyptian pottery.

'Looks like somebody else has been messing around with tana leaves,' someone says.

'And not so long ago.'

Kharis carries Amina through a nearby field, and Tom revives. Peanuts begins to bark and renews his pursuit of Kharis, and they all follow him. Rushing through the swampside reeds, Tom sees Kharis limping away, Amina in his arms. As she is carried onward, Amina is slowly being transformed – her hair turns white, her hands and feet wrinkle and shrivel. Tom and the others carry on the chase to the banks of a swampy pool where they look on helplessly. Kharis steps into the water, wading slowly up to waist-level, and Tom attempts to follow.

'You can't go in that swamp!' the Sheriff shouts. 'It's certain death!'

And Tom steps into the water, when he sees the face of his sweetheart – beak nose, wrinkled skin, warts, the complete appearance of a woman two hundred years old! Kharis sinks under the mud and the water bubbles over their heads.

Tom sadly leaves with the others, going silently, and Peanuts surveys the quicksand grave of Amina and Kharis.

The warning of the High Priest to Youssef echoes, unheard, through the sky:

'The fate of those who disobey the will of the gods shall be a cruel and violent death.'

The last bubbles rise no more.

THE SECRET OF SEBEK

by Robert Bloch

I should never have attended Henricus Vanning's costume ball. Even if the tragedy had not occurred, I would be better off had I refused his invitation that night. Now that I have left New Orleans I can view the episode in saner light, and I know that I made a mistake. The remembrance of that final inexplicable moment is a horror that I still cannot face with a rational mind. Had I suspected beforehand, I might now be spared the recurrent nightmares which afflict me.

But at that time of which I speak there was no premonition to guide me. I was a stranger in the Louisiana city, and very lonely. The Mardi Gras season served only to accentuate my feeling of utter isolation. During the first two evenings of celebration, tired from long vigils at the typewriter, I wandered alien and alone along the quaintly twisted streets, and the crowds that hustled by seemed to mock my solitude.

My work at the time was very exhausting – I was doing a series of Egyptian stories for a magazine – and my mental state was a bit off. During the day I sat in my quiet room and gave my mind over to images of Nyarlathotep, Bubastis, and Anubis; my thoughts were peopled with the priestly pageantries of olden times. And in the evenings I walked unknown amidst thoughtless throngs more unreal than the fanciful figures of the past.

But enough of excuses. To be perfectly frank, when I left the house that third night after a weary day, I expressly intended to get drunk. I entered a café at dusk, dining lavishly with a bottle of peach brandy. The place was hot and crowded; the ribald, costumed masqueraders all seemed to be enjoying the reign of Momus.

After a time this did not disturb me. Four generous goblets of the really excellent liqueur had set the blood running like elixir in my veins; bold, reckless dreams cascaded through my head. I now gazed at the impersonal swarms about me with new interest and understanding. They too were trying to escape tonight – escape from maddening monotony and humdrum commonplace. The fat man in the clown costume near by had looked silly an hour ago; now I seemed to sympathize with him. I sensed the frustration behind the masks these strangers wore; appreciated how valiantly they strove to find forgetfulness in the Mardi Gras.

I would forget, too. The bottle was emptied. I left the café and once more walked the streets, but this time I no longer had any feeling of isolation. I strode along like the carnival king himself, and traded gibe for gibe with chance buffeters.

Here memory is temporarily blurred. I went into a club lounge for scotch and soda, then continued on my way. Where my feet led me I cannot say. I seemed to float along effortlessly, but my mind was crystal-clear.

I was not thinking of mundane things. Through some quirk I recalled work again, and I contemplated ancient Egypt. Through crumbled centuries I moved, in visions of secret splendour.

I lurched down a dim, deserted street.

I walked through templed Thebes, while sphinxes stared.

I turned into a lighted thoroughfare where revellers danced.

I mingled with the white-clad acolytes adoring sacred Apis.

The carousing mob blew paper trumpets, strewed confetti.

To the shrill litany of lutes the temple virgins showered me with roses red as the blood of betrayed Osiris.

Thus I passed through streets of saturnalia, my thoughts still wine-wafted and far away. It was all very much like a dream when at last I entered that obscure thoroughfare in the heart of the Creole district. Tall houses reared deserted on either side; darkened, dingy domiciles deserted by their owners, who mingled with the merrymakers amidst more pleasant surroundings. The buildings were old; in the fashion of ancient days they stood narrowly together, row on row.

They are like untenanted mummy-cases in some forgotten tomb; they stand deserted by the maggot and the worm.

From the steeply gabled roofs little black windows yawned.

They are empty, like the eyeless sockets of a skull, and like a skull they too hide secrets.

Secrets.

Secret Egypt.

It was then that I saw the man. Threading my way down that black and twisted street, I noticed a figure in the shadows before me. It stood silent, as though awaiting my approach. I endeavored to hurry past, but there was something about the motionless man which arrested my attention. He was dressed – unnaturally.

Suddenly, shockingly, my drunken dreams were fused with stark reality.

This waiting man was dressed like a priest of ancient Egypt!

Was it hallucination, or did he wear the triple-crowned insignia of Osiris? That long white robe was unmistakable, and in his lean hands was the sceptered diadem of Set, the Serpent.

Overcome with bewilderment, I stood stock-still and stared. He stared back, his thin, tanned face bland and expressionless. With a quick gesture, his right hand darted under his robe. I shrank back, as he withdrew it once more and pulled out – a cigarette.

'Got a match, stranger?' asked the priest of Egypt.

Then I laughed, remembered, and understood. Mardi Gras! What a scare he had given me, though! Smiling, my head suddenly clear once more, I extended my lighter. He used it, and as the flame flared upward, peered curiously into my countenance.

He started, grey eyes evincing sudden recognition. To my astonishment, he spoke my name in interrogation. I nodded my head.

'What a surprise!' he chuckled. 'You're the writer, aren't you? I've read some of your recent stuff, but I had no idea that you were here in New Orleans.'

I mumbled a few words of explanation. He genially interrupted.

'That's great luck. My name is Vanning – Henricus Vanning. I'm interested in the occult myself; we should have a lot in common.'

We stood chatting for several minutes; or rather, he chatted and I listened. I learned that Mr Vanning was a gentleman of means and leisure. He touched a bit glibly and flippantly on his studies in primitive mythology, but expressed a patently genuine interest in Egyptian lore. There was mention of a social group whose mutual and private researches in metaphysics might interest me.

As if seized with sudden inspiration, he clapped me heartily on the back.

'What are your plans for the evening?' he said.

I confessed my predicament. He smiled.

'Splendid! Just had dinner, myself. I'm on the way back to the house now to play host. Our little group – I told you about them – is holding a costume ball there. Like to come along? Interesting.'

'But I'm not in costume,' I protested.

'Doesn't matter. I think you'd particularly appreciate this affair. Most unusual. Come on.'

He beckoned me to follow and started off down the street. I shrugged, but acquiesced. After all, I had nothing to lose, and my curiosity was aroused.

As we walked, the garrulous Mr Vanning carried on a smooth and intriguing conversation. He spoke in greater detail of his little 'circle' of esoteric friends. I gathered that they rather ostentatiously referred to themselves as *The Coffin Club*, and spent much of their time in pursuit of exotic and macabre phases in art, literature or music.

Tonight, according to my host, the group were celebrating the Mardi Gras in their own unique fashion. Defying the conventional masquerade, all members and invited friends planned to come attired in supernatural garb; instead of the usual clowns, pirates, and Colonial gentlemen, they would represent the more outlandish features of fancy and myth. I would mingle with werewolves, vampires, gods, goddesses, priests and black magicians.

I must confess that this news did not wholly please me. I never could stomach the pseudo-occultist or the quack devotee and metaphysicist. I dislike a bogus interest and a sham knowlege of legendry in others. Petty dabblings in spiritualism, astrology, and 'psychic' charlatanry have always been repellent to my tastes.

I feel that it is not good for fools to mock the old faiths and the secret ways of vanished races. If this was to be one of the usual groups, of middle-aged neurotics and pallid-purple dilettantes, then I would spend a boring evening.

But Henricus Vanning himself seemed to have more than a surface smattering of erudition. His cultured allusions to various myth-sagas in my stories seemed to hint at deep knowledge and sincere research that peered beyond the blacker veils of human thought. He spoke quite fluently of his delvings into Manicheism and primal cult-ceremonials.

I became so absorbed in his words that I failed to heed the direction in which he led me, though I know we walked for some time. When we drew up at last, it was to turn into a long, shrubbery-bordered walk which led to the doors of a well-lighted and imposing mansion.

In simple truth, I must admit to being so seduced by Vanning's picturesque statements, that I cannot remember a single concrete detail of the house's exterior appearance or the environs in which it stood.

Still bemused, I followed Vanning through the opened door and walked into – nightmare.

When I stated that the house was brilliantly lighted, I meant just that. It was lighted – *in flaming red*.

We stood in a hallway; a hallway of hell. Scarlet scimitars of light scintillated from the surface of mirrored walls. Vermilion drapes cloaked inner entrances, and the crimson ceiling seemed to smolder with the crystalline carmine fires of ruby gas-torches that hung in blood-imbrued braziers. A Luciferean butler took my hat, handed me a goblet of cherry brandy.

Alone in the red room, Vanning faced me, glass in hand.

'Like it?' he inquired. 'Gay setting to put my guests in the mood. Little touch I borrowed from Poe.'

I thought of the splendid *Masque of the Red Death*, and winced inwardly at this crude and vulgar desecration.

Still, this evidence of the man's eccentricity did intrigue me. He was *trying* for something. I was almost moved when I lifted my glass to the pseudo-priest of Egypt there in that eery anteroom.

The brandy burned.

'Now – on to our guests.' He pushed a tapestry aside, and we entered the cavernous chamber to the right.

Green and black were the velvet backgrounds of these walls; silver the candles that lighted the niches. The furniture, however, was modern and conventional enough; but when I first surveyed the throng of guests I felt for a moment as if I were again in dreams.

'Werewolves, gods, and black magicians,' Vanning had said. There was more of understatement than exaggeration in that cryptic remark. The occupants of that room constituted a pantheon from all the hells.

I saw an obscene Pan dancing with a withered night-hag; a mad Freya embracing a voodoo priest; a Bacchante clinging lecherously to a wild-eyed dervish from Irem. There were archdruids, dwarfs, nixies and kobolds; lamas, Shamans, priestesses, fauns, ogres, magi, ghouls. It was a sabbat – a resurrection of ancient sin.

Then, as I mingled with the throng and was introduced, the momentary illusion faded. Pan was merely a stout, rather puffy-eyed, middle-aded gentleman with an obvious paunch which no goatskin girdle could obliterate. Freya was a desperately-bright debutante, with the predatory slut-eyes of a common harlot. The voodoo priest was just a nice young man in burnt cork, with a slightly incongruous English lisp.

I met perhaps a dozen guests, and quickly forgot their names. I was a trifle surprised by Vanning's seeming superciliousness; he almost snubbed several of the more talkative.

'Enjoy yourselves,' he called over his shoulder as he dragged me across the floor. 'Those are the fools,' he confided in a lower voice. 'But there are a few I want you to meet.'

Over in the corner sat a little group of four men. All wore priestly raiment similar to Vanning's own, in that religion dominated.

'Doctor Delvin.' An old man, in Babylonian, almost biblical robes.

'Etienne de Marigny.' Dark, handsome priest of Adonis.

'Professor Weildan.' A bearded gnome in a kalender's turban.

'Richard Royce.' A young, bespectacled scholar, monkishly cowled.

The foursome bowed courteously. Upon my being introduced, however, there was an immediate slackening of their reserve. They crowded about Vanning and me in a rather confidential way, while our host spoke softly in my ear.

'These are the real members of the group I spoke about. I saw the way you looked at the others here, and I quite understand and agree with you. Those people are silly fools. We, here, are the initiates. Perhaps, then, you wonder at the reason for their presence. Let me explain. Attack is the best defence.'

'Attack is the best defence?' I echoed, puzzled.

'Yes. Suppose, now, that I and my friends here are really deep students of black magic.'

There was a subtle suggestion in the way he breathed 'suppose'.

'Suppose that is true. Don't you think that our society friends would object, gossip, investigate?'

'Yes,' I admitted. 'That sounds reasonable.'

'Of course. That's why we formulated our attack. By publicly proclaiming an eccentric interest in occultism, and showing it by giving these stupid parties, we are left quite unmolested to carry out our serious work by ourselves. Clever, eh?'

I smiled in agreement. Vanning was no fool.

'It might interest you to know that Doctor Delvin, here, is one of this country's foremost ethnologists. De Marigny is a well-known occultist – you may remember his connection with the Randolph Carter case several years ago. Royce is my personal aide, and Professor Weildan is *the* Weildan, Egyptologist.'

Funny, how Egypt kept recurring in the course of the evening!

'I promised you something interesting, my friend, and you shall have it. First, though, we must endure these cattle for another half-hour or so. Then we'll go up to my room for a real session. I trust you will be patient.'

The four men bowed to me as Vanning again led me into the centre of the room. The dancing had stopped now, and the floor was covered by little groups of idle chatterers. Demons drank mint-juleps, and virgin sacrifices to the Magna Mater artfully applied their lipstick. Neptune passed me, with a cigar in his mouth. The gaiety was shrill.

Masque of the Red Death, I thought. Then I saw – him.

It was all Poe, his entrance. The black and green curtains at the end of the room parted, and he glided in as though emerging from the hidden depths of the hangings rather than the door behind them.

Silver candle-light silhouetted his figure, and as he walked a grisly nimbus seemed to cloak each movement. I had the momentary impression of gazing at him through a prism, since the queer lighting made him appear indistinct and sharply-etched in turn.

He was the soul of Egypt.

The long white robe concealed a body whose contours were elusively problematical. Taloned hands hung from swirling sleeves, and the jewelled fingers clasped a rod of gold, set with the seal of the Eye of Horus.

The top of the robe terminated in a cape-collar of black; it stood, a stiffly hooded background for a head of horror.

The head of a crocodile. The body of an Egyptian priest.

That head was – awful. A slanted, saurian skull, all green and scaly on top; hairless, slimy, slick and nauseous. Great bony ridges socketed the embered eyes, staring from behind a sickening sweep of long, reptilian snout. A rugose muzzle, with great champing jaws half opened to reveal a lolling pinkish tongue and scummy teeth of stiletto-like sharpness.

What a mask!

I have always prided myself on a certain *sensitivity*. I can *feel* quite strongly. Now, gazing at that triumph of morbid mummery, I received a sensory shock. I felt that this masquer was real – more real than his less grotesque fellows. The very outlandishness of his costume seemed to carry added conviction when contrasted with the makeshift pretences of those through which he walked.

He seemed to be alone, nor did anyone attempt to converse with him in passing. I reached forward and tapped Vanning on the shoulder. I wanted to meet this man.

Vanning, however, swung ahead to the platform, where he turned and spoke to the orchestra men. I glanced back, half intending to approach the crocodile-man myself.

He was gone.

I searched the crowd with eager eyes. No use. He had vanished.

Vanished? Had he existed? I saw him – or thought I did –
only for a moment. And I was still a little befuddled. Egypt on
the brain. Perhaps I had been over-imaginative. But why the
queer flooding feeling of reality?

These questions were never answered, for my attention was
distracted by the performance on the platform. Vanning had
started his half-hour of entertainment for the 'guests.' He had
told me it was a mere sop to conceal his real interests, but I
found it more impressive than I expected.

The lights turned blue – haggard, graveyard-misty blue.
The shadows darkened to indigo blurs as the celebrants found
seats. An organ rose from beneath the orchestra platform, and
music throbbed.

It was my favourite number – the superb and sonorously
sepulchral Number One scene from *The Swan Lake*, by
Tchaikovsky. It droned, mocked, shrilled, blared. It
whispered, roared, threatened, frightened. It even impressed
and quieted the milling geese about me.

There was a Devil Dance following; a magician, and a final
Black Mass ritual with a really terrifying illusion of sacrifice.
All very weird, very morbid, and very false. When the lights
went up at last and the band resumed their places, I found
Vanning, and we hastened across the room. The four fellow-
researchers were waiting.

Vanning motioned me to follow them through the curtains
near the platform. We made our exits unobtrusively, and I
found myself walking down a long, darkened hallway.
Vanning halted before an oak-panelled door. A key flashed,
grated, turned. We were in a library.

Chairs, cigars, brandy – indicated in turn by our smiling
host. The brandy – a fine cognac – momentarily sent my
thoughts astray once more. Everything was unreal; Vanning,
his friends, this house, the entire evening. Everything but the
man in the crocodile mask. I must ask Vanning . . .

Abruptly, a voice summoned me back to the present. Vanning
was speaking, addressing me. His voice was solemn, and held an
unusual timbre. It was almost as though I was hearing him
speak for the first time; as if this were the real man, and the other
genial inhabitant of an open house merely a sham as insub-
stantial as the Mardi Gras costumes of the guests.

As he spoke, I found myself the focus of five pairs of eyes; Delvin's Celtic blue, de Marigny's penetrating Gallic brown, Royce's bespectacled grey, Weildan's deep umber, and the gun-metal pinpoints of Vanning himself. Each seemed to ask a question:

'Do you dare?'

But what Vanning said was much more prosaic.

'I promised you an unusual time. Well, that's what you're here for. But I must admit that my motives are not altruistic alone. I – I need you. I've read your tales. I think you are a sincere student, and I want both knowledge and advice. That is why we five are admitting a comparative stranger to our secret. We trust you – we must trust you.'

'You can,' I said, quietly. For the first time I realized that Vanning was not only earnest; he was nervous. The hand holding the cigar shook; perspiration gathered beneath the Egyptian hood. Royce, the scholarly student, was twisting the belt of his monkish costume. The other three men still watched me, and their silence was more disturbing than the unnatural earnestness in Vanning's voice.

What was all this? Was I drugged, dreaming? Blue lights, and crocodile masks, and a melodramatic secret. Yet I believed.

I believed, when Vanning pressed the lever in the great library table so that the false drawers beneath swung outward and revealed the gaping space within. I believed when I saw him hoist out the mummy-case, with de Marigny's aid.

I became interested even before I noted the peculiarities of the case itself. For Vanning went over to a shelf and came back with an armful of books. These he handed to me silently. They were his credentials; they confirmed all that he had told me.

Nobody but a recognized occultist and adept could possess these strange tomes. Thin strips of glass protected the crumbling covers of the ill-famed *Book of Eibon*, the original editions of *Cultes des Goules*, and the almost fabulous *De Vermis Mysteriis*.

Vanning managed a smile when he saw the light of recognition in my face.

'We've gone in pretty deep these past few years,' he said.
'You know what lies in these books.'

I knew. I have written of *De Vermis Mysteriis* myself, and
there are times when the words of Ludvig Prinn fill me with a
vague fright and an indefinable repulsion.

Vanning opened the latter volume. 'You are familiar with
this, I believe. You've mentioned it in your work.'

He pointed to the cryptic chapter that is known as *Saracenic
Rituals*.

I nodded I knew the *Saracenic Rituals* only too well. The
account dealt with Prinn's mysterious sojourn in Egypt and
the Orient in what he claimed were Crusader days. There is
revealed the lore of the *efreet* and the *djinn*, the secrets of the
Assassin sects, the myths of Arabian ghoul-tales, and the
hidden practices of dervish cults. I had found within it a great
wealth of material on the legends of ancient Inner Egypt;
indeed, much story material was culled from those tattered
pages.

Egypt again! I glanced at the mummy-case.

Vanning and the others watched me intently. At last my
host shrugged.

'Listen,' he said. 'I'll put my cards on the table. I – I must
trust you, as I said.'

'Go ahead,' I rejoined, impatiently. Such mystery of manner was irritating.

'It all started with this book,' said Henricus Vanning.
'Royce, here, dug it up for me. We got interested in the
Bubastis legend, at first. For a while I contemplated some
investigations in Cornwall – looking up the Egyptian ruins of
England, you know. But then, I found a more fertile field in
actual Egyptology. When Professor Weildan, here, went on
his expedition last year, I authorized him to obtain anything
of interest he might discover, at any price. He returned last
week, with this.'

Vanning stepped over to the mummy-case. I followed.

He didn't have to explain further. One detailed inspection
of that mummy-case, combined with what I knew of the
Saracenic Rituals chapter, led to an inference that was unmistakable.

The hieroglyphs and markings on the case indicated that it

contained the body of an Egyptian priest; a priest of the god Sebek. And *Saracenic Rituals* told its own story.

For a moment I mentally reviewed my knowledge. Sebek, according to reputable anthropologists, was a lesser deity of Inner Egypt; a fertility god of the Nile. If recognized authorities be correct, only four mummies of his priesthood have ever been found; though numerous statuettes, figurines, and pictures in tombs testify to the veneration accorded this deity. Egyptologists have never fully traced the history of the god, though some unorthodox surmises and wild linkages have been made or hinted at by Wallis-Budge.

Ludvig Prinn, though, had delved further. I recalled his words with an appreciable shudder.

In *Sarecenic Rituals*, Prinn spoke of what he had learned from Alexandrian seers; of his journeyings into the deserts and his secret tomb-looting in hidden valleys of the Nile.

He told a tale, historically authenticated, of the Egyptian priestcraft and its rise to power – how the servants of the dark nature-gods ruled the Pharaohs from behind the throne, and held the land in their grip. For Egyptian gods and religions were based on secret realities. Strange hybrids walked the earth when it was young; gigantic, lumbering creatures – half-beast, half-man. Human imagination alone did not create the gigantic serpent Set, carnivorous Bubastis, and great Osiris. I thought of Thoth, and tales of harpies; thought of jackal-headed Anubis and the legend of werewolves.

No, the ancients trafficked with elemental powers and beasts of the beyond. They could summon their gods, the humans with the heads of animals. And, at times, they did. Hence their power.

In time, they ruled over Egypt; their word was law. The land was filled with rich temples, and every seventh man owed allegiance to the ritual bodies. Incense rose before a thousand shrines – incense, and blood. The beast-mouths of the gods hungered for blood.

Well might the priests adore, for they had made strange and curious bargains with their divine Masters. Unnatural perversions drove the cult of Bubastis out of Egypt, and a never-mentioned abomination caused the symbol and story of Nyarlathotep to be forgotten. But ever the priests waxed stronger and bolder; their sacrifices more outrageous, and their rewards greater.

For the sake of life everlastingly reincarnated, they pleasured the gods and assuaged their curious appetites. To safeguard their mummies with divine curses, they offered up scapegoats filled with blood.

Prinn speaks of the sect of Sebek in particular detail. The priests believed that Sebek, as a fertility deity, controlled the sources of life eternal. He would guard them in their graves until the resurrection-cycle was completed, and he would destroy their enemies who sought to violate their sepulchres. To him they offered virgin maidens, to be torn between the jaws of a golden crocodile. For Sebek, the Crocodile God of the Nile, had the body of a man, the head of a crocodile, and the lustful appetites of both.

The description of these ceremonies is grisly. The priests wore crocodile masks, in emulation of their Lord, for that was his earthly aspect. Once a year, they thought, Sebek himself appeared to the High Priests in the Inner Temple of Memphis, and then he too assumed the form of a man with a crocodile head.

The devout believed that he would guard their graves – and countless screaming virgins died to support their faith.

This I knew, and hurriedly recollected, while glancing at the mummy of the Priest of Sebek.

For now I looked into the case, and saw that the mummy had been unwrapped. It lay under a pane of glass, which Vanning removed.

'You know the story, then,' he said, reading my eyes aright. 'I've had the mummy here a week; it's been chemically treated, thanks to Weildan, here. On its chest, though, I found this.'

He pointed to an amulet of clear jade – a saurian figure, covered with ideographic images.

'What is it?' I asked.

'Secret code of the priesthood. De Marigny thinks it's Nacaal. Translation? A curse – as the Prinn story has it – a curse on the heads of tomb-looters. Threatens them with the vengeance of Sebek himself. Nasty wording.'

Vanning's flippancy was forced. I could tell that by the

restless stirring of the others in the room. Doctor Devlin was coughing nervously; Royce twisted his robe; de Marigny scowled. The gnome-like Professor Weildan approached us. He glanced at the mummy for some time, as if seeking solution to a secret in those eyeless sockets that blindly brooded in the gloom.

'Tell him what I think, Vanning,' he said, softly.

'Weildan, here, has done some investigation. He managed to get this mummy in past the authorities, but it cost him plenty to do it. He told me where he found it, and it's not a pleasant story. Nine of the caravan boys died on the return journey, though it may have been bad water that did that. The professor has gone back on us, I'm afraid.'

'I have not,' interposed Weildan, sharply. 'When I tell you to get rid of the mummy it is because I want to live. We had some notion of using it in ceremonials here, but this is not possible. You see, I believe in the curse of Sebek.

'You know, of course, that only four mummies of his priests have ever been found. That is because the others repose in secret crypts. Well, the four finders are all dead. I knew Partington, who found the third. He was investigating this curse myth quite thoroughly when he returned – but he died before publishing any reports. It was rather curious, his end. Fell off the bridge into a crocodile pit of the London Zoo. When they pulled him out, he was a mess.'

Vanning looked at me. 'Bogey man,' he said, deprecatingly. Then, in more serious tones, he continued. 'That's one of the reasons I asked you here to share this secret. I want your own opinion, as a scholar and occultist. Should I get rid of the mummy? Do you believe in this curse story? I don't, but I have felt quite uneasy of late. I know of too many peculiar coincidences, and I have faith in Prinn's veracity. What we intended to use the mummy for does not matter. It would have been a – a desecration great enough to anger any god. And I wouldn't like to have a crocodile-headed creature at my throat. What do you say?'

Abruptly, I remembered. The man in the mask! He had been dressed like a priest of Sebek, in emulation of the god.

I told Vanning what I had seen of him. 'Who is he?' I asked. 'He should really be here. It makes things – appropriate.'

Vanning's horror was not feigned. I regretted having spoken, after observing his terrified reaction.

'I never saw *that!* I swear I didn't! We must find the man at once.'

'Perhaps it's a polite form of blackmail,' I said. 'He may have the goods on you and Weildan, and frighten you into paying hush-money.'

'Perhaps.' Vanning's voice held no note of sincerity. He turned to the others.

'Quickly,' he said. 'Go back into the other room and look among the guests. Collar this elusive – stranger; bring him here.'

'Police?' suggested Royce, nervously.

'No, you fool. Hurry, all of you!'

The four men left the room, and their footsteps echoed in the outer corridor as they receded.

A moment's silence. Vanning tried to smile. I was in a strange oblivious fog. The Egypt of my dreams – *was it real?* Why had that one glimpse of the mysterious man in the mask so impressed me? The priests of Sebek spilt blood to bind a bargain of vengeance; could they satisfy an ancient curse? Or was Vanning mad?

A soft sound . . .

I turned. And there in the doorway stood the man in the crocodile mask.

'That's the fellow!' I exclaimed. 'That's – '

Vanning leaned against the table, his face the colour of wet ash. He just stared at the figure on the threshold, but his tormented eyes telepathically conveyed a dreadful message to me.

The man in the crocodile mask . . . nobody had seen him but myself. And I was dreaming in Egypt. Here, in this room, was the stolen mummy of Sebek's priest.

The god Sebek was – *a crocodile-headed god.* And his priests were dressed in his image – *they wore crocodile masks.*

I had just warned Vanning about the vengeance of the old priests. He himself had believed and was afraid when I told him what I had seen. And now, in the doorway, stood the silent stranger. What was more logical than to believe it was a resurrected priest, come to avenge this insult to his kind?

Yet I could not believe it. Even when the figure entered, sinister and still, I did not guess its purpose. Even when Vanning cowered and moaned against the mummy-case, I was not convinced.

Then, everything happened so swifly that I had no time to act. Just as I was about to challenge the unnatural intruder, doom was unleashed. With a darting, reptilian movement, the body beneath the white robe *undulated* across the room. In a second it towered above the cringing figure of my host. I saw clawing hands sink into sagging shoulders; then the jaws of the mask descended and *moved*. Moved – in Vanning's quivering throat.

As I leapt, my thoughts seemed sluggishly calm in contrast. 'Diabolically clever murder,' I mused. 'Unique death-weapon. Cunningly contrived tooth-mechanism in a mask, Fanatic.'

And my eyes, in a detached fashion, observed that monstrous muzzle biting into Vanning's neck. Moving, the squamous horror of the head loomed like a camera close-up.

It took only a second, understand. Then, with sudden purpose, I had seized a sleeve of the white robe, and with my free hand wrenched at the mask of the murderer.

The killer wheeled, ducked. My hand slipped, and for a moment rested on the crocodile snout, the bloody jaw.

Then, in a flash, the invader wheeled and disappeared, while I was left screaming before the ripped and tattered body on the mummy-case of Sebek.

Vanning was dead. His murderer had disappeared. The house was crowded with revellers; I had but to step to the door and call for aid.

I did not. I stood for one stark second in the centre of the room, screaming, while my vision veered. Everything was swimming around and around – the blood-blotched books; the sere mummy, its chest now crushed and crimsoned by the struggle; the red, unmoving thing on the floor. All blurred before my eyes.

Then, and only then, did volition come to me. I turned and ran.

I wish my tale could end there, but it cannot. There is a conclusion to be drawn. It must be revealed so that I can know peace once more.

I'll be frank. I know it would make a better story if I had asked the butler about the man in the crocodile mask and heard him say that no such person entered the place. But this is not a story, but truth.

I *know* he was there, and after I saw Vanning die I did not wait to interview another soul. I made that last desperate clutch at the masked murderer, then screamed and ran from the room. I rushed through the revellers on the floor without even giving an alarm, dashed out of the house and panted up the street. Grinning horror bestrode my shoulders and urged me on, until I lost all consciousness and ran blindly back to the lighted lanes and laughing throngs that dwelt smugly safe from the terrors I knew.

I left New Orleans without investigating any further details. I purposely did not buy a paper, so that I do not even know if the police discovered Vanning's body or investigated his death. I have never attempted to learn anything more, nor dare I. There might be a sane explanation for it all – and then, again . . .

I prefer not to be sure. I desperately try to make myself believe that I was drunk; that the whole incident never happened, or if it did, that part of it was unreal. Even Vanning's death I could bear, but not that legend of Sebek and the mummy-case of Sebek. I told Vanning the truth about that, and my belief has been hideously confirmed.

Knowledge came during that last moment, when I saw the stranger sink his curiously constructed crocodile muzzle in poor Vanning's throat – sink it with sabre-teeth slashing. It was then that I grabbed him for a moment before he slipped away; grabbed at him, screamed, and hysterically fled.

I grabbed him, in that horrible moment, by the bloody muzzle of the frighteningly realistic crocodile mask. Just a single moment of horrid contact, before he disappeared. But it was enough.

For when I seized that bloody, reptilian muzzle, I felt beneath my fingers, *not a mask, but living flesh!*

A LIFE FOR A LIFE

by Dennis Wheatley

'Well, good night, Doctor – it was nice of you to drop in so friendly.' Mrs Sandmeyer's yellowish face broke into an artificial smile as she spoke from the doorway of the parlour. Her pale eyes travelled with faint disapproval to the half-empty whisky bottle among the cheap ornate china on the narrow mantelpiece, then across to her husband.

'You won't be long, Herbert, will you?' She smiled again, half-archly, half-apologetically, at the doctor. 'I can never get off to sleep without him beside me – I'm funny that way.'

The tired-looking little doctor stroked back his scanty hair and nodded to her. 'Not more than a few minutes, Mrs Sandmeyer. Good night to you.'

As the door closed behind his wife, Herbert Sandmeyer heaved a sigh of relief. He had only thought of consulting the doctor about his trouble after supper that evening when it was too late to frame an excuse for leaving the house again. It had needed considerable stage managing to get the doctor round, on an apparently unofficial call and even more to manœuvre his wife off to bed so as to get his visitor alone.

'Well, what's the trouble?' the doctor asked, pulling thoughtfully at his ragged brown moustache as he watched Sandmeyer pour another tot of whisky into his glass.

'I hardly know how to tell you, Doc' – you'll think I'm crazy.'

'Don't be silly, now.' The doctor took the proffered glass. 'I've got a maternity case which should come off about eleven, so I can't give you very long. Out with it, man.'

Sandmeyer poured himself a drink with an unsteady hand, and turning, caught the reflection of his dead-white face in the narrow mirror of the overmantel. He stared at it for a moment and then exclaimed:

'I'm afraid! That's what it is – I'm afraid!'

'What of?' asked the doctor quickly.

Sandmeyer turned upon him with sudden truculence. 'Tell me I'm a loonie! Tell me I ought to be ashamed of myself at my age, if you like, but it's a fact! I'm afraid to go up to bed!'

'You've been overworking, I expect. Can't sleep, eh! I get like that at times, especially when we get an epidemic of 'flu going round the district.'

Sandmeyer gulped down his whisky, then violently shook his head. 'It isn't that. It isn't ordinary nerves, either. Promise – promise you won't laugh at me if I tell you about it.'

'Of course not. As a professional man I'm used to confidences, so you can tell me and it won't go any further. Patients often tell me things they wouldn't care for the rest of the world to know.'

'No – no. It's nothing like that. I've been having dreams lately and I tell you I'm just scared stiff of going up to bed.'

The doctor nodded. 'I can see your nerves are in a pretty rotten state. You need a tonic and a change if you could manage it.' His eye fell again on the whisky bottle from which Sandmeyer was already pouring himself another drink.

'This isn't ordinary nerves, I tell you.' Sandmeyer hit the table angrily with his fist. 'It's psychic trouble. That's the only way I can describe it. Tell me, Doc', do you believe in the old Biblical saying, "an eye for an eye, a tooth for a tooth, and a life for a life"?'

'Well, hardly.' The tired little doctor demurred with a patient smile. 'Although I'm by no means an atheist in the full sense of the word. I take it you have not told your wife anything about this?'

'Not a thing. She's Chapel and set in her beliefs. If I tried to tell her about it, she'd think I was going out of my mind. When I wake from these – these nightmares, gasping for breath and shaking just like I had a fit, she puts it down to chronic indigestion.'

'You are sure that it is not something of that kind?'

'Certain. I've got a digestion like an ostrich. This is psychic, I tell you; I don't suppose you can do me any good but I had to talk it over with someone.'

The doctor adjusted the pince-nez on his bulbous nose. 'Perhaps you had better tell me how it started,' he said, a little wearily.

'That's a long way back.' Sandmeyer regarded him for a moment with a despairing look, then he went on hurriedly. 'You see, I was what they call psychic even as a child. I've always known things about people without being told and at one time I used to do a bit of fortune-telling, just among friends, you know, but I cut it out because sometimes misfortunes I'd predicted came about so that they said afterwards that I'd wished it on them. I can do that, too, if I want, and I did once with a fellow who did me a dirty trick. I wished him ill and he got it – never mind how. A fellow called Dawson, it was. He was after Maggie – Mrs Sandmeyer, that is – and told her all sorts of lies about me, but I got even with him – more than even – and I got her, too. You can say that was coincidence, if you like, but I know better. Anyway, I was so scared afterwards at the thought of what I'd done that I determined to cut it out for the future.

'I've never told her anything, of course, and I thought I'd been clear of the whole business for years now, but my brother-in-law came up from the country to stay for a bit about a month ago and, like a fool, I allowed him to persuade me into going to the British Museum with him to see the Egyptian galleries.

'It's wrong to show those mummies the way they do. I've always thought that. After all, they're dead people – aren't they – and directly I got inside that Egyptian gallery I could feel all sorts of forces moving around me.

'I had a sort of feeling that Frank Dawson was somewhere in the place, watching me, as it were, though I haven't even thought of him for years and he might have been in China for all I know. Then as we were moving round we stopped opposite one of the wall cases. There was a wooden coffin inside, all painted over with hieroglyphics and what-not, made in the shape of a body, and over the head part it had a kind of mask. This wasn't the mummy itself, but the coffin that I'm speaking of.

'Then – well, I can hardly expect you to believe me – but the black eyes in that mask suddenly became alive. They stared up at me out of that painted face deep and dark and liquid. I'm not raving – they were living eyes, black as pitch and full of smouldering fire. They held me rooted there like I was being hypnotized until my brother-in-law said something. It gave me such a turn that I darn near fainted; anyhow, I pulled myself together and got out of the place just as quickly as I could.

'Well, that's just on a month back, and I certainly wasn't thinking about it when I went up to bed three nights ago.

'We turned in about ten as usual and I dropped off to sleep without a worry in the world, but I had an extraordinary dream later.

'I seemed to be walking down a flight of broken stairs into a sort of crypt. All round the walls there were rows of things like great bath tubs, some stone, some wood, and they were carved or painted with hieroglyphics all along their sides, just as you see them in the Egyptian rooms at the museum.

'I walked over to one at the far end of the place and found myself looking down into it. The lid was off. There was just enough light for me to see that it was a woman and that she didn't seem to be dead at all. Instead of being dark and parchmenty, her flesh was white and healthy where it showed through the decayed stuff of her shroud. Then I saw that her head was covered with long golden hair. That was strange, wasn't it, because in a place like that one would naturally have expected her to be black-haired like all the Egyptian women, but perhaps she was one of those slaves that they imported from Greece, or a Princess who had married into Egypt from some country far away in the north.

'After a little time her eyes opened and she lay there staring up at me. I felt a kind of chill run right through my body because they were the same dark living eyes that I had seen on the coffin lid at the museum. There was a horrid sort of soullessness about them.

'She spoke then, or rather, she sent a message to my brain, for her lips never moved although I heard her just as clearly as if she had said the words.

'"You must help me to get up."

'It was terribly cold down in that crypt, and I could feel myself shivering as I stood there. I wanted most terribly to get away from it. Then I found myself stooping down and putting my arms round her naked shoulders.

'She was cold as an icicle, and try as I would I couldn't lift her up; it was as though she was made of marble and screwed down inside that box.

'After a moment, though, a little colour just tinged her cheeks, then, very slowly, she raised her hands and laid them on my shoulders while the faintest flicker of a smile twisted her pale lips. Those hands of hers seemed to weigh on my arms like lumps of solid lead, but her shoulders shifted and raised a little from the bottom of the coffin.

'"Help me – help me," she was saying all the time, and it seemed to me as if I struggled for hours to get her up.

'I'm fairly strong, you know, and I could carry an average-sized woman upstairs without turning a hair, but this girl seemed to weigh a ton. As I hauled at her shoulders her grip on my arms tightened, and she seemed to gain strength, but mine was ebbing from me. With a last frantic heave I managed to pull her into a sitting position. Then I woke up.

'I was panting as though I'd run a mile and shivering in a cold sweat from one end of my body to the other. It took me a good ten minutes to get back my breath and even then I was so exhausted I could hardly turn in my bed. Afterwards I fell into a sort of lethargy and then dropped off to sleep.

'All next day I felt tired and depressed, but then I thought it was only a darned unpleasant nightmare as a kind of after-effect of my visit to the museum. I dismissed it as that more or less and went to bed the following night quite cheerfully as usual, but I had hardly fallen asleep when I had the same dream again.

'There she was, sitting upright in the long wooden box, her white flesh showing through the shreds of her grave clothes just as I had left her.

'You must help me to get up,' she said again.

'I was struggling with myself already to get away, and the chill of the place seemed to eat into my very bones, but I could not help bending down towards her.

'She had some strength of her own, too, now, for before I even touched her she lifted her arms, and next moment, as I stooped there, I felt them close like a vice round my neck.

'For a little I struggled to break away from her, but I had my arms round her body all the time, and, in spite of myself, I was trying to lift her up. I felt the terrible weight of her again just as though she were a life-size stone figure. As she pressed against me I could feel her flesh was cold as ice but soft and yielding. Then as she stood upright I felt her heart suddenly begin to pound and beat just below my breast.

'I seemed to be falling. Then I must have cried out, for I woke to find myself sitting up in bed screaming fit to bring the house down.

'Maggie had woken, of course, and we put on the light. She lectured me for eating too many baked beans for supper, which is what we'd had, and told me to dose myself with bicarbonate. I was so weak that I could hardly crawl out of bed, but she's that fixed in her opinions she would have thought I was going potty if I'd tried to tell her the truth, so I made a pretence of getting the bicarbonate although I knew that it wasn't the least use.

'Afterwards I slept from sheer exhaustion, and next morning I felt like death. I dragged myself off to work as usual, but I couldn't add a column of figures to save my life, and the boss was pretty shirty with me. It wasn't so much that I was scared and obsessed with this thing then but that I was just utterly tired out.

'That evening – last night it was – I began to get the wind up. I made up my mind that somehow I'd got to keep awake. If I had been able to do as I liked I would have gone out to some place where there was a band and a lot of people and when it closed down I would have walked the streets till dawn, but with Maggie being the way she is I simply didn't dare.

'She put her foot down on my going out with my men friends when we first married – years ago – and she even hates me sitting up reading of a night. Says that she can't sleep comfortable without me, and that if I do come up late when she's dropped off it always wakes her and then she can never get to sleep again – you know how it is when you've lived with a woman year in year out as I have. She's a good sort, too,

even if she is narrow in her views. I cudgelled my wits for
hours trying to think up some excuse for going out or staying
down here in the parlour, but I couldn't think of one that
would pass muster with her, so in the end I had to throw my
hand in, and we went up to bed round about half-past ten.

'When I had to pretend to go to sleep, I began to recite
things to myself – bits of songs and poems that I had learnt as
a kid – the names of all the customers in my ledger and all the
seaside places I could remember – working round the British
Isles from John O'Groats.

'It's a ghastly business trying to keep awake when you're
lying in the dark, and hardly dare to turn over. As it was I
stuck it out till after three. Then I was stumbling down those
beastly stairs again.

'I crossed the crypt place, just as I had before, and there
was the golden-haired woman waiting for me on the other
side. I tried not to look at her. I was just terrified by then, but,
standing in her coffin, she stretched out a hand and laid it on
my arm, and I felt her speak again.

'"You must help me out of here."

'Next minute she half-jumped and half-fell out of the
wooden box. I turned and tried to run, but she threw her bare
arms round my neck and staggered along at my side.

'As I tried to unloose her grip I saw her face for a moment
within an inch or two of mine. It was human yet somehow not
human if you understand what I mean. Lovely as that of any
woman that I've ever looked on but set with a positively
devilish determination.

'"Help me out – help me out!" I felt her screaming from
between her white clenched teeth, and she clung to me as if
her slender arms were made of steel.

'"I can't!" I kind of felt myself saying, although I never
even opened my mouth. "You're stonger than I am now. You
must help me."

'She laughed then, and I've never heard anything like it.
People talk about their flesh creeping – well, mine did then –
and with me fighting like mad all the time to get away from
her we stumbled along together until we reached the middle of
the chamber.

'"Up the stairs – up the stairs," she was panting, and those dark eyes of hers were set like flaming things on the entrance of the vault.

Her grip on me was so strong that I can feel it now. Her nails absolutely bit into my arm and shoulder, and every second I felt my strength ebbing from my body into hers. My knees were giving under me, and I suddenly knew with an awful certainty that if I could not free myself from her I should never wake in this life again.

'I remember making a last gigantic effort. I saw her swaying there in the middle of the crypt glaring at me with those wild dark eyes, then everything went black for a moment, and next thing I remember I was lying, too weak to move, upstairs beside Maggie in my bed.

'I didn't sleep again. Something seemed to tell me that if I dropped off I'd have to return to her. She was strong now, powerful with the life she had sucked out of me – and evil. She seemed to be calling to me the whole time that I lay there, with set teeth and my eyes wide open in the darkness – although of course I could hardly lift a limb.

'By five o'clock I'd just strength enough to hoist myself out of bed and douse my face in cold water. That revived me a bit. Maggie had woken naturally and became a bit peevish, but I was too scared to worry much over that. I shut her up by saying that I had the pains again and told her that I was going down to the kitchen to make myself some hot coffee. I did too, although I was so weak that I could hardly lift the saucepan on to the stove.

'When the light came I was still there. The coffee had done me good and I cut myself some cold meat sandwiches. I was hungry as if I hadn't eaten for a week.

'Maggie had fallen into a doze again, she told me afterwards. She couldn't do else, since I found her snoring when I went up to the bedroom round about seven o'clock.

'We breakfasted and I found that the sandwiches hadn't even taken the edge off my appetite. I was ravenous like a starving man. Then I went off to work, leaving Maggie in none too good a temper. At least she *thinks* I went to work. Actually I cut the office for the day. I was so dead beat that I simply could not face it. Instead I slept most of the morning in the free library and, when I was turned out from there, on a park bench well into the afternoon.

'I had to get back home, of course, same time as if I'd been to work, and it just shows how little things can worry you when you're faced with a real big trouble like this. I was scared stiff that Maggie would have heard from the boss some way that I had cut my job.

'He was too busy with other things, I reckon. Anyhow, I didn't have to face the grilling I'd expected, only a lot of questions as to why I'd brought home the bottle of whisky that's on the mantel there. I thought I'd go barmy at supper and begin to break things or rush out of the house, but I'm terribly fond of Maggie. Then I suddenly thought that I might be able to save myself if I could get hold of you.'

Sandmeyer paused, his eyes, purple-rimmed, bore down into those of the doctor. He shivered slightly and then exclaimed:

'Well! There you are! You don't believe me – do you? But I'm afraid, I tell you. Just terrified of going upstairs to bed.'

The doctor was a little man with a little practice, the greater part of which lay in a slum area. In his mind he had already diagnosed the case of Herbert Sandmeyer. A steady fellow who through secret worry had taken to drink. As he stood up his eye fell upon the now nearly empty whisky bottle and then, looking at Herbert again, he decided that given a day or two he might be able to check these alcoholic ravings which were bordering on D.T.s.

'I'm not saying that I don't believe you,' he soothed the haggard man a little wearily. 'But this sort of thing is a bit outside my sphere. I'll give you some stuff which will make you sleep tonight, and then I think you had better come and see me at my consulting-room – round about ten o'clock tomorrow morning.'

'But you don't understand!' Sandmeyer burst out. 'I don't want to sleep. I've got to keep awake all night. If I don't I'll be drawn to that place again. That she-devil will draw all the life I've got left out of me and I'll never come back – never wake up any more.'

A heavy rapping sounded on the floor of the room above. Both men glanced up at the ceiling.

'That's your wife,' said the doctor. 'You had really better take this bromide.' He produced a small bottle from his shabby black bag and shook a few pellets from it into the palm of his hand.

Herbert Sandmeyer's body suddenly seemed to go limp. He leaned heavily on the mantelpiece. The feverish light died out of his eyes, and they took on a dull, glazed, despairing look.

With a feeble gesture he brushed the proffered pellets aside. 'No, thanks. If you don't believe me – but then – I hardly thought you would.'

The doctor glanced at his wrist-watch. 'By Jove! It's just on eleven. I must hurry, or that poor woman may be having her baby with only the district nurse to help her.'

'Life's queer, isn't it, Doc'?' said Sandmeyer slowly. 'Whenever any of us go out of it there's always another coming in to take our place.'

'What?' said the doctor as he shuffled into his worn brown coat.

'Oh, nothing.' Sandmeyer led the way out into the narrow hall.

'I think I know what's wrong with you,' the doctor remarked as they stood on the doorstep. 'Come and see me in the morning.'

'Thanks, Doc',' Herbert Sandmeyer replied evenly. 'It was nice of you to call. Good night.'

As he closed the front door a thin, querulous voice floated down the steep stairs to the hallway.

'Herbert! Are you coming up?'

'All right, Maggie, I'll be with you in a moment,' he called over his shoulder as he went back into the stuffy sitting-room. Then he poured the last of the whisky into his glass.

For a moment he gazed again at his reflection in the mirror of the overmantel. The eyes he saw were panic-stricken and great furrows had appeared in his cheeks.

'By God, she'll get me – I know she will!' he exclaimed hoarsely.

Then the flicker of a smile spread over his pallid features and he murmured to his reflection in a puzzled tone:

'I wonder why I told the Doc' that Frank Dawson might be in China or some place? He's dead as door nails, and I wished it on him, too. But he's getting back on me now after all these years – or something is. It's a Life for a Life all right.'

He tilted his glass and swallowed the neat spirit, then shuddered and coughed a little as the fiery liquid caught his throat.

'Herbert!'

The strident, now angry call came from the room above.

'And to think that I did it to get Maggie,' he whispered to himself.

'HERBERT!' the voice came again.

'All right – I'm coming!' he called back.

Then Herbert Sandmeyer took a last glance round the sitting-room, turned out the gas, and went up to bed.

COLONEL STONESTEEL'S GENUINE
HOME-MADE TRULY EGYPTIAN MUMMY

by Ray Bradbury

That was the autumn they found the genuine Egyptian mummy out past Loon Lake.

How the mummy got there, and how long it had been there, no one knew. But there it was, all wrapped up in its creosote rags, looking a bit spoiled by time, and just waiting to be found by someone.

The day before, it had been just another autumn day with the trees blazing and dropping down their burnt-looking leaves when Charlie Flagstaff, aged twelve, stepped to the middle of a pretty empty street, stared at the sky, the horizon, the whole world, and shouted, 'Okay! I'm waiting. Come on!'

Nothing happened. So Charlie kicked the leaves ahead of him across town until he came to the tallest house on the greatest street, the house where everyone in Green Town came with his troubles. Charlie scowled, shut his eyes, and yelled at the big house windows, 'Colonel Stonesteel!'

The front door burst open, as if the old man had been waiting there, like Charlie, for something incredible to happen in Green Town, Illinois.

'Charlie,' Colonel Stonesteel called. 'You're old enough to knock. What's there about boys makes them shout around houses?'

The door slammed shut.

Charlie sighed, walked up, and knocked softly.

'Why, Charlie Flagstaff, is that you?' The door opened a squint for the Colonel. 'Good gravy, look at that weather!'

The old man strode forth to hone his fine hatchet nose on the sharp wind. 'Don't you just love autumn, son? Just smell that air.'

He remembered to glance down at the boy's pale face.

'Why, son, you look as if your last friend drowned and your dog died. What's wrong? School starts next week? On top of which, Hallowe'en's not coming fast enough?'

'Still eight long weeks off. Might as well be ten years,' the boy sighed, staring out at the autumn town. 'You ever notice, Colonel, not much ever happens around here?'

'Why, hell's bells, son, it's Labor Day tomorrow, big parade, seven almost-brand-new cars, mayor in his next-best suit, fireworks, maybe – er . . .'

The Colonel stopped, not impressed with his own grocery list. 'How old are you, Charlie?'

'Thirteen. Almost.'

'Things do tend to run down, come thirteen. Meanwhile, Charlie, what do we do to survive until noon today?'

'If anyone knows, it's you, Colonel.'

'Charlie . . .' The old man flinched from the boy's clear-water stare. 'I can move politicians big as prize hogs, shake town hall skeletons, make locomotives run back uphill. But small boys on long, dry autumn weekends, suffering from a bad attack of the desperate empties? Well . . .'

Colonel Stonesteel eyed the future in the clouds.

'Charlie,' he said at last, 'I am touched and moved by the circumstances of your lying there on the damn railway tracks, waiting for a murderous train that will never come. So, listen. I'll bet you six Baby Ruth candy bars that Green Town, upper Illinois, population five thousand sixty-two people, one thousand dogs, will be changed forever, changed for the best, by God, sometime in the next twenty-four miraculous hours! Bet?'

'A bet!' Charlie seized and pumped the old man's hand. 'Colonel, I knew you could do it!'

'Ain't done yet, but look. This town's the Red Sea. I herewith order it to part. Gangway!'

The Colonel marched (Charlie ran) into the house, where the Colonel sniffed a vast door leading up to a dry-timber attic. 'Listen, Charlie. Hear. The attic storms.'

The Colonel yanked the door wide on autumn whispers, high winds trapped and shuddering in the beams.

'What's it say?'

Just then a gust of wind hurled the Colonel, like so much flimsy chaff, up the dark stairs. He was philosophical along the way: 'Time, it says, mostly. Oldness. Memory. Dust. Pain. Listen to those beams. When the weather cracks a roof's skeleton on a fine autumn day, you truly got time-talk, Bombay snuffs, tombyard flowers gone to ghost – '

'Boy, Colonel,' Charlie gasped, climbing, 'you oughta write for *Top Notch Magazine!*'

'Did once. Got rejected. Here we are!'

And there they were indeed, in a place with no calendar, no days, no months, no years, but only vast spider shadows and glints of light from collapsed chandeliers lying about like shed tears in the dust.

'Boy!' Charlie cried, scared, and glad of it.

'Charles,' the Colonel said, 'you ready for me to birth you a real live, half-dead, sockdolager, on-the-spot mystery?'

'Ready!'

'Now!'

The Colonel swept charts, maps, agate marbles, glass eyes, and sneezes of dust off a table, then rolled up his sleeves.

'Great thing about midwifing mysteries is you don't have to boil water or wash up. Hand me that papyrus scroll there, boy, that darning needle just beyond, that old rickshaw blueprint on the wall, that plug of fired cannonball-cotton underfoot. Jump!'

'I'm jumping!' Charlie ran and fetched, fetched and ran.

'Here, here, and here! There, there, and there!'

Bundles of dry twigs, clutches of pussy willow, and cattails flew. The Colonel's sixteen hands were wild in the air, flashing sixteen bright suture needles, flakes of meadow grass, flickers of owl feather, glares of bright yellow fox eye.

'There, by God. Half-done!'

The Colonel pointed with a chop of his nose.

'Peel an eye, son. What's it commence to start to re-semble?'

Charlie circled the table, eyes stretched so wide his mouth gaped.

'Why . . . why – ' he sputtered. And then: 'A mummy! Can't be!'

'Is, boy! Is!'

Wrist-deep in his creation, the Colonel listened to its reeds and thistles, its dry-flower whispers.

'Now, why did I build this mummy? You, you inspired it, Charlie. Go look out the attic window.'

Charlie spat on the dusty pane, wiped a clear viewing spot, and peered out.

'What do you see out there in the damn town?' the Colonel asked. 'Any murders being transacted?'

'Heck, no – '

'Anyone falling off church steeples or being run down by maniac lawn mowers?'

'Nope.'

'Any *Monitors* or *Merrimacks* sailing up the dry lake, dirigibles falling on the Masonic Temple and squashing six thousand Masons flat?'

'Heck, there's only five thousand folks in Green Town!'

'Don't unhinge me with facts. Stare, boy. Spy. Report!'

'No dirigibles.' Charlie stared. 'No squashed Masonic temples.'

'Right you are, boy.'

The Colonel trotted over to join Charlie, surveying the dire territory. He pointed with his great hound nose.

'In all Green Town, in all your life, not one murder, not one orphanage fire, not one mad fiend carving his initials on librarian ladies' wooden legs. Face it, son, Green Town, upper Illinois, is the most common, mean, ordinary, plain old bore of a graveyard in the eternal history of the Roman, Greek, Russian, Anglo-American empires. If Napoleon had been born here, he'd have committed hara-kiri by the age of nine. Boredom. If Caesar had been raised here, he'd have raced to the Forum at the age of ten, shoved in his *own* dagger – '

'Boredom,' said Charlie.

'Kee-rect!' Colonel Stonesteel ran back to flailing and pushing and cramming a strange lumpish shape around on the groaning table. 'Boredom by the pound and ton. Boredom by the doomsday yard and the funeral mile.

Lawns, homes, dog fur, men's haircuts, cheap suits in dark store windows, all cut from the same cloth – '

'Boredom,' said Charlie, on cue.

'And what do you do when you're bored, son?'

'Er . . . break a window in a haunted house?'

'We got no haunted houses in Green Town!'

'Used to be. Old Higley's place. Torn down.'

'See my point! What else should we try? Quick!'

'Hold a massacre?'

'No massacre here in dogs' years. Lord, even our police chief's honest. Mayor? Not corrupt. Madness. Whole damn town faced with stark-raving ennuis and lulls. Last chance, Charlie. What's our salvation?'

Charlie smiled. 'Build a mummy?'

'Bulldogs in the belfry! Yes! Lend a hand. Help me to finish, boy!'

While the old man cackled and sewed and swooped, Charlie seized and snatched and grabbed and hauled more lizard tails, old nicotine bandages left from a skiing accident that had busted the Colonel's ankle and broken a romance in 1895, some patches from a 1922 Kissel Kar inner tube, a few burned-out sparklers from the last peaceful summer of 1913, and a collection of gypsy moths and death's-head beetles that once had labels and now flew nameless as Charlie and the old man kneaded and wove, shuttled and tapped and molded a brittle, dry wicker shape.

'*Voilà*, Charlie! Finished. Done.'

'Oh, Colonel!' The boy stared and gasped with love. 'Can I make him a crown?'

'Make him a crown, boy. Make him a crown.'

The sun was setting when the Colonel and Charlie and their Egyptian friend came down the dusky backstairs of the old man's house. Two of them were walking iron-heavy, the third was floating light as toasted cornflakes on the September air.

'Colonel!' Charlie wondered aloud. 'What we going to do with this pharaoh, now we got him? It ain't as if he could talk much, or run around doing things – '

'No need. Let folks talk, let folks run. Peek out.'

They cracked the door and peered out at a town smothered in peace and ruined by nothing to do.

'All right, son, now you have recovered from your almost-fatal seizure of desperate empties. But that whole blasted population out there lies up to its elbows in glum and despond, fearful to rise each morn and find it's always and forever Sunday! Who'll save 'em, boy?'

'Amon Bubastis Rameses Ra the Third, just arrived on the Four O'Clock Limited?'

'God love your sprightly tongue, Charles. What we got here is a giant seed. Seed's no good unless we – '

'*Plant* it?' Charles asked.

'Plant. Then watch it grow. Then what? Harvest time. Harvest! Come on, boy. Er . . . bring your friend.'

The Colonel crept out into the first nightfall.

The mummy came soon after, helped by Charlie.

Labor Day at high noon, Osiris Bubastis Amon-Ra-Tut arrived from the Land of the Dead.

An autumn wind stirred the land and flapped doors wide, not with the sound of the usual Labor Day parade, seven touring cars, a fife-and-drum corps, and the mayor, but with a mob that grew as it flowed through the streets and fell in a tide to inundate the lawn in front of Colonel Stonesteel's house. The Colonel and Charlie were sitting on the front porch; they had been sitting there for some hours, waiting for the conniption fits to arrive, the storming of the Bastille to occur. Now with dogs going mad and biting boys' ankles and boys dancing around the fringes of the mob, the Colonel gazed down upon the Creation (his and Charlie's) and gave his secret smile.

'Well, Charlie. Do I win my bet?'

'You sure do, Colonel!'

'Come on.'

Phones rang all across town and lunches burned on stoves as the Colonel strode forth to give the annual Labor Day parade his papal blessing.

At the centre of the mob was a horse-drawn wagon. On top of the wagon, his eyes wild with discovery, was Tom Tuppen, owner of a half-dead farm just beyond town. Tom was babbling, and the crowd was babbling, because in the back of the wagon was the special harvest delivered out of four thousand lost years of time.

'Well, flood the Nile and plant the Delta,' the Colonel gasped, eyes wide, staring. 'Is or is not that a genuine old Egyptian mummy lying there in its original papyrus and coal-tar wrappings?'

'Sure is!' Charlie cried.

'Sure is!' everyone yelled.

'I was ploughing the field this morning,' said Tom Tuppen. 'Ploughing, just ploughing and – bang! Plough turned this up, right before me! Like to have had a stroke! Think! The Egyptians must've marched through Illinois three thousand years ago, and no one knew! Revelations, I call it! Outa the way, kids! I'm taking this find to the post office lobby. Setting it up on display! Giddap, now, git!'

The horse, the wagon, the mummy, the crowd moved away, leaving the Colonel behind, his eyes still pretend-wide, his mouth open.

'Hot dog,' the Colonel whispered, 'we did it, Charles. This uproar, babble, talk, and hysterical gossip will last for a thousand days or Armageddon, whichever comes first!'

'Yes, *sir*, Colonel!'

'Michelangelo couldn't've done better. Boy David's a castaway, lost and forgotten wonder compared to our Egyptian surprise and –'

The Colonel stopped as the mayor rushed by.

'Colonel, Charlie, howdy! Just phoned Chicago. Newsfolks here tomorrow breakfast! Museum folks by lunch! Glory Hallelujah for the Green Town Chamber of Commerce!'

The mayor ran off after the mob.

An autumn cloud crossed the Colonel's face and settled around his mouth.

'End of Act One, Charlie. Start thinking fast. Act Two coming up. We *do* want this commotion to last forever, don't we?'

'Yes, sir –'

'Crack your brain, boy. What does Uncle Wiggily say?'

'Uncle Wiggily says – ah – go back two hops?'

'Give the boy an A-plus, a gold star, and a brownie! The Lord giveth and the Lord taketh away, eh?'

Charlie looked into the old man's face and saw visitations of plagues there. 'Yes, sir.'

The Colonel watched the mob milling around the post office, two blocks away. The fife-and-drum corps arrived and played some tune vaguely inclined toward the Egyptian.

'Sundown, Charlie,' the Colonel murmured, his eyes shut. 'We make our final move.'

What a day it was! Years later people said, 'That was a day!' The mayor went home and got dressed up and came back and made three speeches and held two parades, one going up Main Street toward the end of the trolley line, the other coming back, and Osiris Bubastis Amon-Ra-Tut was at the centre of both, smiling now to the right as gravity shifted his flimsy weight and then to the left as they rounded a corner. The fife-and-drum corps, now heavily augmented by accumulated brass, had spent an hour drinking beer and learning the Triumphal March from *Aida*, and this they played so many times that mothers took their screaming babies into the house and men retired to bars to soothe their nerves. There was talk of a third parade and a fourth speech, but sunset took the town unawares, and everyone, including Charlie, went home to a dinner mostly talk and short on eats.

By eight o'clock Charlie and the Colonel were driving along the leafy streets in the fine darkness, taking the air in the old man's 1924 Moon, a car that took up trembling where the Colonel left off.

'Where we going, Colonel?'

'Well,' the Colonel mused, steering at ten philosophical miles per hour, nice and easy, 'everyone, including your folks, is out at Grossett's Meadow right now, right? Final Labor Day speeches. Someone'll light the gasbag mayor, and he'll go up about forty feet, kee-rect? Fire Department'll be setting off the big skyrockets. Which means the post office, plus the mummy, plus the sheriff sitting there with him, will be empty and vulnerable. Then the miracle will happen, Charlie. It *has* to. Now ask me why the miracle will happen.'

'Why?'

'Glad you asked. Well, boy, folks from Chicago'll be

jumping off the train steps tomorrow, hot and fresh as pancakes, with their pointy noses and glass eyes and microscopes. Those museum snoopers, plus the Associated Press, will rummage our Egyptian pharaoh seven ways from Christmas and blow their fuse boxes. That being so, Charles –'

'We're on our way to mess around with the evidence.'

'You put it indelicately, boy, but truth is at the core. Look at it this way, child. Life is a magic show, or *should* be if people didn't go to sleep on each other. Always leave folks with a bit of mystery, son. Now, before people get used to our ancient friend, before he wears out the wrong bath towel, like any smart weekend guest, he should grab the next scheduled camel west and hightail it out of town. There!'

The post office stood silent, with one light shining in the foyer. Through the great window they could see the sheriff seated alongside the mummy on display, neither of them talking, abandoned at last by the attentive mobs that had gone for suppers and fireworks.

The Colonel brought forth a brown bag, in which a mysterious liquid gurgled. 'Give me thirty-five minutes to mellow the sheriff down, Charlie. Then you creep in, listen, follow my cues, and work the miracle. Here goes nothing!'

And the Colonel stole away.

Beyond town, the mayor sat down and the fireworks went up.

Charlie stood on top of the Moon and watched them for half an hour. Then, figuring the mellowing time was over, he dog-trotted across the street and moused himself into the post office to stand in the shadows.

'Well, now,' the Colonel was saying, seated between the Egyptian pharaoh and the sheriff, 'why don't you just finish that bottle, sir?'

'It's finished,' said the sheriff, obeying without hesitation.

The Colonel leaned forward in the half-light and peered at the gold amulet on the mummy's breast.

'You believe them old sayings?'

'What old sayings?' the sheriff inquired.

'If you read them hieroglyphics out loud, the mummy comes alive and walks.'

'Horseradish,' said the sheriff.

'Just look at all those fancy Egyptian symbols!' the Colonel pursued.

'Someone stole my glasses,' the sheriff blurted. 'You read that stuff to me. Make the fool mummy walk.'

Charlie took this as a signal to move, and he sidled around through the shadows, closer to the Egyptian king.

'Here goes.' The Colonel bent even closer to the pharaoh's amulet, meanwhile slipping the sheriff's glasses out of his cupped hand into his side pocket. 'First symbol on here is a hawk. Second one's a jackal. That third's an owl. Fourth's a yellow fox eye – '

'Continue,' the sheriff commanded.

The Colonel did so, and his voice rose and fell, and the sheriff's head nodded, and all the ancient Egyptian pictures and words flowed and touched around the mummy until at last the Colonel gave a great gasp and pointed.

'Good grief, Sheriff. Look!'

The sheriff blinked both eyes wide.

'The mummy,' said the Colonel. 'It's going for a walk!'

'Can't be!' the sheriff cried. 'Can't be!'

'Is,' said a voice, somewhere. Maybe the pharaoh under his breath.

And the mummy lifted up, suspended, and drifted toward the door.

'Why,' the sheriff suggested, tears in his eyes, 'I think he might just *fly*!'

'I'd better follow and bring him back,' the Colonel said.

'*Do* that!' the sheriff replied.

The mummy was gone. The Colonel ran. The door slammed.

'Oh, dear.' The sheriff lifted the bottle and shook it. 'Empty.'

They drove through avenues of autumn leaves that were suddenly the temples of dusting Egypt and the lily-sculpted pillars of time. Charlie let the car motor hum in his soul while over his shoulder, in the back seat, taking the ancient air, enjoying the warm river of wind, the mummy leaned this way and that as the car swerved

'Say it, Colonel,' said Charlie at last.

'What?' asked the old man.

'I love to hear you talk. Say what I want to hear. About the mummy. What he truly is. What he's really made of. Where he comes from – '

'Why, boy, you were there, you helped make, you saw – '

But the boy was looking at him steadily with bright autumn eyes. The mummy, their ancient harvest-tobacco dried-up Nile River bottom old-time masterpiece, leaned in the wind over their shoulder, waiting as much as the boy for the talk to come.

'You want to know who he truly was, once upon a time?'

The Colonel gathered a handful of dust in his lungs and softly filtered it out before he answered.

'He was everyone, no one, someone. You. Me.'

'Go on,' Charlie whispered.

Continue, said the lapis-lazuli gleam in the mummy's eyes.

'He was, he is,' the Colonel murmured, 'a bundle of old Sunday comic pages stashed in the attic to spontaneously combust from all those forgotten notions and stuffs. He's a stand of papyrus left in an autumn field long before Moses, a papier-mâché tumbleweed blown out of time, this way long-gone dusk, that way come-again dawn . . . a chart map of Siam, Blue River Nile source, hot desert dustdevil . . . all the confetti from lost trolley transfers, dried-up yellow cross-country road maps petering off in sand dunes . . . dry crushed flowers from wedding memory books . . . funeral wreaths . . . ticker tapes unravelled from gone-off-forever par-ades to Far Rockaway . . . lost scrolls from the great burned library at Alexandria . . . smell the chars? His rib cage, covered with what?! Posters torn off seed barns in North Storm, Ohio, shuttled south toward Fulfilment, Texas . . . dead gold-mine certificates, wedding and birth announce-ments . . . all the things that were once need, hope, dream . . . first nickel in the pocket, dollar on the wall . . . wrapped and ribboned yellow-skinned letters from failed old men, time-orphaned women saying Tomorrow and Tomorrow . . . there'll be a ship in the harbour, horse on the road, knock on the door . . . He's . . . he's telegrams you're afraid to open . . . poems you wrote and threw away . . . all the dumb, strange shadows you ever grew, boy, or I ever inked out inside my head at three A.M., crushed, stashed, and now shaped in one form under our hands and here in our gaze. That, that, that is what old King Pharaoh Seventh Dynasty Holy Dust *is*!

'Wow,' Charlie sighed.

As they drove up and parked in front of his house, Colonel Stonesteel peered out cautiously.

'Your folks ever go up in your attic, boy?'

'Too small. They poke me up to rummage.'

'Good. Hoist our ancient Egyptian friend out of the backseat there. Don't weigh much, twenty pounds at the most. You carried him fine, Charlie. Oh, that was a sight. You running out of the post office, making the mummy walk. You shoulda seen the sheriff's face!'

'I hope he don't get in trouble because of this.'

'Oh, he'll bump his head and make up a fine story. Can't very well admit he saw the mummy go for a walk, can he? He'll think of something – organize a posse. You'll see. But right now, son, get our ancient friend here up, hide him good, visit him weekly. Feed him night talk. Then thirty, forty years from now – '

'What?' Charlie asked.

'In a bad year so brimmed up with boredom it drips out your ears, when the town has long forgotten this first arrival and departure, on a morning, I say, when you lie in bed and don't want to get up, don't even want to twitch your ears or blink you're so damned bored ... well, on *that* morning, Charlie, you just climb up in your rummage-sale attic and shake this mummy out of bed, toss him in a cornfield, and watch new hellfire mobs break loose. Life starts over that hour, that day, for you, the town, everyone. Now grab, git, and hide, boy! Hop to it!'

'I hate for the night to be over,' Charlie said very quietly. 'Can't we circle a few more blocks and then finish off some lemonade on your porch, and *him* along, too?'

'Lemonade!' Colonel Stonesteel banged his heel on the car floor. The car exploded and surged. 'For the Lost and Found King, and the Pharaoh's Illinois Son!'

It was late on Labor Day evening, the two of them seated on the Colonel's front porch again, rocking up a fair breeze, lemonades in hand, ice in mouth, sucking the sweet savour of the night's incredible adventures. A wind blew. The mummy, behind Charlie's rocker, propped against the porch wall, almost seemed to be listening.

'Boy!' Charlie exclaimed. 'I can see tomorrow's *Clarion* headlines: PRICELESS MUMMY KIDNAPPED. RAMESES-TUT VANISHES. GREAT FIND GONE. REWARD OFFERED. SHERIFF NONPLUSSED. BLACKMAIL EXPECTED.'

'Talk on, boy. Like I taught you.'

The last Labor Day fireworks were dying in the sky. Their light faded in the lapis-lazuli eyes of boy and man and their withered friend, all fixed in shadow.

'Colonel.' Charlie gazed into the future. 'What if, even in my old age, I don't ever *need* my own particular mummy?'

'Eh?'

'What if I have a life chock-full of things, never bored, find what I want to do, *do* it, make every day count, every night swell, sleep tight, wake up yelling, laugh lots, grow old, still running fast, what *then*, Colonel?'

'Why then, boy, you'll be one of God's luckiest people!'

'For you see, Colonel,' Charlie said, looking at him with pure round, unblinking eyes, 'I made up my mind. I'm going to be the greatest writer that ever lived.'

The Colonel braked his rocker and searched the innocent fire in that small face.

'Lord, I see it. Yes. You *will*. Well, then, Charles, when you are very old, you must find some lad, not as lucky as you, to give Osiris-Ra to. Your life may be full, but others, lost on the road, will need our Egyptian friend. Agreed? Agreed.'

The last skyrockets soared and fell, the last fire balloons went sailing out among the gentle stars. Cars and people were driving or walking home, some fathers or mothers carrying their tired and already-sleeping children. As the quiet parade passed Colonel Stonesteel's porch, some folks glanced in and waved at the old man and the boy and the tall, dim-shadowed servant who stood between. The night was over forever.

Charlie said, 'Say some more, Colonel.'

'No. I'm shut. Listen to what *he* has to say now. Let *him* tell your future, Charlie. Let him start you on stories. Ready?'

A wind came up and blew in the dry papyrus and sifted the

ancient wrappings and trembled the curious hands and softly twitched the lips of their old/new four-thousand-year night-time visitor, whispering.

'What's he saying, Charles?'

Charlie shut his eyes, waited, listened, nodded, let a single tear slide down his cheek, and at last said, 'Everything . . . Everything I always wanted to hear.'